# FLOYD L. WALLACE RESURRECTED

## The Science Fiction Stories of Floyd Wallace

## By Floyd L. Wallace
### Edited by Greg Fowlkes

Includes the Special Preview of
## THE BLOOD RED SANDS OF MARS
A Science Fiction Novel by Greg Fowlkes

# FLOYD L. WALLACE RESURRECTED

**The Science Fiction Stories of Floyd Wallace**

© 2011 Resurrected Press
www.ResurrectedPress.com

## Published by Resurrected Press

This classic book was handcrafted by Resurrected Press. Resurrected Press is dedicated to bringing high quality classic books back to the readers who enjoy them. These are not scanned versions of the originals, but, rather, quality checked and edited books meant to be enjoyed!

Please visit ResurrectedPress.com to view our entire catalogue!

ISBN 13: 978-1-937022-27-3

Printed in the United States of America

# FOREWORD

Floyd L. Wallace had, for a decade, a prospering career as a science fiction author. During that time he had two dozen stories published, many of them in *Galaxy*, one of the more prestigious magazines of the time. He also had a novel, *Address: Centauri* published. In addition to science fiction, he wrote mysteries and had a number of stories published, as well as two mystery novels, *Three Times a Victim* and *Wired for Scandal*. And then he stopped writing.

It's not clear why this happened. He did have another career as an engineer which undoubtedly paid more. He might just have gotten tired of the work involved. Isaac Asimov, in notes printed in one of his anthologies that included a Wallace story speculated that as Wallace had most of his work published in *Galaxy* while H. L. Gold was the editor, when that editor passed away, he no longer wanted to or felt like he could write for another editor. When several of his works were anthologized in the 80's he indicated that he was thinking of writing again, but as far as I know, nothing ever came of this.

What we are left with is a legacy of two dozen stories. Quite good stories in general. Several of the stories included here have been anthologized, some more than once, in particular, "Student Body," "The Deadly Ones," and "Delay in Transit."

The eleven stories included in this volume are a varied lot. There are short stories, novella length stories, serious stories, humorous stories. Several of the stories, "Bolden's Pet," and "Student Body" deal with alien ecologies. "Mezzerow Loves Company" is about the pitfalls of dealing with a galaxy wide bureaucracy, while "The Deadly Ones" is a tale of Vampires vs. Flying Saucers. Wallace's affinity for mystery and intrigue are evident in "Tangle Hold," "Forget Me Nearly," and "Delay in Transit." In "The Impossible Voyage Home," Wallace presents a surprising solution to the problems radiation present to space travel, and "Accidental Flight" deals with another group for which space flight is the only way out. "Second Landing" is a Christmas story of sorts, while "End As a World" is a thoughtful, gentle look at a young boy as his world changes forever.

With these examples, one could wish that Floyd Wallace had extended his career. He certainly hadn't run out of ideas or talent. Unfortunately, he didn't, so his work is bounded by and limited to that most productive era in science fiction, the 50's. With that in mind, Resurrected Press is proud to bring you this collection of stories in *Wallace Resurrected*.

**About the Author**

Floyd L. Wallace was born in Rock Island, Illinois on February 16, 1914 and died in Tustin California on November 26, 2004. He graduated with a degree in mechanical engineering from the University of Iowa and spent most of his life in California. He wrote some two dozen stories, mostly in the 1950's and one novel, *Address: Centauri*. In addition to science fiction, he also wrote a number of mysteries.

Greg Fowlkes
Editor-In-Chief
Resurrected Press
www.ResurrectedPress.com

# Table Of Contents

# Accidental Flight

Illustrated by Ed Alexander
Originally Published in *Galaxy Science Fiction*
April 1952

*Outcasts of a society of physically perfect people, they couldn't stay and they couldn't go home again—yet there had to be some escape for them. Oddly enough, there was!*

# ACCIDENTAL FLIGHT

Cameron frowned intently at the top of the desk. It was difficult to concentrate under the circumstances. "Your request was turned over to the Medicouncil," he said. "After studying it, they reported back to the Solar Committee."

Docchi edged forward, his face literally lighting up.

Dr. Cameron kept his eyes averted; the man was damnably disconcerting. "You know what the answer is. A flat no, for the present."

Docchi leaned back. "We should have expected that," he said wearily.

"It's not entirely hopeless. Decisions like this can always be changed."

"Sure," said Docchi. "We've got centuries." His face was flushed—*blazing* would be a better description.

Absently, Cameron lowered the lights in the room as much as he could. It was still uncomfortably bright. Docchi was a nuisance.

"But why?" asked Docchi. "You know that we're capable. Why did they refuse?"

Cameron had tried to avoid that question. Now it had to be answered with blunt brutality. "Did you think you would be chosen? Or Nona, or Jordan, or Anti?"

Docchi winced. "Maybe not. But we've told you that we're willing to abide by what the experts say. Surely from a thousand of us they can select one qualified crew."

"Perhaps so," said Cameron. He switched on the lights and resumed staring at the top of the desk. "Most of you are biocompensators. Ninety per cent, I believe. I concede that we ought to be able to get together a competent crew." He sighed.

"But you're wasting your time discussing this with me. I'm not responsible for the decision. I can't do anything about it."

Docchi stood up. His face was colorless and bright.

Dr. Cameron looked at him directly for the first time. "I suggest you calm down. Be patient and wait; you may get your chance."

"You wait," said Docchi. "We don't intend to."

The door opened for him and closed behind him.

Cameron concentrated on the desk. Actually he was trying to look through it. He wrote down the card sequence he expected to find. He opened a drawer and gazed at the contents, then grimaced in disappointment. No matter how many times he tried, he never got better than strictly average results. Maybe there was something to telepathy, but he hadn't found it yet.

He dismissed it from his mind. It was a private game, a method of avoiding involvement while Docchi was present. But Docchi was gone now, and he had better come up with some answers. The right ones.

He switched on the telecom. "Get me Medicouncilor Thorton," he told the robot operator. "Direct, if you can; indirect if you have to. I'll wait."

With an approximate mean diameter of thirty miles, the asteroid was listed on the charts as Handicap Haven. The regular inhabitants were willing to admit the handicap part of the name, but they didn't call it haven. There were other terms, none of them suggesting sanctuary.

It was a hospital, of course, but even more like a convalescent home, *the permanent kind*. A healthy and vigorous humanity had built it for those few who were less fortunate. A splendid gesture, but, like many such gestures, the reality fell somewhat short of the original intentions.

The robot operator interrupted his thoughts. "Medicouncilor Thorton will speak to you."

The face of an older man filled the screen. "On my way to the satellites of Jupiter. I'll be in direct range for the next half hour." At such distance, transmission and reception were practically instantaneous. "You wanted to speak to me about the Solar Committee reply?"

"I do. I informed Docchi a few minutes ago."

"How did he react?"

"He didn't like it. As a matter of fact, he was mad all the way through."

"That speaks well for his mental resiliency."

"They all seem to have enough spirit, though, and nothing to use it on," said Dr. Cameron. "I confess I didn't look at him often, in spite of the fact that he was quite presentable. Handsome, even, in a startling way."

Thorton nodded. "Presentable. That means he had arms."

"He did. Is that important?"

"I think it is. He expected a favorable reply and wanted to look his best. As nearly normal as possible."

"Trouble?"

"I don't see how," said the medicouncilor uncertainly. "In any event, not immediately. It will take them some time to get over the shock of refusal. They can't do anything, really. Individually they're helpless. Collectively—there aren't parts for a dozen sound bodies on the asteroid."

"I've looked over the records," said Dr. Cameron. "Not one accidental has ever *liked* being on Handicap Haven, and that covers quite a few years. But there has never been so much open discontent as there is now."

"Someone is organizing them. Find out who and keep a close watch."

"I know who. Docchi, Nona, Anti, and Jordan. But it doesn't do any good merely to watch them. I want your permission to break up that combination. Humanely, of course."

"How do you propose to do it?"

"Docchi, for instance. With prosthetic arms he appears physically normal, except for that uncanny luminescence. That is repulsive to the average person. Medically there's nothing we can do about it, but psychologically we might be able to make it into an asset. You're aware that Gland Opera is the most popular program in the Solar System. Telepaths, teleports, pyrotics and so forth are the heroes. All fake, of course: makeup and trick camera shots. But Docchi can be made into a real live star. The death-ray man, say. When his face shines, men fall dead or paralyzed. He'd have a chance to return to normal society under conditions that would be mentally acceptable to him."

"Acceptable to him, perhaps, but not to society," reflected the medicouncilor. "An ingenious idea, one which does credit to your humanitarian outlook. Only it won't work. You have Docchi's medical record, but you probably don't know his complete history. He was an electrochemical engineer, specializing in cold lighting. He seemed on his way to a brilliant career when a particularly messy accident occurred. The details aren't important. He was badly mangled and tossed into a tank of cold lighting fluid by automatic machinery. It was some time before he was discovered.

"There was a spark of life left and we managed to save him. We had to amputate his arms and ribs practically to his spinal column. The problem of regeneration wasn't as easy as it usually is. We were able to build up a new rib case; that's as much as we could do. Under such conditions, prosthetic arms are merely ornaments. They can be fastened to him and they look all right, but he can't use them. He has no back or shoulder muscles to anchor them to.

"And add to that the adaptation his body made while he was in the tank. The basic cold lighting fluid, as you know, is semi-organic. It permeated every tissue in his body. By the time we got him, it was actually a necessary part of his metabolism. A corollary, I suppose, of the fundamental biocompensation theory."

The medicouncilor paused and shook his head. "I'm afraid your idea is out, Dr. Cameron. I don't doubt that he would be successful on the program you mention. But there is more to life on the outside than success. Can you picture the dead silence when he walks into a room of normal people?"

"I see," said Cameron, though he didn't, at least not eye to eye. The medicouncilor was convinced and there was nothing Cameron could do to alter that conviction. "The other one I had in mind was Nona," he added.

"I thought so." Thorton glanced at the solar chronometer. "I haven't much time, but I'd better explain. You're new to the post and I don't think you've learned yet to evaluate the patients and their problems properly. In a sense, Nona is more impossible than Docchi. He was once a normal person. She never was. Her appearance is satisfactory; perhaps she's quite pretty, though you must remember that you're seeing her under circumstances that may make her seem more attractive than she really is.

"She can't talk or hear. She never will. She doesn't have a larynx, and it wouldn't help if we gave her one. She simply doesn't have the nervous system necessary for speech or hearing. Her brain is definitely not structurally normal. As far as we're concerned, that abnormality is not in the nature of a mutation. It's more like an anomaly. Once cleft palates were frequent— prenatal nutritional deficiencies or traumas. Occasionally we still run into cases like that, but our surgical techniques are always adequate. Not with Nona, however.

"She can't be taught to read or write; we've tried it. We dug out the old Helen Keller techniques and brought them up to date with no results. Apparently her mind doesn't work in a human fashion. We question whether very much of it works at all."

"That might be a starting point," said Cameron. "If her brain—"

"Gland Opera stuff," interrupted Thorton. "Or Rhine Opera, if you'll permit me to coin a term. We've thought of it, but it isn't true. We've tested her for every telepathic quality that the Rhine people list. Again no results. She has no special mental capacities. Just to make sure of that, we've given her periodic checkups. One last year, in fact."

Cameron frowned in frustration. "Then it's your opinion that she's not able to survive in a normal society?"

"That's it," answered the medicouncilor bluntly. "You'll have to face the truth—you can't get rid of any of them."

"With or without their cooperation, I'll manage," said Cameron.

"I'm sure you will." The medicouncilor's manner didn't ooze confidence. "Of course, if you need help we can send reinforcements."

The implication was clear enough. "I'll keep them out of trouble," Cameron promised.

The picture and the voice were fading. "It's up to you. If it turns out to be too difficult, get in touch with the Medicouncil...."

The robot operator broke in: "The ship is beyond direct telecom range. If you wish to continue the conversation, it will have to be relayed through the nearest main station. At present, that is Mars."

Aside from the time element, which was considerable, it wasn't likely that he would get any better answers than he could supply for himself. Cameron shook his head. "We are through, thanks."

He got heavily to his feet. That wasn't a psychological reaction at all. He really was heavier. He made a mental note. He would have to investigate.

In a way they were pathetic—the patchwork humans, the half or quarter men and women, the fractional organisms masquerading as people—an illusion which died hard for them. Medicine and surgery were partly to blame. Techniques were too good, or not good enough, depending on the viewpoint.

Too good in that the most horribly injured person, if he were still alive, could be kept alive! Not good enough because a percentage of the injured couldn't be returned to society completely sound and whole. There weren't many like that; but there were some, and all of them were on the asteroid.

They didn't like it. At least they didn't like being *confined* to Handicap Haven. It wasn't that they wanted to go back to the society of the normals, for they realized how conspicuous they'd be among the multitudes of beautiful, healthy people on the planets.

What the accidentals did want was ridiculous. They desired, they hoped, they petitioned to be the first to make the long, hard journey to Alpha and Proxima Centauri in rockets. Trails of glory for those that went; a vicarious share in it for those who couldn't.

Nonsense. The broken people, those without a face they could call their own, those who wore their hearts not on their sleeves, but in a blood-pumping chamber, those either without limbs or organs—or too many. The categories seemed endless.

The accidentals were qualified, true. In fact, of all the billions of solar citizens, *they alone could make the journey and return.* But there were other factors that ruled them out. The first point was never safe to discuss with them, especially if the second had to be explained. It would take a sadistic nature that Cameron didn't possess.

*        *        *        *        *

Docchi sat beside the pool. It was pleasant enough, a pastoral scene transplanted from Earth. A small tree stretched shade overhead. Waves lapped and made gurgling sounds against the sides. No plant life of any kind grew and no fish swam in the liquid. It looked like water, but it wasn't. It was acid. In it floated something that monstrously resembled a woman.

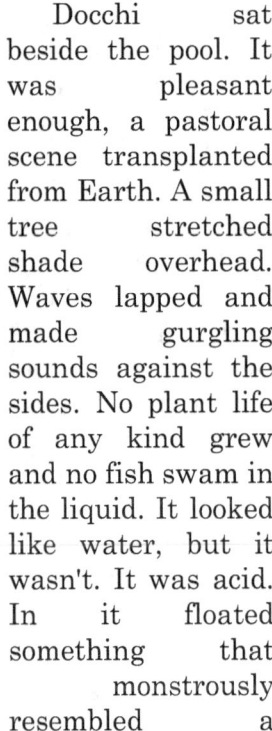

"They turned us down, Anti," Docchi said bitterly.

"Didn't you expect it?" the creature in the pool asked.

"I guess I didn't."

"You don't know the Medicouncil very well."

"Evidently I don't." He stared sullenly at the faintly blue fluid. "Why did they turn us down?"

"Don't you know?"

"All right, I know," he said. "They're pretty irrational."

"Of course, irrational. Let them be that way, as long as we don't follow their example."

"I wish I knew what to do," he said. "Cameron suggested we wait."

"Biocompensation," murmured Anti, stirring restlessly. "They've always said that. Up to now it's always worked."

"What else can we do?" asked Docchi. Angrily he kicked at an anemic tuft of grass. "Draw up another request?"

"Memorandum number ten? Let's not be naive about it. Things get lost so easily in the Medicouncil's filing system."

"Or distorted," grunted Docchi.

"Maybe we should give the Medicouncil a rest. They're tired of hearing us anyway."

"I see what you mean," said Docchi, rising.

"Better talk to Jordan about it."

"I intend to. I'll need arms."

"Good. I'll see you when you leave for far Centauri."

"Sooner than that, Anti. Much sooner."

Stars were beginning to wink. Twilight brought out shadows and tracery of the structure that supported the transparent dome overhead. Soon controlled slow rotation would bring darkness to this side of the asteroid.

*     *     *     *     *

Cameron leaned back and looked speculatively at the gravital engineer, Vogel. The man could give him considerable assistance, if he would. There was no reason why he shouldn't; but any man who had voluntarily remained on Handicap Haven as long as Vogel had was a doubtful quantity.

"Usually we maintain about half Earth-normal gravity," Cameron said. "Isn't that correct?"

Engineer Vogel nodded.

"It isn't important why those limits were set," Cameron continued. "Perhaps it's easier on the weakened bodies of the accidentals. There may be economic factors."

"No reason for those limits except the gravital units themselves," Vogel said. "Theoretically it should be easy to get any gravity you want. Practically, though, we get between a quarter and almost full Earth gravity. Now take the fluctuations. The gravital computer is set at fifty per cent. Sometimes we get fifty per cent and sometimes seventy-five. Whatever it is, it just is and we have to be satisfied."

The big engineer shrugged. "I hear the units were designed especially for this asteroid," he went on. "Some fancy medical reason. Easier on the accidentals to have less gravity change, you say. Me, I dunno. I'd guess the designers couldn't help it and the reason was dug up later."

Cameron concealed his irritation. He wanted information, not a heart-to-heart confession. "All practical sciences try to justify whatever they can't escape but would like to. Medicine, I'm sure, is no exception." He paused thoughtfully. "Now, there are three separate gravital units on the asteroid. One runs for forty-five minutes while the other two are idle. Then it cuts off and another takes over. This is supposed to be synchronized. I don't have to tell you that it isn't. You felt your weight increase suddenly at the same time I did. What is wrong?"

"Nothing wrong," said the engineer. "That's what you get with gravital."

"You mean they're supposed to run that way? Overlapping so that for five minutes we have Earth or Earth-and-a-half gravity and then none?"

"It's not *supposed* to be that way," said Vogel. "But nobody ever built a setup like this that worked any better." He added defensively: "Of course, if you want, you can check with the company that makes these units."

"I'm not trying to challenge your knowledge, and I'm not anxious to make myself look silly. I have a sound reason for asking these questions. There is a possibility of sabotage."

The engineer's grin was wider than the remark seemed to require.

"All right," said Cameron tiredly. "Suppose you tell me why sabotage is so unlikely."

"Well," explained the gravital engineer, "it would have to be someone living here, and he wouldn't like it if he suddenly got double or triple gravity or maybe none at all. But there's another reason. Now take a gravital unit. Any gravital unit. Most people think of it as just that—a unit. It isn't really that at all. It has three parts.

"One part is a power source that can be anything as long as it's big enough. Our power source is a nuclear pile, buried deep in the asteroid. You'd have to take Handicap Haven apart to get to it. Part two is the gravital coil, which actually produces the gravity and is simple and just about indestructible. Part three is the gravital control. It calculates the relationship between the amount of power flowing through the gravital coil and the strength of the created gravity field in any one microsecond. It uses the computed relationship to alter the power flowing through in the next microsecond to get the same gravity. No change of power, no gravity. I guess you could call the control unit a computer, as good a one as is made for any purpose."

The engineer rubbed his chin. "Fatigue," he continued. "The gravital control is an intricate computer that's subject to fatigue. That's why it has to rest an hour and a half to do forty-five minutes of work. Naturally they don't want anyone tinkering with it. It's non-repairable. Crack the case open and it won't work. But first you have to open it. Mind you, that can be done. But I wouldn't want to try it without a high-powered lab setup."

If it didn't seem completely foolproof, neither did it seem a likely source of trouble. "Then we can forget about the gravital units," said Cameron, arising. "But what about hand weapons? Are there any available?"

"You mean toasters?"

"Anything that's lethal."

"Nothing. No knives even. Maybe a stray bar or so of metal." Vogel scratched his head. "There is something dangerous, though. Dangerous if you know how to take hold of it."

Instantly Cameron was alert. "What's that?"

"Why, the asteroid itself. You can't physically touch any part of the gravital unit. But if you could somehow sneak an impulse into the computer and change the direction of the field...." Vogel was very grave. "You could pick up Handicap Haven and throw it anywhere you wanted. At the Earth, say. Thirty miles in diameter is a big hunk of rock."

It was this kind of information Cameron was looking for, though the engineer seemed to regard the occasion as merely a social call. "Is there any possibility of that occurring?" he asked quietly.

The engineer grinned. "Never happened, but they're ready for things like that with any gravital system. They got monitor stations all over—the moons of Jupiter, Mars, Earth, Venus.

"Any time the gravital computer gets dizzy, the monitor overrides it. If that fails, they send a jammer impulse and freeze it up tight. It won't work until they let loose."

Cameron sighed. He was getting very little help or information from Vogel. "All right," he said. "You've told me what I wanted to know."

He watched the engineer depart for the gravity-generating chamber far below the surface of the asteroid.

*　　*　　*　　*　　*

The post on Handicap Haven wasn't pleasant; it wasn't an experience a normal human would desire. It did have advantages—advancement came in sizes directly proportional to the disagreeableness of the place.

Ten months to go on a year's assignment. If Cameron could survive that period with nothing to mar his administration, he was in line for better positions. A suicide or any other kind of unpleasantness that would focus the attention of the outside world on the forgotten asteroid was definitely unwelcome.

He flipped on the telecom. "Rocket dome. Get me the pilot."

When the robot finally answered, it wasn't encouraging. "I'm sorry. There is no answer."

"Then trace him," he snapped. "If he's not in the rocket dome, he's in the main dome. I want you to get him at once."

A few seconds of silence followed. "There is no record of the pilot leaving the rocket dome."

His heart skipped; with an effort he spoke carefully. "Scan the whole area. Understand? You've got to find him."

"Scanning is not possible. The system is out of operation in that area."

"All right," he said, starting to shake. "Send out repair robots." They were efficient in the sense they always did the work they were set to do, but not in terms of speed.

"The robots were dispatched as soon as scanning failed to work. Are there any other instructions?"

He thought about that. He needed help, plenty of it. Vogel? He'd be ready and willing, but that would leave the gravity-generating setup unprotected. Better do without him.

Who else? The sour old nurse who'd signed up because she wanted quick credits toward retirement? Or the sweet young thing who had bravely volunteered because someone ought to help those poor unfortunate men? Not the women, of course. She had a bad habit of fainting when she saw blood. Probably that was why she couldn't get a position in a regular planetary hospital.

That was all, except the robots, who weren't much help in a case like this. That and the rocket pilot. For some reason he wasn't available.

The damned place was under-manned. Always had been. Nobody wanted to come except the mildly psychotic, the inefficient and lazy, or, conceivably, an ambitious young doctor like himself. Mentally, Cameron berated the last category. If anything serious happened here, such a doctor might end his career bandaging scratches at a children's playground.

"Instructions," he said. "Yes. Leave word in gravity-generating for Vogel. Tell him to throw everything he's got around the units. Watch them."

"Is that all?"

"Not quite. Send six general purpose robots. I'll pick them up at the entrance to the rocket dome."

"Repair robots are already in that area. Will they do as well?"

"They will not. I want geepees for another reason." They wouldn't be much help, true, but the best he could manage.

*       *       *       *       *

Docchi waited near the rocket dome. Not hiding, merely inconspicuous among the carefully nurtured shrubbery that was supposed to give the illusion of Earth. If the plants failed in that respect, at least they contributed to the oxygen supply of the asteroid.

"Good girl," said Docchi. "That Nona is wonderful."

Jordan could feel him relax. "A regular mechanical marvel," he agreed. "But we can gas about that later. Let's get going."

Docchi glanced around and then walked boldly into the passageway that connected the main dome with the much smaller, adjacent rocket dome. Normally, it was never dark in the inhabited parts of the asteroid; a modulated twilight was considered more conducive to the slumber of the handicapped. But it wasn't twilight as they neared the rocket dome—it was a full-scale rehearsal for the darkness of interplanetary space.

Docchi stopped before the emergency airlock which loomed solidly in front of them. "I hope Nona was able to cut this out of the circuit," he said anxiously.

"She understood, didn't she?" asked Jordan. He reached out and the great slab moved easily aside in its grooves. "The trouble with you is that you lack confidence."

Docchi, listening with a frown, didn't answer.

"Okay, I hear it, too," whispered Jordan. "We'd better get well inside before he reaches us."

Docchi walked rapidly into the darkness of the rocket dome. He allowed his face to become faintly luminescent, the one part of his altered metabolism that he had learned to control, when he wasn't under emotional strain.

He was nervous now, but his control had to be right. Enough light so that he'd be noticed, not so much that details of his appearance would be plain.

The footsteps came nearer, accompanied by a steady volume of profanity. Docchi flashed his face once and then lowered the intensity almost immediately.

The footsteps stopped. "Docchi?"

"No. Just a lonely little light bulb out for an evening stroll."

The rocket pilot's laughter wasn't altogether friendly. "I know it's you. I meant, what are you doing here?"

"I saw the lights in the rocket dome go out. The entrance was open, so I came in. Maybe I can help."

"They're off, all right. Everything. Even the standby system." The rocket pilot moved closer. The deadly little toaster was in his hand. "You can't help. You'd better get out. It's against regulations for you to be in here."

Docchi ignored the weapon. "What happened? Did a meteor strike?"

The pilot grunted. "Not likely." He peered intently at the barely visible silhouette. "Well, I see you're getting smart. You should do that all the time. You look better that way, even if they're not usable arms. You look...." His voice faded away.

"Sure, almost human," Docchi finished for him. "Not like a pair of legs and a spinal column with a lightning bug stuck on top."

"I didn't say that. So you're sensitive about it, eh? Maybe that's not your fault. Anyway, you'd better get going."

"But I don't want to go," said Docchi deliberately. "I'm not afraid of the dark. Are you?"

"Cut the psycho talk, Docchi. All your circuits are working and you know it. Now get out of here before I take your fake hand and drag you out."

"Now you've hurt my feelings," declared Docchi reproachfully, nimbly stepping away.

"You asked for it," growled the pilot, lunging after him. What he took hold of wasn't an imitation hand, made of plastic. It was flesh and blood. That was why the pilot screamed, once, before he was lifted off his feet and slammed to the floor.

Docchi bent double. The dark figure on his back came over his head like a sword from a scabbard.

"Jor—"

"Yeah," said Jordan.

He wrapped one arm around the pilot's throat and clamped it tight. With the other he felt for the toaster the pilot still held. Effortlessly he tore it away and used the butt with just enough force to knock the pilot unconscious without smashing the skull. Docchi stood by until it was over. All he could offer was an ineffectual kick, not balanced by arms.

It wasn't needed.

"Let there be light," ordered Jordan, laughing, and there was, a feeble, flickering illumination from Docchi.

Jordan was balancing himself on his hands. A strong head, massive, powerful arms and shoulders. His body ended at his chest. A round metal capsule contained his digestive system.

"Dead?" Docchi looked down at the pilot.

Jordan rocked forward and listened for the heartbeat. "Nah," he said. "I remembered in time that we can't afford to kill anyone."

"Good," said Docchi, and stifled an exclamation as something coiled around his leg. His reactions were fast; he broke loose almost instantly.

"Repair robot," said Jordan, looking around. "The place is lousy with them."

Docchi blinked on and off involuntarily and the robot came toward him.

"Friendly creature," observed Jordan. "He's offering to fix your lighting system for you."

Docchi ignored the squat contrivance and stared at the pilot. "Now what?" he asked.

"Agreed," said Jordan. "He needs attention. *Not* the kind I gave him." He balanced the toaster in his hand and burned a small hole in the little wheeled monster. Tentacles emerged from the side of the machine and felt puzzledly at the damaged area. The  tentacles were withdrawn and presently reappeared with a small torch and began welding.

Jordan pulled the unconscious pilot toward him. He leaned against the machine, raised the inert form over his head and laid it gently on the top flat surface. Another tentacle reached out to investigate the body of the pilot. Jordan welded the joints solid with the toaster. Three times he repeated the process until the pilot was fastened to the robot.

"The thing will stay here, repairing itself, until it's completely sound again," remarked Jordan. "However, that can be fixed." He adjusted the toaster beam to an imperceptible thickness. Deftly he sliced through the control case and removed a circular section. He reached inside and ripped out circuits. "No further self-repair," he said cheerfully. "Now I'm going to need your help. From a time stand-point, I think it's a good idea to run the robot around the main dome a few times before it delivers the pilot to the hospital. No point in giving ourselves away before we're ready."

Docchi bent over the robot, and with his help the proper sequence was implanted. The machine scurried erratically away.

Docchi watched it go. "Time for us to be on our way." He bent double for Jordan. The arms folded around his neck, but Jordan made no effort to climb up onto his back. For a panic moment Docchi knew how the pilot felt when strength, where there shouldn't have been strength, reached out from the darkness and gripped his throat.

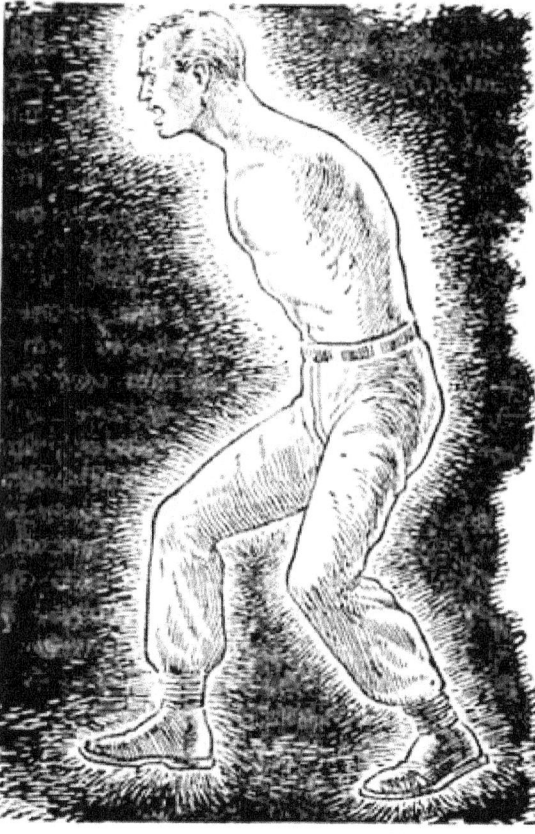

He shook the thought from his mind. "Get on my back," he insisted.

"You're tired," said Jordan. "Half gravity or not, you can't carry me any farther." His fingers worked swiftly and the carrying harness fell to the floor. "Stay down," growled Jordan. "Listen."

Docchi listened. "Geepees!"

"Yeah," said Jordan. "Now get to the rocket."

"What can I do when I get there? You'll have to help me."

"You'll figure something out when the time comes. Hurry up!"

"Not without you," said Docchi stubbornly, without moving.

A huge paw clamped around the back of his skull. "Listen to me," whispered Jordan fiercely. "Together we were a better man than the pilot—your legs and my arms. It's up to us to prove that separately we are a match for Cameron and his geepees."

"We're not trying to *prove* anything," said Docchi.

A brilliant light sliced through the darkness and swept around the rocket dome.

"Maybe we are," said Jordan. Impatiently, he hitched himself along the ground. "I think I am."

"What are you going to do?"

"I'm going up. With no legs, that's where I belong."

He grasped the structural steel member in his great hands, and in the light gravity, ascended rapidly.

"Careful," warned Docchi.

"This is no time to be careful." His voice floated down from high in the lacy structure. It wasn't completely dark; the lights were getting nearer. Docchi decided it was possible for Jordan to see what he was doing.

They hadn't expected to be discovered so soon. But the issue had not yet been settled against them. Docchi settled into a long stride, avoiding the low-slung repair robots that seemed to be everywhere. If Jordan refused to give up, Docchi had to try.

He stayed well ahead of the oncoming general purpose robots.

*     *     *     *     *

He reached the rocket and barely had time to look around. It was enough, however. The ship's passenger and freight locks were closed. Nona had either not understood all their instructions, or she hadn't been able to carry them out. The first, probably. She had put the light and scanning circuits out of commission with no tools except her hands. That and her uncanny knowledge of the inner workings of machines. It was too much to expect that she should also have the ship ready and waiting for them.

It was up to him to get in. If he had the toaster they'd taken from the pilot, he might have been able to soften the proper area of the passenger lock. But he didn't. Not having arms, he couldn't have used it. For that reason Jordan had kept the weapon.

The alternative was to search the surrounding mechanical jungle for an external control of the rocket. There had to be one, at least for the airlocks. Then it was a matter of luck whether he could work it.

The approaching lights warned him that he no longer had that alternative. If Cameron hadn't tried to search the rocket dome as he came along, the geepees would be solidly ringed around the ship now. That was Cameron's mistake, however, and he might make more.

In all probability Jordan was still at large. Perhaps nearby. Would Cameron know that? He might not.

Docchi descended into the shallow landing pit. Until both of them were caught, there was always a chance. He had to hide, but the landing pit seemed remarkably ill-suited for that purpose.

He leaned against the stern tube cluster and tried to shake his brain into activity. The metal pressed hard into the thin flesh that covered his back. In the smooth glazed surface of the landing pit, the only answer was the tubes.

He straightened up and looked into them. A small boy might climb inside and crawl out of sight. Or a grown man who had no shoulders or arms to get wedged in the narrow cylinder.

Out in space, the inner ends of the tubes were closed with a combustion cap wherein the fuel was ignited. But in the dome, where the ship was not used for months at a time....

Yes, there was that possibility.

He tried a lower tube. He lay on the floor and thrust his head inside. He wriggled and shoved with his feet until he had forced himself entirely in. It was dark and terrifying, but no time for claustrophobia.

He stopped momentarily and listened. A geepee descended noisily into the landing pit. The absence of any other sound indicated to Docchi that it was radio-controlled.

He drove himself on, though it was slow progress. The walls were smooth and it was difficult to get much purchase. The going became even tougher—the tube was getting smaller. Not much, but enough to matter.

Again he stopped. Outside, there was the characteristic sputter, like frying, that the toaster beam made when it struck metal. A great clatter followed.

"Get him!" shouted Cameron. "He's up there!"

Jordan had arrived and had picked off a geepee. And it wasn't going to be easy for Cameron to capture him. The diversion would help.

"Don't use heat," ordered Cameron. "Get your lights on him. Blind him. Drive him in a corner and then go up and get him."

Docchi had been wrong; the geepees were controlled by voice, not radio. That would make it easier for him once he got inside the ship. If he did.

It looked as though he would. The tube wasn't getting narrower. More important, the air was not noticeably stale. The combustion cap had been retracted, which was a lucky break. His feet slipped. It didn't matter; somehow he inched along. Blood was pounding in his veins from the constriction, but his head emerged in the rocket.

He stared at the retracted combustion cap a few feet away. If he had arms, he could grasp it and pull himself free. But if he had arms, he would never have gotten this far. He wriggled until his body was nearly out and only his legs were in the tube. He kicked hard, fell to the floor.

He lay there while his head cleared, then rolled to his feet and staggered forward to the control compartment. The rocket was his, but he didn't want it for himself alone.

He stared thoughtfully at the instrument panel. It had been a long time since he had operated a ship. When he understood the controls, he bent down and thrust his chin against the gravital dial. Laboriously he turned it to the proper setting. Then he sat down and kicked on a switch. The ship rocked and rose a few inches.

Chances were that Cameron wouldn't notice that in the confusion outside. If he did, he had thirty seconds in which to stop Docchi. That wouldn't be enough for Cameron.

"Rocket landing," said Docchi when the allotted time passed. "Emergency instructions. Emergency instructions. Stand by." Strictly speaking, that wasn't necessary, for the frequency he was using assured him of complete control.

"All energized geepees lend assistance. This order supersedes previous orders. Additional equipment necessary." After listing the equipment, he sat back and chuckled.

With his knee he turned on the external lights, got up and walked to the passenger lock, brushing against the switch. The airlock opened. He stood boldly at the threshold and looked out. The rocket dome was floodlighted by the ship.

"All right, Jordan, you can come down now," he called.

Jordan appeared overhead, hanging from a beam. He swung along it until he reached a column, down which he descended. He propelled himself over the floor and up the ramp in his awkward fashion. Balancing on his hands, he gazed up at Docchi.

"Well, monster, how did you do it?"

"Monster yourself," said Docchi. "Do what?"

"I saw you crawl in the rocket tubes," said Jordan. "But what did you do after you got inside?"

"Cameron's a medic," said Docchi, "not mechanically inclined. He forgot that an emergency rocket landing cancels any verbal orders. So I took the ship up a few inches. Geepees aren't very bright; that satisfied them that I was coming in for a landing. What Cameron should have done was splash some heat against a gravital unit, and then, having created an artificial emergency condition in the main dome, he could have directed the geepees from the gravity control center. After that, he would have had top priority, not me."

"But they rushed off, carrying Cameron with them." Jordan looked puzzled.

"Easy. I told the geepees that there was danger of crashing and that they must remove any human beings nearby, whether they were willing or not. You weren't nearby and that let you out. They took Cameron because he was."

"It's ours!" breathed Jordan. "But what about Anti and Nona?"

"Anti's taken care of. As far as the geepees are concerned, she comes under the heading of emergency landing material. They'll bring her. Nona is supposed to be waiting with Anti." Docchi frowned. "There's nothing we can do if she isn't. Meanwhile you'd better get ready to take the ship off."

Jordan swung himself inside.

Docchi remained at the passenger lock, waiting. He heard the geepees first and saw them seconds later. They came into sight half pushing, half carrying a huge rectangular tank. With unexpected robotic ingenuity, they had mounted it on four of their smaller brethren, the squat repair robots, which served to support the tremendous weight.

The tank was filled with blue liquid. Twisted pipes dangled from the ends; it had been torn and lifted from its foundation. Broken plants still clung to the narrow ledge on top and moist soil adhered to the sides. Five geepees pushed it rapidly toward the ship, mechanically oblivious to the disheveled man who frustratedly shouted and struck at them.

"Jordan, open the freight lock."

In response the ship rose a few more inches and hung quivering. A section of the ship hinged outward and downward to form a ramp. The ship was ready to take on cargo.

Docchi stood at his post. That damn fool Cameron should have stayed in the main dome where the geepees had released him. His presence added an unwelcome complication. Still, it should be easy enough to get rid of him when the time came.

It was Nona who really worried him. She wasn't anywhere to be seen. He took an uncertain step down the ramp, came back, shaking his head. It was impossible to look for her now, though he wanted to.

The tank neared the ship. A few feet of it projected onto the ramp. The geepees stopped; their efforts lost momentum. They looked bewildered.

The tank rolled backward. The geepees shook, buzzed and looked around, primarily at Docchi. He didn't wait any longer. He leaped into the ship.

"Close the passenger lock!" he shouted.

Jordan looked up questioningly from the controls.

"Vogel, the engineer," explained Docchi. "He must have seen the geepees on scanning when they entered the main dome. He's trying to do what Cameron should have done, but didn't have enough sense to do."

The passenger lock swung ponderously shut behind him.

"Now what?" Jordan asked, worried.

"First, let's see what you can get on the telecom," said Docchi.

The angle was impossible, so close to the ship, but they did manage to get a corner of the tank on the screen. Apparently it was resting where Docchi had last seen it, though it was difficult to be sure because the curve of the ship loomed so large.

"Maybe we'd better get out of here," suggested Jordan nervously.

"Without the tank? Not a chance. Vogel hasn't got complete control of them yet." That seemed to be true. The geepees were nearly motionless, paralyzed.

"What shall I do?" asked Jordan.

"Give me full power on the radio," said Docchi. "Burn it out if you have to. I think the engineer is at the wrong angle to broadcast much power to them. Besides, the intervening structure is absorbing most of his signal."

He waited until Jordan had complied. "The tank must be placed in the ship," he added.

Geepees were not designed to sift contradictory commands that were nearly at the same level of urgency. Their reasoning power was feeble, but the mechanism was complicated enough. In that respect they resembled humans. Borderline decisions were difficult.

"More power," whispered Docchi.

Sweating, Jordan obeyed.

Marionettes. This string led toward a certain action. Another, intrinsically more important, but suddenly far less powerful, pulled for something else. Circuits burned within electronic brains. Micro-relays fluttered under the stress.

Choice....

Stiffly the geepees moved and grasped the tank. The quality of decision, in this case, was strained. Inch by inch the tank rolled up the ramp.

"When it's completely on, raise the ramp," Docchi whispered to Jordan in an even lower voice.

One geepee wavered and fell. Motionless, it lay there. The remaining four were barely equal to the task.

"Now," said Docchi.

The freight ramp began to rise. The tank picked up speed as it rolled into the ship.

"Geepees, save yourselves!" shouted Docchi.

They leaped from the ramp.

Jordan breathed deeply. "I don't think they can hurt us now."

Docchi nodded. "Get me ship-to-asteroid communication, if there's any radio left."

"There is." Jordan made the adjustment.

"Vogel, we're going out. Give us the proper sequence and save the dome some damage."

There was no reply.

"He's trying to bluff," said Jordan. "He knows the airlocks to the main dome will automatically close if we do break through."

"Sure," said Docchi. "Everyone in the main dome is safe, *if* everyone is in there. Vogel, we'll give you time to think about that."

Jordan gave him the time until it hurt, waiting. Meanwhile he flipped on the telecom and searched the rocket dome. Nothing was moving; no geepee was in sight. Docchi watched the screen with interest. What he thought didn't show on his face.

Still there was no reply from Vogel.

"All right," Docchi said in a low, hard voice. "Jordan, take it out. Hit the shell with the bow of the rocket."

The ship hardly quivered as it ripped through the transparent covering of the rocket dome. The worst sound was unheard: the hiss of air escaping through the great hole in the envelope.

Jordan sat at the controls, gripping the levers. "I couldn't tell," he said slowly. "It happened too fast for me to be sure. Maybe Vogel did have the inner shell out of the way. In that event, it's all right because it would close immediately. The outer shell is supposed to be self-sealing, but I doubt if it could handle that much damage."

He twisted the lever and the ship leaped forward.

"Cameron I don't mind. He had enough time to get out if he wanted to. But I keep thinking that Nona might be in there."

Docchi avoided his eyes. There was no light at all in his face. He walked away.

Jordan rocked back and forth. The hemisphere that held what remained of his body was well suited for that. He set the auto-controls and reduced the gravity to one-quarter Earth normal. He bent his great arms and shoved himself into the air, deftly catching hold of a guide rail. He would have to go with Docchi. But not at the moment. He felt bad.

That is, he did until he saw a light blinking at a cabin door. He had to investigate that first.

\*　　\*　　\*　　\*　　\*

Jordan caught up before Docchi reached the cargo hold. In the lesser gravity of the ship Jordan was truly at home.

Docchi turned and waited for him. Jordan still carried the weapon he had taken from the pilot. It was clipped to the sacklike garment he wore, dangling from his midsection, which, for him was just below his shoulders. Down the corridor he flew, swinging from the guide rails lightly, though gravity on the ship was as erratic as on the asteroid.

Docchi braced himself. Locomotion was not so easy for him.

Jordan halted beside him and dangled from one hand. "We have another passenger."

Docchi stiffened. "Who?"

"I could describe her," said Jordan. "But why, when a name will do at least as well?"

"Nona!" said Docchi. He slumped in sudden relief against the wall. "How did she get in the ship?"

"A good question," said Jordan. "Remind me to ask her that sometime when she's able to answer. But since I don't know, I'll have to use my imagination. My guess is that, after she jammed the lights and scanners in the rocket dome, she walked to the ship and tapped the passenger lock three times in the right places, or something just as improbable. The lock opened for her whether it was supposed to or not."

"As good a guess as any," agreed Docchi.

"We may as well make our assumptions complete. Once inside, she felt tired. She found a comfortable cabin and fell asleep in it. She remained asleep throughout our skirmish with the geepees."

"She deserves a rest," said Docchi.

"She does. But if she had waited a few minutes to take it, she'd have saved you the trouble of crawling through the tubes."

"She did her part and more," Docchi argued. "We depend too much on her. Next we'll expect her to escort us personally to the stars." He straightened up. "Let's go. Anti is waiting for us."

The cargo hold was sizable. It had to be to contain the tank, battered and twisted though it was. Equipment had been jarred from storage racks and lay in tangled heaps on the floor.

"Anti!" called Docchi.

"Here."

"Are you hurt?"

"Never felt a thing," came the cheerful reply.

*     *     *     *     *

Jordan scaled the side of the tank. He reached the top and peered over. "She seems all right," he called down. "Part of the acid's gone. Otherwise no damage."

Damage enough, however. Acid was a matter of life for Anti. It had been splashed from the tank and, where it had spilled, metal was corroding rapidly. The wall against which the tank had crashed was bent and partly eaten through. That was no reason for alarm; the scavenging system of the ship would handle acid. The real question was what to do for Anti.

"I've stewed in this soup for years," said Anti. "Get me out of here."

"How?"

"If you weren't as stupid as doctors pretend to be, you'd know how. No gravity, of course. I've got muscles, more than you think. I can walk as long as my bones don't break from the weight."

No gravity would be rough on Docchi; having no arms, he would be virtually helpless. The prospect of floating free without being able to grasp something was terrifying.

"As soon as we can manage it," he said, forcing down his fear. "First we've got to drain and store the acid."

Jordan had anticipated that. He'd swung off the tank and was busy expelling the water from an auxiliary compartment into space. As soon as the compartment was empty, he led a hose from it to the tank.

The pumps sucked and the acid level fell slowly.

Docchi felt the ship lurch familiarly. "Hurry," he called out to Jordan.

The gravital unit was acting up. Presumably it was getting ready to cut out. If it did—well, a free-floating globe of acid would be as destructive to the ship and those in it as a high velocity meteor cluster.

Jordan jammed the lever as far as it would go and held it there. "All out," said Jordan presently, and let the hose roll back into the wall. Done in plenty of time. The gravital unit remained in operation for a full minute.

As soon as she was weightless, Anti rose out of the tank.

In all the time Docchi had known her, he had seen no more than a face framed in blue acid. Periodic surgery, where it was necessary, had trimmed the flesh from her face. For the rest, she lived submerged in a corrosive liquid that destroyed the wild tissue as fast as it grew. Or nearly as fast.

Docchi averted his eyes.

"Well, junkman, look at a real monster," snapped Anti.

*     *     *     *     *

Humans were not meant to grow that large. But it was not obscene to Docchi, merely unbelievable. Jupiter is not repulsive because it is the bulging giant of planets; it is overwhelming, and so was Anti.

"How will you live out of the acid?" he stammered.

"How really unobservant some men are," said Anti loftily. "I anticipated our little journey and prepared for it. If you look closely, you will notice I have on a special surgery robe. It's the only thing in the Solar System that will fit me. It's fabricated from a spongelike substance and holds enough acid to last me about thirty-six hours."

She grasped a rail and propelled herself toward the corridor. Normally that was a spacious passageway. For her it was a close fit.

Satellites, one glowing and the other swinging in an eccentric orbit, followed after her.

*     *     *     *     *

Nona was standing before the instrument panel when they came back. There was an impressive array of dials, lights and levers in front of her, but she wasn't interested in these. A single small dial, separate from the rest, held her complete attention. She seemed disturbed by what she saw or didn't see. Disturbed or excited, it was difficult to say which.

Anti stopped. "Look at her. If I didn't know she's a freak like the rest of us, the only one, in fact, who was born that way, it would be easy to hate her—she's so disgustingly normal."

Normal? True and yet not true. Surgical techniques that could take a body apart and put it back together again with a skill once reserved for the repair of machines had made beauty commonplace. No more sagging muscles, wrinkles; even the aged were attractive and youthful-seeming until the day they died. No more ill-formed limbs, misshapen bodies. Everyone was handsome or beautiful. No exceptions.

None to speak of, at least.

The accidentals didn't belong, of course. In another day most of them would have been candidates for a waxworks or the formaldehyde of a specimen bottle.

Nona fitted neither category; she wasn't a repair job. Looking at her closely—and why not?—she was an original work as far from the normal in one direction as Anti, for example, was in the other.

"Why is she staring at the little dial?" asked Anti as the others slipped past her and came into the compartment. "Is there something wrong with it?" She shrugged. "I would be interested in the big dials. The ones with colored lights."

"That's Nona." Docchi smiled. "I'm sure she's never been in the control room of a rocket before, and yet she went straight to the most curious thing in it. She's looking at the gravital indicator. Directly behind it is the gravital unit."

"How do you know? Does it say so?"

"It doesn't. You have to be trained to recognize it, or else be Nona."

Anti dismissed that intellectual feat. "What are you waiting for? You know she can't hear us. Go stand in front of her."

"How do I get there?" Docchi had risen a few inches from the floor, now that Jordan had released him from his grip.

"A good engineer would have enough sense to put on magneslippers. Nona did." Anti grasped his jacket. How she was able to move was uncertain. The tissues that surrounded the woman were too vast to permit the perception of individual motions. Nevertheless, she proceeded to the center of the compartment, and with her came Docchi.

Nona turned before they reached her.

"My poor boy," sighed Anti. "You do a very bad job of concealing your emotions, if that's what you're trying to do. Anyway, stop glowing like a rainbow and say something."

"Hello," said Docchi.

Nona smiled at him, though it was Anti that she came to.

"No, not too close, child. Don't touch the surgery robe unless you want your pretty face to peel off like a plastiwrapper."

Nona stopped; she said nothing.

Anti shook her head hopelessly. "I wish you would learn to read lips or at least recognize written words. It's so difficult to communicate with you."

"She knows facial expressions and actions, I think," said Docchi. "She's good at emotions. Words are a foreign concept to her."

"What other concepts does anyone think with?" asked Anti dubiously.

"Maybe mathematical relationships," answered Docchi. "Though she doesn't. They've tested her for that." He frowned. "I don't know what concepts she does think with. I wish I did."

"Save some of that worry and apply it to our present situation," said Anti. "The object of your concern doesn't seem to be interested in it."

That was true. Nona had wandered back and was staring at the gravital indicator again. What she saw to hold her attention was a puzzle.

In some ways she seemed irresponsible and childlike. That was an elusive thought, though: whose child? Not really, of course. Her parents were obscure technicians and mechanics, descendants of a long line of mechanics and technicians. The question he had asked himself was this: where and how does she belong? He couldn't answer.

With an effort Docchi came back to reality. "We appealed to the Medicouncil," he said. "We asked for a ship to go to the nearest star. It would have to be a rocket, naturally. Even allowing for a better design than any we now have, the journey would take a long time, forty or fifty years going and the same length of time back. That's entirely too long for a normal, but it wouldn't matter to a biocompensator."

"Why a rocket?" interrupted Jordan. "Why not some form of gravity drive?"

"An attractive idea," admitted Docchi. "Theoretically, there's no limit to gravity drive except light speed, and even that's not certain. If it would work, the time element could be cut to a fraction. But the last twenty years have proved that gravity drives won't work at all outside the Solar System. They function very poorly even when the ship is as far out as Jupiter's orbit."

"I thought the gravity drive on a ship was nearly the same as the gravital unit on the asteroid," said Jordan. "Why won't they function?"

"I don't know why," answered Docchi impatiently. "If I did, I wouldn't be marooned on Handicap Haven. Arms or no arms, biocompensator or not, I'd be the most important scientist on Earth."

"With a multitude of pretty women competing for your affections," added Anti.

"I think he'd settle for one. A certain one," suggested Jordan.

"Poor, unimaginative boy," said Anti. "In my youth...."

"We've heard about your youth," said Jordan.

"Youth and love are long since past, for both of you. Talk about them privately if you want, but not now." Docchi glowered at them. "Anyway," he resumed, "gravity drive is out. One time they had hopes for it, but no longer. It should be able to drive this ship. Actually, its sole function is to provide an artificial gravity *inside* the ship, for passenger comfort. So rocket ship it is. That's what we asked for. The Medicouncil refused. Therefore we're going to appeal to a higher authority."

"Fine," said Anti. "How?"

"We've discussed it," answered Docchi. "Ultimately the Medicouncil is responsible to the Solar Government. And in turn—"

"All right, I'm in favor of it," said Anti. "I just wanted to know."

"Mars is closer," continued Docchi. "But Earth is the seat of government. As soon as we get there...." He stopped suddenly and listened.

Anti listened with him and waited until she could stand it no longer. "What's the matter?" she asked. "I don't hear anything."

Jordan leaned forward in his seat and looked at the instrument panel. "That's the trouble, Anti. You're not supposed to hear anything. But you should be able to *feel* the vibration from the rocket exhaust, as long as it's on."

"I don't feel anything, either."

"Yeah," said Jordan. He looked at Docchi. "There's plenty of fuel."

\*    \*    \*    \*    \*

Momentum of the ship didn't cease when the rockets stopped, of course. They were still moving, but not very fast and not in the direction they wanted to go. Gingerly Docchi tried out the magneslippers; he was clumsy, but no longer helpless in the gravityless ship. He stared futilely at the instruments as if he could wring more secrets than the panel had electronic access to.

"It's mechanical trouble of some sort," he said uneasily. "There's one way of finding out."

Before he could move, Anti was in the corridor that led away from the control compartment.

"Stay here, Anti," he said. "I'll see what's wrong."

She reached nearly from the floor to the ceiling. She missed by scant inches the sides of the passageway. Locomotion was easy enough for her; turning around wasn't. Anti didn't turn.

"Look, honey," her voice floated back. "You brought me along for the ride. That's fine, but I'm not satisfied with it. I want to earn my fare. You stay and run the ship because you know how and I don't. I'll find out what's wrong."

"But you won't know what to do, Anti." There was no answer. "All right," he said in defeat. "Both of us ought to go. Jordan, you stay at the controls."

Anti led the way because Docchi couldn't get around her. Determinedly he shuffled along. There was a trick to magneslippers that he had nearly forgotten. Slowly it was coming back to him—shuffle instead of striding.

It was a dingy, poorly lighted passageway in an older ship. Handicap Haven definitely didn't rate the best equipment that was produced. On one side was the hull of the ship; on the other, a few small cabins. None were occupied. Anti stopped. The passageway ended in a cross corridor that led to the other side of the ship.

"We'd better check the stern rocket tubes," he said, still unable to see around her. "Open it up and we'll take a look."

"I can't," said Anti. "There are handles, but the thing won't open. There's a red light, too. Does that mean anything?"

His heart sank. "It does. Don't try to open it. With your strength, you might be unlucky enough to do it."

"That's a man for you," said Anti sharply. "First he wants me to open it, and then he tells me not to."

"There's a vacuum in there. The combustion cap has been retracted. That's the only thing that will actuate the warning signal. You'd die in a few seconds if you somehow managed to open the lock to the rocket compartment."

"What are we waiting for? Let's get busy and fix it."

"Sure, fix it. You see, Anti, that didn't happen by itself. Someone, or something, was responsible."

"Who?"

"Did you see anyone when we were loading your tank in the ship?"

"Nothing. I heard Cameron shouting, a lot of noise. All I could see was what was directly overhead. What does that have to do with it?"

"I think it has to do with a geepee. I thought they all dropped outside. Maybe there was one that didn't."

"Why a geepee?" she asked blankly.

"In the first place, no man is strong enough to move the combustion cap. But if he should somehow manage to exert super-human effort, as soon as the cap cleared the tubes, rocket action would cease. The air in the compartment would exhaust into space and anyone in there would die."

"So we have a dead geepee in there."

"A geepee doesn't die. Not even become inactive; it doesn't need air." Docchi tried to think the thing through. "Not only that, a geepee might be able to escape from the compartment. The lock would close as soon as the pressure dropped. But a geepee...."

Anti settled down grimly. "Then there's a geepee on the loose, intent on sabotage?"

"I'm afraid so," he admitted worriedly.

"What are we standing here for? We'll go back to controls and pick up the robot on radio. What it damaged, it can repair." She was partly turned around now and saw Docchi's face. "Don't tell me," she said. "I suppose I should have thought of it. The signal doesn't work inside the ship."

Docchi nodded. "It doesn't. Robots are never used aboard, so the control is set in the bow antenna and the ship, of course, is insulated."

"Well," said Anti happily, "we've got a robot hunt ahead of us."

"We do. And our bare hands to hunt it with."

"Oh, come now! It's not as bad as all that. Look, the geepee was back here when the rockets stopped. Could it get by the control compartment without our seeing it?"

"It couldn't. There are two corridors leading through the compartment, one on each side of the ship."

"That's what I thought. We came down one corridor and no geepee was in it. It has to be in the other. If it goes into a cabin, a light will shine on the outside. It can't really hide from us."

"Sure, we'll find out where it is. But what are we going to do with it when we find it?"

"I was thinking," said Anti. "Can you get around me when I'm standing like this?"

"I can't."

"Neither can a geepee. All I need is a toaster, or something that looks like one, and I can drive the robot into the control compartment for Jordan to pick off." Determinedly, she began to move toward the opposite corridor. "Hurry back to Jordan and tell him what we're doing. There ought to be another toaster on the ship. Probably there's one somewhere in the control compartment. Bring it back to me."

Docchi bit his lip and stared at the back of the huge woman. "All right," he answered. "But stay where you are. Don't try anything until I get back."

Anti laughed. "I value my big, fat life," she said. There were other things she valued, but she didn't mention them.

Docchi went as fast as the magneslippers would allow, which wasn't very fast. The strategy was simple, but it didn't follow that it was sound—a toaster for Jordan and one for Anti, if another could be found.

Anti would block the corridor. A geepee might go through her, but it could never squeeze past her. The robot would have to run for it. If it came toward Anti, she might be able to burn it down. But she would be firing directly into the control room. If she missed even partially—

The instruments were delicate.

It wasn't better if Jordan got the chance to bring down the robot. Anti would be in the line of fire. No, that wasn't good, either. They'd have to think of something else.

"Jordan," called Docchi as he entered the control compartment. Jordan wasn't there. Nona was, still gazing serenely at the gravity indicator.

Lights were streaming from the corridor on the opposite side of the compartment. Docchi hurried over. Jordan was just inside the entrance, the toaster clutched grimly in his hand. He was hitching his truncated body slowly toward the stern.

Coming to meet him was Anti—unarmed, enormously fat Anti. She wasn't walking; somehow it seemed more like swimming, a bulbous, flabby sea animal moving through the air. She waved her fins against the wall and propelled herself forward.

"Melt him down!" she cried.

It was difficult to make out the vaguely human form of the geepee. The powerful, shining body blended into the structure of the ship itself—unintentional camouflage, though the robot wasn't aware of that. It was crouched at the threshold of a cabin, hesitating between the approaching dangers.

Jordan raised the weapon and as instantly lowered it. "Get out of the way," he told Anti.

There was no place for her to go. She was too big to enter a cabin, too massive to let the geepee squeeze by her even if she wanted it to.

"Never mind that. Get him," she answered.

A geepee was not a genius even by robot standards. It didn't need to be. Heat is deadly; a human body is a fragile thing. This it knew. It ran toward Anti. Unlike man, it didn't need magneslippers. It had magnetic metal feet which could move fast, and did.

Docchi couldn't close his eyes, though he wanted to. He had to watch. The geepee torpedoed into Anti. And it was the robot that was thrown back. Relative mass favored the monstrous woman.

The electronic brain obeyed its original instructions, whatever those were. It got to its feet and rushed toward Anti. Metal arms shot out with dazzling speed and crashed against the flesh of the fat woman. Docchi could hear the thud. No ordinary person could take that kind of punishment and live.

Anti wasn't ordinary; she was strange, even for an accidental, living far inside a deep armor of flesh. It was possible

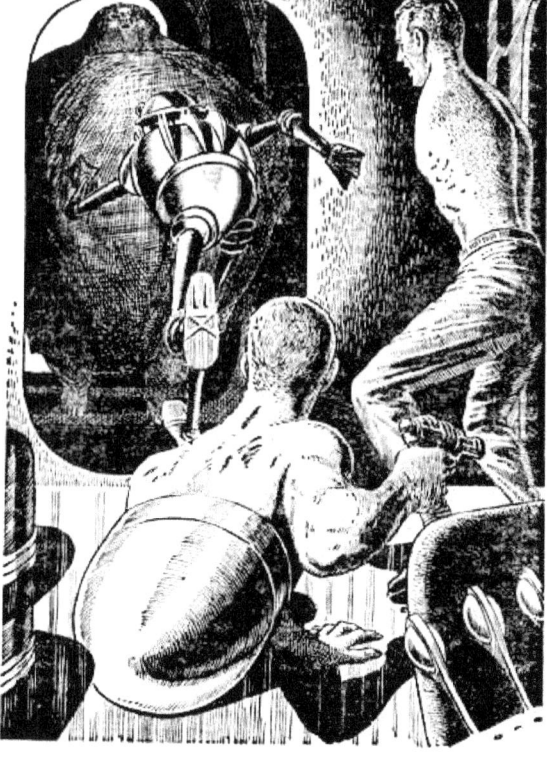

that she never felt the crushing force of those blows. Amazingly, she grasped the robot and drew it to her. And the geepee lost the advantage of leverage. The bright arms didn't flash so fast nor with such lethal power.

"Gravity!" cried Anti. "All you've got!"

She leaned against the struggling machine.

Gravity. That was something he could do. Docchi turned, took two steps before the surge of gravity hit him. It came in waves, the sequence of which he was never able to disentangle. The first wave staggered him; at the second his knees buckled and he sank to the floor. After that his eardrums hurt. He thought he could feel the ship quiver. He knew dazedly that an artificial gravity field of this magnitude was impossible, but that knowledge didn't help him move.

It vanished as suddenly as it had come. Painfully his lungs expanded. Each muscle ached. He rolled to his feet and lurched past Jordan.

He didn't find the mass of broken flesh he expected. Anti was already standing.

"Oof!" she grunted and gazed with satisfaction at the twisted grotesque shape at her feet. The electronic brain had been smashed, the body flattened.

"Are you hurt?" asked Docchi gently, awed.

She waggled the extremities of her body. "Nope, I can't feel anything broken," she said solemnly. She moved back to get a better view of the robot. "I'd call that throwing my weight around. At the right time, of course. The secret's timing. And I must say you picked up your cue with the gravity well." Her laughter rolled through the ship.

"It wasn't I," said Docchi.

"Jordan? No, he's just getting up. Then who?"

"Nona," said Docchi. "It had to be her. She saw what had to be done and did it. But how she got that amount of gravity—"

"Ask her," said Anti with fond irony.

Docchi grimaced and limped back into the control room, followed by Anti and Jordan. Nona was at the gravity panel, her face pleasant and childlike.

"Gravity can be turned on or off," said Docchi puzzledly, searching her face for some sign. "And regulated, within certain narrow limits. But somehow you doubled or tripled the normal amount. How?"

Nona smiled questioningly.

"Gravity engineers would like to know that too," said Jordan.

"Everybody would like to know," Anti interrupted irritably. "Except me. I'm too pragmatic, I suppose, but I want to know when we start the rockets and be on our way."

"It isn't that easy," sighed Jordan. "A retracted combustion cap in flight generally means at least one burned-out tube." He made his way to the instrument panel and looked at it glumly. "Three."

"A factor." Docchi nodded. "But I was thinking about the robot."

Anti was impatient. "An interesting subject, no doubt. What about it?"

"Where did it get instructions? Not radio; the hull of the ship cuts off all radiation. The last we knew, it was in our control."

"All right, how?"

"Voice," said Docchi. "Cameron's voice, to be exact."

"But he was in the rocket dome," Jordan objected.

"Think back to when we were loading the tank. We had to look through the telecom and the angle of vision was bad. We couldn't see much of the cargo lock. Anti couldn't see anything that wasn't directly overhead. Both Cameron and the geepee managed to get inside and we didn't know it."

Jordan hefted his weapon. "Looks like we've got another hunt on our hands. This time a nice normal doctor."

"Keep it handy," said Docchi, glancing at the toaster. "But be careful how you use it. One homicide and we can forget what we came for. I think he'll be ready to surrender. The ship's temporarily disabled; he'll consider that damage enough."

*     *     *     *     *

Jordan found the doctor in the forward section of the ship. Cameron knew better than to argue with a toaster. In a matter of minutes he was in the control room.

"Now that you've got me, what are you going to do with me?" he asked.

Docchi swiveled away from the instrument panel. "I don't expect active cooperation, of course, but I like to think you'll give your word not to hinder us hereafter."

Cameron glared. "I promise nothing of the kind."

"We can chain him to Anti," suggested Jordan. "That will keep him out of trouble."

"Like leading a poodle on a leash? Nope," said Anti indignantly. "A girl has to have some privacy."

"Don't wince, Cameron," objected Docchi. "She really was a girl once, an attractive one."

"We can put him in a spacesuit and lock his hands behind his back," said Jordan. "Something like an ancient straitjacket."

Cameron laughed.

"No, that's inhuman," said Docchi.

Jordan juggled the toaster. "I can weld with this. Let's put him in a cabin and weld the door closed. We can cut a slot to shove food in. A very narrow slot."

"Excellent. I think you have the solution. That is, unless Dr. Cameron will reconsider his decision."

Cameron shrugged. "They'll pick you up in a day or less anyway. I suppose I'm not compromising myself by agreeing to your terms."

"Good."

"A doctor's word is as good as his oath," observed Anti. "Hippocratic or hypocritic."

"Now, Anti, don't be cynical. Doctors have an economic sense as well as the next person," said Docchi gravely. He turned to Cameron. "You see, after Anti grew too massive for her skeletal structure, doctors reasoned she'd be most comfortable in the absence of gravity. That was in the early days, before successful ship gravital units were developed. They put her on an interplanetary ship and kept transferring her before each landing.

"But that grew troublesome and—expensive. They devised a new treatment; the asteroid and the tank of acid. Not being aquatic by nature, Anti resented the change. She still does."

"I knew nothing about that," Cameron pointed out defensively.

"It was before your time." Docchi frowned at the doctor. "Tell me, why did you laugh when Jordan mentioned a spacesuit?"

Cameron grinned. "That was my project while you were busy with the robot."

"To do what? Jordan—"

But Jordan was already on his way. He was gone for some time.

"Well?" asked Docchi on his return. It really wasn't necessary; Jordan's gloomy face told the story.

"Cut to ribbons."

"All of them?"

"Every one. Beyond repair."

"What's the excitement about?" rumbled Anti. "We don't need spacesuits unless something happens to the ship and we have to go outside."

"Exactly, Anti. How do you suppose we go about replacing the defective tubes? From the outside, of course. By destroying the spacesuits, Cameron made sure we can't."

Anti opened her mouth with surprise and closed it in anger. She glowered at the doctor.

"We're still in the asteroid zone," said Cameron. "In itself, that's not dangerous. Without power to avoid stray rocks, it is. I advise you to contact the Medicouncil. They'll send a ship to pick us up and tow us in."

"No, thanks. I don't like Handicap Haven as well as you do," Anti said brusquely. She turned to Docchi. "Maybe I'm stupid for asking, but exactly what is it that's deadly about being out in space without a spacesuit?"

"Cold. Lack of air pressure. Lack of oxygen."

"Is that all? Nothing else?"

His laugh was too loud. "Isn't that enough?"

"I wanted to be sure," she said.

She beckoned to Nona, who was standing near. Together they went forward, where the spacesuits were kept.

Cameron scowled puzzledly and started to follow. Jordan waved the toaster around.

"All right," said the doctor, stopping. He rubbed his chin. "What is she thinking about?"

"I wouldn't know," said Docchi. "She's not scientifically trained, if that's what you mean. But she has a good mind, as good as her body once was."

"And how good was that?"

"We don't talk about it," said Jordan shortly.

*     *     *     *     *

It was a long time before the women came back—if the weird creature that floated into the control compartment with Nona *was* Anti.

Cameron stared at her and saw shudderingly that it was. "You need a session with the psycho-computer," he said. "When we get back, that's the first thing we do. Can't you understand...."

"Be quiet," growled Jordan. "Now, Anti, explain what you've rigged up."

"Any kind of pressure is good enough as far as the outside of the body is concerned," answered Anti, flipping back the helmet. "Mechanical pressure will do as well as air pressure. I had Nona cut the spacesuits into strips and wind them around me—hard. Then I found a helmet that would fit over my head when the damaged part was cut away. It won't hold much air pressure, even taped very tight to my skin. But as long as it's pure oxygen—"

"It might be satisfactory," admitted Docchi. "But the temperature?"

"Do you think I'm going to worry about cold?" asked Anti. "Me? Way down below all this flesh?"

"Listen to me," said Cameron through his teeth. "You've already seriously threatened my career with all this childish nonsense. I won't permit you to ruin it altogether by a deliberate suicide."

"You and your stinking career," retorted Jordan tiredly. "We're not asking your permission to do anything." He turned away from the doctor. "You understand the risk, Anti? It's possible that it won't work at all."

"I've thought about it," Anti replied soberly. "On the other hand, I've thought about the asteroid."

"All right," said Jordan. Docchi nodded. Nona bobbed her head; it was doubtful that she knew what she was agreeing to.

"Let's have some telecom viewers outside," said Docchi. "One directly in back, one on each side. We've got to know what's happening."

Jordan went to the control panel and flipped levers. "They're out and working," he said, gazing at the screen. "Now, Anti, go to the freight lock. Close your helmet and wait. I'll let the air out slowly. The pressure change will be gradual. If anything seems wrong, let me know over the helmet radio and I'll yank you in immediately. Once you're outside I'll give you further instructions. Tools and equipment are in a compartment that opens into space."

Anti waddled away.

Jordan looked down at his legless body. "I suppose we have to be realistic about it—"

"We do," answered Docchi. "Anti is the only one of us who has a chance of doing the job and surviving."

Jordan adjusted a dial. "It was Cameron who was responsible for it. If Anti doesn't come back, you can be damn sure he'll join her."

"No threats, please," said Docchi. "When are you going to let her out?"

"She's out," said Jordan. Deliberately, he had diverted their attention while he had taken the burden of emotional strain.

Docchi glanced hastily at the telecom. Anti was hanging free in space, wrapped and strapped in strips torn from the useless spacesuits—that, and more flesh than any human had ever borne. The helmet sat jauntily on her head; the oxygen cylinder was strapped to her back. She was still intact.

"How is she?" he asked anxiously, unaware that the microphone was open.

"Fine," came Anti's reply, faint and ready. "The air's thin, but it's pure oxygen."

"Cold?" asked Docchi.

"It hasn't penetrated yet. No worse than the acid, at any rate. What do I do?"

Jordan gave her directions. The others watched. It was work to find the tools and examine the tubes for defectives, to loosen the tubes in the sockets and pull them out and push them spinning into space. It was still harder to replace them, though there was no gravity and Anti was held to the hull by magneslippers.

But it seemed more than work. To Cameron, who was watching, an odd thought occurred: In her remote past, of which he knew nothing, Anti had done something like this before. Ridiculous, of course. Yet there was a rhythm to her motions, this shapeless giant creature whose bones would break with her weight if she tried to stand at even only half Earth gravity. Rhythm, a sense of purpose, a strange pattern, an incredible gargantuan grace.

The whale plowing the waves is graceful; it cannot be otherwise in its natural habitat. The human race had produced, accidentally, one unlikely person to whom interplanetary space was not an alien thing. Anti was at last in her element.

"Now," said Jordan, keeping the tension out of his voice, "go back to the outside tool compartment. You'll find a lever. Pull. That will set the combustion cap in place."

"Done," said Anti, some minutes later.

"That's all. You can come in now."

"That's all? But I'm not cold. It hasn't reached any nerves yet."

"Come in," repeated Jordan, showing the anger of alarm.

She walked slowly over the hull to the cargo lock and, while she did, Jordan reeled in the telecom viewers. The lock was no sooner closed to the outside and the air hissing into the compartment than Jordan was there, opening the inner lock.

"Are you all right?" he asked.

She flipped back the helmet. There was frost on her eyebrows and her nose was a bright red. "Of course. My hands aren't a bit cold." She stripped off the heated gloves and waggled her fingers.

"It *can't* be!" protested Cameron. "You should be frozen stiff!"

"Why?" asked Anti, laughing. "It's a matter of insulation and I have plenty of that."

Cameron turned to Docchi. "When I was a kid, I saw a film of a dancer. She did a ballet, Life of the Cold Planets, I believe it was called. For some cockeyed reason, I thought of it when Anti was out there. I hadn't thought of it in years."

He rubbed his hand fretfully over his forehead. "It fascinated me when I first saw it. I couldn't get it out of my mind. When I grew older, I found out a tragic thing happened to the dancer. She was on a tour of Venus and the ship she was in disappeared. They sent out searching parties, of course. They found her after she had spent a week on a fungus plain. You know what that meant. The great ballerina was a living spore culture medium."

"Shut up," growled Jordan.

Cameron didn't seem to hear. "Naturally, she died. I can't remember her name, but I've always remembered the ballet she did. And that's funny, because it reminded me of Anti out there—"

A fist exploded in his face. If there had been more behind the blow than shoulders and a fragment of a body, his jaw would have been broken. As it was he floated through the air and crashed against the wall.

Angrily, he got to his feet. "I gave my word I wouldn't cause any trouble. The agreement evidently doesn't work both ways." He glanced significantly at the weapon Jordan carried. "Maybe you'd better be sure to have that around at all times."

"I told you to shut up," said Jordan. After that he ignored the doctor. He didn't have a body with which to do it, but somehow Jordan managed a bow. "A flawless performance. One of your very best, Antoinette."

"Do you think so?" sighed Anti. The frost had melted from her eyebrows and was trickling down her cheek. She left with Jordan.

Cameron remained behind. He felt his jaw. It was too bad about his ambitions. He knew now that he was never going to be the spectacular success he had once imagined. Not after these accidentals had escaped from Handicap Haven. Still, he would always be able to practice medicine somewhere in the Solar System. He'd done his best on the asteroid and this ship, and he'd been a complete ass both times.

The ballerina hadn't really died, as he had been told. It would have been better for her if she had. He succeeded in recalling her name. It had been Antoinette.

Now it was Anti. He could have found that out by checking her case history—*if* Handicap Haven had one on file. Probably not, he comforted himself. Why keep case histories of hopeless cases?

*　*　*　*　*

"We'll stick to the regular lanes," said Docchi. "I think we'll get closer. They have no reason to suspect that we're heading toward Earth. Mars is more logical, or one of the moons of Jupiter, or another asteroid."

Jordan shifted uneasily. "I'm not in favor of it. They'll pick us up before we have a chance to say anything."

"But there's nothing to distinguish us from an ordinary Earth-to-Mars rocket. We have a ship's registry on board. Pick out a ship that's in our class. Hereafter, we're going to be that ship. If Traffic blips us, and they probably won't unless we try to land, have a recording ready. Something like this: 'ME 21 zip crackle 9 reporting. Our communication is acting up. We can't hear you, Traffic.' Don't overdo the static effects but repeat that with suitable variations and I don't think they will bother us."

Shaking his head dubiously, Jordan swung away toward the repair shops.

"You look worried," said Anti.

Docchi turned around. "Yeah."

"Won't it work?"

"Sure. We'll get close to Earth. They're not looking for us around here. They don't really know why we escaped in the rocket. That's why they can't figure out where we're going."

His face was taut and his eyes were tired. "It's not that. The entire Solar Police Force has been alerted for us."

"Which means?"

"Look. We planned to bypass the Medicouncil and take our case directly to the Solar Government. If they want us as much as the radio indicates, it's not likely they'll be very sympathetic. If the Solar Government doesn't support us all the way, we'll never get another chance."

"Well?" said Anti. She seemed trimmer, more vigorous. "What are we waiting for? Let's take the last step first."

He raised his head. "The Solar Government won't like it."

"They won't, but there's nothing they can do about it."

"I think there is—simply shoot us down. When we stole the ship, we automatically stepped into the criminal class."

"We knew that in advance."

"Is it worth it?"

"I think so," said Anti.

"In that event," he said, "I'll need time to get ready."

She scrutinized him carefully. "Maybe we can fix you up."

"With fake arms and grease-paint? No. They'll have to accept us as we are."

"A good idea. I hadn't thought of the sympathy angle."

"Not sympathy. Reality. I don't want them to approve of us as handsome accidentals and have them change their minds when they discover what we're really like."

Anti looked doubtful, but she kept her objections to herself as she waddled away.

Sitting in silence, he watched her go. She, at least, would derive some benefit. Dr. Cameron apparently hadn't noticed that exposure to extreme cold had done more to inhibit her unceasing growth than the acid bath. She'd never be normal again; that was obvious. But some day, if the cold treatment were properly investigated, she might be able to stand gravity.

He examined the telecom. They were getting closer. No longer a bright point of light, Earth was a perceptible disc. He could see the outline of oceans, shapes of land; he could imagine people.

Jordan came in. "The record is rigged up, though we haven't had to use it. But we have a friend behind us. An official friend."

"Has he blipped us?"

"Not yet. He keeps hanging on."

"Is he overtaking us?"

"He would like to."

"Don't let him."

"With this bag of bolts?"

"Shake it apart if you have to," Docchi impatiently said. "How soon can you break into a broadcasting orbit?"

"I thought that was our last resort."

"Right. As far as Anti and I are concerned, this is it. Any argument against?"

"None that I can think of," answered Jordan. "With a heavy cruiser behind us, no argument at all."

\*    \*    \*    \*    \*

They were all in the control compartment. "I don't want a focus exclusively on me," Docchi was saying. "To a world of perfect normals I may look strange, but we have to avoid the family portrait effect."

"Samples," suggested Anti.

"In a sense, yes. A lot depends on whether they accept those samples."

For the first time Dr. Cameron began to realize what they were up to. "Wait!" he exclaimed. "You've got to listen to me!"

"We're not going to wait and we've already done enough listening to you," said Docchi. "Jordan, see that Cameron stays out of the telecom transmitting angle and doesn't interrupt. We've come too far for that."

"Sure," Jordan promised harshly. "If he makes a sound, I'll melt the teeth out of his mouth." He held the toaster against his side, out of line with the telecom, but aimed at Cameron's face.

Cameron began to shake with urgency, but he kept still.

"Ready?" Docchi asked.

"Flip the switch and we will be, with everything we've got. If they don't read us, it'll be because they don't want to."

The rocket slipped out of the approach lanes. It spun down, the stern tubes pulsing brightly, coming toward Earth in a tight trajectory.

"Citizens of the Solar System!" began Docchi. "Everyone on Earth! This is an unscheduled broadcast, an unauthorized appeal. We are using the emergency bands because, for us, it is an emergency. Who are we? Accidentals, of course, as you can see by looking at us. I know the sight isn't pretty, but we consider other things more important than appearance. Accomplishment, for example. Contributing to progress in ways normals cannot do.

"Shut away on Handicap Haven, we're denied this right. All we can do there is exist in frustration and boredom; kept alive whether we want to be or not. Yet we have a gigantic contribution to make ... if we are allowed to leave the Solar System for Alpha Centauri! You can't travel to the stars now, although eventually you will.

"You must be puzzled, knowing how slow our present rockets are. No normal person could make the round trip; he would die of old age. But we accidentals can go! We would positively *not* die of old age! The Medicouncil knows that is true ... and still will not allow us to go!"

At the side of the control compartment, Cameron opened his mouth to protest. Jordan, glancing at him, imperceptibly waggled the concealed weapon. Cameron swallowed his words and subsided without a sound.

"Biocompensation," continued Docchi evenly. "You may know about it, but in case information on it has been suppressed, let me explain: The principle of biocompensation has long been a matter of conjecture. This is the first age in which medical technology is advanced enough to explore it. Every cell, every organism, tends to survive, as an individual, as a species. Injure it and it strives for survival according to the seriousness of the injury. We accidentals have been maimed and mutilated almost past belief.

"Our organisms had the assistance of medical science. *Real* medical science. Blood was supplied as long as we needed it, machines did all our breathing, kidneys were replaced, hearts furnished, glandular products supplied in the exact quantities necessary, nervous and muscular systems were regenerated. In the extremity of our organic struggle, because we had the proper treatment, our bodies were wiped virtually free of death."

Sweat ran down his face. He longed for hands to wipe it away.

"Most accidentals are nearly immortal. Not quite—we'll die four or five hundred years from now. Meanwhile, there is no reason why we can't leave the Solar System. Rockets are slow; you would die before you got back from Alpha Centauri. We won't. Time doesn't matter to us.

"Perhaps better, faster rockets will be devised after we leave. You may get to there long before we do. We won't mind. We will simply have made our contribution to progress as best we could, and that will satisfy us."

With an effort Docchi smiled. The instant he did, he felt it was a mistake, one that he couldn't rectify. Even to himself it felt more like a snarl.

"You know where we're kept That's a politer word than imprisoned. We don't call it Handicap Haven; our name for it is the *junkpile*. And to ourselves we're junkmen. Does this give you a clue to how we feel?

"I don't know what you'll have to do to force the Medicouncil to grant their permission. We appeal to you as our last resort. We have tried all other ways and failed. Our future as human beings is at stake. Whether we get what we want and need is something for you to settle with your conscience."

He nudged the switch and sat down.

His face was gray.

"I don't like to bother you," said Jordan, "but what shall we do about them?"

Docchi glanced at the telecom. "They" were uncomfortably close and considerably more numerous than the last time he had looked.

"Take evasive action," he said wearily. "Swing close to Earth and use the planet's gravity to give us a good push. We've got to keep out of their hands until people have time to react."

"I think you ought to know—" began Cameron. There was an odd tone to his voice.

"Save it for later," said Docchi. "I'm going to sleep." His body sagged. "Jordan, wake me up if anything important happens. And remember that you don't have to listen to this fellow unless you want to."

Jordan nodded and touched the controls. Nona, leaning against the gravital panel, paid no attention to the scene. She seemed to be listening to something nobody else could hear. That was nothing new, but it broke Docchi's heart whenever he saw it. His breath drew in almost with a sob as he left the control room.

*　*　*　*　*

The race went on. Backdrop: planets, stars, darkness. The little flecks of light that edged nearer didn't seem cheerful to Jordan. His lips were fixed in a straight, hard line. He could hear Docchi come in behind him.

"Nice speech," said Cameron.

"Yeah." Docchi glanced at the telecom. The view didn't inspire further comment.

"That's the trouble, it was just a speech. It didn't do you any good. My advice is to give up before you get hurt."

"It would be."

Cameron stood at the threshold. "I may as well tell you," he said reluctantly. "I tried to before the broadcast, as soon as I found out what you were going to do. But you wouldn't listen."

He came into the control compartment. Nona was huddled in a seat, motionless, expressionless. Anti was absent.

"You know why the Medicouncil refused to let you go?"

"Sure," said Docchi.

"The general metabolism of accidentals is further from normal than that of creatures we dredge from the bottom of the sea. Add to that an enormously elongated life span and you ought to see the Medicouncil's objection."

"Get to the point!"

"Look at it this way," Cameron continued almost desperately. "The Centauri group contains quite a few planets. From what we know of cosmology, intelligent life probably exists there to a greater or lesser extent. You will be our representatives to them. What *they* look like isn't important; it's their concern. But our ambassadors have to meet certain minimum standards. They at least—damn it, don't you see that they at least have to *look* like human beings?"

"I know you feel that way," said Jordan, rigid with contempt.

"I'm not talking for myself," Cameron said. "I'm a doctor. The medicouncilors are doctors. We graft on or regenerate legs and arms and eyes. We work with blood and bones and intestines. We know what a thin borderline separates normal people from—from you.

"Don't you understand? They're perfect, perhaps too much so. They can't tolerate even small blemishes. They rush to us with things like hangnails, pimples, simple dandruff. Health—or rather the appearance of it—has become a fetish. They may think they're sympathetic to you, but what they actually feel is something else."

"What are you driving at?" whispered Docchi.

"Just this: if it were up to the Medicouncil, you would be on your way to the Centauri group. But it isn't. The decision always had to be referred back to the Solar System as a whole. And the Medicouncil can't go counter to the mass of public opinion."

Docchi turned away in loathing.

"Don't believe me," said Cameron. "You're not too far from Earth. Pick up the reaction to your broadcast."

Worriedly, Jordan looked at Docchi.

"We may as well find out," said Docchi. "It's settled now, one way or the other."

They searched band after band. The reaction was always the same. Obscure private citizen or prominent one, man or woman, they all told how sorry they were for the accidentals, but—

"Turn it off," said Docchi at last.

"Now what?" Jordan asked numbly.

"You have no choice," said the doctor.

"No choice," repeated Docchi dully. "No choice but to give up. We misjudged who our allies were."

"We knew you had," said Cameron. "It seemed better to let you go on thinking that way while you were on the asteroid. It gave you something to hope for. It made you feel you weren't alone. The trouble was that you got farther than we thought you would ever be able to."

"So we did," Docchi said. His lethargy seemed to lift a little. "And there's no reason to stop now. Jordan, pick up the ships behind us. Tell them we've got Cameron on board. A hostage. Play him up as a hero. Basically, he's not with those who are against us."

Anti came into the control compartment. Cheerfulness faded from her face. "What's the matter?" she asked.

"Jordan will explain to you. I've got to think."

Docchi closed his eyes. The ship lurched slightly, though the vibration from the rockets did not change. There was no reason for alarm; the flight of a ship was never completely steady. Docchi paid no attention.

At last he opened his eyes. "If we were properly fueled and provisioned," he said without much hope, "I would be in favor of the four of us heading for Alpha or Proxima. Maybe even Sirius. It wouldn't matter where, since we wouldn't intend to come back. But we can't make it with our small fuel reserve. If we can shake the ships behind us, we might be able to hide until we can steal the necessary fuel and food."

"What'll we do with Doc?" asked Jordan.

"We'd have to raid an unguarded outpost, of course. Probably a small mining asteroid. We can leave him there."

"Yeah," said Jordan. "A good idea, *if* we can run away from our personal escort of bloodhounds. Offhand, that doesn't seem very likely. They didn't come any closer when I told them we had Doc with us, but they didn't drop back—"

He stopped and raised his eyes to the telecom. He blinked, not believing what he saw.

"They're gone!" His voice broke with excitement.

Almost instantly Docchi was beside him. "No," he corrected. "They're still following, but they're very far behind." Even as he looked, the pursuing ships visibly lost ground.

"What's our relative speed?" asked Jordon. He looked at the dials himself, frowned, tapped them as if the needles had gone crazy.

"What did you do to the rockets?" demanded Docchi.

"Nothing! There wasn't a thing I *could* do. We were already running at top speed."

"We're above it. Way above it. How?"

There was nothing to explain their astonishing velocity. Cameron, Anti, and Jordan were in the control compartment. Nona still sat huddled up, hands pressed tight against her head. There was no explanation at all, yet power was pouring into the gravital unit, as a long unused, actually useless dial was indicating.

"The gravital drive is working," Docchi blankly pointed out.

"Nonsense," said Anti. "I don't feel any weight."

"You don't," answered Docchi. "You won't. The gravital unit was originally installed to drive the ship. When that proved unsatisfactory, it was converted. The difference is slight but important. An undirected general field produces weight effects inside the ship. That's for passenger comfort. A directed field, outside the ship, will drive it. You can have one or the other, not both."

"But I didn't turn on the gravital drive," said Jordan in flat bewilderment. "I couldn't if I wanted to. It's disconnected."

"I would agree with you, except for one thing. It's working." Docchi stared at Nona, whose eyes were closed. "Get her attention," he said.

It was Jordan who gently touched her shoulder. She opened her eyes. On the instrument board, the needle of a once useless dial rose and fell.

"What's the matter with the poor dear?" asked Anti. "She's shaking."

"Let her alone," said Docchi.

No one moved. No one said anything at all. Minutes passed while the ancient ship creaked and groaned and ran away from the fastest rockets in the Solar System.

"I think I know," said Docchi at last, still frowning. "Consider the gravity-generating plant. Part of it is an electronic computer, capable of making the necessary calculations and juggling the proportion of power required to produce, continuously, directed or undirected gravity. In other words, a brain, a complex mechanical intelligence. From the viewpoint of that intelligence, why should it perform *ad infinitum* a complicated but meaningless routine? It didn't know why, and because it didn't, very simply, it refused to do so.

"Now consider Nona. She's deaf, can't speak, can't communicate. In a way she's comparable to the gravital computer. Like it, she has a very high potential intelligence. Like it, she's had difficulty grasping the facts of her environment. Unlike it, though, she has learned something. How much, I don't know, but it's far more than the Medicouncil psychologists credit her with."

"Yeah," said Jordan dubiously. "But what's happening now?"

"If there were two humans involved, you would call it telepathy," answered Docchi hesitantly, fumbling for concepts he could only sense without grasping. "One intelligence is electronic, the other organic. You'll have to coin a new term, because the only one I know is extrasensory perception, and that's obviously ridiculous. It is, isn't it?"

Jordan smiled and flexed his arms. Under the shapeless garment his muscles rippled. "It isn't," he said. "The power was there, but we're the only ones who know how to use it. Or rather Nona is."

"Power?" repeated Anti, rising majestically. "You can keep it. I want just enough to get to Centauri."

"I think you'll get it," Docchi promised. "A lot of things seem clearer now. For example, in the past, why didn't gravital units work well at considerable distances from the Sun? As a matter of fact, the efficiency of each unit was inversely proportional to the square of the distance between it and the Sun.

"The gravital computer is a deaf, blind, mass-sensitive brain. The major fact in its existence is the Sun, the greatest mass in the Solar System. To such a brain, leaving the Solar System would be like stepping off the edge of a flat world, because it couldn't be aware of stars.

"Now that it knows about the Galaxy, the drive will work anywhere. With Nona to direct it, even Sirius isn't far away."

"Doc," said Jordan carelessly, "you'd better be figuring a way to get off the ship. Remember, we're going faster than man ever went before." He chuckled. "Unless, of course, you *like* our company and don't want to leave."

"We've got to do some figuring ourselves," interposed Docchi. "Such as where we are heading now."

"A good idea," said Jordan. He busied himself with charts and calculations. Gradually his flying fingers slowed. His head bent low over his work. At last he stopped and folded his arms.

"Where?" asked Docchi.

"There." Jordan dully punched the telecom selector and a view became fixed on the screen. In the center glimmered a tiny world, a fragment of a long-exploded planet. Their destination was easily recognizable.

It was Handicap Haven.

"But why do we want to go there?" asked Anti. She looked in amazement at Docchi.

"We're not going voluntarily," he answered, his voice flat and spent. "We're going where the Medicouncil wants us to go. We forgot about the monitor system. When Nona activated the gravital unit, that fact was indicated at some central station. All the Medicouncil had to do was use the monitor to take the gravital drive away from Nona."

"We thought we were running away from the ships, which we were, but only to beat them back to the junkpile?" asked Anti.

Docchi nodded.

"Well, it's over. We did our best. There's no use crying about it." Yet she was. She passed by Nona, patting her gently. "It's all right, darling. You tried."

Jordan followed her from the compartment.

Cameron remained; he came over to Docchi. "Everything isn't lost," he said, somewhat awkwardly. "You're back where you started from, but Nona at least will benefit."

"Benefit?" said Docchi. "Someone will. It won't be Nona."

"You're wrong. Now that she is an important factor—"

"So is a special experimental machine. Very valuable. I don't think she'll like that classification."

Silence met silence. It was Dr. Cameron who turned away.

"That ghastly glow of yours when you're angry always did upset me. I'll come back when it's dimmer."

Docchi glared after him. Cameron was the only normal aware that it was Nona who controlled the gravital unit. All the outside world could realize was that it was in operation, as it had been designed to work, but never had. If Cameron could be disposed of—

He shook his head. It wouldn't solve anything. He might fool them for a while. They might think he was responsible. In the end, they'd find out. Nona wasn't capable of that much deception, for she never knew what a test was.

He went over to her. Once he had hoped.... It didn't matter what he had hoped.

She looked up and smiled. She had a right to. No word had ever broken the silence of her mind, but now she was communicating with something, whatever it was that an electronic brain could say. Of course she didn't understand that the conversation was taking place between two captives, herself and the gravital computer.

Abruptly he turned away. He stopped at the telecom panel and methodically kicked it apart. Delicate tubes smashed into powder. The emergency radio he thoroughly demolished.

The ship was firmly in the grip of the gravital monitor. There was nothing he could do about that. All that remained was to protect Nona from their prying minds as long as he could.

She didn't hear the noise, or didn't care. She sat there, head in her hands, calm and smiling.

*     *     *     *     *

The outer shell of the rocket dome opened before and closed behind them. Jordan set the controls in neutral and lifted his hands, muttering to himself. They were gliding through the lip of the inner shell. Home.

"Cheer up," said Cameron breezily. "You're not really prisoners, you know."

Nona seemed content, though Jordan didn't. Docchi said nothing, the light gone from his face. Anti wasn't with them; she was floating in the tank of acid. The gravity field of the asteroid made that necessary.

The ship scraped gently and they were down. Jordan touched a lever; passenger and freight locks were open.

"Let's go," said Dr. Cameron. "I imagine there's a reception committee for you."

There was. The little rocket dome held more ships than normally came in a year. The precise confusion of military discipline was everywhere in evidence. Armed guards lined either side of the landing ramp down which they walked.

At the bottom, a large telecom unit had been set up. If size indicated anything, someone considered this an important occasion. From the screen, larger than life, Medicouncilor Thorton looked out approvingly.

The procession from the ship halted in front of the telecom unit.

"A good job, Dr. Cameron," said the medicouncilor. "We were quite surprised at the escape of the four accidentals, and your disappearance, which coincided with it. From what we were able to piece together, you deliberately followed them. A splendid example of quick thinking, Doctor. You deserve recognition for it."

"Thank you," said Cameron.

"I'm sorry I can't be there to congratulate you in person, but I will be soon." The medicouncilor paused discreetly. "At first the publicity was bad. Very bad. We thought it unwise to conceal an affair of such magnitude. Of course the unauthorized broadcast made it impossible. Fortunately, the gravital discovery came along at just the right time. I don't mind telling you that the net effect is now in our favor."

"I hoped it would be," said Cameron. "Nona—"

"You've spoken about her before." The medicouncilor frowned. "We can discuss her later. For the moment, see that she and the rest of the accidentals are returned to their usual places. Bring Docchi to your office at once. I want to question him privately."

Cameron stared at him in bewilderment. "But I thought—"

"No objections, Doctor," snapped Thorton. "Important people are waiting for you. That is all." The telecom darkened.

"I think you heard what he said, Dr. Cameron." The officer at his side was very polite. He could afford to be, with the rank of three big planets on his tunic.

"Very well," Cameron answered. "But as commander of the asteroid, I request that you furnish a guard for the girl."

"Commander?" repeated the officer. "That's funny—my orders indicate that I am, until further notice. I haven't got that notice." He looked around at his men and crooked a finger. "Lieutenant, see that the little fellow—Jordan, I think his name is—gets a lift back to the main dome. And you can walk the pretty lady to her room. Or whatever it is she lives in." He smiled negligently at Cameron. "Anything to oblige another commander."

\* \* \* \* \*

The medicouncilor, Thorton, was waiting impatiently on the telecom when they got to Cameron's office.

"We will arrive in about two hours," he said immediately. "When I say we, I mean a number of top governmental officials and scientists. Meanwhile, let's get on with this gravital business." He caught sight of the commander. "General Judd, this is a technical matter. I don't think you'll be interested in it."

"Very well, sir. I'll stand guard outside."

The medicouncilor was silent until the door closed behind General Judd. "Sit down, Docchi," he said with unexpected kindness. He paused to note the effect. "I can sympathize with you. You had everything you wanted nearly within your reach. And, after that, to return to Handicap Haven—well, I can understand how you feel. But since you did return, I think we can arrange to do something for you."

Docchi stared at the man on the screen. A spot of light pulsed on his cheek and then flared rapidly over his face.

"Sure," he said casually. "But there are criminal charges against me."

"A formality," said the medicouncilor. "With a thing like the discovery—or rediscovery—of the gravital drive to think about, no one is going to worry much about your unauthorized departure from the asteroid."

Medicouncilor Thorton sounded pleased. "I don't want to mislead you. We can't do any more for you medically than has already been done. However, you will find yourself the center of a more adequate social life. Friends, work, whatever you want. Naturally, in return for this, we will expect your full cooperation."

"Naturally." Docchi blinked at him and got to his feet. "Sounds interesting. I'd like to think about it for a minute."

Cameron planted himself squarely in front of the screen. "Maybe I don't understand. I think you've got the wrong person."

"Dr. Cameron!" Thorton glowered. "Please explain."

"It was an easy mistake to make," said Cameron. "Cut off from communication, the gravital drive began to work. How? Why? Mostly, who did it? You knew it wasn't I. I'm a doctor, not a physicist. Nor Jordan, he's at best a mechanic. Therefore it had to be Docchi, because he's an engineer. He could make it work. But it wasn't Docchi. He had nothing to do with—"

"Look out!" cried Thorton too late.

Cameron fell to his knees. The same foot that brought him down crashed into his chin. His head snapped back and he sprawled on the floor. Blood trickled from his face.

"Docchi!" shouted Thorton from the screen.

Docchi didn't answer. He was crashing through the door. The commander was lounging against the wall. Head down, Docchi ran into him. The toaster fell from his belt to the floor. With scarcely a pause, Docchi stamped on it and continued running.

The commander got to his feet and retrieved the weapon. He aimed it tentatively at the retreating figure; a thought occurred to him and he lowered it. He examined the damaged mechanism. After that, it went gingerly into a tunic pocket.

Muffled shouts were coming from Cameron's office. The general broke in.

The medicouncilor glared at him from the screen. "I can see that you let him get away."

The disheveled officer straightened his uniform. "I'm sorry, sir. I'll alert the guards immediately."

"Never mind now. Revive that man."

The general wasn't accustomed to giving resuscitation; it was out of his line. Nevertheless, in a few minutes Cameron was conscious, though somewhat dazed.

"Now then, Doctor, if it wasn't Docchi who was responsible for the sudden functioning of the gravital drive, who was it?"

With satisfaction, Cameron told him. He had not been wrong about the girl. Listening to the detailed explanation of Nona's mental abilities, the general was perplexed, as generals sometimes are.

"I see." The medicouncilor nodded. "We overlooked that possibility altogether. Not the mechanical genius of an engineer. Instead, the strange telepathic sense of a girl. That puts the problem in a different light."

"It does." Cameron pressed his aching jaw. "She can't tell us how she does it. We'll have to experiment. Fortunately, it won't involve any danger. With the monitor system we can always control the gravital drive."

The medicouncilor leaned perilously backward and shook his head. "You're wrong. It's supposed to, but it doesn't. We tried. For a microsecond, the monitor did take over, but the gravital computer is smarter than we thought, if it *was* the computer that figured out the method. It found a way of cutting the power from the monitor circuit. It didn't respond at all."

Cameron forgot his jaw. "If you didn't bring the rocket back on remote, why did she come?"

"Docchi knows," growled the medicouncilor. "He found out in this room. That's why he escaped." He tapped on his desk with blunt fingers. "She could have taken the ship anywhere she pleased and we couldn't have stopped her. Since she voluntarily came back, it's obvious that she wants the asteroid!"

Medicouncilor Thorton tried to shove his face out of the screen and into the room. "Don't you ever think, General? There isn't any real difference between gravital units except size and power. What she did to the ship she can do as easily to the asteroid." He thrust out a finger and pointed angrily. "Don't stand there, General Judd. Find that girl!"

It was late for that kind of command. The great dome overhead trembled and creaked in countless joints. The little world shivered, groaned as if it had lain too long in an age-old orbit. It began to move.

\*     \*     \*     \*     \*

Vague shapes stirred, crawled, walked if they could. Fantastic and near-fantastic figures came to the assembly. Huge or tiny, on their own legs or borrowed ones, they arrived, with or without arms, faces. The word had spread by voice, by moving lips, by sign languages of every sort.

"Remember, it will be hours or perhaps days before we're safe," said Docchi. His voice was growing hoarse. "It's up to us to see that Nona has all the time she needs."

"Where is she hiding?" asked someone from the crowd.

"I don't know. If I did, I still wouldn't tell you. It's our job to keep them from finding her."

"How?" demanded one near the front. "Fight the guards?"

"Not directly," said Docchi. "We have no arms in the sense of weapons. Many of us have no arms in any sense. All we can hope to do is obstruct their search. Unless someone has a better idea, this is what I plan:

"I want all the men, older women, and the younger ones who aren't suitable for reasons I'll explain later. The guards won't be here for another half hour—it will take that long to get them together and give them the orders that the Medicouncil must be working out now. When they do come, get in their way.

"How you do that, I'll leave to your imagination. Appeal to their sympathy as long as they have any. Put yourself in dangerous situations. They have ethics; at first they'll be inclined to help you. When they do, try to steal their weapons. Avoid physical violence as much as you can. We don't want to force them into retaliation. Make the most of that phase of their behavior. It won't last long."

Docchi paused and looked over the crowd. "Each of you will have to decide for himself when to drop that kind of resistance and start an active battle campaign. We have to disrupt the light and scanning and ventilation systems, for instance. They'll be forced to keep them in repair. Perhaps they'll try to guard these strategic points. So much the better for us—there will be fewer guards to contend with."

"What about me?" called a woman from far in back. "What do I do?"

"You are in for a rough time," Docchi promised her. "Is Jerian here?"

She elbowed her way to his side through the crowd.

"Jerian," said Docchi to the accidentals, "is a normal, pretty woman—outwardly. She has, however, no trace of a digestive system. The maximum time she can go without food and fluid injections is ten hours. That's why she's here."

Again Docchi scanned the group. "I need a cosmetech, someone who has her equipment with her."

A legless woman propelled herself forward. Docchi conferred with her. She seemed startled, but she complied. Under her deft fingers Jerian was transformed—into Nona.

"She will be the first Nona they'll find," explained Docchi, "because she can get away with the disguise longer. I think—I hope—they'll call off the search for a few hours while they test her. Eventually they are sure to find out. In Jerian's case, fingerprints or X-rays would reveal who she is. But that won't occur to them immediately. Nona is impossible to question, as you know, and Jerian will act exactly as Nona would.

"As soon as they discover that Jerian isn't Nona—well, they won't bother to be polite, if that's the word for it. The guards will like the idea of finding an attractive girl they can manhandle in the line of duty, especially if they think that will help them find Nona. It won't, of course. But it will hold up the search and that's what we want."

They stood still, no one moving. Women looked at each other in silent apprehension.

"Let's go," said Jordan grimly.

"Wait," advised Docchi. "I have one volunteer Nona. I need about fifty more. It doesn't matter if you're physically sound or not—we'll raid the lab for plastissue. If you think you can be made up to look like Nona, come forward."

Slowly, singly and by twos and threes, they came to him. There were few indeed who wouldn't require liberal use of camouflage.

The rest followed Jordan out.

Mass production of an individual. Not perfect in every instance. Good enough to pass in most. Docchi watched approvingly, suggesting occasional touches of makeup.

"She can't speak or hear," he reminded the volunteers. "Remember that at all times, no matter what they do. Hide in difficult places. After Jerian is taken and the search called off and then resumed, let yourselves be found one at a time. Every guard that has to take you for examination is one less to look for the real Nona. They have to find her soon or get off the asteroid."

The cosmetechs were busy; none stopped. There was one who looked up.

"Get off?" she asked. "Why?"

"The Sun is getting smaller."

"Smaller!" exclaimed the woman.

He nodded. "Handicap Haven is leaving the Solar System."

Her fingers flew and molded the beautiful curve of a jaw where there had been none. Next, plastissue lips were applied.

Nona was soon hiding in half a hundred places.

And one more....

\*    \*    \*    \*    \*

The orbit of Neptune was far behind and still the asteroid was accelerating. Two giant gravital units strained at the core of Handicap Haven. The third clamped an abnormally heavy gravity on the isolated world. Prolonged physical exertion was awkward and doubly exhausting. Hours turned into a day, but the units never faltered.

"Have you figured it out as precisely as you should?" asked Docchi easily. "You share our velocity away from the Sun. You'll have to overcome it before you can start going back."

The general ignored him. "If we could only turn off that damned drive!"

Engineer Vogel shrugged sickly. "You try it," he suggested. "I don't want to be around when you do. It sounds easy: just a gravital unit. But remember there's a good-sized nuclear pile involved."

"I know we can't," admitted the general, morosely looking at the darkness overhead. "On the other hand, we can take off and blow this rock apart from a safe distance."

"And lose all hope of finding her?" taunted Docchi.

"We're losing her anyway," Cameron commented sourly.

"It's not as bad as all that," consoled Docchi. "Now that you know where the difficulty is, you can always build another computer and furnish it with auxiliary senses. Or maybe build into it the facts of elementary astronomy."

Cautiously, he shifted his frail body under the heavy gravity. "There's another solution, though it may not appeal to you. I can't believe Nona is altogether unique. There must be others like her. So-called 'born' mechanics, maybe, whose understanding of machinery is a form of empathy we've never suspected. Look hard enough and you may find them, perhaps in the most unlikely or unlovely body."

General Judd grunted wearily, "If I thought you knew where she is—"

"You can try to find out," Docchi invited, glowing involuntarily.

"Forget about the dramatics, General," said Cameron in disgust. "We've questioned him thoroughly. Resistance we would have had in any event. He's responsible merely for making it more effective than we thought possible."

He added slowly: "At the moment, obviously, he's trying to tear down our morale. He doesn't have to bother. The situation is so bad that it looks hopeless. I can't think of a thing we can do that would help us."

The Sun was high in the center of the dome. Sun? More like a very bright star. It cast no shadows; the lights in the dome did. They flickered and with monotonous regularity went out again. The general swore constantly and emotionlessly until service was restored.

A guard approached with his captive. "I think I've found her, sir."

Cameron looked at the girl in dismay. "Guard, where's your decency?"

"Orders, sir," the man said.

"Whose orders?"

"Yours, sir. You said she was sound of body. How else could I find out?"

Cameron scowled and thrust a scalpel deep into the girl's thigh. She looked at him with a tear-stained face, but didn't move a muscle.

"Plastissue, as any fool can see," he commented dourly.

The guard looked revolted and started to lead her out.

"Let her go," snapped the doctor. "Both of you will be safer, I think."

The girl darted away. The guard followed her, shuddering, his eyes filled with a self-loathing that Cameron realized would require hours of psychiatric work to remove.

Docchi smiled. "I have a request to make."

"Go ahead and make it," snorted the general. "We're likely to give you anything you want."

"You probably will. You're going to leave without her. Very soon. When you do go, don't take all your ships. We'll need about three when we come to another solar system."

General Judd opened his mouth in rage.

"Don't you say anything you'll regret," cautioned Docchi. "When you get back, what will you report to your superiors? Can you tell them that you left in good order, while there was still time to continue the search? Or will they like it better if they know you stayed until the last moment? So late that you had to abandon some of your ships?"

The general closed his mouth and stamped away. Wordlessly, Cameron dragged after him.

\*     \*     \*     \*     \*

The last ship had blasted off and the rocket trails had faded into overwhelming darkness. The Sun, which had been trying to lose itself among the other stars, finally succeeded. The asteroid was no longer the junkpile. It was a small world that had become a swift ship.

"We can survive," said Docchi. "Power and oxygen, we have, and we can grow or synthesize our food."

He sat beside Anti's tank, which had been returned to the usual place. A small tree nodded overhead in the artificial breeze. It was peaceful enough. But Nona wasn't there.

"We'll get you out of the tank," promised Jordan. "When she comes back, we'll rig up a place where there's no gravity. And we'll continue cold treatment."

"I can wait," said Anti. "On this world I'm normal."

Docchi stared forlornly about. The one thing he wanted to see wasn't there.

"If you're worrying about Nona," advised Anti, "don't. The guards were pretty rough with the women, but plastissue doesn't feel pain. They didn't find her."

"How do you know?"

"Listen," said Anti. The ground shivered with the power of the gravital units. "As long as they're running, how can you doubt?"

"If I could be sure—"

"You can start now," Jordan said. "First, though, you'd better get up and turn around."

Docchi scrambled to his feet. She was coming toward him.

She showed no sign of strain. Except for a slight smudge on her wonderfully smooth and scar-less cheek, she might just have stepped out of a beauty cubicle. Without question, she was the most beautiful woman in the world. This world, of course, though she could have done well on any world—if she could have communicated with people as well as with machines.

"Where were you hiding?" Docchi asked, expecting no answer.

She smiled. He wondered, with a feeling of helplessness, if machines could sense and appreciate her lovely smile, or whether they could somehow smile themselves.

"I wish I could take you in my arms," he said bitterly.

"It's not as silly as you think," said Anti, watching from the surface of the tank. "You don't have any arms, but she has two. You can talk and hear, but she can't. Between you, you're a complete couple."

"Except that she would never get the idea," he answered unhappily.

Jordan, rocking on his hands, looked up quizzically. "I must be something like her. They used to call me a born mechanic; just put a wrench in my hand and I can do anything with a piece of machinery. It's as if I sense what the machine wants done to it. Not to the extent that Nona can understand, naturally. You might say it's reversed, that she's the one who can hear while I have to lip-read."

"You never just gabble," Docchi prompted. "You have something in mind."

Jordan hesitated. "I don't know if it's stupid or what. I was thinking of a kind of sign language with machines. You know, start with the simple ones, like clocks and such, and see what they mean to her. Since they'd be basic machines, she'd probably have pretty basic reactions. Then it's just a matter of—"

"You don't have to blueprint it," Docchi cut in excitedly. "That would be fine for determining elementary reactions, but I can't carry around a machine shop; it wouldn't be practical. There ought to be one variable machine that would be portable and yet convey all meanings to her."

"An electronic oscillator?"

Acid waves washed at the sides of the tank as Anti stirred impatiently. "Will you two great brains work it out in the lab, please? And when you get through with that problem, you'll have plenty more to keep you occupied until we get to the stars. Jordan and me, for instance. What future is there for a girl unless she can get married?"

"That's right," Docchi said. "I've got an idea we can do better than normal doctors. Being accidentals ourselves, we won't stop experimenting till we succeed. And we have hundreds of years to do it in."

Glowing, literally, with pleasure, he bent over for Jordan to climb on his back. Then he kissed Nona and headed for the laboratory.

Nona smiled and followed.

"There are some things you don't need words or machines to express," Anti called out. "Keep that in mind, will you?"

She submerged contentedly in the acid bath. Above the dome, the stars gleamed a bright welcome to the little world that flashed through interstellar space..

# DELAY IN TRANSIT

ORIGINALLY PUBLISHED IN *GALAXY SCIENCE FICTION*,
SEPTEMBER 1952

# DELAY IN TRANSIT

"Muscles tense," said Dimanche. "Neural index 1.76, unusually high. Adrenalin squirting through his system. In effect, he's stalking you. Intent probably assault with a deadly weapon."

"Not interested," said Cassal firmly, his subvocalizations inaudible to anyone but Dimanche. "I'm not the victim type. He was standing on the walkway near the brink of the thoroughfare. I'm going back to the habitat hotel and sit tight."

"First you have to get there," Dimanche pointed out. "I mean, is it safe for stranger to walk through the city."

"Now that you mention it, no," answered Cassal. He looked around apprehensively. "Where is he?"

"Behind you. At the moment he's pretending interest in a merchandise display.

A native stamped by, eyes brown and incurious. Apparently he was accustomed to the sight of an Earthman standing alone, Adam's apple bobbing up and down silently. It was a Godolphian axiom that all travelers were crazy.

Cassal looked up. Not an air taxi in sight, Godolph shut down at dusk. It would be pure luck if he found a taxi before morning. Of course he *could* walk to the hotel, but was that such a good idea?

A Godolphian city was peculiar. And, though not intended, it was peculiarly suited to certain kinds of violence. A human pedestrian was at a definite disadvantage.

"Correction," said Dimanche. "Not simple assault. He has murder in mind."

"It still doesn't appeal to me," said Cassal. Striving to look unconcerned, he strolled toward the building side of the walkway and stared into the interior of a small café. Warm, bright and dry. Inside, he might find safety for a time.

Damn the man who followed him! It would be easy enough to elude him in a normal city. On Godolph, nothing was normal. In an hour the streets would be brightly lighted—for native eyes. A human would consider it dim.

"Why did he choose me?" asked Cassal plaintively. "There must be something he hopes to gain."

"I'm working on it," said Dimanche. "But remember, I have limitations. At short distances I can scan nervous systems, collect and interpret physiological data. I can't read minds. The best I can do is report what a person says or subvocalizes. If you're really interested in finding out why he wants to kill you, I suggest you turn the problem over to the godawful police."

"Godolph, not godawful," corrected Cassal absently.

That was advice he couldn't follow, good as it seemed. He could give the police no evidence save through Dimanche. There were various reasons, many of them involving the law, for leaving the device called Dimance out of it. The police would act as if they found a body. His own, say, floating face-down on some quiet street. That didn't seem the proper approach, either.

"Weapons?"

"The first thing I searched him for. Nothing very dangerous. A long knife, a hard striking object. Both concealed on his person."

Cassal strangled slightly. Dimanche needed a good stiff course in semantics. A knife was still the most silent of weapons. A man could die from it. His hand strayed toward his pocket. He had a measure of protection himself.

"Report," said Dimanche. "Not necessarily final. Based, perhaps, on tenuous evidence."

"Let's have it anyway."

"His motivation is connected somehow with your being marooned here. For some reason you can't get off this planet."

That was startling information, though not strictly true. A thousand star systems were waiting for him, and a ship to take him to each one.

Of course, the one ship he wanted hadn't come in. Godolph was a transfer point for stars nearer the center of the Galaxy. When he had left Earth, he had known he would have to wait a few days here. He hadn't expected a delay of nearly three weeks. Still, it wasn't unusual. Interstellar schedules over great distances were not as reliable as they might be.

Was this man, whoever and whatever he might be, connected with that delay? According to Dimanche, the man thought he was. He was self-deluded or did he have access to information that Cassal didn't?

Denton Cassal, sales engineer, paused for a mental survey of himself. He was a good engineer and, because he was exceptionally well matched to his instrument, the best salesman that Neuronics, Inc., had. On the basis of these qualifications, he had been selected to make the long journey, the first part of which already lay behind him. He had to go to Tunney 21 to see a man. That man wasn't important to anyone save the company that employed him, and possibly not even to them.

The thug trailing him wouldn't be interested in Cassal himself, his mission which was a commercial one, nor the man on Tunney, And money wasn't the objective, if Dimanche's analysis was right. What *did* the thug want?

Secrets? Cassal had none, except, in a sense, Dimanche. And that was too well kept on Earth, where the instrument was invented and made, for anyone this far away to learn about it.

And yet the thug wanted to kill him. Wanted to? Regarded him as good as dead. It might pay him to investigate the matter further, if it didn't involve too much risk.

"Better start moving." That was Dimanche. "He's getting suspicious.

Cassal went slowly along the narrow walkway that bordered each side of that boulevard, the transport tide. It was raining again. It usually was on Godolph, which was a weather-controlled planet where the natives like rain.

He adjusted the controls of the weak force field that repelled the rain. He widened the angle of the field until water slanted through it unhindered. He narrowed it around him until it approached visibility and the drops bounced away. He swore at the miserable climate and the near amphibians who created it.

A few hundred feet away, a Godolphian girl waded out of the transport tide and climbed onto the walkway. It was this sort of thing that made life dangerous for a human—Venice revised, brought up to date in a faster-than-light age.

Water. It was a perfect engineering material. Simple, cheap, infinitely flexible. With a minimum of mechanism and at breakneck speed, the ribbon of the transport tide flowed at different levels throughout the city. The Godolphian merely plunged in and was carried swiftly and noiselessly to his destination. Whereas a human—Cassal shivered. If he were found drowned, it would be considered an accident. No investigation would be made. The thug who was trailing him had certainly picked the right place.

The Godolphian girl passed him. She wore a sleek brown fur, her own. Cassal was almost positive she muttered a polite "Arf?" as she sloshed by. What she meant by that, he didn't know and didn't intend to find out.

"Follow her, " instructed Dimanche. "We've got to investigate our man at closer range."

Obediently, Cassal turned and began walking after the girl. Attractive in an anthropomorphic, seal-like way, even from behind. Not graceful out of her element, though.

The would-be assassin was still looking at merchandise as Cassal retraced his steps. A man, or at least man type. A big fellow, physically quite capable of violence, if his size had anything to do with it. The face, though, was out of character. Mild, almost meek. A scientist or scholar. It didn't fit with murder.

"Nothing," said Dimanche disgustedly. "His mind froze when we got close. I could feel his shoulder blades twitching as we passed. Anticipating guilt, of course. Projecting to you the action of his plans. That makes the knife definite."

Well beyond the window at which the thug watched and waited, Cassal stopped. Shakily he produced a cigarette and funbled for a lighter.

"Excellent thinking," commented Dimanche. "He won't attempt anything on the street. Too dangerous. Turn aside at the next deserted intersection and let him follow the glow of your cigarette."

The lighter flared in his hand. "That's one way of finding out," said Cassal. "But wouldn't I be a lot safer if I just concentrated on getting back to the hotel?"

"I'm curious. Turn here."

"Go to hell," said Cassal nervously. Nevertheless, when he came to that intersection, he turned there.

It was a Godolphian equivalent to an alley, narrow and dark, oily slow-moving water gurgling at one side, high cavernous walls looking on the other.

He would have to adjust the curiosity factor of Dimanche. It was all very well to be interested in the man who trailed him, but there was also the problem of coming out of this adventure alive. Dimanche, an electronic instrument, naturally wouldn't consider that.

"Easy," warned Dimanche. "He's at the entrance to the alley, walking fast. He's surprised and pleased that you took this route."

"I'm surprised, too," remarked Cassal. "But I wouldn't say I'm pleased. Not just now."

"Careful, Even subvocalized conversation is distracting." The mechanism concealed within his body was silent for an instant and then continued: "His blood pressure is rising, breathing is faster. At a time like this, he may be ready to verbalize why he wants to murder you. This is critical."

"That's no lie," agreed Cassal bitterly. The lighter was in his hand. He clutched it grimly. It was difficult not to look back. The darkness assumed an even more sinister quality.

"Quiet," said Dimanche. "He's verbalizing about you."

"He's decided I'm a nice fellow after all. He's going to stop and ask me for a light."

"I don't think so," answered Dimanche. "He's whispering: 'Poor devil. I hate to do it. But it's really his life or mine.'"

"He's more right than he knows. Why all this violence, though? Isn't there any clue?"

"None at all," admitted Dimanche. "He's very close. You'd better turn around."

Cassal turned, pressed the stud on his lighter. It should have made him feel more secure, but it didn't. He could see very little.

A dim shadow rushed at him. He jumped away from the water side of the alley, barely in time. He could feel the rush of air as the assailant shot by.

"Hey!" shouted Cassal.

Echoes answered; nothing else did. He had the uncomfortable feeling that no one was going to come to his assistance.

"He wasn't expecting that reaction," explained Dimanche. "That's why he missed. He's turned around and is coming back."

"I'm armed!" shouted Cassal.

"That won't stop him. He doesn't believe you."

Cassel grabbed the lighter. That is, it had been a lighter a few seconds before. Now a needle-thin blade had snapped out and projected stiffly. Originally it had been designed as an emergency surgical instrument. A little imagination and a few changes had altered its function, converting it into a compact, efficient stiletto.

"Twenty feet away," advised Dimanche. "He knows you can't see him, but he can see your silhouette by the light from the main thoroughfare. What he doesn't know is that I can detect every move he makes and keep you posted below the level of his hearing."

"Stay on him," growled Cassal nervously. He flattened himself against the wall.

"To the right," whispered Dimanche. "Lunge forward. About five feet. Low."

Sickly, he did so. He didn't care to consider the possible effects of a miscalculation. In the darkness, how far was five feet? Fortunately, his estimate was correct. The rapier encountered yielding resistance, the soggy kind: flesh. The tough blade bent, but did not break. His opponent gasped and broke away.

"Attack!" howled Dimanche against the bone behind his ear. "You've got him. He can't imagine how you know where he is in the darkness. He's afraid."

Attack he did, slicing about wildly. Some of the thrusts landed; some didn't. The percentage was low, the total amount high. His opponent fell to the ground, gasped and was silent.

Cassal fumbled in his pockets and flipped on a light. The man lay near the water side of the alley. One leg was crumpled under him. He didn't move.

"Heartbeat slow," said Dimanche solemnly. "Breathing barely perceptible."

"The he's not dead," said Cassal in relief.

Foam flecked from the still lips and ran down the chin. Blood oozed from cuts on the face.

"Respiration none, heartbeat absent," stated Dimanche.

Horrified, Cassal gazed at the body. Self-defense, of course, but would the police believe it? Assuming they did, they'd still have to investigate. The rapier was an illegal concealed weapon. And they would question him until they discovered Dimanche. Regrettable, but what could he do about it?

Suppose he were detained long enough to miss the ship bound for Tunney 21?

Grimly, he laid down the rapier. He might as well get to the bottom of this. Why had the man attacked? What did he want?

"I don't know," replied Dimanche irritably. "I can interpret body data—a live body. I can't work on a piece of meat."

Cassal searched the body thoroughly. Miscellaneous personal articles of no value in identifying the man. A clip with a startling amount of money in it. A small white card with something scribbled on it. A picture of a woman and a small child posed against a background which resembled no world Cassal had ever seen, That was all.

Cassal stood up in bewilderment. Dimanche to the contrary, there seemed to be no connection between this dead man and his own problem in getting to Tunney 21.

Right now, though, he had to dispose of the body. He glanced toward the boulevard. So far no one had been attracted by the violence.

He bent down to retrieve the lighter-rapier. Dimanche shouted at him. Before he could react, someone landed on him. He fell forward, vainly trying to grasp the weapon. Strong fingers felt for his throat as he was forced to the ground.

He threw the attacker off and staggered to his feet. He heard footsteps rushing away. A slight splash followed. Whoever it was, he was escaping by way of the water.

Whoever it was. The man he had thought he has slain was no longer in sight.

"Interpret body data, do you? Muttered Cassal. "Liveliest dead man I've ever been strangled by."

"It's just possible there are some breeds of men who can control the basic functions of their body," said Dimanche defensively. "When I checked him, he had no heartbeat."

"Remind me not to accept your next evaluation so completely." Grunted Cassal. Nevertheless, he was relieved, in a fashion. He hadn't *wanted* to kill the man. And now there was nothing he'd have to explain to the police.

He needed the cigarette he stuck between his lips. For the second time he attempted to pick up the rapier-lighter. The time he was successful. Smoke swirled into his lungs and quieted his nerves. He squeezed the weapon into the shape of a lighter and put it away.

Something, however, was missing—his wallet.

The thug had relieved him of it in the second round of the scuffle. Persistent fellow. Damned persistent.

It really didn't matter. He fingered the clip he had taken from the supposedly dead body. He had intended to turn it over to the police. Now he might as well keep it to reimburse him for his loss. It contained more money than his wallet had.

Except for the identification tab he always carried in his wallet, it was more than a fair exchange. The identification, a rectangular piece of plastic, was useful in establishing credit, but with the money he now had, he wouldn't need credit. If he did, he could always send away for another tab.

A white card fluttered from the clip. He caught it as it fell. Curiously he examined it. Blank except for one crudely printed word, STAB. His unknown assailant had tried.

\*     \*     \*     \*     \*

The old man stared at the door, an obsolete visual projector wobbling precariously on his head. He closed his eyes and the lettering on the door disappeared. Cassal was too far away to see what it had been. The technician opened his eyes and concentrated. Slowly a new sign formed on the door.

TRAVELERS AID BUREAU
Murra Foray, First Counselor

It was a drab sign, but, then it was a dismal, backward planet. The old technician passed on to the next door and closed his eyes again.

With a sinking feeling, Cassal walked towards the entrance. He needed help and he had to find it in this dingy rathole.

Inside, though, it wasn't dingy and it wasn't a rathole. More like a maze, an approved scientific one. Efficient, though not comfortable. Travelers Aid was busier than he thought it would be. Eventually he managed to squeeze unto one of the many small counseling rooms.

A woman appeared on the screen, crisp and cool. "Please answer everything the machine asks. When the tape is complete, I'll be available for consultation."

Cassal wasn't sure he was going to like her. "Is this necessary?" he asked. "It's merely a matter of information."

"We have certain regulations we abide by." The woman smiled frostily. "I can't give you any information until you comply with them."

"Sometimes regulations are silly," Cassal said firmly. "Let me speak to the first counselor."

"You are speaking to her," she said. Her face disappeared from the screen.

Cassal sighed. So far he hadn't made a good impression.

Travelers Aid Bureau, in addition to regulations, was abundantly supplied with official curiosity. When the machine finished with him, Cassal had the feeling that he could be recreated from the record it had of him. His individuality had been captured into a series of questions and answers. One thing he drew the line at—why he wanted to go to Tunney 21 was his own business.

The first counselor reappeared. Age, indeterminate. Not, he supposed, that anyone would be curious about it. Slightly taller than average, rather on the slender side. Face was broad at the brow, narrow at the chin and her eyes were enigmatic. A dangerous woman.

She glanced down at the data. "Denton Cassal, native of Earth. Destination, Tunney 21." She looked up at him. "Occupation, sales engineer. Isn't that an odd combination?" Her smile was quite superior.

"Not at all. Scientific training as an engineer. Special knowledge of customer relations."

"Special knowledge of a thousand races? How convenient." Her eyebrows arched.

"I think so," he agreed blandly. "Anything else you'd like to know?"

"Sorry. I didn't mean to offend you."

He could believe that or not as he wished. He didn't.

"You refused to answer why you were going to Tunney 21. Perhaps I can guess. They're the best scientists in the Galaxy. You wish to study them"

Close—but wrong on two counts. They were good scientists, though not necessarily the best. For instance, it was doubtful that they could build Dimanche, even if they had ever thought of it, which was even less likely.

There, however, one relatively obscure research worker on Tunney 21 that Neuronics wanted on their staff. If the fragment of his studies that had reached Earth across the vast distance meant anything, he could help Neuronics perfect instantaneous radio. The company that could build a radio to span the reaches of the Galaxy with no time lag could set its own price, which would be control of all communications, transport, trade—a galactic monopoly. Cassal's share would be a cut of all that.

His part was simple, on the surface. He was to persuade that researcher to come to Earth, *if he could*. Literally he had to guess the Tunnesian's price before the Tunnesian himself knew it. In addition, the reputation of the Tunnesian scientists being exceeded only by their arrogance, Cassal had to convince him that he wouldn't be working for ignorant Earth savages. The existence of such as instrument as Dimanche was a key factor.

Her voice broke through his thoughts. "Now, then, what is your problem?"

"I was told on Earth I might have to wait a few days on Godolph. I've been here three weeks. I want information on the ship bound for Tunney 21."

"Just a moment." She glanced at something below the angle of the screen. She looked up and her eyes were grave. "*Rickrock C* arrived yesterday. Departed for Tunney early this morning."

"Departed?" He got up and sat down again, swallowing hard.

"When will the next ship arrive?"

"Do you know how many stars there are in the Galaxy?" she asked.

He didn't answer.

"That's right," she said. "Billions. Tunney, according to the notation, is near the center of the Galaxy, inside the third ring. You've covered about a third of the distance to it. Local traffic, anything within a thousand light-years, is relatively easy to manage. At longer distances, you take a chance. You've had yours and missed it. Frankly, Cassal, I don't know when another ship bound for Tunney will show up on or near Godolph. Within five years—maybe."

He blanched. "How long would it take to get there using local transportation, star-hopping?"

"Take my advice; don't try it. Five years, if you're lucky."

"I don't need that kind of luck."

"I suppose not." She hesitated. "You're determined to go on?" A the emphatic nod, she sighed. "If that's your decision, we'll try to help you. To start things moving, we'll need a print of your identification tab."

"There's something funny about her," Dimanche decided. It was the usual speaking voice of the instrument, no louder than the noise the blood made in coursing through arteries and veins. Cassal could hear it plainly, because it was virtually inside his ear.

Cassal ignored his private voice. "Identification tab? I don't have it with me. In fact, I may have lost it."

She smiled in instant disbelief. "We're not trying to pry into any part of your past you may wish concealed. However, it's much easier for us to help you if you have your identification. Now if you can't *remember* your real name and where you put your identification—" She arose and left the screen. "Just a moment."

He glared uneasily at the spot where the first counselor wasn't. His *real* name!

"Relax," Dimanche suggested. "She didn't mean it as a personal insult."

Presently she returned.

"I have news for you, whoever you are."

"Cassal," he said firmly. "Denton Cassal, sales engineer, Earth. If you don't believe it, send back to—" He stopped. It had taken him four months to get to Godolph, non-stop, plus a six-month wait on Earth for a ship to show up that was bound in the right direction. Over distances such as these, it just wasn't practical to send back to Earth for anything.

"I see you understand." She glanced at the card in her hand. "The spaceport records indicate that when *Rickrack C* took off this morning, there was a Denton Cassal on board, bound for Tunney 21."

"It wasn't I," he said dazedly. He knew who it was, though. The man who had tried to kill him last night. The reason for the attack now became clear. The thug had wanted his identification tab. Worse, he had gotten it.

"No doubt it wasn't," she said wearily. "Outsiders don't seem to understand what galactic travel entails. Outsiders? Evidently what she called those who lived beyond the second transfer ring. Were those who lived at the edge of the Galaxy, beyond the first ring, called Rimmers? Probably.

                    *       *       *       *       *

She was still speaking: "Ten years to cross the Galaxy, without stopping. At present, no ship is capable of that. Real scheduling is impossible. Populations shift and have to be supplied. A ship is taken off a run for repairs and is never put back on. It's more urgently needed elsewhere. The man who depended on it is left waiting; years pass before he learns it's never coming."

"If we had instantaneous radio, that would help. Confusion wouldn't vanish overnight, but it would diminish. We wouldn't have to depend on ships for all the news. Reservations could be made ahead of time, credit established, lost identification replaced—"

"I've traveled before," he interrupted stiffly. "I've never had any trouble."

She seemed to be exaggerating the difficulties. True, the center was more congested. Taking each star as the starting point for a limited number of ships and using statistical probability as a guide—why, no man would arrive at his predetermined destination.

But that wasn't the way it worked. Manifestly, you couldn't compare galactic transportation to the erratic path of an air molecule in a giant room. Or could you?

For the average man, anyone who didn't have his own interstellar ship, was the comparison too apt? It might be.

"You've traveled outside, where there are still free planets waiting to be settled. Where a man is welcome, if he's able to work." She paused. "The center is different. Populations are excessive. Inside the third ring, no man is allowed off a ship without an identification tab. They don't encourage immigration."

In effect, that meant no ship bound for the center would take a passenger without identification. No ship owner would run the risk of having a permanent guest on board, someone who you couldn't be rid of when his money was gone.

Cassel held his head in his hands. Tunney 21 was inside the third ring.

"Next time," she said, "don't let anyone take your identification."

"I won't," he promised grimly.

The woman looked directly at him. Her eyes were bright. He revised his estimate of her age dramatically downward. She couldn't be as old as he. Nothing outward had happened, but she no longer seemed dowdy. Not that he was interested. Still, it might pay him to be friendly to the first counselor.

"We're a philanthropic agency," said Murra Foray. "Your case is special, though—"

"I understand," he said gruffly. "You accept contributions."

She nodded. "If the donor is able to give. We won't ask so much that you'll have to compromise your standard of living." But she named a sum that would force him to do just that if getting to Tunney 21 took any appreciable time.

He stared at her unhappily. "I suppose it's worth it. I can always work, if I have to."

"As a salesman?" she asked. "I'm afraid you'll find it difficult to do business with Godolphians."

"Not just another salesman," he answered definitely. "I have special knowledge of customer reactions. I can tell exactly—"

He stopped abruptly. Was she baiting him? For what reason? The instrument he called Dimanche was not known to the Galaxy at large. From the business angle, it would be poor policy to hand out that information at random. Aside from that, he needed every advantage he could get. Dimanche was that special advantage.

"Anyway," he finished lamely, " I'm a first-class engineer. I can always find something in that line."

"A scientist, maybe," murmured Murra Foray. "But in this part of the Milky Way, an engineer is regarded as merely a technician who hasn't yet gained practical experience." She shook her head. "You'll do better as a salesman."

He got up, glowering. "If that's all—"

"It is. We'll keep you informed. Drop your contribution in the slot provided for that purpose as you leave."

A door, which he hadn't noticed in entering the counseling cubicle, swung open. The agency was efficient.

"Remember," the counselor called out as he left, "identification is hard to work with. Don't accept a crude forgery."

He didn't answer, but it was an idea worth considering. The agency was eminently practical.

The exit path guided him firmly to an inconspicuous and yet inescapable contribution station. He began to doubt the philanthropic aspect of the bureau.

*     *     *     *     *

"I've got it," said Dimanche as Cassal gloomily counted out the sum the first counselor had named.

"Got what?" asked Cassal. He rolled the currency into a neat bundle, attached his name, and dropped it in the chute.

"The woman, Murra Foray, the first counselor. She's a Huntner."

"What's a Huntner?"

"A sub-race of men on the other side of the Galaxy. She was vocalizing about her planet when I managed to locate her."

"Any other information?"

"None. Electronic guards were sliding into place as soon as I reached her. I got out as fast as I could."

"I see." The significance of that, if any escaped him. Nevertheless, it sounded depressing.

"What I want to know is," said Dimanche, "why such precautions as electronic guards? What does Travelers Aid have that's so secret?"

Cassal grunted and didn't answer. Dimanche could be annoyingly inquisitive at times.

Cassal had entered one side of a block square building. He came out on the other side. The agency was larger than he had thought. The old man was staring at a door as Cassal came out. He had apparently changed every sign in the building. His work was finished, the technician was removing the visual projector from his head as Cassal came up to him. He turned and peered.

"You stuck here, too?" he asked in the uneven voice of the aged.

"Stuck?" repeated Cassal. "I suppose you can call it that. I'm waiting for my ship." He frowned. He was the one who wanted to ask questions. "Why all the redecoration? I thought Travelers Aid was an old agency. Why did you change so many signs? I could understand it if the agency was new."

"The previous counselor resigned suddenly, in the middle of the night, they say. The new one didn't like the name of the agency, so she ordered it changed."

She would do that, thought Cassal. "What about this Murra Foray?"

The old man winked mysteriously. He opened his mouth and then seemed overcome with senile fright. Hurriedly he shuffled away.

Cassal gazed after him, baffled. The old man was afraid for his job, afraid of the first counselor. Why he should be, Cassal didn't know. He shrugged and went on. The agency was now in motion on his behalf, but he didn't intend to depend on that alone.

"The girl ahead of you is making unnecessary wriggling motions as she walks," observed Dimanche. "Several men are looking with approval. I 'don't understand."

Cassal glanced up. They walked that way back in good old L. A. A pang of homesickness swept through him.

"Shut up," he growled plaintively. "Attend to the business at hand."

"Business? Very well," said Dimanche. "Watch out for the transport tide."

Cassal swerved back from the edge of the water. Murra Foray had been right. Godolphians didn't want or need his skills, at least not on terms that were acceptable to him. The natives didn't have to exert themselves. They lived off the income provided by travelers, with which the planet was abundantly supplied by ship after ship.

Still, that didn't alter his need for money. He walked the streets at random while Dimanche probed.

"Ah!"

"What is it?"

"That man. He crinkles something in his hands. Not enough, he is subvocalizing."

"I know how he feels," commented Cassal.

"Now his throat tightens. He bunches his muscles. 'I know where I can get more,' he tells himself. He is going there."

"A sensible man," declared Cassal. "Follow him."

Boldly the man headed toward a section of the city which Cassal had not previously entered. He believed opportunity lay there. Not for everyone. The shrewd, observant, and the courageous could succeed if—The word the quarry used was a slang term, unfamiliar to either Cassal or Dimanche. It didn't matter as long as it led to money.

Cassal stretched his stride and managed to keep the man in sight. He skipped nimbly over the narrow walkways that curved through the great buildings. The section grew dingier as they proceeded. Not slums; not the showplace city frequented by travelers, either.

Abruptly the man turned into a building. He was out of sight when Cassal reached the structure.

He stood at the entrance and stared in disappointment. "Opportunities Inc.," Dimanche quoted softly in his ear. "Science, thrills, chance. What does that mean?"

"It means that we followed a gravity ghost!"

"What's a gravity ghost?"

"An unexplained phenomenon," said Cassal nastily. "It affects the instruments of spaceships, giving the illusion of a massive dark body that isn't there."

"But you're not a pilot. I don't understand."

"You're not a very good pilot yourself. We followed the man to a gambling joint."

"Gambling," mused Dimanche. "Well, isn't it an opportunity of a sort? Someone inside is thinking of the money he's winning."

"The owner, no doubt."

Dimanche was silent, investigating. "It is the owner," he confirmed finally. "Why not go in, anyway. It's raining. And they serve drinks." Left unstated was the admission that Dimanche was curious, as usual.

\*     \*     \*     \*     \*

Cassal went in and ordered a drink. It was a variable place, depending on the spectator—bright, cheerful, and harmonious if he was winning, garish and depressingly vulgar if he was not. At the moment Cassal belonged to neither group. He reserved judgment.

An assortment of gaming devices were in operation. One in particular seemed interesting. It involved the counting of electrons passing through an aperture, based on probability.

"Not that," whispered Dimanche. "It's rigged."

"But it's not necessary," Cassal murmured. "Pure chance alone is good enough."

"They don't take chances, pure or adulterated. Look around. How many Godolphians do you see?"

Cassal looked. Natives were not even there as servants. Strictly a clip joint, working travelers.

Unconsciously, he nodded. "That does it. It's not the kind of opportunity I had in mind."

"Don't be hasty," objected Dimanche. "Certain devices I can't control. There may be others in which my knowledge will help you. Stroll around and sample some games."

Cassal equipped himself with a supply of coins and sauntered through the establishment, disbursing them so as to give himself the widest possible acquaintance with the layout.

"That one," instructed Dimanche.

It received a coin. In return, it rewarded him with a large shower of change. The money spilled to the floor with a satisfying clatter. An audience gathered rapidly, ostensibly to help him pick up the coins.

There was a circuit in it," explained Dimanche. "I gave it a shot of electrons and it paid out.

"Let's try it again," suggested Cassal.

"Let's not," Dimanche said regretfully. "Look at the man on your right."

Cassal did so. He jammed the money back in his pocket and stood up. Hastily. He began thrusting the money back into the machine. A large and very unconcerned man watched him.

"You get the idea," said Dimanche. "It paid off two months ago. It wasn't scheduled for another this year." Dimanche scrutinized the man in a multitude of ways while Cassal continued play. "He's satisfied," was the report at last. "He doesn't detect any sign of crookedness."

"*Crookedness?*"

"On your part, that is. In the ethics of a gambling house, what's done to insure profit is merely prudence.

\*      \*      \*      \*      \*

They moved on to other games, though Cassal lost his briefly acquired enthusiasm. The possibility of winning seemed to grow more remote.

"Hold it," said Dimanche. "Let's look into this."

"Let me give *you* some advice," said Cassal. "This is one thing we can't win at. Every race in the Galaxy has a game like this. Pieces of plastic with values printed on them are distributed. The trick is to get certain arbitrarily selected sets of values in the plastics dealt to you. It seems simple, but against a skilled player a beginner can't win."

"Every race in the Galaxy," mused Dimanche. "What do men call it?"

"Cards," said Cassal, "though there are many varieties within that general classification." He launched into a detailed exposition of the subject. If it were something he was familiar with, all right, but a foreign deck and strange rules—

Nevertheless, Dimanche was interested. They stayed and observed.

The dealer was clumsy. His great hands enfolded the cards. Not a Godolphian nor quite a human, he was an odd type, difficult to place. Physically burly, he wore a garment chiefly remarkable for its ill-fitting appearance. A hard round hat jammed closely over his skull completed the outfit. He was dressed in a manner that somewhere in the Universe was evidently considered the height of fashion.

"It doesn't seem bad," commented Cassal. "There might be a chance."

"Look around," said Dimanche. "Everyone thinks that. It's the classic struggle, person against person and everyone against the house. Naturally, the house doesn't lose."

"Then why are we wasting our time?"

"Because I've got an idea," said Dimanche. "Sit down and take a hand."

"Make up your mind. You said the house doesn't lose."

"the house hasn't played against us. Sit down. You get eight cards, with the option of two more. I'll tell you what to do."

Cassal waited until a disconsolate player relinquished his seat and stalked moodily away. He played a few hands and bet small sums in accordance with Dimanche's instructions. He held his own and won insignificant amounts while learning.

It was simple. Nine order, or suits, of twenty-seven cards each. Each suit would build a different equation. The lowest hand was a quadratic. A cubic would beat it. All he had to remember was his math, guess at what he didn't remember, and draw the right cards.

"What's the highest possible hand?" asked Dimanche. There was a note of abstraction in his voice, as if he were paying more attention to something else.

Cassal peeked at the cards that were face-down on the table. He shoved some money into the betting square in front of him and didn't answer.

"You had it last time," said Dimanche. "A three dimensional encephalocurve. A time modulated brainwave. If you had bet right, you could have owned the house now."

"I did? Why didn't you tell me?"

"Because you had it three successive times. The probabilities against that are astronomical. I've got to find out what's happening before you start betting recklessly."

"It's not the dealer," declared Cassal. "Look at those hands."

They were huge hands, more suitable, seemingly, for crushing the life from some alien beast than the delicate manipulation of cards. Cassal continued to play, betting brilliantly by the only standard that mattered; he won.

*    *    *    *    *

One player dropped out and was replaced by a recruit from the surrounding crowd. Cassal ordered a drink. The waiter was placing it in his hand when Dimanche made a discovery.

"I've got it!"

A shout from Dimanche was roughly the equivalent to a noiseless kick in the head. Cassal dropped the drink. The player next to him scowled but said nothing. The dealer blinked and ent on dealing.

"What have you got?" asked Cassal, wiping up the mess and trying to keep track of the cards.

"How he fixes the deck," explained Dimanche in a lower and less painful tone. "Clever."

"Muttering, Cassal shoved a bet in front of him.

"Look at that hat," said Dimanche.

"Ridiculous, isn't it? But I see no reason to gloat because I have better taste."

"That's not what I meant. It's pulled down low over his knobby ears and touches his jacket. His jacket rubs against his trousers, which in turn come in contact with the stool on which he sits."

"True," agreed Cassal, increasing his wager. "But except for his physique, I don't see anything unusual.

"It's a circuit, a visual projector broken down into components. The hat is a command circuit which makes contact, via his clothing, with the broadcasting unit built into the chair. The existence of a visual projector is completely concealed."

Cassal bit his lip and squinted at his cards. "Interesting. What does it have to do with anything?"

"The deck," exclaimed Dimanche excitedly. "The backs are regular, printed with an intricate design. The front is a special plastic, susceptible to the influence of the visual projector. He doesn't need manual dexterity. He can make any value appear on any card he wants. It will stay there until he changes it."

Cassal picked up the cards. "I've got a Loreenaroo equation. Can he change that to anything else?"

"He can, but he doesn't work that way. He decides before he deals who's going to get what. He concentrates on each card as he deals it. He can change a hand after a player gets it, but it wouldn't look good."

"It wouldn't." Cassal wistfully watched the dealer rake in his wager. His winnings were gone, plus. The newcomer to the game won.

He started to get up. "Sit down," whispered Dimanche. "We're just beginning. Now that we know what he does and how he does it, we're going to take him."

The next hand started in the familiar pattern, two cards of fairly good possibilities, a bet, and then another card. Cassal watched the dealer closely. His clumsiness was only superficial. At no time were the faces of the cards visible. The real skill was unobservable, of course—the swift bookkeeping that went on in his mind. A duplication in the hands of the players, for instance would be ruinous.

Cassal received his last card. "Bet high," said Dimanche. With trepidation, Cassal shoved the money into the betting area.

The dealer glanced at his hand and started to sit down. Abruptly he stood up again. He scratched his cheek and stared puzzledly at the players around him. Gently he lowered himself onto the stool. The contact was even briefer. He stood up in indecision. An impatient murmur arose. He dealt himself a card, looked at it, and paid off all the way around. The players buzzed with curiosity.

"What happened?" asked Cassal as the next hand started.

"I induced a short in the circuit," said Dimanche. "He couldn't sit down to chant the last card he got. He took a chance, as he had to, and dealt himself a card, anyway."

"But he paid off without asking to see what we had."

"It was the only thing he could do," explained Dimanche. "He had duplicate cards."

The dealer was scowling. He didn't seem quite so much at ease. The cards were dealt and the betting proceeded almost as usual. True, the dealer was nervous. He couldn't sit down and stay down. He was sweating. Again he paid off. Cassal won heavily and he was not the only one.

The crowd around them grew almost in a rush. There is an indefinable sense that tells one gambler when another is winning.

This time the dealer stood up. His leg contacted the stool occasionally. He jerked it away each time he dealt to himself. At the last card he hesitated. It was amazing how much he could sweat. He lifted a corner of the cards. Without indicating what he had drawn, determinedly and deliberately he sat down. The chair broke. The dealer grinned weakly as a waiter brought him another stool.

"They still think it may be a defective circuit," whispered Dimanche.

The dealer sat down and sprang up from the new chair in one motion. He gazed bitterly at the players and paid them.

"He had a blank hand," explained Dimanche. "He made contact with the broadcasting circuit long enough to erase, but not long enough to put anything in its place."

The dealer adjusted his coat. "I have a nervous disability," he declared thickly. "If you'll pardon me for a few minutes while I take a treatment—"

"Probably going to consult with the manager," observed Cassal.

"He is the manager. He's talking to the owner."

"Keep track of him."

*     *     *     *     *

A blonde, pretty, perhaps even Earth-type human, smiled and wriggled closer to Cassal. He smiled back.

"Don't fall for it," warned Dimanche. "She's an undercover agent for the house."

Cassal looked her over carefully. "Not much under cover."

"But if she should discover—"

"Don't be stupid. She'll never guess you exist. There's a small lump behind my ear and a small round tube cleverly concealed elsewhere."

"All right," sighed Dimanche resignedly. "I suppose people will always be a mystery to me."

The dealer reappeared, followed by an unobtrusive man who carried a new stool. The dealer looked subtly different, though was the same person. It took close inspection to determine what the difference was. His clothing was new, unrumpled, unmarked by perspiration. During his brief absence, he had been furnished with new visual projector equipment, and it had been thoroughly checked out. The house intended to locate the source of the disturbance.

Mentally, Cassal counted his assets. He was solvent again, but un other ways his position was not so good.

"Maybe," he suggested, "we should leave. With no further interference from us, they might believe defective equipment is the cause of their loss."

"Maybe," replied Dimanche, " you think the crowd around us is composed solely of patrons?"

"I see," said Cassal soberly.

He stretched his legs. The crowd pressed closer, uncommonly aggressive and ill-tempered for mere spectators. He decided against leaving.

"Let's resume play." The dealer-manager smiled blandly at each player. He didn't suspect any one player—yet.

"He might be using an honest deck," said Cassal hopefully.

"They don't have that kind," answered Dimanche. He added absently: "During his conference with the owner, he was given authority to handle the situation in any way he sees fit."

Bad, but not too bad. At least Cassal was opposing someone who had authority to let him keep his winnings, *if he could be convinced.*

The dealer deliberately sat down on the stool. Testing. He could endure the charge that trickled through him. The bland smile spread into a triumphant grin.

"While he was gone, he took a sedative," analyzed Dimanche. "He also had the strength of the broadcasting circuit reduced. He thinks that will do it."

"Sedatives wear off," said Cassal. "By the time he knows it's me, see that it has worn off. Mess him up."

\*     \*     \*     \*     \*

The game went on. The situation was too much for the others. They played poorly and bet atrociously, on purpose. One by one they lost and dropped out. They wanted badly to win, but they wanted to live even more.

The joint was jumping, and so was the dealer again. Sweat rolled down his face and there were tears in his eyes, So much liquid began to erode his fixed smile. He kept replenishing it from some inner source of determination.

Cassal looked up. The crowd had drawn back, or had been forced by hirelings who mingled with them. He was alone with the dealer at the table. Money was piled high around him. It was more than he needed, more than he wanted.

"I suggest one last hand," said the dealer-manager, grimacing. It sounded a little stronger than a suggestion.

Cassal nodded.

"For a substantial sum," said the dealer, naming it.

Miraculously, it was an amount that equaled everything Cassal had. Again Cassal nodded.

"Pressure," muttered Cassal to Dimanche. "The sedative has worn off. He's back at the level at which he started. Fry him if you have to."

The cards came out slowly. The dealer was jittering as he dealt. Soft music was lacking, but not the motions that normally accompanied it. Cassal couldn't believe that cards could be so bad. Somehow the dealer was rising to the occasion. Rising and sitting.

"There's a nerve in your body," Cassal began conversationally, "which, if it were overloaded, would cause you to drop dead."

The dealer didn't examine his own cards. He didn't have to. "In that event, someone would be arrested for murder," he said. "You."

That was the wrong tack; the humanoid had too much courage. Cassal passed his hand over his eyes. "You can't do this to men, but strictly speaking, the dealer's not human. Try suggestion on him. Make him change the cards. Play him like a piano. Pizzicato on the nerve strings."

Dimanche didn't answer; presumably he was busy scrambling circuits.

The dealer stretched out his hand. It never reached the cards. Danger: Dimanche at work. The smile dropped from his face. What remained was pure anguish. He was too dry for tears. Smoke curled up faintly from his jacket.

"Hot, isn't it?" asked Cassal. "It might be cooler if you took off your cap."

The cap tinkled to the floor. The mechanism in it was destroyed. What the cards were, they were. Now they couldn't be changed.

"That's better," said Cassal.

He glanced at his hand. In the interim it had changed slightly. Dimanche had got there.

The dealer examined his cards one by one. His face changed color. He sat utterly still on a cool stool.

"You win," he said hopelessly.

"Let's see what you have."

The dealer-manager roused himself. "You won. That's good enough for you, isn't it?"

Cassal shrugged. "You have Bank of the Galaxy service here. I'll deposit my money with them *before* you pick up your cards."

The dealer nodded unhappily and summoned an assistant. The crowd, which had anticipated violence, slowly began to drift away.

"What did you do?" asked Cassal silently.

"Men have no shame," sighed Dimanche. "Some humanoids do. The dealer was one who did. I forced him to project onto his cards something that wasn't a suit at all."

"Embarrassing if that got out," agreed Cassal. "What did you project?"

Dimanche told him. Cassal blushed, which was unusual for a man.

The dealer-manager returned and the transaction was completed. His money was safe in the Bank of the Galaxy.

"Hereafter, you're not welcome," said the dealer morosely. "Don't come back."

Cassal picked up the cards without looking at them. "And no accidents after I leave," he said extending the cards face-down. The manager took them and trembled.

"He's an honorable humanoid, in his own way," whispered Dimanche. "I think you're safe."

It was time to leave, "One question," Cassal called back. "What do you call this game?"

Automatically the dealer started to answer. "Why everyone knows..." He sat down, his mouth open.

It was more than time to leave.

Outside, he hailed an air taxi. No point in tempting the management.

"Look," said Dimanche as the cab rose from the surface of the transport tide.

A technician with a visual projector was at work on the sign in front of the gaming house. Huge words took shape: WARNING—NO TELEPATHS ALLOWED.

There were no such things anywhere, but now there were rumors of them.

*     *     *     *     *

Arriving at the habitat wing of the hotel, Cassal went directly to his room. He awaited the delivery of the equipment he had ordered and checked through it thoroughly. Satisfied that everything was there, he estimated the size of the room. Too small for his purpose.

He picked up the intercom and dialed Services, "Put a Life Stage Cordon around my suite," he said briskly.

The face opposite his went blank. "But you're an Earthman. I thought—"

"I know more about my own requirements than your Life Stage Bureau/ Earthmen do have life stages. You know the penalty if you refuse that service."

There were some races who went without sleep for five months and then had to make up for it. Others grew vestigial wings for brief periods and had to fly with them or die; reduced gravity would suffice for that. Still others—"

But the one common feature was always a critical time in which certain conditions were necessary. Insofar as there was a universal law, from one end of the Galaxy to the other, this was it. The habitat hotel had to furnish appropriate conditions for the maintenance of any life-form that requested it.

The Godolphian disappeared from the screen. When he came back, he seemed disturbed.

"You spoke of a suite. I find that you're listed as occupying one room."

"I am. It's too small. Convert the rooms around me into a suite."

"That's very expensive."

"I'm aware of that. Check the Bank of the Galaxy for my credit rating."

He watched the process take place. Service would be amazingly good from now on.

"Your suite will be converted in about two hours. The Life Stage Cordon will begin as soon after that as you want. If you tell me how long you'll need it, I can make arrangements now."

"About ten hours is all I'll need." Cassal rubbed his jaw reflectively. "One more thing. Put a perpetual service at the spaceport. If a ship comes in bound for Tunney 21 r the vicinity of it, get accommodations on it for me. And hold it until I get ready, no matter what it costs."

He flipped off the intercom and promptly went to sleep. Hours later, he was awakened by a faint hum. The Life Stage Cordon had just been snapped safely around his newly created suite.

"Now what?" asked Dimanche.

"I need an identification tab."

"You do. And forgeries are expensive and generally crude, as that Huntner woman, Murra Foray, observed."

Cassal glanced at the equipment. "Expensive, yes. Not crude when we do it."

"*We* forge it?" Dimanche was incredulous.

"That's what I said. Consider it this way. I've seen my tab a countless number of times. If I tried to draw it as I remember it, it would be inept and wouldn't pass. Nevertheless, that memory is in my mind, recorded in neuronic chains, exact and accurate." He paused significantly. "You have access to my memory."

"At least partially. But what good does that do."

"Visual projector and plastic which will take the imprint. I think hard about the identification as I remember it. You record and feed it back to me while I concentrate on projecting it on the plastic. After we get it down, we change the chemical composition of the plastic. It will then pass everything except destructive analysis, and they don't often do that."

Dimanche was silent. "Ingenious," was its comment. "Part of that we can manage, the official engraving., even the electron stamp. That, however, is gross detail. The print of the brain area is beyond our capacity. We can put down what you remember, and you remember what you saw. You didn't see fine enough, though. The general area will be recognizable, but not the fine structure, nor the charges stored there nor their interrelationships."

"But we've got to do it," Cassal insisted, pacing about nervously.

"With more equipment to probe—"

"Not a chance. I got one Life Stage Cordon on a bluff. If I ask for another, they'll look it up and refuse."

"All right, said Dimanche, humming. The mechanical attempt at music made Cassal's head ache. "I've got an idea. Think about the identification tab."

Cassal thought.

"Enough," said Dimanche. "Now poke yourself."

"Where?"

"Everywhere," replied Dimanche irritably. "One place at a time."

Cassal did so, though it became monotonous.

Dimanche stopped hi,. "Just above your right knee."

"What about my right knee?"

"The principle access to that part of your brain we're concerned with," said Dimanche. "We can't photomeasure your brain the way it was originally done, but we can investigate it remotely. The result will be simplified, naturally. Something like a scale model as compared to the original. A more apt comparison might be that of a relief map to an actual locality."

"Investigate it remotely?" murmured Cassal. A horrible suspicion touched on his consciousness. He jerked away from that touch. "What does that mean?"

"What it sounds like. Stimulus and response. From that I can construct an accurate chart of the proper portion of your brain. Our probing instruments will be crude out of necessity, but effective."

"I've already visualized those probing instruments," said Cassal worriedly. "Maybe we'd better work first on the official engraving and the electron stamp, while I'm fresh. I have a feeling . . ."

"Excellent suggestion," said Dimanche.

Cassal gathered the articles slowly. His lighter would burn and it would also cut. He needed a heavy object to pound with. A violent irritant for the nerve endings. Something to freeze his flesh. . .

Dimanche interrupted: "there are also a few glands we've got to pick up. See if there's a stimi in the room."

"Stimi? Oh yes, a stimulator. Never use the damn things." But he was going to. The next few hours weren't going to be pleasant. Nor dull, either.

Life could be difficult on Godolph.

*     *     *     *     *

As soon as the Life Stage Cordon came down, Cassal called for a doctor. The native looked at him professionally.

"Is it a part of the Earth life process?" he asked incredulously. Gingerly, he touched the swollen and lacerated leg.

Cassal nodded wearily. "A matter of life and death," he croaked.

"If it is, then it is," said the doctor, shaking his head. "I , for one, am glad to be a Godolphian."

"To each his own habitat," Cassal quoted the motto of the hotel.

Godolphians were clumsy, good-natured caricatures of seals. There was nothing wrong with their medicine, however. In a matter of minutes he was feeling better. By the time the doctor left, the swelling had subsided and the open wound was fast closing.

Eagerly, he examined the identification tab. As far as he could tell, it was perfect. What the scanner would reveal was, of course, another matter. He had to check that as best he could without exposing himself.

Services came up to the suite right after he laid the intercom down. A machine was place over his head and the identification slipped into the slot. The code on the tab was noted; the machine hunted and found the corresponding brain area. Structure was mapped, impulses recorded, scrambled, converted into a ray of light which danced over a film.

The identification tab was similarly recorded. There was now a means of comparison.

Fingerprints could be duplicated—that is, if the race in question had fingers. Every intelligence, however much it differed from its neighbors, had a brain, and tampering with that brain was easily detected. Each identification tab carried a psychometric number which corresponded to the total personality. Alteration of any part of the brain could only subtract from the personality index.

The technician removed the identification and gave it to Cassal. "Where shall I send the strips?"

"You don't," said Cassal. I have a private message to go with them."

"But that will invalidate the process."

"I know. This isn't a formal contract."

Removing the two strips and handing them to Cassal, the technician wheeled the machine away. After due thought, Cassal composed the message:

Travelers Aid Bureau
Murra Foray, first counselor:
If you were considering another identification tab for me, don't. As you can see, I've located the missing item.

He attached the message to the strips and dropped them into the communications chute.

*     *     *     *     *

He was wiping his whiskers away when the answer came. Hastily he finished and wrapped himself, noting but not approving the amused glint in her eyes as she watched. His morals were his own, wherever he went.

"Denton Cassal," she said. "A wonderful job. The two strips were in register to within one percent. The best previous forgery I've seen was six per cent, and that was merely a lucky accident. It couldn't be duplicated. Let me congratulate you."

His dignity was professional. "I wish you weren't so fond of the word 'forgery.' I told you I mislaid the tab. As soon as I found it, I sent you the proof. I want to get to Tunney 21. I'm willing to do anything I can to speed up the process."

Her laughter tinkled. "You don't *have* to tell me how you did it or where you got it. I'm inclined to think you made it. You understand that I'm not concerned with the legality as such. From time to time the agency has to furnish missing documents. If there's a better way that we have, I'd like to know it."

He sighed and shook his head. For some reason, his heart was beating fast. He wanted to say more, but there was nothing to say.

When he failed to respond, she leaned towards him. "Perhaps you'll discuss this with me. At greater lengths."

"At the agency?"

She looked at him in surprise. "Have you been sleeping? The agency is closed for the day. The first counselor can't work all the time, you know."

Sleeping? He glanced at the remembrance of the self-administered beating. No, he hadn't been sleeping. He brushed the thought aside and boldly named a place. Dinner was acceptable.

Dimanche waited until the screen was dark. The words were carefully chosen.

"Did you notice," he asked, "that there was no apparent change in clothing or makeup, yet she seemed younger, more attractive?"

"I didn't think you could trace her that far."

"I can't. I looked at her through your eyes."

"Don't trust my reaction," advised Cassal. "It's likely to be subjective."

"I don't," answered Dimanche. "It is."

Cassal hummed thoughtfully. Dimanche was a business neurological instrument. It didn't follow that it was an expert at human psychology.

                    *    *    *    *    *

Cassal stared at the woman coming toward him. Center-of-the-Galaxy fashion. Decadent, of course, or maybe ultra-civilized. As an Outsider, he wasn't sure which. Whatever it was, it did to the human body what should have been done a long time ago.

And the body wasn't exactly human. The subtle skirt of proportions betrayed it as an offshoot or deviation from the human race. Some of the new subraces staked up against the original stock much in the same way Cro-Magnons did against Neanderthals, in beauty, at least.

Dimanche spoke a single syllable and subsided, an event Cassal didn't notice. His consciousness was focused on another discovery; the woman was Murra Foray.

He knew vaguely that the first counselor was not necessarily what she had seemed that first time at the agency. That she was capable of such a metamorphosis was hard to believe, though pleasant to accept. His attitude must have shown on his face.

"Please," said Murra Foray. "I'm a Huntner. We're adept at camouflage."

"Huntner," he repeated blankly. "I knew that. But what's a Huntner?"

She wrinkled her lovely nose at the question. "I didn't expect you to ask that. I won't answer it now." She came closer. "I thought you'd ask which was the camouflage—the person you see here, or the one at the Bureau?"

He never remembered the reply he made. It must have been satisfactory, for she smiled and drew her fragile wrap closer. The reservations were waiting.

Dimanche seized the opportunity to speak. "There's something phony about her. I don't understand it and I don't like it."

"You," said Cassal, "are a machine. You don't have to like it."

"That's what I mean. You *have* to like it. You have no choice."

Murra Foray looked back questioningly. Cassal hurried to her side.

The evening passed swiftly. Food that he ate and didn't taste. Music he heard and didn't listen to. Geometric light fugues that were seen and not observed. Liquor that he drank— and here the sequence ended, in the complicated chemistry of Godolphian stimulants.

Cassal reacted to that smooth liquid, though his physical reactions were not slowed. Certain mental centers were depressed, others left wide open, subject to acceleration at whatever speed he demanded.

Murra Foray, in his eyes at least, might look like a dream, the kind men have and never talk about. She was, however, interested slowly in her work, or so it seemed.

"Godolph is a nice place," she said, toying with a drink. "If you like rain. The natives are happy enough. But the Galaxy is big and there are lots of strange planets in it, each of which seems ideal to those who are adapted to it. I don't have to tell you what happens when people travel. They get stranded. It's not the time spent in actual flight that's important; it's waiting for the right ship to show up and then having the necessary documents. Believe me, that can be important, as you found out."

He nodded. He had.

"That's the origin of Travelers Aid Bureau," she continued. "A loose organization, propagated mainly by example. Sometimes it's called Star Travelers Aid. It may have other names. The aim, however, is always the same: to see that stranded persons get where they want to go."

She looked at him wistfully, appealingly. "That's why I'm interested in your method of creating identification tabs. It's the thing most commonly lost. Stolen, if you prefer the truth."

She seemed to anticipate his question "How can anyone use another's identification> It can be done under certain circumstances. By neural lobotomy, a portion of one brain may be made to match, more or less exactly, the code are of another brain. The person operated on suffers a certain loss of function, of course. How great that loss is depends on the degree of similarity between the two brain areas before the operation took place."

She ought to know, and he was inclined to believe her. Still, it didn't sound feasible.

"You haven't accounted for the psychometric index," he said.

"I thought you'd see it. That's diminished, too."

Logical enough, though not a pretty picture. A genius could always be made into an average man or lowered to the level of an idiot. There was no operation, however, that could raise an idiot to the level of a genius.

The scramble for the precious identification tabs went on, from the higher to the lower, a game of musical chairs with grim overtones.

She smiled gravely. "You haven't answered my implied question."

The company that employed him wasn't anxious to let the secret of Dimanche get out. They didn't sell the instrument; they made it for their own use. It was an advantage over their competitors they intended to keep. Even on his recommendation. They wouldn't sell to the agency.

Moreover, it wouldn't help Travelers Aid Bureau if they did. Since she was first counselor, it was probably that she'd be the one to use it. She couldn't make identification for anyone except herself, and then only if she developed exceptional skill.

The alternative was to surgery it in and out of whoever needed it. When that happened, secrecy was gone, Travelers couldn't be trusted.

He shook his head. "It's an appealing idea, but I'm afraid I can't help you."

"Meaning you won't."

The was intriguing. Not it was the agency, not he, who wanted help.

"Don't overplay it," cautioned Dimanche, who had been consistently silent.

She leaned forward attentively. He experienced and uneasy moment. Was it possible she had noticed his private conversation? Of course not. Yet—

"Please," she said, and the tone allayed his fears. "there's an emergency situation and I've got to attend to it. Will you go with me?"

She smiled understandingly at his quizzical expression. "Travelers Aid is always having emergencies."

She was rising. "It's too late to go to the Bureau. My place has a number of machines with which I keep in touch with the spaceport."

"I wonder," said Dimanche puzzledly. "She doesn't subvocalize at all. I haven't been able to get a line on her. I'm certain she didn't receive any sort of call. Be careful."

"This might be a trick."

"Interesting," said Cassal. He wasn't in the mood to discuss it.

*   *   *   *   *

Her habitation was luxurious, though Cassal wasn't impressed. Luxury was found everywhere in the Universe. Huntner women weren't. He watched as she adjusted the machines grouped at one side of the room. She spoke in a low voice; he couldn't distinguish the words. She actuated levers, pressed buttons; impediments of communications.

At last she finished. "I'm tired. Will you wait till I change?"

Inarticulately he nodded.

"I think her 'emergency' was a fake," said Dimanche flatly as soon as she left. "I'm positive she wasn't operating the communicator. She merely went through the motions."

"Motions," murmured Cassal dreamily, leaning back. "And what motions."

"I've been watching her," said Dimanche. "She frightens me."

"I've been watching her, too. Maybe in a different way."

"Get out of here while you can," warned Dimanche. "She's dangerous."

Momentarily, Cassal considered it. Dimanche had never failed him. He ought to follow that advice. And yet there was another explanation.

"Look," said Cassal. "A machine is a machine. But among humans there are men and women. What seems dangerous to you may be merely a pattern of normal behavior. . .: He broke off, Murra Foray had entered.

Strictly from the other side of the Galaxy, which she was. A woman can be slender and still be womanly beautiful, without being obvious about it. Not that Murra disdained the obvious, technically. But he could see through technicalities.

The tendons in his hands ached and his mouth was dry, though not with fear. An urgent ringing pounded in his ears He shook it out of his head and got up.

She came to him.

The ringing was still in his ears. It wasn't a figment of imagination; it was a real voice—that of Dimanche, howling.

"Huntner! It's a word variant. In their language it means Hunter. *She can hear me!*"

"Hear you?" repeated Cassal vacantly.

She was kissing him.

"A descendant of carnivores. An audiosensitive. She's been listening to you and me all this time."

"Of course I have, ever since the first interview at the bureau," said Marra. "In the beginning I couldn't see what value it was, but you convinced me." She laid her hand gently over his eyes. "I hate to do this to you dear, but I've got to have Dimanche."

She had been smothering him with caresses. Now deliberately, she began smothering him in actuality.

Cassal had thought he was an athlete. For an Earthman, he was. Murra Foray, however, was a Huntner, which meant hunter, a descendant of incredibly strong carnivores.

He didn't have a chance. He knew that when he couldn't budge her hands and fell into the airless blackness of space.

Alone and naked. Cassal awakened. He wish he hadn't. He turned over and, though he tried hard not tom promptly woke up again. His body was willing to sleep, but his mind was panicked and disturbed. About what, he wasn't sure.

He sat up shakily and held his roaring head in his hand. He ran aching fingers through his hair. He stopped. The lump behind his ear was gone.

"Dimanche?" he called, and looked at his abdomen.

There was a thin scar, healing visibly before his eyes.

"Dimanche!," he cried again. "Dimanche!"

There was no answer. Dimanche was no longer with him

He staggered to his feet and stared at the wall. She'd been kind enough to return him to his own rooms. At length he gathered enough strength to rummage through his belongings. Nothing was missing. Money, identification—all were there.

He couldn't go to the police. He grimaced as he thought of it. The neighborly Godolphian police were hardly a match for the Huntner; she 'd fake them out of their skins.

He couldn't prove she's taken Dimanche. Nothing else normally considered valuable was missing. Besides, there might even be a local prohibition against Dimanche. Not by name, of course; but they could dig up an ancient ordinance—invasion of privacy or something like that. Anything would do if it gave them an opportunity to confiscate the device for intensive study.

For the police to believe his story was the worst that could happen. They might locate Dimanche, but he'd never get it.

He smiled bitterly and the effort hurt. "Dear," she had called him as she had strangled and beaten him into unconsciousness. Afterward singing, very likely, as she had sliced the little instrument out of him.

He could picture her not very remote ancestors springing from cover and overtaking a fleeing herd—

No use pursuing that line of thought.

Why did she want Dimanche? She had hinted that the agency wasn't always concerned with legality as such. He could believe her. If she wanted it for making identification tabs, she'd soon find that it was useless. Not that that was much comfort— she wasn't likely to return Dimanche after she'd made that discovery.

For that matter, what was the purpose of Travelers Aid Bureau? It was a front for another kind of activity. Philanthropy had nothing to do with it.

If he still had possession of Dimanche, he'd be able to find out. Everything seemed to hinge on that. With it, he was nearly a superman, able to hold his own in practically all situations— anything that didn't involve a Huntner woman, that is.

Without it—well, Tunney 21 was still far away.  Even if he should manage to get there without it, his mission on the planet was certain to fail.

He dismissed the idea of trying to recover it immediately from Murra Foray.  She was an audio-sensitive.  At twenty feet, unaided, she could hear his heartbeat, the internal noise muscles made in sliding over each other.  With Dimanche, she could hear electrons rustling.  As an antagonist she was altogether too formidable.

*     *     *     *     *

He began pulling on his clothing, wincing as he did so.  The alternative was to make another Dimanche.  *If* he could.  It would be a tough job even for a neuronic expert familiar with the process.  Hw wasn't that expert, but it still had to be done.

The new instrument would have to be better than the original.  Maybe not such a slick machine, but more comprehensive.  More wallop.  He grinned as he thought hopefully about giving Murra Foray a surprise.

Ignoring his aches and pains, he went right to work.  With money not a factor, it was an easy matter to line up the best electronic and neuron concerns on Godolph.  Two were put on a standby basis.  When he gave them the plans, they were to rush construction at all possible speed.

Each concern was to build a part of the new instrument.  Neither part was of value without the other.  The slow-thinking Godolphians weren't likely to make the necessary mental connection between the seemingly unrelated projects.

He retired to his suite and began to draw diagrams.  It was harder than he thought.  He knew the principles, but the actual details were far more complicated that he remembered.

Functionally, the Dimanche instrument was divided into three main phases.  There was a brain and memory unit that operated much as the human counterpart did.  Unlike the human brain, however, it had no body to control, hence more of it was available for thought processes.  Entirely neuronic in construction, it was far smaller than an electronic brain of the same capacity.

The second function was electronic, akin to radar. Instead of material objects, it traced and recorded distant nerve impulses. It could count the heartbeat, measure the rate of respiration, was even capable of approximate analysis of the contents of the bloodstream. Properly focused on the nerves of the tongue, lips, or larynx, it transmitted that data back to the neuronic brain, which then reconstructed it into speech. Lip reading, after a fashion, carried to the ultimate.

Finally, there was the voice of Dimanche, a speaker under the control of the neuronic brain.

For convenience of installation in the body, Dimanche was packaged in two units. The larger package was usually surgeried into the abdomen. The small one, containing the speaker was attached to the skull just behind the ear. It worked by bone conduction, allowing silent communication between operator and instrument. A real convenience.

It wasn't enough to know this, as Cassal did. He'd talked to company experts, had seen the symbolic drawings, the plans for an improve version. He needed something better than the best though, that had been planned.

The drawback was this: Dimanche *was powered directly by the nervous system of the body in which it was housed.* Against Murra Foray, he'd be overmatched. She was stronger than he physically, probably also in the production of nervous energy.

One solution was to make available to the new instrument a larger fraction of the neural currents of the body. That was dangerous—a slight miscalculation and the user was dead. Yet he had to have an instrument that would overpower her.

Cassal rubbed his eyes wearily. How could he find some way to supply additional power.

Abruptly, Cassal sat up. That was the way, of course—an auxiliary power pack that need not be surgeried into his body, extra power that he would use only in emergencies.

Neuronics, Inc., had never done this, had never thought that such an instrument would ever be necessary. They didn't need to overpower their customers. They merely wanted advance information via subvocalized thoughts.

It was easier for Cassal to conceive this idea than to engineer it. At the end of the first day, he knew it would be a slow process.

Twice he postponed deadlines to manufacturing concerns he'd engaged. He locked himself in his rooms and took Anti-Sleep against the doctor's vigorous protests. In one week he had the necessary drawings, crude but legible. An expert would have to make innumerable corrections, but the intent was plain.

One week. During that time Murra Foray would be growing hourly more proficient in the use of the Dimanche.

*     *     *     *     *

Cassal followed the neuronics expert groggily, seventy-two hours' sleep still clogging his reactions. Not that he hadn't needed sleep after that week. The Godolphian showed him proudly through the shops, though he wasn't at all interested in their achievements. The only noteworthy aspect was the grand scale of their architecture.

"We did it, though I don't think we'd have the job if we'd known how hard it was going to be," the neuronics expert chattered. "It works exactly as you specified. We had to make substitutions, of course, but you understand that was inevitable."

He glanced anxiously at Cassal, who nodded. That was to be expected. Components that were common on Earth wouldn't necessarily be available here. Still, any expert worth his pay could always make the proper combinations and achieve the same results.

Inside the lab, Cassal frowned. "I thought you were keeping my work separate. What is the planetary drive doing here?"

The Godolphian spread his broad hands and looked hurt. "Planetary drive?" He tried to laugh. "This is the instrument you ordered."

Cassal started. It was supposed to fit under a flap of skin behind his ear. A three World saurian couldn't carry it.

He turned savagely on the expert. "I told you it had to be small."

"But it is. I quote your orders exactly: 'I'm not familiar with your system of measurements, but make it tiny, very tiny. Figure the size you think it will have to be and cut it in half. And then cut *that* in half. This is the fraction remaining.'"

It certainly was. Cassal glanced at the Godolphian's hands. Excellent for swimming. No wonder they built on such a grand scale. Broad, blunt, webbed hands weren't exactly suited for precision work.

Valueless. Completely valueless. He knew now what he would find at the other lab. He shook his head in dismay, personally saw to it that the instrument was destroyed. He paid for the work and retrieved the plans.

*　　*　　*　　*　　*

Back in his rooms again, he sat and thought. It was still the only solution. If the Godolphians couldn't do it, he'd have to find some race that could. He grabbed the intercom and jangled it savagely. In half an hour he had a dozen leads.

The best seemed to be Spirella. A small, insect-like race, about three feet tall, they were supposed to have excellent manual dexterity. And were technically advanced. They sounded as if they were acquainted with the necessary fields. Three light years away, they could be reached by readily available local transportation within the day. Their idea of what was small was likely to coincide with his.

He didn't bother to pack. The suite would remain his headquarters. Home was where his enemies were.

He made a mental correction—enemy.

He rubbed his sensitive ear, grateful for the discomfort. His stomach was sore, but it wouldn't be for long. The Spirella made the new instrument just as he wanted it. They had built an even better auxiliary power unit than he had specified. He fingered the flat case in his pocket. In an emergency, he could draw on these, whereas Murra Foray would be limited to the energy in her nervous system.

What he had now was hardly the same instrument. A military version of it, perhaps. It didn't seem right to use the same name. Call it something staunch and crisp, suggestive of raw power. Manche. As good a name as any. Manche against Dimanche. Cassal against a queen.

He swung confidently along the walkway beside the transport tide. It was raining. He decided to test the new instrument. The Godolphian across the way bent double and wondered why his knees wouldn't work. They had suddenly become swollen and painful to move. Maybe it was the climate.

And maybe it wasn't, thought Cassal. Eventually the pain would leave, but he hadn't meant to be so rough on the native. He'd have to watch how he used Manche.

*     *     *     *     *

He scouted the vicinity of Travelers Aid Bureau, keeping at least one building between him and possible detection. Purely precautionary. There was no indication that Murra Foray had spotted him. For a Huntner, she wasn't very alert, apparently.

He sent Manche out on exploration at maximum strength. The electronic guards which Dimanche had spoken of were still in place. Manche went through easily and didn't disturb an electron. Behind the guards there was no trace of the first counselor.

He went closer. Still no warning of danger. The same old technician shuffled in front of the entrance. A horrible thought hit him. It was easy enough to verify. Another "reorganization: had taken place. The new sign read:

STAR TRAVELERS AID BUREAU
STAB Your Hour
Of Need
Delly Mortinbras, first counselor

Cassal leaned against the building, unable to understand what it was that frightened and bewildered him. Then it gradually became, if not clear, at least not quite so muddy.

STAB was the word that had been printed on the card in the money clip that his assailant had left behind. Cassal had naturally interpreted it as an order to the thug. It wasn't, of course.

The first time Cassal had visited the Travelers Aid Bureau, it had been in the process of reorganization. The only purpose of the reorganization, he realized now, had been to change the name so he wouldn't translate the word on the slip into the original initials of the Bureau.

Now it probably didn't matter any more whether or not he knew so the name had been changed back to the Star Travelers Aid Bureau—STAB.

That, he saw bitterly, was why Murra Foray had been so positive that the identification tab he'd made with the aid of Dimanche had been a forgery.

*She had known the man who robbed Cassal of the original one, perhaps had even helped him plan the theft.*

That didn't make sense to Cassal. Yet it had to. He'd suspected the organization of being a racket, but it obviously wasn't. By whatever name it was called, it was actually dedicated to helping the stranded traveler. The question was— which travelers?

There must be agency operatives at the spaceport, checking every likely prospect who arrived, finding out where they were going, whether their papers were in order. Then, just as had happened to Cassal, the prospect was robbed of his papers so somebody stranded here could go on to the next destination!

\* \* \* \* \*

The shabby, aging technician finished changing the last door sign and hobbled over to Cassal. He peered through the rain and darkness.

"You stuck here, too?" he quavered.

"No," said Cassal with dignity, shaky dignity. "I'm not stuck. I'm here because I want to be."

"You're crazy," declared the old man. "I remember—"

Cassal didn't wait to find out what it was he remembered. An impossible land, perhaps, a planet which swings in perfect orbit around an ideal sun. A continent which reared a purple mountain range to hold up a honey sky. People with whom anyone could relax easily and without worry or anxiety. In short, his own native world from which, at night, all the constellations were familiar.

\* \* \* \* \*

Somehow, Cassal managed to get back to his suite, tumbled wearily into his bed. The showdown wasn't going to take place.

Everyone connected with the agency—including Murra Foray—had been "stuck here" for one reason or another: no identification tab, no money, whatever it was. That was the staff of the Bureau, a pack of desperate castaways. The "philanthropy" extended to them and nobody else. They grabbed their tabs and money from the likeliest travelers, leaving them marooned here—and they in turn had to join the Bureau and use the same methods to continue their journeys through the Galaxy.

It was an endless belt of stranded travelers robbing and stranding other travelers, who then had to rob and strand still others, and so on and on . . .

*       *       *       *       *

Cassal didn't have a chance of catching up with Murra Foray. She had used the time—and Dimanche—to create her own identification tab and escape. She was going back to Kettikat, home of the Huntners, must already be light-years away.

Or was she? The signs on the Bureau had just been changed. Perhaps the ship was still in the spaceport, or cruising along below the speed of light. He shrugged defeatedly. It would do him no good, he could never get on board.

He got up suddenly on one elbow. He couldn't. but Manche could! Unlike his old instrument, it could operate at tremendous distances. Its power no longer dependent only on his limited nervous energy.

With calculated fury, he let Manche strike out into space.

*       *       *       *       *

"There you are!" exclaimed Murra Foray. "I thought you could do it."

"Did you?" he asked coldly. "Where are you now?"

"Leaving the atmosphere. If you can call the stuff around this planet an atmosphere."

"It's not the atmosphere that's bad," he said as nastily as he could. "It's the philanthropy."

"Please don't feel that way," she appealed. "Huntners are rather unusual people, I admit, but sometimes even we need help. I had to have Dimanche and I took it."

"At the risk of killing me."

Her amusement was strange, it held a sort of sadness. "I didn't hurt you. I couldn't. You were too cute, like a—well, the animal native to Kettikat that would be called a teddy bear on Earth. A cute, lovable teddy bear."

"Teddy bear," he repeated, really stung now. "Careful. This one may have claws."

"Long claws?  Long enough to reach from here to Kettikat? She was laughing, but it sounded thin and wistful.

Manche struck out at Cassal's unspoken command. The laughter was canceled.

"Now you've done it," said Dimanche. "She's out cold."

There was no reason for remorse; it was strange that he felt it. His throat was dry.

"So you, too, can communicate with me.  Through Manche, of course. I built a wonderful instrument, didn't I?"

"A fearful one," said Dimanche sternly.  "She's unconscious."

"I heard you the first time." Cassal hesitated. "Is she dead?"

Dimanche investigated. "Of course not. A little thing like that wouldn't hurt her. Her nerve system is marvelous. I think it could carry the current of a city. Beautiful!"

"I'm aware of the beauty," said Cassal.

An awkward silence followed. Dimanche broke it. "Now that I know the facts, I'm proud to be her chosen instrument. Her need was greater than yours."

Cassal growled, "As first counselor, she had access to every—"

"Don't interrupt with your half truths," said Dimanche. "Huntners *are* special; their brain structure too. Not necessarily better, just different. Only the auditory and visual centers of their brains resemble that of man. You can guess the results of even superficial tampering with those parts of her mind. And stolen identification would involve lobotomy."

He could imagine?  Cassal shook his head.  No, he couldn't.  A blinded and deaf Murra would not go back to the home of the Huntners.  According to her racial conditioning, a sightless young tiger should creep away and did.

Again there was silence.  "No, she's not pretending unconsciousness," announced Dimanche.  "For a moment I thought—but never mind."

The conversation was lasting longer than he expected.  The ship must be obsolete and slow.  There were still a few things he wanted to find out, if there was time."

"When are you going on Drive?" he asked.

"We've been on it for some time," answered Dimanche.

"Repeat that?" said Cassal, stunned.

"I said that we've been on faster-than-light drive for some time.  Is there anything wrong with that?"

Nothing wrong with that at all.  Theoretically, there was only one means of communicating with a ship hurtling along faster than light, and that hadn't been invented.

*Hadn't been invented until he had put together the instrument he called Manche.*

Unwittingly, he had created far more than he intended.  He ought to feel elated.

Dimanche interrupted his thoughts.  "I suppose you know what she things of you."

"She made it plain enough," said Cassal wearily.  "A teddy bear.  A brainless, childish toy."

"Among the Huntners, women are vigorous and aggressive," said Dimanche.  The voice grew weaker as the ship, already light-years away, slid into unfathomable distances.  "Where words are concerned, morals are very strict.  For instance, 'dear' is never used unless the person means it.  Huntner men are weak and not overburdened with intelligence."

The voice was barely audible, but it continued": "The principal romantic figure in the dreams of women . . ." Dimanche failed altogether.

"Manche!" cried Cassal.

Manche responded with everything it had, ". . .is the teddy bear."

The elation that had been missing, and the triumph, came now.  It was no time for hesitation, and Cassal didn't hesitate. Their actions had been directed against each other, but their emotions, which each had tried to ignore, were real and strong.

The gravitator dropped him to the ground floor. In a few minutes, Cassal was at the Travelers Aid Bureau.

Correction. Now it was the Star Travelers Aid Bureau.

And, though no one but himself knew it, even that was wrong. Quickly he found the old technician.

"There's been a reorganization," said Cassal bluntly. "I want the sign changed?"

The old man drew himself up. "Who are you?"

"I've just elected myself," said Cassal. "I'm the new first counselor."

He hoped no one would be foolish enough to challenge him. He wanted an organization that could function immediately, not a hospital full of cripples.

The old man thought about it. He was merely a menial, but he had been with the bureau for a long time. He was nobody, nothing, but he could recognize power when it was near him. He wiped his eyes and shambled out into the fine cold rain. Swiftly the new signs went up.

STAR TRAVELERS AID BUREAU
S.T.A. WITH US
DENTON CASSAL, FIRST COUNSELOR

Cassal sat at the control center. Every question cubicle was visible at a glance. In addition there was a special panel, direct from the spaceport, which recorded essential data about every newly arrived traveler. He could think of a few minor improvements, but he wouldn't have time to put them in effect. He'd mention them to his assistant, a man with a fine, logical mind. Not really first-rate, of course, but well suited to his secondary position. Every member quickly rose or sank to his proper level in this organization, and this one had, without a struggle.

Business was dull. The last few ships had brought travelers who were bound for unimaginably dreary destinations, nothing he need be concerned with.

He thought about the instrument. It was the addition of power that had made the difference. Dimanche plus power equaled Manche, and Manche raised the user far above the level of other men. There was little to fear.

But essentially the real value of Manche lay in this—it was a beginning. Through it, he had communicated with a ship traveling far faster than light. The only one instrument capable of that was instantaneous radio. Actually it wasn't radio, but the old name had stuck to it.

Manche was really a very primitive model of instantaneous radio. It was crude; all first steps were. Limited in range, it was practically valueless for that purpose now. Eventually the range would be extended. Hitch a neuronic manufactured brain to a human one, add the power of a tiny atomic battery, and Manche was created.

The last step was his share of the invention. Or maybe the credit belonged to Murra Foray. If she hadn't stolen Dimanche, it never would have been necessary to put together the new instrument.

The stern lines on his face relaxed. Murra Foray. He wondered about the marriage customs of the Huntners. He hoped marriage was a custom on Ketticat.

Cassal leaned back; officially, his mission was complete. There was no longer any need to go to Tunney 21. The scientist he was sent to bring back might as well remain there in obscure arrogance. Cassal knew he should return to Earth immediately. But the Galaxy was wide and there were lots of places to go.

Only one he was interested in, though—Kettikat, as far from the center of the Galaxy as Earth, but in the opposite direction, incredibly far away in terms of trouble and transportation. It would be difficult even for a man who had the services of Manche.

Cassal glanced at the board. Someone wanted to go to Zombo.

"Delly." He called to his assistant. "Try 13. This may be what you want to get back to your own planet."

Delly Mortinbras nodded gratefully and cut in.

Cassal continued scanning. There was more to it than he imagined, though he was learning fast. It wasn't enough to have identification, money and a destination. The right ship might come in with standing room only. Someone had to be "persuaded" that Godolph was a cozy little place, as good as any for an unscheduled stopover.

It wouldn't change appreciably during his lifetime. There were too many billions of stars. First he had to perfect it, isolate from dependence on the human element, and then there would come installation. A slow process, even with Murra to help him.

Someday he would go back to Earth. He should be welcome. The information he was sending back to his former employer, Neuronics, Inc., would more than compensate them for the loss of Dimanche.

Suddenly he was alert. A report had just come in.

Once upon a time, he thought tenderly, scanning the report, there was a teddy bear that could reach to Kettikat. With claws—but he didn't think they would be needed.

# Student Body

ILLUSTRATED BY WILLIAM ASHMAN
ORIGINALLY PUBLISHED IN *GALAXY SCIENCE FICTION*
MARCH 1953

*When a really infallible scientific bureau makes a drastically serious error, the data must be wrong ... but wrong in what way?*

# Student Body

The first morning that they were fully committed to the planet, the executive officer stepped out of the ship. It was not quite dawn. Executive Hafner squinted in the early light; his eyes opened wider, and he promptly went back inside. Three minutes later, he reappeared with the biologist in tow.

"Last night you said there was nothing dangerous," said the executive. "Do you still think it's so?"

Dano Marin stared. "I do." What his voice lacked in conviction, it made up in embarrassment. He laughed uncertainly.

"This is no laughing matter. I'll talk to you later."

The biologist stood by the ship and watched as the executive walked to the row of sleeping colonists.

"Mrs. Athyl," said the executive as he stopped beside the sleeping figure.

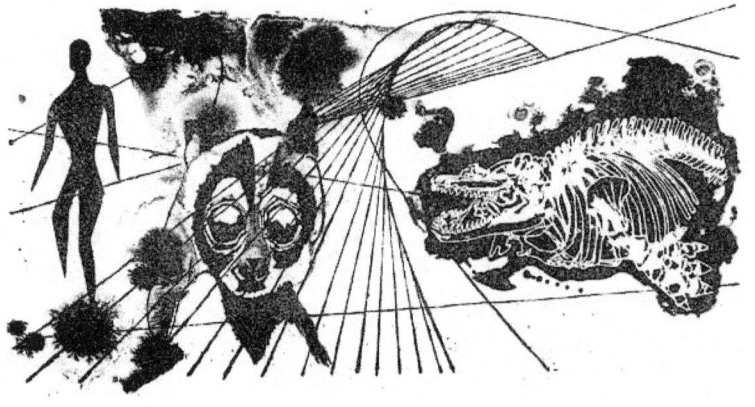

She yawned, rubbed her eyes, rolled over, and stood up. The covering that should have been there, however, wasn't. Neither was the garment she had on when she had gone to sleep. She assumed the conventional position of a woman who is astonished to find herself unclad without her knowledge or consent.

"It's all right, Mrs. Athyl. I'm not a voyeur myself. Still, I think you should get some clothing on." Most of the colonists were awake now. Executive Hafner turned to them. "If you haven't any suitable clothing in the ship, the commissary will issue you some. Explanations will be given later."

The colonists scattered. There was no compulsive modesty among them, for it couldn't have survived a year and a half in crowded spaceships. Nevertheless, it was a shock to awaken with no clothing on and not know who or what had removed it during the night. It was surprise more than anything else that disconcerted them.

On his way back to the spaceship, Executive Hafner paused. "Any ideas about it?"

Dano Marin shrugged. "How could I have? The planet is as new to me as it is to you."

"Sure. But you're the biologist."

As the only scientist in a crew of rough-and-ready colonists and builders, Marin was going to be called on to answer a lot of questions that weren't in his field.

"Nocturnal insects, most likely," he suggested. That was pretty weak, though he knew that in ancient times locusts had stripped fields in a matter of hours. Could they do the same with the clothing of humans and not awaken them? "I'll look into the matter. As soon as I find anything, I'll let you know."

"Good." Hafner nodded and went into the spaceship.

*     *     *     *     *

Dano Marin walked to the grove in which the colonists had been sleeping. It had been a mistake to let them bed down there, but at the time the request had been made, there had seemed no reason not to grant it. After eighteen months in crowded ships everyone naturally wanted fresh air and the rustle of leaves overhead.

Marin looked out through the grove. It was empty now; the colonists, both men and women, had disappeared inside the ship, dressing, probably.

The trees were not tall and the leaves were dark bottle-green. Occasional huge white flowers caught sunlight that made them seem larger than they were. It wasn't Earth and therefore the trees couldn't be magnolias. But they reminded Marin of magnolia trees and thereafter he always thought of them as that.

The problem of the missing clothing was ironic. Biological Survey never made a mistake—yet obviously they had. They listed the planet as the most suitable for Man of any so far discovered. Few insects, no dangerous animals, a most equitable climate. They had named it Glade because that was the word which fitted best. The whole land mass seemed to be one vast and pleasant meadow.

Evidently there were things about the planet that Biological Survey had missed.

Marin dropped to his knees and began to look for clues. If insects had been responsible, there ought to be a few dead ones, crushed, perhaps, as the colonists rolled over in their sleep. There were no insects, either live or dead.

He stood up in disappointment and walked slowly through the grove. It might be the trees. At night they could exude a vapor which was capable of dissolving the material from which the clothing had been made. Far-fetched, but not impossible. He crumbled a leaf in his hand and rubbed it against his sleeve. A pungent smell, but nothing happened. That didn't disprove the theory, of course.

He looked out through the trees at the blue sun. It was bigger than Sol, but farther away. At Glade, it was about equal to the Sun on Earth.

He almost missed the bright eyes that regarded him from the underbrush. Almost, but didn't—the domain of biology begins at the edge of the atmosphere; it includes the brush and the small creatures that live in it.

He swooped down on it. The creature fled squealing. He ran it down in the grass outside the grove. It collapsed into quaking flesh as he picked it up. He talked to it gently and the terror subsided.

It nibbled contentedly on his jacket as he carried it back to the ship.

*       *       *       *       *

Executive Hafner stared unhappily into the cage. It was an undistinguished animal, small and something like an undeveloped rodent. Its fur was sparse and stringy, unglamorous; it would never be an item in the fur export trade.

"Can we exterminate it?" asked Hafner. "Locally, that is."

"Hardly. It's ecologically basic."

The executive looked blank. Dano Marin added the explanation: "You know how Biological Control works. As soon as a planet has been discovered that looks suitable, they send out a survey ship loaded with equipment. The ship flies low over a good part of the planet and the instruments in the ship record the neural currents of the animals below. The instruments can distinguish the characteristic neural patterns of anything that has a brain, including insects.

"Anyway, they have a pretty good idea of the kinds of animals on the planet and their relative distribution. Naturally, the survey party takes a few specimens. They have to in order to correlate the pattern with the actual animal, otherwise the neural pattern would be merely a meaningless squiggle on a microfilm.

"The survey shows that this animal is one of only four species of mammals on the planet. It is also the most numerous."

Hafner grunted. "So if we kill them off here, others will swarm in from surrounding areas?"

"That's about it. There are probably millions of them on this peninsula. Of course, if you want to put a barrier across the narrow connection to the mainland, you might be able to wipe them out locally."

The executive scowled. A barrier was possible, but it would involve more work than he cared to expend.

"What do they eat?" he asked truculently.

"A little bit of everything, apparently. Insects, fruits, berries, nuts, succulents, and grain." Dano Marin smiled. "I guess it could be called an omnivore—now that our clothing is handy, it eats that, too."

Hafner didn't smile. "I thought our clothing was supposed to be verminproof."

Marin shrugged. "It is, on twenty-seven planets. On the twenty-eighth, we meet up with a little fella that has better digestive fluids, that's all."

Hafner looked pained. "Are they likely to bother the crops we plant?"

"Offhand, I would say they aren't. But then I would have said the same about our clothing."

Hafner made up his mind. "All right. You worry about the crops. Find some way to keep them out of the fields. Meanwhile, everyone sleeps in the ship until we can build dormitories."

Individual dwelling units would have been more appropriate in the colony at this stage, thought Marin. But it wasn't for him to decide. The executive was a man who regarded a schedule as something to be exceeded.

"The omnivore—" began Marin.

Hafner nodded impatiently. "Work on it," he said, and walked away.

The biologist sighed. The omnivore really was a queer little creature, but it was by no means the most important thing on Glade. For instance, why were there so few species of land animals on the planet? No reptiles, numerous birds, and only four kinds of mammals.

Every comparable planet teemed with a wild variety of life. Glade, in spite of seemingly ideal conditions, hadn't developed. Why?

He had asked Biological Controls for this assignment because it had seemed an interesting problem. Now, apparently, he was being pressed into service as an exterminator.

He reached in the cage and picked up the omnivore. Mammals on Glade were not unexpected. Parallel development took care of that. Given roughly the same kind of environment, similar animals would usually evolve.

In the Late Carboniferous forest on Earth, there had been creatures like the omnivore, the primitive mammal from which all others had evolved. On Glade, that kind of evolution just hadn't taken place. What had kept nature from exploiting its evolutionary potentialities? There was the real problem, not how to wipe them out.

Marin stuck a needle in the omnivore. It squealed and then relaxed. He drew out the blood and set it back in the cage. He could learn a lot about the animal from trying to kill it.

*     *     *     *     *

The quartermaster was shouting, though his normal voice carried quite well.

"How do you know it's mice?" the biologist asked him.

"Look," said the quartermaster angrily.

Marin looked. The evidence did indicate mice.

Before he could speak, the quartermaster snapped, "Don't tell me they're only mice-like creatures. I know that. The question is: how can I get rid of them?"

"Have you tried poison?"

"Tell me what poison to use and I'll use it."

It wasn't the easiest question to answer. What was poisonous to an animal he had never seen and knew nothing about? According to Biological Survey, the animal didn't exist.

It was unexpectedly serious. The colony could live off the land, and was expected to. But another group of colonists was due in three years. The colony was supposed to accumulate a surplus of food to feed the increased numbers. If they couldn't store the food they grew any better than the concentrates, that surplus was going to be scanty.

Marin went over the warehouse thoroughly. It was the usual early construction on a colonial world. Not esthetic, it was sturdy enough. Fused dirt floor, reinforced foot-thick walls, a ceiling slab of the same. The whole was bound together with a molecular cement that made it practically airtight. It had no windows; there were two doors. Certainly it should keep out rodents.

A closer examination revealed an unexpected flaw. The floor was as hard as glass; no animal could gnaw through it, but, like glass, it was also brittle. The crew that had built the warehouse had evidently been in such a hurry to get back to Earth that they hadn't been as careful as they should have been, for here and there the floor was thin. Somewhere under the heavy equipment piled on it, the floor had cracked. There a burrowing animal had means of entry.

Short of building another warehouse, it was too late to do anything about that. Mice-like animals were inside and had to be controlled where they were.

The biologist straightened up. "Catch me a few of them alive and I'll see what I can do."

\* \* \* \* \*

In the morning, a dozen live specimens were delivered to the lab. They actually did resemble mice.

Their reactions were puzzling. No two of them were affected by the same poison. A compound that stiffened one in a matter of minutes left the others hale and hearty, and the poison he had developed to control the omnivores was completely ineffective.

The depredations in the warehouse went on. Black mice, white ones, gray and brown, short-tailed and long-eared, or the reverse, they continued to eat the concentrates and spoil what they didn't eat.

Marin conferred with the executive, outlined the problem as he saw it and his ideas on what could be done to combat the nuisance.

"But we can't build another warehouse," argued Hafner. "Not until the atomic generator is set up, at any rate. And then we'll have other uses for the power." The executive rested his head in his hands. "I like the other solution better. Build one and see how it works."

"I was thinking of three," said the biologist.

"One," Hafner insisted. "We can't spare the equipment until we know how it works."

At that he was probably right. They had equipment, as much as three ships could bring. But the more they brought, the more was expected of the colony. The net effect was that equipment was always in short supply.

Marin took the authorization to the engineer. On the way, he privately revised his specifications upward. If he couldn't get as many as he wanted, he might as well get a better one.

In two days, the machine was ready.

It was delivered in a small crate to the warehouse. The crate was opened and the machine leaped out and stood there, poised.

"A cat!" exclaimed the quartermaster, pleased. He stretched out his hand toward the black fuzzy robot.

"If you've touched anything a mouse may have, get your hand away," warned the biologist. "It reacts to smell as well as sight and sound."

Hastily, the quartermaster withdrew his hand. The robot disappeared silently into the maze of stored material.

In one week, though there were still some mice in the warehouse, they were no longer a danger.

*        *        *        *        *

The executive called Marin into his office, a small sturdy building located in the center of the settlement. The colony was growing, assuming an aspect of permanency. Hafner sat in his chair and looked out over that growth with satisfaction.

"A good job on the mouse plague," he said.

The biologist nodded. "Not bad, except there shouldn't be any mice here. Biological Survey—"

"Forget it," said the exec. "Everybody makes mistakes, even B. S." He leaned back and looked seriously at the biologist. "I have a job I need done. Just now I'm short of men. If you have no objections...."

The exec was always short of men, would be until the planet was overcrowded, and he would try to find someone to do the work his own men should have done. Dano Marin was not directly responsible to Hafner; he was on loan to the expedition from Biological Controls. Still, it was a good idea to cooperate with the executive. He sighed.

"It's not as bad as you think," said Hafner, interpreting the sound correctly. He smiled. "We've got the digger together. I want you to run it."

Since it tied right in with his investigations, Dano Marin looked relieved and showed it.

"Except for food, we have to import most of our supplies," Hafner explained. "It's a long haul, and we've got to make use of everything on the planet we can. We need oil. There are going to be a lot of wheels turning, and every one of them will have to have oil. In time we'll set up a synthetic plant, but if we can locate a productive field now, it's to our advantage."

"You're assuming the geology of Glade is similar to Earth?"

Hafner waggled his hand. "Why not? It's a nicer twin of Earth."

Why not? Because you couldn't always tell from the surface, thought Marin. It seemed like Earth, but was it? Here was a good chance to find out the history of Glade.

Hafner stood up. "Any time you're ready, a technician will check you out on the digger. Let me know before you go."

*     *     *     *     *

Actually, the digger wasn't a digger. It didn't move or otherwise displace a gram of dirt or rock. It was a means of looking down below the surface, to any practical depth. A large crawler, it was big enough for a man to live in without discomfort for a week.

It carried an outsize ultrasonic generator and a device for directing the beam into the planet. That was the sending apparatus. The receiving end began with a large sonic lens which picked up sound beams reflected from any desired depth, converted it into electrical energy and thence into an image which was flashed onto a screen.

At the depth of ten miles, the image was fuzzy, though good enough to distinguish the main features of the strata. At three miles, it was better. It could pick up the sound reflection of a buried coin and convert it into a picture on which the date could be seen.

It was to a geologist as a microscope is to a biologist. Being a biologist, Dano Marin could appreciate the analogy.

He started at the tip of the peninsula and zigzagged across, heading toward the isthmus. Methodically, he covered the territory, sleeping at night in the digger. On the morning of the third day, he discovered oil traces, and by that afternoon he had located the main field.

He should probably have turned back at once, but now that he had found oil, he investigated more deliberately. Starting at the top, he let the image range downward below the top strata.

It was the reverse of what it should have been. In the top few feet, there were plentiful fossil remains, mostly of the four species of mammals. The squirrel-like creature and the far larger grazing animal were the forest dwellers. Of the plains animals, there were only two, in size fitting neatly between the extremes of the forest dwellers.

After the first few feet, which corresponded to approximately twenty thousand years, he found virtually no fossils. Not until he reached a depth which he could correlate to the Late Carboniferous age on Earth did fossils reappear. Then they were of animals appropriate to the epoch. At that depth and below, the history of Glade was quite similar to Earth's.

Puzzled, he checked again in a dozen widely scattered localities. The results were always the same—fossil history for the first twenty thousand years, then none for roughly a hundred million. Beyond that, it was easy to trace the thread of biological development.

In that period of approximately one hundred million years, something unique had happened to Glade. What was it?

On the fifth day his investigations were interrupted by the sound of the keyed-on radio.

"Marin."

"Yes?" He flipped on the sending switch.

"How soon can you get back?"

He looked at the photo-map. "Three hours. Two if I hurry."

"Make it two. Never mind the oil."

"I've found oil. But what's the matter?"

"You can see it better than I can describe it. We'll discuss it when you get back."

\*      \*      \*      \*      \*

Reluctantly, Marin retracted the instruments into the digger. He turned it around and, with not too much regard for the terrain, let it roar. The treads tossed dirt high in the air. Animals fled squealing from in front of him. If the grove was small enough, he went around it, otherwise he went through and left matchsticks behind.

He skidded the crawler ponderously to halt near the edge of the settlement. The center of activity was the warehouse. Pickups wheeled in and out, transferring supplies to a cleared area outside. He found Hafner in a corner of the warehouse, talking to the engineer.

Hafner turned around when he came up. "Your mice have grown, Marin."

Marin looked down. The robot cat lay on the floor. He knelt and examined it. The steel skeleton hadn't broken; it had been bent, badly. The tough plastic skin had been torn off and, inside, the delicate mechanism had been chewed into an unrecognizable mass.

Around the cat were rats, twenty or thirty of them, huge by any standards. The cat had fought; the dead animals were headless or disemboweled, unbelievably battered. But the robot had been outnumbered.

Biological Survey had said there weren't any rats on Glade. They had also said that about mice. What was the key to their error?

The biologist stood up. "What are you going to do about it?"

"Build another warehouse, two-foot-thick fused dirt floors, monolithic construction. Transfer all perishables to it."

Marin nodded. That would do it. It would take time, of course, and power, all they could draw out of the recently set up atomic generator. All other construction would have to be suspended. No wonder Hafner was disturbed.

"Why not build more cats?" Marin suggested.

The executive smiled nastily. "You weren't here when we opened the doors. The warehouse was swarming with rats. How many robot cats would we need—five, fifteen? I don't know. Anyway the engineer tells me we have enough parts to build three more cats. The one lying there can't be salvaged."

It didn't take an engineer to see that, thought Marin.

Hafner continued, "If we need more, we'll have to rob the computer in the spaceship. I refuse to permit that."

Obviously he would. The spaceship was the only link with Earth until the next expedition brought more colonists. No exec in his right mind would permit the ship to be crippled.

But why had Hafner called him back? Merely to keep him informed of the situation?

\*     \*     \*     \*     \*

Hafner seemed to guess his thoughts. "At night we'll floodlight the supplies we remove from the warehouse. We'll post a guard armed with decharged rifles until we can move the food into the new warehouse. That'll take about ten days. Meanwhile, our fast crops are ripening. It's my guess the rats will turn to them for food. In order to protect our future food supply, you'll have to activate your animals."

The biologist started. "But it's against regulations to loose any animal on a planet until a complete investigation of the possible ill effects is made."

"That takes ten or twenty years. This is an emergency and I'll be responsible—in writing, if you want."

The biologist was effectively countermanded. Another rabbit-infested Australia or the planet that the snails took over might be in the making, but there was nothing he could do about it.

"I hardly think they'll be of any use against rats this size," he protested.

"You've got hormones. Apply them." The executive turned and began discussing construction with the engineer.

\*     \*     \*     \*     \*

Marin had the dead rats gathered up and placed in the freezer for further study.

After that, he retired to the laboratory and worked out a course of treatment for the domesticated animals that the colonists had brought with them. He gave them the first injections and watched them carefully until they were safely through the initial shock phase of growth. As soon as he saw they were going to survive, he bred them.

Next he turned to the rats. Of note was the wide variation in size. Internally, the same thing was true. They had the usual organs, but the proportions of each varied greatly, more than is normal. Nor were their teeth uniform. Some carried huge fangs set in delicate jaws; others had tiny teeth that didn't match the massive bone structure. As a species, they were the most scrambled the biologist had ever encountered.

He turned the microscope on their tissues and tabulated the results. There was less difference here between individual specimens, but it was enough to set him pondering. The reproductive cells were especially baffling.

Late in the day, he felt rather than heard the soundless whoosh of the construction machinery. He looked out of the laboratory and saw smoke rolling upward. As soon as the vegetation was charred, the smoke ceased and heat waves danced into the sky.

They were building on a hill. The little creatures that crept and crawled in the brush attacked in the most vulnerable spot, the food supply. There was no brush, not a blade of grass, on the hill when the colonists finished.

*      *      *      *      *

Terriers. In the past, they were the hunting dogs of the agricultural era. What they lacked in size they made up in ferocity toward rodents. They had earned their keep originally in granaries and fields, and, for a brief time, they were doing it again on colonial worlds where conditions were repeated.

The dogs the colonists brought had been terriers. They were still as fast, still with the same anti-rodent disposition, but they were no longer small. It had been a difficult job, yet Marin had done it well, for the dogs had lost none of their skill and speed in growing to the size of a great dane.

The rats moved in on the fields of fast crops. Fast crops were made to order for a colonial world. They could be planted, grown, and harvested in a matter of weeks. After four such plantings, the fertility of the soil was destroyed, but that meant nothing in the early years of a colonial planet, for land was plentiful.

The rat tide grew in the fast crops, and the dogs were loosed on the rats. They ranged through the fields, hunting. A rush, a snap of their jaws, the shake of a head, and the rat was tossed aside, its back broken. The dogs went on to the next.

Until they could not see, the dogs prowled and slaughtered. At night they came in bloody, most of it not their own, and exhausted. Marin pumped them full of antibiotics, bandaged their wounds, fed them through their veins, and shot them into sleep. In the morning he awakened them with an injection of stimulant and sent them tingling into battle.

It took the rats two days to learn they could not feed during the day. Not so numerous, they came at night. They climbed on the vines and nibbled the fruit. They gnawed growing grain and ravaged vegetables.

The next day the colonists set up lights. The dogs were with them, discouraging the few rats who were still foolish enough to forage while the sun was overhead.

An hour before dusk, Marin called the dogs in and gave them an enforced rest. He brought them out of it after dark and took them to the fields, staggering. The scent of rats revived them; they were as eager as ever, if not quite so fast.

The rats came from the surrounding meadows, not singly, or in twos and threes, as they had before; this time they came together. Squealing and rustling the grass, they moved toward the fields. It was dark, and though he could not see them, Marin could hear them. He ordered the great lights turned on in the area of the fields.

The rats stopped under the glare, milling around uneasily. The dogs quivered and whined. Marin held them back. The rats resumed their march, and Marin released the dogs.

The dogs charged in to attack, but didn't dare brave the main mass. They picked off the stragglers and forced the rats into a tighter formation. After that the rats were virtually unassailable.

The colonists could have burned the bunched-up rats with the right equipment, but they didn't have it and couldn't get it for years. Even if they'd had it, the use of such equipment would

endanger the crops, which they had to save if they could. It was up to the dogs.

The rat formation came to the edge of the fields, and broke. They could face a common enemy and remain united, but in the presence of food, they forgot that unity and scattered—hunger was the great divisor. The dogs leaped joyously in pursuit. They hunted down the starved rodents, one by one, and killed them as they ate.

When daylight came, the rat menace had ended.

The next week the colonists harvested and processed the food for storage and immediately planted another crop.

Marin sat in the lab and tried to analyze the situation. The colony was moving from crisis to crisis, all of them involving food. In itself, each critical situation was minor, but lumped together they could add up to failure. No matter how he looked at it, they just didn't have the equipment they needed to colonize Glade.

The fault seemed to lie with Biological Survey; they hadn't reported the presence of pests that were endangering the food supply. Regardless of what the exec thought about them, Survey knew their business. If they said there were no mice or rats on Glade, then there hadn't been any—*when the survey was made.*

The question was: when did they come and how did they get here?

Marin sat and stared at the wall, turning over hypotheses in his mind, discarding them when they failed to make sense.

His gaze shifted from the wall to the cage of the omnivores, the squirrel-size forest creature. The most numerous animal on Glade, it was a commonplace sight to the colonists.

And yet it was a remarkable animal, more than he had realized. Plain, insignificant in appearance, it might be the most important of any animal Man had encountered on the many worlds he had settled on. The longer he watched, the more Marin became convinced of it.

He sat silent, observing the creature, not daring to move. He sat until it was dark and the omnivore resumed its normal activity.

*Normal?* The word didn't apply on Glade.

The interlude with the omnivore provided him with one answer. He needed another one; he thought he knew what it was, but he had to have more data, additional observations.

He set up his equipment carefully on the fringes of the settlement. There and in no other place existed the information he wanted.

He spent time in the digger, checking his original investigations. It added up to a complete picture.

When he was certain of his facts, he called on Hafner.

The executive was congenial; it was a reflection of the smoothness with which the objectives of the colony were being achieved.

"Sit down," he said affably. "Smoke?"

The biologist sat down and took a cigarette.

"I thought you'd like to know where the mice came from," he began.

Hafner smiled. "They don't bother us any more."

"I've also determined the origin of the rats."

"They're under control. We're doing nicely."

\*     \*     \*     \*     \*

On the contrary, thought Marin. He searched for the proper beginning.

"Glade has an Earth-type climate and topography," he said. "Has had for the past twenty thousand years. Before that, about a hundred million years ago, it was also like Earth of the comparable period."

He watched the look of polite interest settle on the executive's face as he stated the obvious. Well, it *was* obvious, up to a point. The conclusions weren't, though.

"Between a hundred million years and twenty thousand years ago, something happened to Glade," Marin went on. "I don't know the cause; it belongs to cosmic history and we may never find out. Anyway, whatever the cause—fluctuations in the sun, unstable equilibrium of forces within the planet, or perhaps an encounter with an interstellar dust cloud of variable density—the climate on Glade changed.

"It changed with inconceivable violence and it kept on changing. A hundred million years ago, plus or minus, there was carboniferous forest on Glade. Giant reptiles resembling dinosaurs and tiny mammals roamed through it. The first great change wiped out the dinosaurs, as it did on Earth. It didn't wipe out the still more primitive ancestor of the omnivore, because it could adapt to changing conditions.

"Let me give you an idea how the conditions changed. For a few years a given area would be a desert; after that it would turn into a jungle. Still later a glacier would begin to form. And then the cycle would be repeated, with wild variations. All this might happen—did happen—within a span covered by the lifetime of a single omnivore. This occurred many times. For roughly a hundred million years, it was the norm of existence on Glade. This condition was hardly conducive to the preservation of fossils."

Hafner saw the significance and was concerned. "You mean these climatic fluctuations suddenly stopped, twenty thousand years ago? Are they likely to begin again?"

"I don't know," confessed the biologist. "We can probably determine it if we're interested."

The exec nodded grimly. "We're interested, all right."

Maybe we are, thought the biologist. He said, "The point is that survival was difficult. Birds could and did fly to more suitable climates; quite a few of them survived. Only one species of mammals managed to come through."

"Your facts are not straight," observed Hafner. "There are four species, ranging in size from a squirrel to a water buffalo."

"One species," Marin repeated doggedly. "They're the same. If the food supply for the largest animal increases, some of the smaller so-called species grow up. Conversely, if food becomes scarce in any category, the next generation, which apparently can be produced almost instantly, switches to a form which does have an adequate food supply."

"The mice," Hafner said slowly.

*     *     *     *     *

Marin finished the thought for him. "The mice weren't here when we got here. They were born of the squirrel-size omnivore."

Hafner nodded. "And the rats?"

"Born of the next larger size. After all, we're environment, too—perhaps the harshest the beasts have yet faced."

Hafner was a practical man, trained to administer a colony. Concepts were not his familiar ground. "Mutations, then? But I thought—"

The biologist smiled. It was thin and cracked at the edges of his mouth. "On Earth, it would be mutation. Here it is merely normal evolutionary adaptation." He shook his head. "I never told you, but omnivores, though they could be mistaken for an animal from Earth, have no genes or chromosomes. Obviously they do have heredity, but how it is passed down, I don't know. However it functions, it responds to external conditions far faster than anything we've ever encountered."

Hafner nodded to himself. "Then we'll never be free from pests." He clasped and unclasped his hands. "Unless, of course, we rid the planet of all animal life."

"Radioactive dust?" asked the biologist. "They have survived worse."

The exec considered alternatives. "Maybe we should leave the planet and leave it to the animals."

"Too late," said the biologist. "They'll be on Earth, too, and all the planets we've settled on."

Hafner looked at him. The same pictures formed in his mind that Marin had thought of. Three ships had been sent to colonize Glade. One had remained with the colonists, survival insurance in case anything unforeseen happened. Two had gone back to Earth to carry the report that all was well and that more supplies were needed. They had also carried specimens from the planet.

The cages those creatures were kept in were secure. But a smaller species could get out, must already be free, inhabiting, undetected, the cargo spaces of the ships.

There was nothing they could do to intercept those ships. And once they reached Earth, would the biologists suspect? Not for a long time. First a new kind of rat would appear. A mutation could account for that. Without specific knowledge, there would be nothing to connect it with the specimens picked up from Glade.

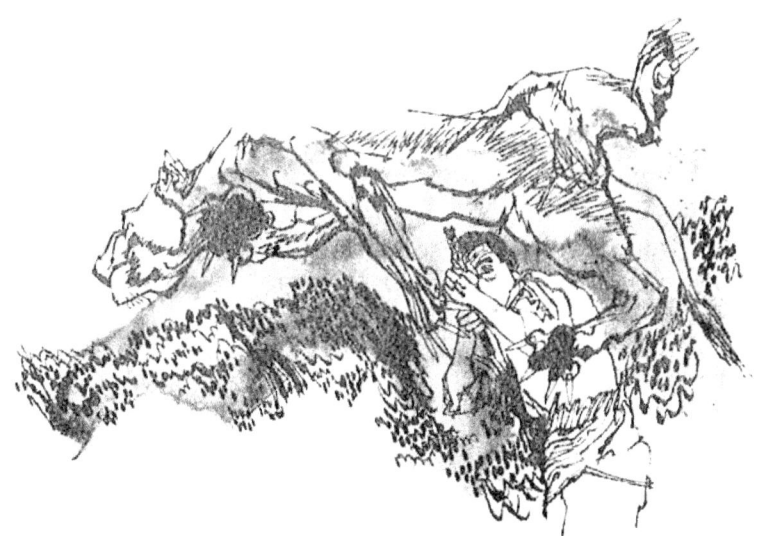

"We have to stay," said the biologist. "We have to study them and we can do it best here."

He thought of the vast complex of buildings on Earth. There was too much invested to tear them down and make them verminproof. Billions of people could not be moved off the planet while the work was being done.

They were committed to Glade not as a colony, but as a gigantic laboratory. They had gained one planet and lost the equivalent of ten, perhaps more when the destructive properties of the omnivores were finally assessed.

A rasping animal cough interrupted the biologist's thoughts. Hafner jerked his head and glanced out the window. Lips tight, he grabbed a rifle off the wall and ran out. Marin followed him.

\*     \*     \*     \*     \*

The exec headed toward the fields where the second fast crop was maturing. On top of a knoll, he stopped and knelt. He flipped the dial to *extreme charge*, aimed, and fired. It was high; he missed the animal in the field. A neat strip of smoking brown appeared in the green vegetation.

He aimed more carefully and fired again. The charge screamed out of the muzzle. It struck the animal on the forepaw. The beast leaped high in the air and fell down, dead and broiled.

They stood over the animal Hafner had killed. Except for the lack of markings, it was a good imitation of a tiger. The exec prodded it with his toe.

"We chase the rats out of the warehouse and they go to the fields," he muttered. "We hunt them down in the fields with dogs and they breed tigers."

"Easier than rats," said Marin. "We can shoot tigers." He bent down over the slain dog near which they had surprised the big cat.

The other dog came whining from the far corner of the field to which he had fled in terror. He was a courageous dog, but he could not face the great carnivore. He whimpered and licked the face of his mate.

The biologist picked up the mangled dog and headed toward the laboratory.

"You can't save her," said Hafner morosely. "She's dead."

"But the pups aren't. We'll need them. The rats won't disappear merely because tigers have showed up."

The head drooped limply over his arm and blood seeped into his clothing as Hafner followed him up the hill.

"We've been here three months," the exec said suddenly. "The dogs have been in the fields only two. And yet the tiger was mature. How do you account for something like that?"

Marin bent under the weight of the dog. Hafner never would understand his bewilderment. As a biologist, all his categories were upset. What did evolution explain? It was a history of organic life on a particular world. Beyond that world, it might not apply.

Even about himself there were many things Man didn't know, dark patches in his knowledge which theory simply had to pass over. About other creatures, his ignorance was sometimes limitless.

Birth was simple; it occurred on countless planets. Meek grazing creatures, fierce carnivores—the most unlikely animals gave birth to their young. It happened all the time. And the young grew up, became mature and mated.

He remembered that evening in the laboratory. It was accidental—what if he had been elsewhere and not witnessed it? They would not know what little they did.

He explained it carefully to Hafner. "If the survival factor is high and there's a great disparity in size, the young need not ever be young. They may be born as fully functioning adults!"

*     *     *     *     *

Although not at the rate it had initially set, the colony progressed. The fast crops were slowed down and a more diversified selection was planted. New buildings were constructed and the supplies that were stored in them were spread out thin, for easy inspection.

The pups survived and within a year shot up to maturity. After proper training, they were released to the fields where they joined the older dogs. The battle against the rats went on; they were held in check, though the damage they caused was considerable.

The original animal, unchanged in form, developed an appetite for electrical insulation. There was no protection except to keep the power on at all times. Even then there were unwelcome interruptions until the short was located and the charred carcass was removed. Vehicles were kept tightly closed or parked only in verminproof buildings. While the plague didn't increase in numbers, it couldn't be eliminated, either.

There was a flurry of tigers, but they were larger animals and were promptly shot down. They prowled at night, so the colonists were assigned to guard the settlement around the clock. Where lights failed to reach, the infra-red 'scope did. As fast as they came, the tigers died. Except for the first one, not a single dog was lost.

The tigers changed, though not in form. Externally, they were all big and powerful killers. But as the slaughter went on, Marin noticed one astonishing fact—the internal organic structure became progressively more immature.

The last one that was brought to him for examination was the equivalent of a newly born cub. That tiny stomach was suited more for the digestion of milk than meat. How it had furnished energy to drive those great muscles was something of a miracle. But drive it had, for a murderous fifteen minutes before the animal was brought down. No lives were lost, though sick bay was kept busy for a while.

That was the last tiger they shot. After that, the attacks ceased.

The seasons passed and nothing new occurred. A spaceship civilization or even that fragment of it represented by the colony was too much for the creature, which Marin by now had come to think of as the "Omnimal." It had evolved out of a cataclysmic past, but it could not meet the challenge of the harshest environment.

Or so it seemed.

\*     \*     \*     \*     \*

Three months before the next colonists were due, a new animal was detected. Food was missing from the fields. It was not another tiger: they were carnivorous. Nor rats, for vines were stripped in a manner that no rodent could manage.

The food was not important. The colony had enough in storage. But if the new animal signaled another plague, it was necessary to know how to meet it. The sooner they knew what the animal was, the better defense they could set up against it.

Dogs were useless. The animal roamed the field they were loose in, and they did not attack nor even seem to know it was there.

The colonists were called upon for guard duty again, but it evaded them. They patrolled for a week and they still did not catch sight of it.

Hafner called them in and rigged up an alarm system in the field most frequented by the animal. It detected that, too, and moved its sphere of operations to a field in which the alarm system had not been installed.

Hafner conferred with the engineer, who devised an alarm that would react to body radiation. It was buried in the original field and the old alarm was moved to another.

Two nights later, just before dawn, the alarm rang.

Marin met Hafner at the edge of the settlement. Both carried rifles. They walked; the noise of any vehicle was likely to frighten the animal. They circled around and approached the field from the rear. The men in the camp had been alerted. If they needed help, it was ready.

They crept silently through the underbrush. It was feeding in the field, not noisily, yet they could hear it. The dogs hadn't barked.

They inched nearer. The blue sun of Glade came up and shone full on their quarry. The gun dropped in Hafner's hand. He clenched his teeth and raised it again.

Marin put out a restraining arm. "Don't shoot," he whispered.

"I'm the exec here. I say it's dangerous."

"Dangerous," agreed Marin, still in a whisper. "That's why you can't shoot. It's more dangerous than you know."

Hafner hesitated and Marin went on. "The omnimal couldn't compete in the changed environment and so it evolved mice. We stopped the mice and it countered with rats. We turned back the rat and it provided the tiger.

"The tiger was easiest of all for us and so it was apparently stopped for a while. But it didn't really stop. Another animal was being formed, the one you see there. It took the omnimal two years to create it—how, I don't know. A million years were required to evolve it on Earth."

Hafner hadn't lowered the rifle and he showed no signs of doing so. He looked lovingly into the sights.

"Can't you see?" urged Marin. "We can't destroy the omnimal. It's on Earth now, and on the other planets, down in the storage areas of our big cities, masquerading as rats. And we've never been able to root out even our own terrestrial rats, so how can we exterminate the omnimal?"

"All the more reason to start now." Hafner's voice was flat.

Marin struck the rifle down. "Are their rats better than ours?" he asked wearily. "Will their pests win or ours be stronger? Or will the two make peace, unite and interbreed, make war on us? It's not impossible; the omnimal could do it if interbreeding had a high survival factor.

"Don't you still see? There is a progression. After the tiger, it bred this. If this evolution fails, if we shoot it down, what will it create next? This creature I think we can compete with. *It's the one after this that I do not want to face.*"

\*     \*     \*     \*     \*

It heard them. It raised its head and looked around. Slowly it edged away and backed toward a nearby grove.

The biologist stood up and called softly. The creature scurried to the trees and stopped just inside the shadows among them.

The two men laid down their rifles. Together they approached the grove, hands spread open to show they carried no weapons.

It came out to meet them. Naked, it had had no time to learn about clothing. Neither did it have weapons. It plucked a large white flower from the tree and extended this mutely as a sign of peace.

"I wonder what it's like," said Marin. "It seems adult, but can it be, all the way through? What's inside that body?"

"I wonder what's in his head," Hafner said worriedly.

It looked very much like a man.

# TANGLE HOLD

ILLUSTRATED BY EMSH
ORIGINALLY PUBLISHED IN *GALAXY SCIENCE FICTION*,
JUNE 1953

*Jadiver objected to being the greatest influence for good on Venus ... because what was good for Venus was bad for Jadiver!*

# TANGLE HOLD

Somebody was wrapping him in a sheet of ice and spice. Somebody was pulling it tight so that his toes ached and his fingers tingled. He still had fingers, and eyes too. He opened his eyes and they turned in opposite directions and couldn't focus on what they saw. He made an effort, but couldn't keep it up and had to let his eyes flutter shut again.

"Rest. You're all right." That's where he got the idea of ice and spice—from that voice.

"Mmmm," said Jadiver. He tried to raise his hand, but it wouldn't move. It was good advice—to rest; he couldn't do otherwise. "What happened?" he whispered.

"You had an accident. Remember?"

He didn't. It was his mind playing tricks, of course. It couldn't have been pleasant if his memory didn't have access to it.

"Mmmm," he evaded.

"Go to sleep. We'll talk later."

He thought he felt something shoved deep in his flesh, but he may have been wrong. In any event, the light that filtered through his closed eyelids faded away and the external world, of which there wasn't much in the first place, vanished completely.

\*      \*      \*      \*      \*

Later, he awakened. How much later, he didn't know, but it may have been days. The oppressive languor had left him and he felt capable of movement. To prove it to himself, he turned his head. He was alone, and he thought he recognized where he was. He didn't like it.

There was an odor in the room, but this time it was the kind that lingers in all hospitals. He tried to sit up, but that was more than he could manage. He lay there a long time, looking through the heavily reinforced window; then someone came in.

"You'll live," said the voice behind him—the same voice.

"Think so?" He hadn't intended to turn around, but the spice was back and he wanted to see. It was only the fragrance she wore—there was none in her voice or demeanor. That was still ice.

When she sat down, he could see that her hair was a shade of copper and the uniform she wore a dark green. She was not a robot and therefore not a nurse or a guard. It was logical to assume she was a doctor, police variety—definitely the police.

Thadeus Jadiver sighed. "What am I in for?"

"You're not in for anything. Maybe you should be, but that's not my business," she said in a flat voice. That was the only thing about her that was flat; the rest curved nicely even under the uniform. "This is an emergency as well as a police hospital. We were close, so we took you in."

That was reassuring. Jadiver tried to smile as he lifted a curiously bandaged arm. "Thanks for this."

"I'll take only half the credit. That was a combo job."

He was going to have difficulty if she insisted on using technical slang. "What's a combo job?"

"Just what it sounds like. A combination robot-human surgeon. All hospitals use them. The robot is more precise and delicate, but it lacks the final margin of judgment that's supplied by the human. Two of us work together in critical cases."

He still couldn't remember what had happened, but it would come back in time. "I was critical?"

Her mouth was firm and her cheekbones a trifle too broad. Just the same, the total effect was pleasing, would have been more so with a little warmth stirred in. "To give you an idea, you'll notice that every square inch of your skin is now synthetic." She leaned over and took his hand, which was encased in a light spongy cocoon. Expertly, she peeled back the end and exposed the tips of his fingers.

Jadiver looked, then turned away. "Cellophane," he said. "A man can be born, live, die, and be shoveled away; begot and beget, completely untouched by human hands."

She looked blank at the mention of cellophane. Probably didn't know what it was, thought Jadiver. So few people did any more.

"Don't worry about it," she said. "Your skin's transparent now, but in a few days it will be normal."

"That's nice," said Jadiver. "I suppose it would be educational, but I'd just as soon not be an anatomy model of the first layer of the human body."

She stood up and managed to work up a creditable imitation of interest. "We had to peel off the burned part, and when you were completely raw, we fitted the synthetic skin to your body. Over that we sprayed the bandage. New body cells form with this synthetic substance as the matrix. You'll gradually return to normal or better. Your new skin may be more resistant to corrosive chemicals and microbe invasions."

"Glad to hear it," said Jadiver. "Superman."

For the first time, she smiled. "Don't count on it. This stuff is too new for us to know how it reacts in all cases." She turned around at the door. "In a few days I'll take off the bandages and you can go home. Meanwhile, you know what to do if you need anything."

\*　　\*　　\*　　\*　　\*

Jadiver lay there after she left, thinking. He hadn't asked what the accident was and she had assumed he remembered. He ought to, but he didn't. He frowned and tried to recall the last thing he had been doing.

They had removed his skin and replaced it with a synthetic substance. Why? Take it from there and work back.

He stirred uneasily. The last he remembered, he'd been in his apartment. That didn't help much; he was often there. He shook his head. He was in the apartment, preparing to leave. That meant he must have used the autobath. That was it. The picture came into focus:

He touched the door of the autobath and it swung open. He went inside. "Shave, massage, bath," he ordered.

The mechanism reached out of the wall to enfold him. He leaned back. It gripped him, not comfortably, as usual—but tightly. He squirmed, but when the grip didn't adjust, he relaxed.

The autobath rumbled familiarly and a jet of water spouted up from the floor. It was icy cold and Jadiver shivered.

"You didn't listen," he said firmly. "I asked for the bath last."

The autobath paid no attention. The top and side jets turned on. The force was greater than he had ever experienced. It was difficult to breathe. The water got hotter rapidly, and then, seconds later, steam blew out of the nozzles.

Jadiver shouted and tried to struggle free. The autobath did not let go. Instead, it ground at his muscles with hard inflexible hands. Here and there his skin began parting from his flesh. The autobath kept on kneading him. It was when it reached for his face—Jadiver remembered very clearly—he lost consciousness.

He lay on the bed in the hospital, sweat soaking into the bandages. He could understand why he'd had a memory block—being boiled alive was frightful enough for his mind to repress.

It was not only the accident that was disturbing, but the manner in which it occurred. He knew robot machinery and the principles used in the construction of it. The autobath was one of the best—foolproof, if there was such a mechanism.

Someone had tampered with it—object: *to try to kill him*.

That was one possibility and he could face it with equanimity.

There was also another, but he didn't like to think about that.

*     *     *     *     *

He looked out over Venicity. From his apartment, the topography resembled that of a lunar crater. In the middle was a giant concrete plain, the rocketport. From the edges of the rocketport, the size of the buildings increased gradually; at a third of the distance from the center, they were at maximum height; thereafter, they decreased gradually until one and two story structures nibbled at the surrounding forest.

Five million people and in ten years there would undoubtedly be seven, a sizable metropolis even for Earth. That didn't mean that the population of Venus could compare with the home planet. Venus was settled differently. Newcomers started with the cities; only later did they venture out into the vast wild lands. Venus was civilized, after a fashion, but it wasn't a copy of Earth.

The screen glimmered at his back. "Thadeus Jadiver, consulting engineer?"

He turned. "That's right. Can I help you?"

The man on the screen closed one eye slowly and opened it again the same way. "This is Vicon Burlingame. I've been doing some experimenting and am now at the point where I can use some technical assistance."

"I'm not sure. I've been in the hospital until this morning. I think I need a checkup."

"I called while you were gone," said Burlingame. "I know about the hospital; however, I don't think my work will be strenuous. Perhaps you'd come over and we'll discuss it."

"I'll take the chance I can help you."

"Good." Vicon Burlingame gave him the address before fading out of the screen.

Jadiver dressed slowly. Weak, but better than he expected. Physically, his recovery was far advanced. It wasn't he who was taking a chance, of course; it was Burlingame. Jadiver had warned him and if Burlingame was willing to risk it, that was up to him.

Before he left, Jadiver checked his office. A few calls in the last week, but nothing important. It was a routine check and he gave the robot routine instructions.

A tiny thing, that office, located on the ground floor of a building fronting a principal thoroughfare. A space large enough for a client to sit down, if one should come, which wasn't often. Behind the desk was the upper half of a robot. Tiny though the office was, it was not inexpensive, and the business that passed through it was barely enough to pay the rent.

There were other advantages in maintaining it, though. As long as he had a business address, he was spared certain legal embarrassments.

\*      \*      \*      \*      \*

Five minutes later, he was greeted by Vicon Burlingame. "Come in." Jadiver did so.

Burlingame silently studied Jadiver closely. "Maybe you're tired," he said at last. "A little sun would relax you."

"It might," agreed Jadiver. "This cloudy Venus."

"It's not so bad when you're home," said Burlingame. "But public places are bad for ultraviolet." He indicated the next room. "The lamp is in there."

Jadiver went in and began to remove his clothing. Before he finished, a little man came in, nodding silently at Jadiver. Without comment, Jadiver stood in front of the machine. While the little man methodically examined him, his clothing disappeared.

The little man looked up at the end of the intensive investigation. "You'll do," he said.

"Clear?" asked Jadiver.

"Clear as the atmosphere of the Moon. We were afraid they'd planted you while you were in the hospital, but we decided to take the chance."

For the first time since the accident, Jadiver felt relaxed. "Thanks, Cobber. I was hoping to contact someone to check it for me."

Cobber shrugged. "Who can you trust? If you go to a doctor good enough to find a gadget that small, what is he? A high-powered professional and he's got his problems. He sees something inside and smiles and says you're fine and charges you a fat fee. Even if he tells you that you've been planted, there's nothing you can do. No one's going to cut it out—not while the police can hear everything through it."

"Thanks for taking the chance."

Burlingame came in smiling confidently. "Now we can talk," he said. Behind him were three other men Jadiver had never seen.

"Where are my clothes?" Jadiver wanted to know.

"They'll be ready," promised Burlingame. "The police have got all kinds of cute tricks, only we don't fall for them. We're systematic."

They were that, decided Jadiver, and something more. They had to be to survive so long. Burlingame was good.

A gamin's face peered through the doorway and one hand thrust his clothing into the room and waved it. "Here. They didn't try to conceal anything." She sounded disappointed.

Jadiver dressed as Burlingame relayed the clothing to him. The gamin wrinkled her nose and disappeared. By the time Jadiver was completely dressed, she came back with refreshments.

They sat down at the table. "I want faces," said Burlingame, across from him—"five faces."

Jadiver looked around. There were six. "None of my business, except in a professional way, but who do I leave out?"

"Cobber. We have other plans for him."

It wasn't a good idea to pry. He had to know the human material on which he was expected to work, but it was safer not to know what they were planning.

He tapped his glass. "What kind of faces? Soft faces, hard faces, space faces? And do you want anything else?"

"Society faces," said Burlingame. "Emily wants to wear a low-cut gown. The rest of us just need faces."

"Real low," the gamin insisted, wriggling.

"Society," mused Jadiver. "I always did think it was better to rob the rich ... like Robin Hood."

"Sure," Burlingame said.

Jadiver tilted the glass. "Especially since the poor don't have much money."

"That has something to do with it," Burlingame cheerfully agreed.

Cobber broke in. He was a little gnarled man, older than the others. "A point, Jadiver. The poor don't have much money, but there's so many more of them. You can actually be more successful robbing them. But you have to keep at it every day in the year, and then you don't call it robbery; you say you're governing them."

"Don't have that kind of stamina," said Burlingame.

"A good point, Cobber." Jadiver leaned on the table. "I don't want specific information, but how can you make robbery pay off these days?"

\*     \*     \*     \*     \*

Burlingame looked at him astutely. "Considering it yourself?"

Jadiver shook his head. "Intellectual curiosity. I'm doing all right in my own line."

"It's a theory," said Burlingame. "You can't touch banks or financial institutions. Too many electronic safeguards, robots, and what have you. In order to get past that kind of equipment, you have to be a top-notch scientist—and one that can do better at a top-notch job.

"Now, who's got money? The rich, and they *want* to show it off wherever they go. Naturally they take precautions, too, but people are always involved and that's the weakness. You can build a machine that does one thing perfectly, but people make mistakes—they get rattled. Teamwork can take advantage of it. A feint here, and a block there, and before anyone knows what's happening, we're through their defenses. With, of course, their money."

Jadiver looked at him, at his handsome, ruddy, respectable face. "You played football?"

Burlingame grinned. "Twenty-five years ago."

"It's changed. You wouldn't recognize it now."

"Perhaps not. But the principle is still the same, and it's the principle that pays off."

Jadiver stood up. "I'd better get started. Where do I work?"

"Here," said Burlingame. "We have the tools ready for you."

"Mind if I look at the setup?"

"Go ahead."

The gamin bounced up and took charge of Jadiver, leading him to a small workshop screened off in a corner of one of the larger rooms. The layout was authentic enough to justify the equipment—a few robot forms in the rough state, handbooks on design, several robot heads in various stages of completion, and an assortment of the specialized tools of the trade. It was standard for the tinkerer, for the would-be designer of robot bodies. Burlingame always covered himself in every detail.

Jadiver inspected it thoroughly, the gamin standing impatiently at his side.

"I'm first when you're ready," she said.

He eyed her amusedly. "What's the hurry?"

"There's more to do on me and you'll do your best work when you're not tired."

"I'll start soon. Let me see the plastic."

She opened a cabinet and there it was. Jadiver squatted and read the instructions on the containers. He shook his head in despair. Every amateur always did this.

He stood up. "You've got the worst kind," he said.

She shrugged. "They told me it was the best."

"That depends. There are two kinds, and this one does look more real than the other. In fact, for a time this actually becomes a part of your body, a pseudo-flesh. But it's quite dangerous."

"The other kind is just a cosmetic, isn't it?"

"That's right, but—"

"Then I'm not worried," she said, tossing her head. "The way I see it, it's dangerous not to use the best disguise we can get."

She might be right. At least he'd warned her, and as long as she had the facts straight, the decision was hers to make.

Jadiver peeled off his jacket and slid into a protective smock. "Ask Burlingame to come in. This is going to be delicate, you know."

The gamin grinned. "I've never been overly concerned about Vicon, and he knows I can take care of myself." She stepped behind a screen and presently came out again, nude. "Where do you want me to stand?"

"On the pedestal, under the light." He looked at her closely. He had thought she was a little girl, a tired little girl who hadn't slept much recently. It was the pert face that had fooled him, with the upturned nose, because she wasn't young. Forty he would say, maybe more, nearly as old as Burlingame.

Her body was slight, but not much was wrong with it. Here and there were a few wrinkles, though in general her figure appeared youthful. It would require all his skill to make her as spectacular in a low-cut gown as she wanted to be. And her legs, though well shaped, were slightly bowed, a sure sign of Venusian rickets. Early settlers hadn't realized that the soil was deficient in some essential trace elements.

He would have to straighten her legs if she expected to mingle with society. It was beyond his power to change the bones, but he could add pseudo-flesh to give the same effect.

He slipped on the mask, attached the various containers, thrust his hand into the glovelike control valve, and began to work.

She winced involuntarily as the spray tingled against her body and adhered with constrictive force. He blocked out the areas he had to alter and then began to fill in and build up.

"I don't see it," said Emily. "I know you must be good. That's why Burlingame wanted you. But it seems to me this is out of your line."

He brought the spray up in a straight line along the edge of her shin. "How good I am is a matter of opinion. Mine and the places I've worked."

"What places, for instance?"

"Mostly Earth."

"I've never been there," she said wistfully.

"You haven't missed much." He knew that, while he believed that with part of his mind, essentially he was wrong. As the spray was drying on her legs, he started filling out her breasts. "However, this isn't as much out of my line as you think. Engineers specialize, you know. Mine's industrial design. We don't usually monkey with the internal mechanism of a machine, though we're able to. Mostly, we design housings for the machines, robots as a rule."

He proceeded to her face and changed the upturned nose to a straight one. "The ideal external appearance of a machine ought to establish the function of that machine, and do so with the most efficient distribution of space and material."

He stood back and eyed the total effect. She was coming along. "The human body is a good design—for a human. It doesn't belong on a robot. That, for most purposes, should be a squat container with three wheels or treads, with eye-stalks and tentacles on top. I designed one like that, but it was never built. Robots always look like beautiful girls or handsome men, and the mechanism is twice as clumsy as it should be, in order to fit in with that conception."

He squinted at the spray. "In other words, I design robot bodies and faces. Why should it be strange I can do the same with humans?"

The spray was neither a liquid nor a dustlike jet. She shivered under it. "Why don't you like robots? I don't see anything wrong with them. They're so beautiful."

He laughed. "I'll give you an idea. I got tired of the meaningless perfection of the bodies I was turning out. Why shouldn't the bodies be beautiful, considering how they're made? Anyway, I put a pimple on one model. Not on her face. Her shoulder."

She extended her hands and he took off the fine wrinkles with a sweeping motion of the spray. "What happened?"

"I had to start looking for another job. But somebody higher up began to think about what I'd done. Now, on Earth, all robots that model clothing have some perceptible skin defects. More lifelike, they say."

"Is that why you came to Venus?"

"I'd been considering it for some time. It seemed to me that there ought to be a place for a good designer, even if I did have to work on robots." He smiled wryly. "A lot of other engineers had the same idea."

"Too much competition?"

"Sort of." He grimaced. "My first job here was designing female bodies for so-called social clubs."

"Oh, those," she said scornfully.

"It's legitimate on Venus. Anyway, I tried out that idea again. Customers didn't like it. Said they could get women with blemishes any time. When they got a robot, they wanted perfection."

"Don't blame them," Emily said practically. She looked at him with sudden suspicion. "Don't give *me* pimples."

"Not a one," he assured her. "You're flawless."

And she was—with only one item missing. He flexed his fingers in the control glove and sprayed on nipples. She was finished.

He shucked off the mask and laid aside the spray gun. "Look at yourself."

She went to the mirror and turned in front of it. She smoothed her hands across her face and smiled with pleasure. "It feels like flesh."

"It is, almost. Tomorrow you'll bleed there if you cut yourself."

She nodded. "Is that all?"

"Except for instructions, yes."

She looked at him with curious shyness and hurriedly slipped into her clothing. She hadn't minded nudity before, when she wasn't as lovely as she wanted to be. What she didn't know was that Jadiver liked her better as she had been.

*       *       *       *       *

Dressed, she came back to him. "What are those instructions?"

He tore off two envelopes attached to the container. He checked the spray gun to determine how much had been used.

"Pseudo-flesh is highly poisonous," he said, handing her the envelopes. "The tablets in the white package neutralize the toxic effects. Take one every eight hours. And don't forget to take it, unless you want to end up in convulsions on the floor."

"I'll remember. When do I begin?"

"In three hours. And now for some advice I know you don't want. You can keep yourself as you are for two months. But you'll be healthier if you get rid of the pseudo-flesh as soon as you can."

She looked longingly at the face in the mirror. "How do I do that?"

"When you're ready, take the tablets in the green package, one every hour until the pseudo-flesh is absorbed. After it's gone, take three more at the same interval. The total time should be about thirteen hours." She was not paying attention. He eased between her and the mirror. "Get a complete checkup before you try this again. It takes years off your life."

"I know that. How many?"

"I can't say exactly. It's a body, pseudo-flesh weight ratio, plus some other factors that no one knows anything about. I'd estimate that you'll lose about three years for every two weeks you keep it."

"It's worth it," she said, gazing again into the mirror. She turned away in indecision. "I've always known Burlingame was mine, even if I wasn't pretty. Now I'm not so sure, after this."

It wasn't exactly Burlingame she was concerned with, thought Jadiver. For a while she was going to be beautiful beyond her expectations. The irony was that almost any robot outshone her temporary beauty. She was jealous of machines that had no awareness of how they looked.

Jadiver straightened up. He hadn't fully recovered from his accident and he was tired. And the artificial skin, no matter what they said, hadn't been completely integrated to his body. It itched.

"Send the rest of them in, one at a time," he said as she went out.

It wasn't going to take long, for which he was grateful. Now that he knew a spying device hadn't been surgeried into him, there were certain aspects of the accident that demanded investigation.

\*   \*   \*   \*   \*

Jadiver limped into the apartment. The chair unfolded and came to meet him as he entered. He relaxed in the depths of it and called out for food. Soon he had eaten, and shortly after that he dozed.

When he awakened, refreshed, he began the thinking he'd put off until now. The fee from Burlingame was welcome. It was dangerous business, so Jadiver had charged accordingly. Now his economic problem was solved for about a month.

In the hospital he had been sure of a motive for the accident. It had seemed simple enough: the police had planted a spying device in him. However, since he had been examined thoroughly at Burlingame's and nothing had been found, that theory broke down.

There was still another possibility—someone had tried to kill him and had failed. If so, that put the police in the clear and he would have to look elsewhere. He might as well start there.

He walked over to the autobath and began inspecting it. It wasn't the one he'd been injured in. That had been removed and replaced by the management. It would have helped if he had been able to go over the original one.

The new autobath was much like the old, a small unit that fitted decoratively into the scheme of the room, not much taller than an upright man, or longer than a man lying down. The mechanism itself, and there was plenty, was effectively sealed. Short of an atomic torch, there wasn't any way to get into it.

Jadiver pried and poked, but learned nothing. In response to the human voice, it automatically provided all the services necessary to human cleanliness, but there was no direct way to check on the involved mechanism.

*    *    *    *    *

He finally called the firm that made it. The usual beautiful robot answered: "Living Rooms, Incorporated. Can I help you?"

"Information," he said. "Autobath unit."

"Sales? New or replacement?"

"Service. I want to see about repairs."

"We have no repair department. Nothing ever wears out."

"Perhaps not, but it becomes defective and has to be replaced."

"Defective parts are a result of wear. Since nothing wears out, no repair is necessary. Occasionally an autobath is damaged, but then it doesn't work at all, even if the damage is slight. It has to be replaced."

That was what he thought, but it was better to be sure. "This is hypothetical," he said. "Suppose there was an accident in an autobath. Is there an alarm system which would indicate that something was wrong?"

The robot was smooth and positive. "Your question is basically misleading, according to our statistics. In eight hundred and forty one million plus installations, on all the inhabited planets of the Solar System, there has never been one accident.

"The autobath is run by a small atomic motor and is not connected in any way to an outside power source. There are plumbing connections, but these are not suitable for the transmission of a signal. To answer your question specifically: There is no alarm system of any kind, local or general, nor is there any provision for someone else to attach one."

"Thanks," said Jadiver, and cut the screen.

He was nearly certain now. One check remained.

*    *    *    *    *

He flipped on a switch and walked out of the room to the hall and stood there listening. He could hear nothing. He came closer to the door and there was still no sound. He pressed his ear against the juncture of the door and jamb. Not the slightest noise.

He winced when he opened the door. The music he had switched on was deafening. He hurried inside and turned it off. He had known his apartment was sound-proofed. Just how good that soundproofing was, he hadn't tested until now.

The so-called accident had happened in the autobath. The unit couldn't signal that anything was wrong. No one passing in the hall could hear his yells.

The evidence indicated that no accident could happen in the autobath—yet it had.

Logically, he should have died in that accident that couldn't happen—yet he hadn't.

What did they want? And was it the police? In the hospital he had been sure—certain, too, of what they were attempting. Now the facts wouldn't fit.

Tiredness came back, reinforced by doubt. His skin itched— probably from nervous tension. He finally fell into an uneasy sleep with the help of a sedative.

\*     \*     \*     \*     \*

In the morning, the itch was still there. He looked curiously at his skin; it appeared normal. It was definitely not transparent, hadn't been even in the hospital when the bandages were removed. He'd had a glimpse of it in the original transparent stage only once, when the doctor had exposed the tips of his fingers.

Briefly he wondered about it. Did it really itch that bad, or was it an unconscious excuse to see the doctor? She was a sullen, indifferent creature, but without doubt worth seeing again. He didn't know her name, but he could find out easily enough.

As if in answer to the silent question, his whole body twitched violently. He raked his fingers across his forearm and the nails broke off. She was at least partly right in her predictions; his skin was considerably tougher than it had been, though nothing appeared different.

He didn't like communicating with the police, but he had little choice. He flipped on the screen and made a few inquiries.

The name he wanted was Doctor Doumya Filone. She was off duty at present. However, if it was an emergency—? His skin crawled and he decided it was just that and identified himself. There were a number of persons with whom he had contacts who wouldn't approve his doing this, but they didn't have to live in his skin.

He dialed her quickly. He couldn't place the number, but figured it was probably across town, in one of the newer districts. He didn't fully remember what she was like until she appeared on the screen. With that face to put on a robot, he might make a fortune. That is, if he could capture the expression as well as the features.

"How's the patient?" she asked. Behind her briskness he thought he could detect a flicker of concern.

"You can take back that skin you gave me," he said. "It itches."

She frowned. "I told you it was very new. We aren't able to anticipate all the reactions." She paused. "However, it shouldn't itch. By now it ought to be well integrated with your body and new cell growth should be occurring with the synthetic substance as the matrix."

"Thanks," he said dryly. "That doesn't explain how I feel."

Unperturbed, she looked down at a desk he could imagine, but could not see. She got up and walked out of the field of vision. She was gone for quite some time.

A disturbing thought formed in his mind. Was she calling elsewhere for instructions? There was no reason why she should, yet the thought persisted.

She came back. "Get a detergent. What kind doesn't matter. Put it in the autobath and take a hot bath, plenty of lather. Soak in it for at least fifteen minutes."

* * * * *

Her prescription was primitive in the extreme. Did she really expect it to be effective, or did she have something else in mind?

"Do you think I'm going to trust myself to that machine?" he said. "I've got myself a little enamel basin. Had to steal it out of a museum."

Nothing was outwardly changed, but she seemed slightly sympathetic. "I can understand how you feel, but you'll have to get over it or go pioneering in the wild lands. As long as you're in a city, you can't rent, buy or build accommodations that have no autobath. Besides, I've been assured that the odds are against that happening again."

That was an understatement, if his information was correct. Actually, he had wanted her reaction, but it didn't tell him a thing.

"Feel better already," he said.

She nodded. "Suggestion at work. Take your bath now and call me tomorrow if it doesn't work. Sooner, if you need to." She cut their connection before he could answer.

In addition to physical relief, he had hoped that she would let slip some information. She hadn't done so. Of course, she might not know anything more than the purely medical aspects of the police plan. If it was the police.

He left the screen and checked the autobath for supplies. Satisfactory for the present. He removed his clothing, stepped inside, and followed her instructions. A tub rose out of the floor, filled with water, and the mechanism immersed him in it. Thick soapy suds billowed up and warm water laved his skin. The rubbery hands of the autobath were soft and massaged him gently and expertly.

He tried to relax. So far, he had suffered no irreparable harm. He tried to avoid the memory of his accident, but that was impossible. The one comfort was that his death was not the objective. He corrected himself—not the *immediate* objective.

Anyway, he'd been rescued and placed under good medical care. How the rescue had been effected was unknown, unless it had been included in the plan from the beginning. If so, he could assume that the autobath had been tampered with and fixed with a signal that would indicate when he was unconscious.

"Fifteen minutes and ten seconds," said the autobath. "Do you wish to remain longer?"

"That'll do," he said. "The rinse, please."

He lay back and curled up his legs, stretching his arms while clear water flowed soothingly over him. In spite of his skepticism, this primitive prescription of Doumya Filone seemed to work. The itch had stopped completely; although his skin was now mottled. No scars; the hospital and Doumya Filone had done a good job.

He scrutinized his skin carefully. The marks were not actually on his skin; they were beneath it. So faint as to be almost invisible, it was nevertheless a disturbing manifestation. The marks gradually became more distinct. It looked like a shadowy web thrown over and pressed deep into his body.

*     *     *     *     *

The autobath lifted him and he stood in front of the mirror. There was no mistake—a network spread over his body, arms, legs, face too; perhaps on his head as well, though he couldn't see that. His skin was not transparent—it was translucent for a certain depth.

Disfigurement didn't concern him. Even if the condition persisted, it wasn't noticeable enough to constitute a handicap. It was not the superficial nervous system showing through, nor the capillary blood vessels. The web effect was strikingly regular, almost mathematical in appearance.

As he looked, the translucence faded and his skin switched to normal, the marks disappearing. That was the word, switched. He ought to be thankful for that, he supposed. Somehow he wasn't.

He was out of the autobath and half dressed before the realization came to him. He knew what the network was, the patterned marks beneath his skin.

A circuit.

A printed circuit, or, since it was imposed on flesh, possibly tattooed.

A circuit. What did anyone use a circuit for? To compute, to gather data, to broadcast, to control. How much of that applied to him, to the body it was concealed in? The first he could eliminate. Not to compute. As for the rest, he was not certain. It seemed possible that everything could be included in the function of the network beneath his skin. He hadn't been controlled up to now, but that didn't mean control wasn't there, quiescent, waiting for the proper time. However, it didn't seem likely. Human mentality was strong, and a reasonably intact mind was difficult to take over.

What else? To gather data and broadcast it. Of that he could be almost positive. The data came from his nervous system. He suspected where it was broadcast to—back to the police.

How the circuit on his body gathered data was unknown. The markings appeared to parallel his central nervous system. It seemed reasonable that it operated by induction.

That meant it involved chiefly tactile sensations, unless, of course, there were other factors he didn't know about. He felt his forehead carefully, his temples, and his skull around his ears. Nothing, but that didn't mean that infinitesimal holes hadn't been drilled through his skull and taps run to the optic and auditory nerves.

It could be done and he wouldn't know about it, couldn't feel it. The broadcasting circuits could then be spread over his head, or, for that matter, over any part of his body.

If his suppositions were correct, then he was a living, walking broadcasting station. Everything he felt, saw or heard was relayed to some central mechanism which could interpret the signals.

The police.

Cobber had been looking for a spy mechanism, a mechanical device in Jadiver's body. He hadn't found it, but it was there, almost impossible to locate. A surgeon might find it by performing an autopsy, but even then he would have to know what to look for.

How Jadiver had been able to find it was a pure puzzle. Obviously, the police hadn't been as thorough as they had meant to be. Their mechanism had somehow gone awry at precisely the time Jadiver was most conscious of his skin. Without the itch, he would never have noticed it.

At least one thing was clear now—the purpose. He'd been boiled into unconsciousness, his skin removed, the circuit put in place, and then had the synthetic substance carefully fitted over his body.

His tension increased, for he knew now that he had betrayed Burlingame without meaning to—but it was betrayal nonetheless. It wasn't only a question of professional ethics; it was how long he would remain alive. Burlingame's survivors, if there were any, would have an excellent idea of who was responsible.

This thing went with him wherever he went. Did it also sleep when he did? That wasn't important, really.

He had to try to warn Burlingame.

Even these thoughts might be a mistake. The police might know what he was thinking. This was one way to determine whether there was such a thing as mechanically induced telepathy, but he couldn't work up much enthusiasm for the experiment.

His own problem was essentially the same as if a mechanical spying device had been planted in him—with one difference. A mechanical part was a foreign object and could be cut out by any competent surgeon willing to risk police retaliation. But only those who had installed this complicated circuit would know how to take it out.

*     *     *     *     *

Burlingame didn't answer. It was probably useless trying to trace him—he very likely had arranged to drop out of sight. He was good at that. The police hadn't caught up with him in twenty years.

There was Cobber. He'd be elsewhere, setting up a rendezvous to which Burlingame and the rest could return and hide while their faces and figures were absorbed into their normal bodies. Cobber would be even tougher to locate.

The only place Burlingame could be found with any degree of certainty, Jadiver reasoned, would be at the scene of the robbery. Jadiver went to the screen and spent an intensive half hour in front of it. At the end of that time, he had narrowed it down to two society events, one of which would occur in a few hours. He made a decision to cover it and warn them, if he could. After that, it was up to Burlingame.

Jadiver rubbed his chin; the stubble had to come off. He went to the autobath, but it wouldn't open. A figure in bas-relief appeared on the door. The surface had been smooth an instant before.

"Sorry," said the voice of the lifelike, semi-nude girl, "the autobath is out of certain supplies. It won't function properly until these are replaced."

"Let's have the list," growled Jadiver. He was jumpy.

The bas-relief figure extended a hand with a slip in it. "If I may suggest, these can be placed on perpetual order to avoid future inconvenience."

What the future held was unknown. It wasn't likely to include a comfortable existence in a well-furnished apartment. "I'll think about it," he grunted.

"If there's any other way I can help you—"

"There isn't," said Jadiver.

The door shivered and the figure snapped back into the memory plastic from which it was made. The surface was smooth again.

\*       \*       \*       \*       \*

He went to the screen and punched a code. The counter display flashed on and then was replaced by a handsome neuter face. That face studied him, ascertained his maximum susceptibility, and promptly faded.

The next face was that of a robot harem girl. Sex sells, that was always the axiom. "Is there anything I can do for you?" she asked huskily.

"Yes," said Jadiver. "You can get off the screen and let me see some merchandise."

"We're not allowed to do that."

Jadiver grumbled in defeat. "I want something for my whisk—"

"Just the thing," she said enthusiastically, reaching out of his field of vision. The hand came back with a package. "Tear off a capsule, crush it, and apply to your face. It removes whiskers permanently for two days, and leaves your face as soft and smooth as Martian down."

Jadiver shuddered. "I'd rather be a man than a bird. Do you have anything that leaves a face feeling like skin?"

The robot harem girl stabbed out frantically, but nothing came to hand. She turned around and went off to search. Jadiver sighed with relief and started to scan the shelves. The robot returned before he could make a selection.

"We have nothing like that," she said, crestfallen. "Asteroid alabaster or hydroponic grapes and several other things, but no whiskoff that will leave your face feeling like skin."

"Then order something that will," said Jadiver. "Meanwhile I'll settle for a face of hydroponic grapes. Two weeks supply will be enough."

The robot complied eagerly. "Anything else? Shampoo?"

Jadiver looked at the list and nodded.

"No need to open the bottle," she rushed on. "Just place in the autobath dispenser and let the machine do the rest. The bottle will dissolve, adding to the secret ingredients. Foams in micro-seconds as proven by actual test, and when you're through, only an expert can tell your hair from mink."

"Mink?" he repeated. "Don't think I'd like it. What about raccoon? I've always admired the legendary Daniel Boone, alone in the terrestrial wilderness with a single-shot rifle. Sure, make it raccoon."

"I know we have none of that." The clerk was positive.

"Then order it," he snapped. "You don't have to furnish the rifle, though."

She seemed confused. "There is a ten per cent extra charge for non-standard merchandise."

"All right. Just don't stand there arguing."

When the clerk left the screen to place the order, Jadiver hastily selected what he wanted. He validated the purchases and snapped off the screen. The merchandise arrived in a few minutes.

He loaded it into the autobath. This time the door opened and the bas-relief figure didn't appear on it. Within a half hour he was ready to leave.

* * * * *

The door was not a door. It was a mirror, three-dimensional. The difference to the eye was slight, but since he knew what to expect, it was not difficult to detect. It was a legitimate piece of staging, but it cost plenty to maintain the illusion. A society event, he supposed, called for such precautions. There must be more inside.

He ignored the mirror and pressed a blank section of the wall directly opposite. The wall faded and a robot in an impressive black-and-white livery stared at him with the proper insolence.

"Your invitation, sir."

"What?" he said tipsily.

"Your invitation, sir." The voice was louder and the insolence increased. If he asked again, the robot would very likely shove him out and close the door. Delicately adjusted and unhumanly strong, it was a bit too invariable in the behavior department to be consistently efficient.

His knowledge of robots was more than fair. In a few seconds he sized up the model facing him. A thin slip fluttered from his hand to the floor. The robot bent over to pick it up. At that instant Jadiver thrust a long, thin, double-tined fork deep into the back of the robot's neck, probing for the right place. He found it. Time became static for the robot; it remained bent over and could not move.

Jadiver rifled the pockets, removed all the invitations, glanced at them, found one that would do, and thrust the rest back. Shadows of figures passed across the field behind the robot. Could they see what Jadiver was doing? Probably not; privacy was too highly regarded. Nevertheless, some people were coming down the corridor and *they* could see when and if they got close. Stepping back, he took away the double-tined fork and the robot straightened up.

"You dropped something, sir," said the robot, handing him the slip from the floor.

"It was nothing," said Jadiver, taking it. That was the best description of what he had dropped. He extended the invitation he had just filched.

The robot grasped the invitation and seemed unable to focus. It tried to examine the markings invisible to human eyes. It passed a trembling hand across a troubled forehead.

"Didn't you come in half an hour ago?" it asked in bewilderment.

Someone had—the person to whom the invitation had been issued. The robot, of course, had remembered.

"Nonsense," said Jadiver sharply. "Do you feel right? Are you sure of your equilibrium?"

If it was sure, he had miscalculated badly. Robots were so much more or less than humans. It should be possible to design a perfect robot, one that would realize all the potentialities of a mechanical personality. It had never been done; anthropomorphic conceptions had always interfered.

"Must be mistaken," mumbled the robot, and swayed. It would collapse in twenty minutes. The robot pressed a button and the field behind him flickered off. Jadiver passed through it and the field fell back in place.

*       *       *       *       *

Inside, he looked around. The usual swank, or maybe more so. Impressive, if he cared to be impressed by it. At the moment he didn't. He had to find Burlingame or Emily. He had created the faces of the other three as well, but he had made them into handsome nonentities. Among so many others who resembled them, he doubted that he could recognize them.

For an instant he thought he saw Emily and made his way through the crowd. When he got there, he saw his mistake. This girl's flesh hadn't been put on with a spray gun.

Burlingame was after jewels, of course, to be carefully selected from two or three of the wealthier guests. He must also have currency in mind, something negotiable for immediate use. He'd need cash to drop out of sight for a while.

Time was growing short for a word with Burlingame, just one word, whispered or spelled out silently: "Police." That was all Burlingame would need.

Jadiver was weaponless, and aside from warning Burlingame, he couldn't help. Until now he'd steered clear of violence and illegality. He'd known the use to which his disguises had been put, but that was the business of those who paid him.

Now it was different. The police had a line to him, direct. How much they knew was impossible to estimate. He could visualize a technician sitting in front of a screen, seeing everything that Jadiver saw. That, however, was a guess, for he didn't actually know how the circuit beneath his skin functioned. Until he learned, he would have to continue guessing, and blunder accordingly.

He made his way to the balcony that encircled half the huge high room. He didn't know the entire layout or the habits of those who lived here, but it was reasonably certain that they kept a large amount of cash on hand and that it would be safeguarded in a room not accessible to all the guests. It might even be up here.

The few people on the balcony were at the far end. He looked down on the milling guests. Still no sign of Burlingame or any of his crew. Jadiver had done his work too well. They were indistinguishable from the others.

At that moment, the lights brightened glaringly. The guests looked less glamorous. Women bulged excessively, top-heavy, and the tanned faces of the men turned an unpleasant gray.

Magically, uniforms appeared at every exit.

"Attention," a harsh voice rang out. "Please line up. There are criminals among you and we can identify them."

*     *     *     *     *

Jadiver didn't listen to the rest. His eyes were on the uniformed men. Mercifully, they carried tangle guns. That much he was thankful for. Burlingame and his crew would be taken alive. They might not like what would happen later, but at least they would live.

The tangle gun was the most effective and least lethal weapon ever conceived. It would bring down a butterfly at two hundred yards and hold it there, without crumpling a wing or disturbing the dustlike scales. It would do the same with a Venusian saurian or a Martian windbeast, either of which outbulked an elephant and outsavaged a tiger.

It didn't have to hit the target. With proximity fuses—and it was usually furnished that way—it was sufficient for the bullet to pass near. Jadiver drew a deep breath. No one was going to get killed because of him. Nevertheless, his skin crawled.

He gazed down at the guests lining up. They, too, knew what tangle guns were.

Suddenly a man darted out of line and headed toward one of the exits. He collided with an officer and the policeman went down. A tangle gun snapped. The running man fell headlong. Three more times the tangle gun fired at the man writhing on the floor—at his hands, at his face, and again at his legs.

The tangle gun propelled a plastic bullet, and that plastic was a paradox. It was the stickiest substance known and would adhere to a sphere of polished platinum, tearing away the solid metal if it were forcibly removed without first being neutralized. It also extruded itself into fine, wire-like strands on a moving object. The more anything moved, the tighter it wrapped around. The victim was better off to relax. He couldn't escape; no one ever had.

Jadiver watched the man threshing on the floor. One shot would have been enough. Someone on the Venicity force liked to see men squirm.

As nearly as Jadiver could determine, the man on the floor was not Burlingame. The leader hadn't been taken, but he didn't have long to enjoy his freedom. The theory he had about teamwork was tarnished now—a feint here and a block there—

and they were all headed into the arms of the Venicity police. It couldn't work against superior force, and an ambush set unwittingly by Jadiver.

Then Jadiver saw them. They moved as a unit— Burlingame, Emily and two others. They smashed through the guests with a formation that had the flying wedge as a remote ancestor. Burlingame was leading it, tangle gun in hand. The guests were thrown back and a policeman went down.

It was hard to fire into the mob through which Burlingame and his crew were bulling. In that respect, the tangle gun was not selective. It seized on any motion.

They couldn't make it, but Jadiver hoped for them. They were at the edge of the crowd. Between them and freedom was a thin cordon of police. Beyond the police was a planted area where jungle vines and shrubs, considerably taller than a man, grew dense. Just past that area were two exits leading to the street.

From the balcony, Jadiver could see it clearly. If they could reach the exits, they had a chance for flight.

They broke through the cordon. They shouldn't have, for superior trained men were opposing them. But it was another kind of training that Burlingame was using and with it he split the police. The group plunged into the jungle shrubs and emerged on the other side. The police on the floor couldn't see them, the planted area screened off the view. They were almost safe.

The exits opened before they could reach them—more police. Burlingame went down, a cloud around his face, weaving wire shapes that tightened on his throat. The other two stumbled as police fired at their feet.

*     *     *     *     *

Emily alone was not hit. She was close and moving too fast. She escaped the tangle guns, but ran directly into the arms of a burly officer. He laughed and grabbed her as if she were a robot. She bit him.

He swore at her and swiftly looked around. The guests couldn't see. He hit her solidly in the middle. She gasped for breath. He took out his tangle gun and fired into her mouth.

Jadiver sicklily knew he had been wrong about the tangle gun; it could kill if the person who used it had sufficient experience and brutality.

Emily would never have to lose that beautiful face and figure. She could keep it until she died, which wouldn't be long. Nobody could stop the peristaltic motion of the digestive system, voluntarily or otherwise, or of the lungs in trying to breathe.

Burlingame wouldn't know. Policemen were cooperative, and it would be listed as an accident.

Jadiver closed his eyes. Emily was dying and no one could help her. Or himself, either, when they came to pick him up. They had to know exactly where he was. He waited, expecting a tap on the shoulder or the snap of the tangle gun.

The lights dimmed and the same harsh voice spoke. "The danger is over, thanks to the efficient work of the Venicity police force. You are now safe."

Nothing like advertising yourself, thought Jadiver.

No one came near him. Apparently the police didn't want him yet—they expected him to do more for them.

He went down the stairs and mingled with the excited guests. It had been a good show, unexpected entertainment, especially since it hadn't involved any real danger for them. He circulated through the chattering men and women until he came near the planted area. At an opportune moment, he slipped in.

It was a miniature jungle; he was safe from ordinary detection as long as he stayed there. He went quietly through the vines and shrubs toward the other side. The broad back of a policemen loomed up in front of him.

Jadiver was an industrial engineer, a specialist in the design of robot bodies and faces, robots that had to look like humans. He knew anatomy, not in the way a doctor did, but it was nonetheless the knowledge of an expert. He reached out and the policeman toppled.

He dragged the unconscious man deeper into the little jungle and listened. No one had noticed. Physically a large man, the policeman might be the one who had shot Emily—and then again he might not be. He did have a tangle gun, which was the important thing. Jadiver took it and rifled the man's pockets for ammunition.

He knelt for a final check on the body. The chest rose and fell with slow regularity. For insurance, Jadiver again pressed the nerve. This man wouldn't trouble anyone for a few hours.

Jadiver looked out. When he was sure he wasn't observed, he walked out and joined the guests. He moved politely from one group to another and in several minutes stood beside the door. He left the way he came.

It was that simple. He had to assume that until events proved he was mistaken.

\*     \*     \*     \*     \*

Outside, he walked briskly. It was not late and the city overflowed with men and women walking, flying, skimming. Roughly dressed men down from the north polar farms, explorers from the temperate jungles, government girls—the jumbled swarm that comes to a planet in the intermediate stages of exploitation. It was a background through which he could pass unnoticed.

The circuit, though—always the circuit. He couldn't escape that by walking away from it. But at least he'd proved that telepathy wasn't possible by means of it, or he wouldn't still be free.

Other than that, he didn't know how it operated. If it was purely electronic in nature, then it had a range. He might be able to get beyond that range, if he knew how far it extended.

A lot depended on the power source. He hadn't been able to check closely, hadn't really known what he was looking at when he'd seen it in the autobath. He remembered that the circuit seemed to be laid over his own nervous system. Considering the power available, the range was apt to be quite limited.

That was pure supposition and might be wrong. There was nothing to preclude an external power source, say a closed field blanketing the city or even the entire planet. If so, it represented a technical achievement beyond anything he was familiar with. That didn't disprove it, of course. The circuit itself indicated a startling advance and he knew *it* existed.

There was still another possibility. The circuit might not be entirely electronic. It might operate with the same forces that existed inside a single nerve cell. If so, all bets were off; there was no way he could determine the range. It might be anything at all, micro-inches or light-years.

With unlimited equipment and all the time in the worlds, he could answer some of those questions floating around in his mind. He had neither, but there were solutions he could make use of. Limited solutions, but it was better than waiting to be caught.

Jadiver headed toward one such solution.

The robot clerk looked up, smiling and patient, as he entered. It could afford to be patient. There was no place it wanted to be other than where it was at the moment. "Can I help you?"

"Passage to Earth," said Jadiver.

The clerk consulted the schedule. That was pretense. The schedule and not much else had been built into its brain. "There's an orbit flight in two weeks."

In two weeks, Jadiver could be taken, tried, and converted ten times over. "Isn't there anything sooner?"

"There's an all-powered flight leaving tomorrow, but that's for Earth citizens only."

"Suits me. Book me for it."

"Be glad to," said the robot. "Passport, please."

\*      \*      \*      \*      \*

It was going to cost more than just the fare, Jadiver knew. He would arrive on Earth with very little money and could expect to start all over. He was no longer fresh out of training, willing to start at the bottom. He was a mature man, experienced beyond the ordinary, and most organizations he could work for would be suspicious of that.

But it was worth it, aside from the escape. No future for him there, jammed in on a crowded world, but it was his planet, always would be, and he wouldn't mind going back.

"Sorry," said the clerk, flipping over the passport and studying it. "I can't book you. The flight's only for Earth citizens."

"I was born there," Jadiver impatiently said. "Can't you see?"

"You were?" asked the robot eagerly. "I was built there." It handed him back the passport. "However, it doesn't matter where you were born. You've been here three years without going back. Automatically, you became a citizen of Venus two and a half years ago."

Jadiver hadn't known that. He doubted that many did. It was logical enough. Earth was overflowing and the hidden citizenship clause was a good way of getting rid of the more restless part of the population and making sure they didn't come back.

"There's still the orbit flight," said the clerk, smiling and serene. "For that you need a visitor's visa, which takes time. Shall I make the arrangements?"

Aside from the time element, which was vital, he couldn't tip the police off that he intended to leave.

"Thanks," he said, taking the passport. "I'll call back when I make up my mind."

Down the street was another interplanetary flight office and he wandered into it. It might have been the same office he had just left, robot and all.

"Information on Mars," he said, his manner casual.

The clerk didn't bother to consult the schedule. There was a difference, after all. "There'll be an orbit flight in four months," it said pleasantly. "Rate, four-fifths of the standard fare to Earth."

Nothing was working out as expected. "What about the moons of Jupiter?" This was the last chance.

"Due to the position of the planets, for the next few months there are no direct flights anywhere beyond Mars. You have to go there and transfer."

That escape was closed. "I can't make plans so far in advance."

The robot beamed at him. "I can see that you're a gentleman who likes to travel." It grew confidential and leaned over the counter. "I have a bargain here, truly the most sensational we've ever offered."

Jadiver drew away from that eagerness. "What is this bargain?"

"Did you notice the fare to Mars? Four-fifths of that to Earth, and yet it's farther away. Did you stop to think why?"

\*      \*      \*      \*      \*

He had noticed and he thought he knew why. It was another side of the citizenship program. Get them away from Earth, the farther the better, and don't let them come back. If necessary, shuttle them between colonies, but don't let them come back.

"I hadn't," he said. "Why?"

The voice throbbed throatily and robot eyes grew round. "To induce people to travel. Travel is wonderful. I love to travel."

Pathetic thing. Someone had erred in building it, had implanted too much enthusiasm for the job. It loved to travel and would never get farther than a few feet from the counter. Jadiver dismissed that thought.

"What's this wonderful offer?" he asked.

"Just think of it," whispered the robot. "We have another destination, much farther than Jupiter, but only one-tenth the fare to Earth. If you don't have the full fare in cash, just give us verbal assurance that you'll pay when you get the money. No papers to sign. We have confidence in your personal integrity."

"Sounds intriguing," Jadiver said, backing away. It sounded more like a death sentence. Alpha Centauri or some such place— hard grubbing labor under a blazing or meager sun, it didn't matter which. Exile forever on planets that lagged and would always lag behind Earth. It took years to get there, even at speeds only a little below that of light, time in which the individual was out of touch.

"I hope you won't forget," said the robot. "It's hard to get people to understand. But I can see that you do."

He understood too well. He ducked out of the flight office. He'd stay and take it here if he had to, escape some way if he could. Nothing was worth that kind of sacrifice.

He went slowly back to the apartment. It was not so strange that the police hadn't arrested him. They knew that he'd stay on the planet, that he had to. They'd had it figured out long before he did.

He fell into the bed without removing his clothing. The bed made no effort to induce him to sleep. It wasn't necessary.

*   *   *   *   *

In the morning, Jadiver awakened to the smell of food. The room he slept in was dark, but in the adjacent room he could hear the Kitch-Hen clucking away contentedly as it prepared breakfast.

He rolled over and sat up. He was not alone.

"Cobber?" he called.

"Yeah," said Cobber. He was very close, but Jadiver couldn't see him.

"The police got them," Jadiver said, reaching for the tangle gun. It was gone. He'd expected that.

"I heard. I was waiting for them and they didn't come." He was silent for a moment. "It had to be you, didn't it?"

"It was," Jadiver said. "When I found out, I tried to tell them. But it was too late."

"Glad you tried," said Cobber. At that instant, so was Jadiver. "I checked you myself. I couldn't find anything," Cobber added thoughtfully. "They must have something new."

"It is new," Jadiver wearily confirmed. "I can't get rid of it."

"Mind telling me? I figure I ought to know."

Hunched up in the darkness, Jadiver told him what he could. At present, he was defenseless. Cobber was a little man, but he was no stranger to violence and he had the weapons. Perhaps that was what the police counted on—that Cobber would save them an arrest.

"Bad," said Cobber after an interval. It sounded like a reprieve.

Jadiver waited.

"I liked Burlingame," continued Cobber. "Emily, too."

Burlingame was a decent fellow. Emily he had seen only once, twice if he counted last night. She deserved better than she got.

"I don't know who it was," Jadiver said. "Some big policeman."

"I know a lot of people—I'll find out," Cobber promised. "I liked Emily."

It wouldn't do any good, though Jadiver approved. For a while there'd be one less sadist on the force, and after that they'd hire another.

"You'd better leave while you can," said Jadiver.

Cobber laughed. "I'll get away. I know Venus and I don't have a spy inside." He got up, turned on the lights and tossed the tangle gun on the bed. "Here. You need this worse than I do."

Jadiver blinked gratefully and took it. Cobber believed him. If the police wanted to eliminate him, they'd have to come for him, after all.

He stood up. "Breakfast?"

"No breakfast," said Cobber. "I'm going to take your advice and get out of here." He went to the door, opened it a fraction and listened. Satisfied, he closed it and turned back to Jadiver. "Tell that cop I know a few tricks with a tangle gun he never heard of. I'll show him what they are."

"I won't see him, I hope."

"You don't have to. They're taking everything down. They'll tell him. That is, I hope they do."

He slipped out the door and was gone.

\*   \*   \*   \*   \*

The Kitch-Hen tired of waiting for Jadiver to come out. It cackled disgustedly and sent a table into his room. Mechanically he sat down and began to eat.

Not only how far but also what kind of data did the circuit transmit? That was one unanswered problem. If he couldn't outrun it, he might outthink it.

First, the data was transmitted to the police with some degree of accuracy. They had been able to anticipate the robbery. Not completely, but they did know it was Burlingame and how many men he was using. They also knew the approximate date.

From that, it was a matter of logic to determine what specific society event he was aiming at. Jadiver had been able to do the same.

Thoughts, visual and auditory impressions, tactile and other sensory data—that was the sum of what the circuit could transmit, theoretically.

He could almost positively rule out thoughts. It had never been proved that thoughts could be transferred from one person to another, mechanically or otherwise. But that was not his reason for rejecting it. If they could read his thoughts, it was useless for him to plan anything. And he was going to plan ahead, whether it was useless or not.

Tactile sensations, temperature, roughness, and the like were unimportant except to a scientist. He doubted that police were that scientifically interested in him. He could forget about the sense of touch.

Sight and hearing. Neither of these could be eliminated at present. They could see what he saw, hear what he heard. As long as they could, escape was out of the question. It wouldn't take much to betray him—a street sign glimpsed through his eyes, for instance, and they knew where he was.

As long as they could see what he saw.

But there was such a thing as a shield. Any known kind of radiation could be shielded against.

He was working with intangibles. He didn't know the nature of the phenomenon he had to fight. He had to extrapolate in part, guess the rest. One thing was certain, though: If he was successful in setting up a shield against the circuit, the police would arrive soon after. Arrive here.

His value to them was obvious. Through him they could make an undetected contact with the shadowy world of illegality. If that contact was cut off or if he seemed about to escape, his usefulness came to an end and they would want one more arrest while they could get it.

Once he started to work on the shield, he would have to work fast.

Jadiver went to the screen. There could be no hesitation; the decision was ready-made.

The bank robot appeared on the screen and Jadiver spoke to him briefly, requesting that his account be cleared. He scribbled his signature and had it recorded.

*     *     *     *     *

While waiting, he began to pack, sorting what he wanted to take. It wasn't much, some special clothing. His equipment, except for a few small tools, he had to leave. No matter. With luck, he could replace it; without luck, he wouldn't need it.

In a few minutes he was ready, but the money hadn't arrived. He sat down and nervously scrawled on a scrap of paper. Presently the delivery chute clattered and the money was in it, crisp new bills neatly wrapped, the total of his savings over the years. He stuffed the money in his pocket.

The scrap of paper was still in his hand. He started to throw it away, but his fingers were reluctant to let it go. He stared curiously at the crumpled wad and on impulse smoothed it out.

There were words on it, though he hadn't remembered writing any. The handwriting was shaky and stilted, as if he were afflicted with some nervous disease; nevertheless, it was unmistakably his own.

There was a message on it, from himself to himself. No, not from himself. But it was intended that he read it. The note said:

RUN, JADIVER. I'LL HELP.    YOUR FRIEND

He sat down. A picture rose involuntarily in his mind: The face was that of Doumya Filone.

He couldn't prove it, but it seemed certain that she was the one. She knew about the circuit, of course, had known long before he did. He remembered the incident when his skin had itched.

He had called her about it and she hadn't seemed surprised. She had left the screen for some time—for what purpose? To adjust the mechanism, or have someone else adjust it. The last, probably; the mechanism was almost certainly at the police end, and at the time he called she had been at home. In any event, the mechanism had originally been set too strong and she had ordered the setting to be reduced. That suggested one thing: the power to activate the circuit came from the mechanism—a radarlike device.

Then what? His skin had momentarily become translucent, allowing him to see the circuit. How she achieved that, he didn't know, but the reason was obvious. It had been her way of warning him and it had worked.

The message in his hand told him one thing. He had known about the danger, but he hadn't guessed that he didn't have to face it alone. Something else was evident: her control was limited—perhaps she could step in at a critical moment, but the greater part was up to him.

He moved quickly. He opened the delivery chute and put in the small bag that held his clothing, then punched a code that dispatched it to the transportation terminal. In return, he received a small plastic strip with the same code on it. The bag could be traced, but not without trouble, and he should be able to pick it up before then. At this stage he didn't want to be encumbered.

He took a last look around and stepped into the hall. He leaped back again.

A heavy caliber slug crashed into the door.

*    *    *    *    *

That had been meant to kill. He was lucky it hadn't.

Who was it? Not the police. By law they were restricted to tangle guns, though they sometimes forgot. In this case, their memory should be good—they'd have difficulty explaining away the holes in his body. Not that they'd have to, really; if they wanted, they could toss him into an alley and claim they had found his body later.

Still, there was no particular reason why they should want to kill him outright when they could do it by degrees scientifically and with full legal protection. They didn't call it killing. There was another term: converting.

The converting process was not new; the principles had existed for centuries. The newness lay in the proper combination of old discoveries. Electric shock was one ingredient, a prolonged drastic application of it during the recreation of a situation that the victim had a weakness for. In the case of an adulterer, say, the scene was hypnotically arranged with the cooperation of a special robot that wouldn't be short-circuited. At the proper moment, electric shock was applied, repeatedly. Rigorous and somewhat rough on the criminal's wife, but the adulterer would be saddled all his life with an unconditional reflex.

That was only one ingredient. There were others, among them a pseudo-religious brotherhood, membership in which was compulsory. C. C.—Confirmed Converters. *They* kept tab on one another with apocalyptic fervor. Transgressions were rare. Death came sooner.

Jadiver stood there thinking. It wasn't the police, because they had converting with which to threaten him. It wasn't Cobber, either. He could have killed Jadiver earlier and hadn't.

Cobber might have talked, though. There were enough people who now regretted that Jadiver had once given them new faces. As far as they were concerned Jadiver was in the hands of the police.

The identity of the man outside didn't matter. He was not from the police, but he did want Jadiver dead.

Jadiver stood back and pushed the door open. Another slug crashed into it, tiny, but with incredible velocity.

He knelt, thrust his hand outside the door near the bottom and fired a random fusillade down the corridor. Then he took his finger off the trigger and listened. There wasn't a sound. The man had decided to be sensible.

Jadiver stepped out. The man was crouched in an inconspicuous corner and he was going to stay in that position for a long time. He couldn't help breathing, though, and his chest was a tangle of wires. There were some on his face, too, where his eyelids flickered and his mouth twitched.

The gun was in his hand and it was aimed nearly right. There was nothing to prevent his squeezing the trigger—except the tangle extruded loosely over his hand. And he could move faster than it could. Once, at any rate.

"I wouldn't," said Jadiver. "You're going to have a hard time explaining that illegal firearm. And it'll look worse if I'm here with my head wrapped around a hole that just fits the slug."

The man reaffirmed his original decision to be sensible about it by remaining motionless. Jadiver didn't recognize him. Probably a hired assassin.

The man paled with the effort not to move. He teetered and the tangle stuff coiled fractionally tighter.

"Take care of yourself," Jadiver said, and left him there.

\*     \*     \*     \*     \*

Jadiver headed toward the transportation terminal. The police could trace him that far. Let them; he intended that they should. It would confuse them more when he walked right off their instruments.

Once inside the underground structure, he lost himself in the traffic. That was just in case he had been followed physically as well as by radiation. People coming from Earth, fewer going back. They arrived in swarms from the surface, overhead from the concrete plain where rockets roared out on takeoff or hissed in for landing. Transportation shunted the mob in one direction for interplanetary travel, in another for local air routes.

Jadiver reclaimed his bag, boarded the moving belts and hopped on and off several times, again just in case. The last time off, he had coins ready. He slipped around a corner and walked down a long quiet corridor. There were doors on either side, a double deck with a narrow balcony on the second story. At intervals, stairs led to the balcony.

He walked a third of the way down the corridor, inserted coins in the slot, and a door opened. He went inside the sleep locker and the door closed behind, locking automatically.

It was miserable accommodation if he intended to sleep, but he didn't. It was also a trap if the police were trailing him. He didn't think they were—they were too certain of him. Nevertheless, the sleep locker had one advantage: it was all metal. Considering the low power that probably went into the circuit, it should be a satisfactory temporary shield.

He changed into clothes that looked ordinary—out of style, in fact, though that was not noteworthy in a solarwide economy—but the material, following a local terrestrial fad of a few years back, contained a high proportion of metallic fiber. That solved only part of the problem, of course. His hands and his head were uncovered.

The pseudo-flesh that he had used on Emily was not for him. In a way, it was the best disguise, but he was playing this one to live, as much as he could, all the way. A standard semi-durable cosmetic would do; that is, it would when he finished altering it to suit his purpose.

The chief addition was a flaky metallic powder, lead. However the signal worked, radar or not, that should be effective in dampening the signal. He squeezed the mixture into a tube and attached the tube to a small gun which he plugged into a wall socket. Standing in front of the tiny mirror, with everything else cramped in the sleep locker, he went over his face and hands. He had trouble getting it on his scalp and under his hair, but it went on.

He looked himself over. He now appeared older, respectable, but not successful, which fitted neatly into the greatest category on Venus—or anywhere, for that matter. He stuffed the clothing he'd worn back into the bag and walked out. He'd been in the sleep locker half an hour.

He was operating blind, but it was all he could do. He had to assume that the metallic fiber in his clothing and the lead flakes in the cosmetic would scramble the circuit signal. If they didn't, then he was completely without protection.

He'd soon know how correctly he had analyzed the problem.

*     *     *     *     *

He walked out of the transportation terminal and hailed an air cab which took him over the city and left him at the edge of a less reputable section.

It was not an old slum—Venicity hadn't endured long enough to have inherited slums; it built them quickly out of shoddy material and then tore them down again as the need for living space expanded outward.

He checked in at a hotel neither more nor less disreputable than the rest. The structure made up in number of rooms what it lacked in size and appearance.

This was the test period and he had to wait it out. If he passed, he was on an equal footing with any other person wanted by the police. He'd take his chances on that, his wits against their organization; he could disappear if he didn't carry a beacon around with him. This was the best place to spend the interim period, crowded together with people coming and going to and from the wild lands of Venus.

But if he didn't pass the test—

He refused to think about it.

He walked aimlessly in the grayness of the Venusian day. Different people from those in the bright new sections of Venicity, quieter, grimmer, more bewildered. Tough, but not the hardness of the criminal element. These people had no interest in either making or breaking the law.

After nightfall, he loitered on the streets for a few hours, watching faces. When policemen began appearing in greater numbers, he checked into his room.

It was a grimy, unpleasant place. Considering the comfort it offered, the rate was exorbitant. Safety, however, if it did afford, and that was beyond price. He lay down, but couldn't sleep. The room, apparently, was designed on the acoustical principle of an echo chamber or a drum.

The adjacent room on one side was occupied by a man and woman. The woman, though, was not a woman. There was a certain pitch to the laughter that could come only from a robot. The management obviously offered attractions other than sleep.

The room on the other side was quieter. Somebody coughed twice, somebody sniffled once. Two of them, decided Jadiver, a man and a woman, both human. They weren't talking loud or much. He couldn't hear the words, but the sounds weren't gay.

In the hall, other voices intruded. Jadiver lay still. He could recognize the way of walking, the tone of voice. Cops. His test period wasn't lasting as long as he'd hoped.

"What good is it?" grumbled one, down the hall, but Jadiver could hear distinctly. "We had him dead center and now we've lost him. If I had my way, we'd have taken him sooner."

\*　　\*　　\*　　\*　　\*

Jadiver's reasoning was not so good if the police were this close. He got up and crept noiselessly toward the door, fully dressed, as he had to be at all times if he expected to scramble the circuit signal.

The companion of the first policeman was more cheerful. "He's not lost. We've just mislaid him. We know the direction he's in. Follow the line and there he is at the end of it."

"Sounds good, but have we got him?"

"We will."

That was the fallacy. He'd scrambled the signal, but he hadn't eliminated it. He still showed up on the police instrument as a direction. He could imagine a technician sitting in front of a crazily wavering screen. The instrument could no longer pick up what he saw through his eyes, but it hadn't lost him altogether.

Jadiver clutched the tangle gun.

"Better check where we are," said the first officer.

"Going to," answered the second. Jadiver couldn't see, but he could visualize the pocket instrument. "This is Lieutenant Parder. How close are we?"

The voice came back, almost inaudible. What he could hear, though, was disturbing. It sounded like someone he knew, but not Doumya Filone. "You're off a hundred yards to your left," said the voice. "Also, he's a mile farther out. Either that or a hundred and fifty miles."

"He's really moving," said the lieutenant. "A hundred and fifty miles is in the middle of the swamp."

"I know that," said the tantalizing familiar voice. "I can't choose between outside and inside the city. If he's inside, I want him to move. That motion, extended a hundred and fifty miles, by simple mathematics will indicate a distance he couldn't possibly travel in the jungle." The voice paused. "We'll send a party to check the swamp. You go to the point a mile farther on. We want him tonight. If we don't get him, we'll probably have to wait until tomorrow night."

"I'll find him," said the lieutenant. "Report when I get there."

Jadiver could hear footsteps receding down the hall.

He breathed in relief. The makeshift shield hadn't been a total failure. They knew the direction, but not the distance from some central location. The scramble had affected the strength of the signal and they couldn't be sure.

The impromptu visit told him this as well: there was only one instrument on him. With two, they could work a triangulation, regardless of the signal strength.

He could hazard a guess as to why they had to get him at night. During the day, there were radiological disturbances originating in the atmosphere that made reception of the signals difficult. That meant that the day was safest for him.

*   *   *   *   *

He went back to the bed and lay down, to puzzle over the familiar voice, to sleep if he could. Sleep didn't come easily. The man and the female robot had left, but the quiet couple on the other side had been awakened by the noise in the hall.

The woman sniffled. "I don't care, Henry. We're going back to Earth."

It was not an old voice, though he couldn't be sure, not seeing her. Thirty-five, say. Jadiver resented the intrusion at a time like this. He was trying to sleep, or think, he wasn't sure which.

"Now, hon, we can't," Henry whispered back. "We've bought the land and nobody's going to buy it back."

"We bought it when they told us there would be roses," said the woman, loud and bitter. "Great big roses, so big that most of the plant grew below ground, only the flower showing. So big, no stem could support them."

"Well, hon—"

"Don't hon me. There *are* roses, ten feet across, all over our land, just like they said." Her voice rose higher. "Mud roses, that's what they are. Stinking mud roses that collapse into a slimy hole in the ground."

She sniffled again. "Did you notice the pictures they showed us? People standing by the roses with their heads turned away. And you know why the pictures were like that? Because they didn't dare show us the expressions on those people's faces, that's why."

"It's not so bad," said the man soothingly. "Maybe we can do something about it."

"What can we do? The roses poison cattle and dogs run away from the smell. And we're humans. We're stronger, we're supposed to take it."

"I've been thinking," said Henry quietly. "I could take a long pipe and run it at an angle to the roots. I could force concrete through the pipe and seal it off below ground. When it collapsed, the rose wouldn't grow back."

The woman asked doubtfully, "Could you?"

"I think so. Of course I'd have to experiment to get the right kind of concrete."

"But what would we do with the hole it left?" There was a faint tremor of hope.

"We could haul away the slime," he said. "It would stop smelling after a while. We might even be able to use it for fertilizer."

"But there's still the hole."

"It would fill with water after the next rain. We could raise ducks in it."

"White ducks?"

"If you like."

The woman was silent. "If you think we can do it, then we'll try," she said. "We'll go back to our farm and forget about Earth."

Henry was silent, too. "They're kind of pretty, even if they do smell bad," he said after a long interval. "Maybe I could pump a different kind of cement, real thin, directly into the stem. It might travel up into the flower instead of down."

"And make them into stone roses," enthused the woman. "Mud roses into stone. I'd like that—a few of them—to remind us of what our farm was like when we came to it." She wasn't sniffling.

They had their own problems, decided Jadiver, and their own solution, which, in their ignorance, might actually work. He'd been like that when he first came to Venus, expecting great things. With him it had been different. He was an engineer, not a farmer, and he didn't want to be a farmer. There was nothing on Venus for him.

He couldn't stay much longer on Venus in any capacity. Earth was out of the question. Mars? If he could escape capture in the months that followed and then manage to get passage on a ship. It wasn't hopeless, but his chances weren't high.

The puzzling thing was why the police wanted him so badly. He was an accessory to a crime—several of them, in fact. But even if they regarded him as a criminal, they couldn't consider him an important one.

And yet they were staging a manhunt. He hated to think of the number of policemen looking for him. There must be a reason for it.

He had a few days left, possibly less. In that time, he would have to get off the planet or shed the circuit. Without drastic extensive surgery, there was not much hope he could peel off the circuit.

Unless—

He had received a message from someone self-identified as a friend. And that friend knew about the circuit and claimed to be willing to help.

He kept seeing gray eyes and a strong, sad, indifferent face, even in his sleep.

\*     \*     \*     \*     \*

He awakened later than he intended. Since daylight was safest for him, that was a serious error. He wasted no time in regret, but went immediately to the mirror. Under the makeup, his face was dirty and sweating. He didn't dare to remove the disguise for an instant, since to do so would be to expose himself to the instrument. He sprayed on a new face, altering the facial characteristics as best he could. His clothing, too, had to stay on. He roughed it up a bit, adding a year's wear to it.

For what it was worth, he didn't look quite the same as yesterday. Seedier and older. It was a process he couldn't keep extending indefinitely. He would not have to, of course. One way or the other, it would be decided soon.

He shredded the bag and his extra clothing, tossing them into the disposal chute. No use giving the police something to paw over, to deduce from it what they could. The tiny spray gun he kept, and the tube of makeup. He might need them once more.

It was close to noon when he left the room. There were lots of people on the streets and only a few policemen. Again he had an advantage.

He found a pay screen and began the search. Doctor Doumya Filone wasn't listed with the police and that seemed strange. A moment's reflection showed that it wasn't. If she were officially connected, she might not show the sympathy she had.

Neither was she listed on the staff of the emergency hospital in which he'd been a patient. He had a number through which he could reach her, but he resisted an impulse to use it. It was certain the police wouldn't confine their efforts to the instrument check. They knew he had that number and they'd have someone on it, tracing everyone who called her.

Noon passed and his stomach called attention to it. He hadn't eaten since yesterday. He took a short break, ate hurriedly, and resumed the search.

Doumya Filone was difficult to find. It was getting late and he had ascertained she wasn't on the staff of any hospital not listed for private practice.

He finally located her almost by accident. She had an office with Medical Research Incorporated. That was the only thing registered under her name.

Evening came early to Venus, as it always did under the massive cloud formations. He got off the air cab a few blocks from his destination and walked the rest of the way.

Inside the building, he paused in the lobby and found her office. Luckily it was in a back wing. He wandered through the corridors, got lost once, and found the route again. The building was almost empty by this time.

Her name was on the door. Dr. Doumya Filone. Research Neurological Systems, whatever that meant. There was a light in the office, a dim one. He eased the door open. It wasn't locked, which meant, he hadn't tripped an alarm.

*     *     *     *     *

No one was inside. He looked around. There was another door in back. He walked over to it. It didn't lead to a laboratory, as he expected. Instead, there were living quarters. A peculiar way to conduct research.

The autobath was humming quietly. He sat down facing it and waited. She came out in a few minutes, hair disarranged, damp around her forehead. She didn't see him at first.

"Well," she said coolly, staring at him. There was no question that she recognized him through the disguise. She slipped quickly into a robe that, whatever it did for her modesty, subtracted nothing from the view. He wished he was less tired and could appreciate it.

She found a cigarette and lighted it. "You're pretty good, you know."

"Yeah." But not good enough, he thought.

"Why are you here?" she asked. She was nervous.

"You know," he said. She had promised him help once before. Now let her deliver. But she had to volunteer.

"I know." She looked down at her hands, long skilled hands. "I put in the circuit. But I didn't choose you."

He began to understand part of it. The 'Medical Research' business was just a cover. The real work was done at the police emergency hospital. That was why she had no laboratory. And the raw material—

"Who did choose me?"

"The police. I have to take what they give me."

There were certain implications in that statement he didn't like. "Have there been others?"

"Two before you."

"What happened to them?"

"They died."

He didn't like where this was taking him. His hand slid toward the tangle gun in his pocket. "Maybe I should die, too."

She nodded. "That would be one solution." She added harshly: "They shouldn't have taken you. Legally speaking, you're not a criminal. But I couldn't investigate you personally before I put the circuit in."

Why not? Was she an automaton that reacted in response to a button? In a way she was, but the button was psychological.

"That doesn't help me," he said tiredly. "The police wanted to catch Burlingame through me. That's right, isn't it?"

She indicated that it was.

"I did, without knowing what I was doing," he went on. "Now I want out. Even if I cooperated with the cops, which I'm not going to do, I'm of no further value to them. Every criminal on Venus knows about me by now."

"That's part of it," she said. "But there's more. You've tied up the machine and neither I nor the police can use it."

\*      \*      \*      \*      \*

Explanations were coming faster. It was no wonder the police wanted him badly. They had a perfect device to use against criminals, which was all they were concerned with, and they couldn't use it as long as the circuit was in him. It made sense, but that kind of logic was deadly—for him.

"I'll face it," he said. "I'll take whatever charge they hang on me. It shouldn't be more than a few years. You can use the time to take this damn thing out of me. Only I want a guarantee first."

She got up and stood with the light behind her. It was deliberately intended to distract him. Under other circumstances, it would have.

"If it were a small circuit, over just a fraction of your body, I could cut it out," she said. "But the way it is, I can't. It would kill you."

At least she was honest about it. And he still didn't know what she meant when she had written, with his hands in the apartment, that she would help him. He would have to find out.

"I can smash the machine," he said. "That's the other solution."

She leaned against the wall. "You can't. And neither can I, though it's technically my machine. It's in the police department with an armed guard around it at all times. Besides, the machine can defend itself."

He looked at her without understanding. It didn't sound right. He was sweating under the makeup and part of it was coming loose.

"Then what did you mean when you said you'd help?" he asked. "You promised, but what can you do?"

"I never promised to help." It was her turn not to understand. Her hand slipped down and so did the robe.

She was lying to him, had been lying all along. She never intended to help, though she said she would. The purpose? To lead him into a trap. She'd been successful enough. He looked up in anger, in time to see an object hurtling from her hand.

It struck him on the side of the head, hard. Some of the makeup chipped and fell off, but that was less important than yanking out the tangle gun. He fired twice, once at her feet and once at her shoulders. He had aimed at her head, but the shot went low.

Her face was still pretty, though no longer indifferent or so strong. "What do you want?" she screamed. "Why don't you leave me alone? I can't help you. Nobody can."

She was standing there rigid, not daring to move. The robe rippled in a breeze from the vent and the tangle stuff gripped it and the fabric tore. She'd stand there a few more hours and then topple over. They'd find her in the morning and remove the tangle with the special tongs.

As for himself, it was too late. He might have got off Venus at one time if he had concentrated on it. He hadn't tried harder because of Doumya Filone. He had *wanted* to believe her because—well, because.

"I told you I'd help, Jadiver. I will." The voice was distinct.

It wasn't Doumya Filone who'd said it. A tangle strand had worked up her throat and gripped her face. She couldn't speak if she tried. Her gray eyes weren't gray; they were the color of tears.

*       *       *       *       *

He looked around. It wasn't Doumya Filone—and there wasn't any other person in the room.

"I've kept the police away," said the familiar voice. "I can protect you for a while longer. There's still time to save yourself. But you have to guess right. You can't make any more mistakes."

Strictly speaking, it wasn't a voice. Doumya Filone didn't hear it; that was obvious. It was the circuit then. Someone was making use of the machine to actuate the auditory nerve directly. That was what he seemed to hear.

Jadiver was tired and his body grimy, muscles twitching under the tension. But if his unknown friend—real, after all—could out-wit a room full of police and tinker with the mechanism which was supposed to spot him, he couldn't do less.

He grinned. "I'll make it this time. I know what to do."

"The police haven't given up," said the voice. "I'm going to be busy with them. Don't expect further communication from me."

He didn't know who the person was, in spite of the haunting familiarity of the voice. And he wasn't going to find out soon. Probably never. It was enough, however, to know that he had a friend.

He left Doumya Filone standing there, which was a mistake, he realized as he reached the front office. He should have fired once more at her hands. The screen was crackling; her hands had been free and she'd managed to turn the screen on before the tangle strands interfered with her movement.

He'd made a grave error, but not necessarily fatal. It would be some time before anyone got there. By then he hoped to be safe.

He slipped through the corridors, went out the rear of the building and looked around for an air cab. The place was deserted at this hour and no cabs were in the nearby sky.

He had to walk and he didn't have that much time. He headed toward the nearest main thoroughfare. It was in the opposite direction to his destination, but he should be able to find an air cab there. He was walking too fast, for a light flashed down on him. He wasn't presentable and his haste was suspicious.

"Stop," said the amplified voice. It was probably just a routine check, but he couldn't risk even that.

He dodged into a space between two buildings and began to run. In the center of town, this would be a blind alley, but in this section it wasn't. There was a chance he could lose them. The buildings were just high enough so that they couldn't use the air car and they'd have to follow on foot.

The patrol car alighted almost instantly and one of the policemen started after him. The man following him knew his business and was in good physical condition, better than Jadiver was after days of tension and little sleep.

Jadiver turned and snapped a half dozen shots at his pursuer. He was lucky, a couple were close enough. The policeman crashed to the ground and began to swear. His voice was choked off in seconds.

The other one got out of the patrol car and let it stand. It was the principle of the thing: nobody did that to a policeman. Jadiver had a substantial lead and it was dark, but he didn't know the route. Jadiver was enormously tired and this was the policeman's regular beat. The gap between them closed rapidly.

Out of breath and time and space to move around in, Jadiver took the wrong turn because the man was so close—and found himself boxed in.

\*    \*    \*    \*    \*

Crouching, Jadiver fired at the oncoming man, a dark shape he sensed rather than saw. The tangle gun clicked futilely, out of ammunition. He fumbled hastily for a clip; before he could reload, the policeman squeezed the trigger and held it down.

The bullets didn't hit him, they were set to detonate a fraction of an inch away. He gave up and awaited the constricting violence of the tangle strands.

The bullets detonated and the strands flashed out, glowing slightly in the darkness. They never touched him; instead, they bent into strange shapes and flipped away. The stickiest substance known, and one of the strongest, from which there was no escape, yet it would not adhere to him—was, in fact, forcefully repelled!

It was that skin, of course, the synthetic substance they had put on him over the circuit. They should have tested it under these conditions. They might not have been so anxious to boil men alive.

He felt that he was almost invincible. It was an exhilarating feeling. He stopped trying to reload the tangle gun and stood up. He sprinted at the policeman, who stood his ground, firing frantically at a target he could not miss and yet did not hit. The tangle strands shattered all around the target.

Jadiver swung the gun with his remaining strength; the butt connected with the policeman's forehead.

Jadiver scooped up the discarded tangle gun and fired twice at close range, in case the man should decide to revive too soon, which was doubtful. He went back and entered the idling patrol car. He hadn't lost much time, after all.

He sat the car down on top of a building near the edge of the rocketport, straightened his clothing and wiped the grime off his face. Some of the disguise went, too, but that no longer mattered much.

He stepped out of the elevator and walked casually along the street until he came to the interplanetary flight office. The same robot was there—would be there every hour, day and night, until the rocketport was expanded and the building torn down and rebuilt, or the robot itself wore out and had to be replaced.

The clerk looked up eagerly. "You're back. I knew I could count on you."

"I'm interested in that flight you were telling me about," said Jadiver.

"We've changed rates," the robot clerk replied, beaming. "It was a bargain before, but just listen to the revised offer. We pay you, on a per diem basis—subjective, of course. When you arrive, you actually have a bank account waiting for you."

Per diem, subjective—the time that *seemed* to elapse when the rocket was traveling near the speed of light. It wasn't as good as the robot made it sound.

"Never mind that," said Jadiver. "I'll take it if it's going far."

"Going far!" echoed the clerk.

A policeman sauntered by outside, just looking, but that was enough.

"I said I'd take it," Jadiver repeated in a loud voice.

The clerk deflated. "I wish I could go with you," it explained wistfully. It reached under the counter and pulled out a perforated tape. "This will get you on the ship, and it also constitutes the contract. Just present it at the other end and collect your money. You can send for your baggage after you're on board."

Jadiver opened his mouth and then closed it. His baggage was intangible, mostly experience, not much of it pleasant.

"I'll do that," he said.

The clerk came out from behind the counter and watched Jadiver leave. Lights from the rocketport glittered in its robot eyes.

*     *     *     *     *

Jadiver paced about the ship. It was not enough to be on it, for the police could still trace him. And if they did, they could get him off. It was not only himself, there was his unknown friend. They had ways to learn about that.

He passed a vision port on his way through the ship. It was night, but it didn't seem so on the vast, brightly lighted concrete plain. A strange vehicle streaked across the surface of the rocketport in defiance of all regulations and common sense.

It was coming his way. It dodged in and out of rockets landing and taking off, escaping blazing destruction with last minute, intricate maneuvers. The driver had complete control of the vehicle and was fantastically skillful.

It was a strange machine. Jadiver had never seen anything quite like it. As far as he knew, it resembled nothing the police used.

It didn't halt outside the ship. The loading ramp was down and the machine came up without hesitation. The entrance was too narrow and the vehicle would never get through—that seemed evident. An instant later, he was not so sure. The ship quivered and groaned and vibrations ran throughout the structure.

He leaned over the railing and looked down. The machine was inside, dented and scraped.

"Captain," bellowed a voice from the vehicle. It was an authoritative voice and it puzzled Jadiver.

The captain came running, either in response to the command or to find out how much damage had been done in the crash and why.

"Take off, Captain," said the voice. "Take off at once."

The captain sputtered. "I give orders here. I'll take off when I get ready."

"You're ready when the ship reaches a certain mass. As soon as I came on board, you attained it. Check your mass gauges, Captain."

The captain hurried to the gauges and glanced at them. He stared back at the machine.

"Captain," purred the machine, "you have a little daughter. By the time you get back, she will be grown and will have children of her own. The sooner you leave, the sooner you will see her again. I will regard it as a personal favor if you see that we take off immediately."

The captain looked at the machine. Tentacles and eye stalks rose up out of the tip as he watched. It was a big machine, well put together, and it appeared quite capable of handling a roomful of armed men. As a matter of fact, it just had.

The captain shrugged and gave the order to lift ship.

*　　*　　*　　*　　*

It was none too soon. Out of the visionport, Jadiver could see uniformed men edging up from the underground shelters. They backed out of sight when the rockets began to flame.

Faster the ship rose and higher. They were in the dense clouds and then through them, out in the clear black of space, away from Venus.

Jadiver looked down at the machine. It wasn't a vehicle. It was a robot, and it was familiar.

"It ought to be familiar," said the robot softly. That voice was for him alone, directly on the auditory nerve. "You designed most of it back on Earth, remember?"

He remembered. It was not a pretty imitation of a human—it was his perfect robot. And it was also, his unknown friend, the one who had watched over him.

He walked slowly down the stairs and stood beside it.

The robot switched to the regular speaking voice. "They built your design, after all. They needed a big and powerful mobile robot, one that could house, in addition to the regular functions, an extensive and delicate mechanism."

That was the voice that had haunted him so long and in so many situations. It was not Jadiver's own voice, but it resembled his. A third person might not recognize the difference.

"That other mechanism," said Jadiver. "Is that the one that monitors the circuit in my body?"

"That *parallels* the circuit in your body." Tentacles were busy straightening out the dents. "When I was built, they gave me a good mind, better than your own in certain respects. What I lacked was sensory perception. Eyes and ears, to be sure, good ones in a way, but without the delicate shadings a human has, particularly tactile interpretations. I didn't need better, they thought, because my function was to observe and report on the parallel circuit I mentioned.

"In the beginning, that circuit was a formless matrix and only faintly resembled your nervous system. As nerve data was exchanged back and forth, it began to resemble you more and more, especially your mind. Now, for practical purposes, it is you and I can look into it at will."

Jadiver stirred uneasily.

"Don't you understand?" asked the robot. "My mind isn't yours, and vice versa. But we do have one thing in common, a synthetic nervous system which, if you were killed, would begin to disintegrate slowly and painfully. And now that it's developed as much as it is, I would probably die, too, since that synthetic nervous system is an otherwise unused part of my brain."

"There were two other victims before me," said Jadiver.

"There were, but they were derelicts—dead, really, before the experiment got started. They lasted a few hours. I tried to help them, but it was too late. It was not pleasant for me."

\*     \*     \*     \*     \*

Not only was it a friend; it had a vital interest in keeping him alive. He could trust it, had to. After what had happened, doubt wasn't called for.

Jadiver rubbed his weary eyes. "That shield I used," he said. "Did it work?"

The robot laughed—Jadiver's laughter. It had copied him in many ways. "It worked to your disadvantage. The circuit signals got through to me, but I couldn't send any back until Doumya Filone chipped off part of your disguise. Then I spoke to you. Before that, I had to misdirect the police. I built up a complete and false history for you and kept them looking where you weren't."

If he had thought, he would have known it had to be that way. The police were efficient; they could have taken him long ago without the aid of the circuit. But it had seemed so easy and they had trusted the robot—had to where the circuit was concerned. No man could sit in front of a screen and interpret the squiggles that meant his hand was touching an apple.

Jadiver sat down. The strain was over and he was safe, bound for some far-off place.

"The police used you, though not as much as you used them," he said. "Still, they didn't develop the theory."

"They didn't. There was a man on Earth, a top-notch scientist. He worked out the theory and set up the mechanism. He had a surgical assistant, a person who would never be more than that on Earth because she wasn't good on theory, though she was a whiz at surgery. She realized it and got his permission to build another machine and take it to Venus. Originally it was intended to accumulate data on the workings of the human nervous system.

"On Venus, things were different. Laws concerning the rights of individuals are not so strict. She got the idea of examining the whole nervous system at once, not realizing what it meant because it had never been done that way. She discussed it with officials from the police department who saw instantly what she didn't—that once an extensive circuit was in a human, there was no way to get it out, except by death. They had no objections and were quite willing to furnish her with specimens, for their own purposes and only incidentally hers. Once the first man died, they had her and wouldn't let her back out, though she wanted to."

"Specimen," repeated Jadiver. "Yeah, I was a specimen to her." His head was heavy. "Why didn't you tell me this in the beginning?"

"Would you have listened when I first contacted you?" asked the robot. "Later, perhaps. But once you put on the shield, I couldn't get in touch with you until you were with Doumya Filone."

*     *     *     *     *

Would Jadiver have listened? Not until it became a matter of raw survival. Even now he hated to leave Earth and what it meant for the unknown dangers and tedium of a planet circling an alien sun. It was more than that, of course. Just as he'd had a design for a perfect robot, he had in mind a perfect woman. He could recognize either when he saw it.

"Doumya Filone was the assistant?"

"She was." The robot was his now, Jadiver knew. Others had built it, but it belonged to him by virtue of a nervous system. It had as good a mind as his, but it wouldn't dispute his claim. "Like yourself," continued the robot, "in the Solar System she would never have been more than second rate, and she wanted to be first. Hardly anyone recognizes it, but the Solar System is not what it once was. It's like a nice neighborhood that decays so slowly that the people in it don't notice what it's become. There are some who can rise even in a slum, but they're the rare exceptions.

"Others need greater opportunity than slums offer. They have to leave if they expect to develop freely. But the hold of a whole culture is strong and it's hard to persuade them that they have to go." The robot paused. "Take a last look at a blighted area."

Outside planets glimmered in the distance.

Jadiver was tired and his eyes were closing. Now he could sleep safely, but not in peace.

"Don't regret it," advised the robot. "Where you're going, you'll have real designs to work on. No more pretty robot faces."

"Where is it—Alpha Centauri?" Jadiver asked disinterestedly.

"That ship left yesterday. They got their quota and left within the hour, before any of the passengers could change their minds. We're going farther, to Sirius."

\*       \*       \*       \*       \*

Sirius. A mighty sun, with planets to match. It was a place to be big. Big and lonely.

"I can't force you to do anything," said the robot. It sounded pleased. "But I have no inhibitions about others."

The robot flipped up its cowl. There was a storage space and a woman in it.

Except for her hands, she was bound tightly by tangle strands.

"I don't think she likes you at the moment," said the robot. "She'll tell you that as soon as she's able to speak. She may relent later, when she realizes what it's really like on Sirius. You've got the whole voyage to convince her."

The eye-stalks of the robot followed Jadiver interestedly. "Are you looking for the tongs? Remember that the tangle stuff is repelled by your skin."

Jadiver willingly used his hands and the tangle strands fell off.

As the robot had predicted, Doumya Filone was not silent— at first.

# Forget Me Nearly

Illustrated by Emsh
Originally Published In *Galaxy Science Fiction*,
June 1954

*What sort of world was it, he puzzled, that wouldn't help victims find out whether they had been murdered or had committed suicide?*

# FORGET ME NEARLY

The police counselor leaned forward and tapped the small nameplate on his desk, which said: *Val Borgenese.* "That's my name," he said. "Who are you?"

The man across the desk shook his head. "I don't know," he said indistinctly.

"Sometimes a simple approach works," said the counselor, shoving aside the nameplate. "But not often. We haven't found anything that's effective in more than a small percentage of cases." He blinked thoughtfully. "Names are difficult. A name is like clothing, put on or taken off, recognizable but not part of the person—the first thing forgotten and the last remembered."

The man with no name said nothing.

"Try pet names," suggested Borgenese. "You don't have to be sure—just say the first thing you think of. It may be something your parents called you when you were a child."

The man stared vacantly, closed his eyes for a moment and then opened them and mumbled something.

"What?" asked Borgenese.

"Putsy," said the man more distinctly. "The only thing I can think of is Putsy."

The counselor smiled. "That's a pet name, of course, but it doesn't help much. We can't trace it, and I don't think you'd want it as a permanent name." He saw the expression on the man's face and added hastily: "We haven't given up, if that's what you're thinking. But it's not easy to determine your identity. The most important source of information is your mind, and that was at the two year level when we found you. The fact that you recalled the word Putsy is an indication."

"Fingerprints," said the man vaguely. "Can't you trace me through fingerprints?"

"That's another clue," said the counselor. "Not fingerprints, but the fact that you thought of them." He jotted something down. "I'll have to check those re-education tapes. They may be defective by now, we've run them so many times. Again, it may be merely that your mind refused to accept the proper information."

The man started to protest, but Borgenese cut him off. "Fingerprints were a fair means of identification in the Twentieth Century, but this is the Twenty-second Century."

*    *    *    *    *

The counselor then sat back. "You're confused now. You have a lot of information you don't know how to use yet. It was given to you fast, and your mind hasn't fully absorbed it and put it in order. Sometimes it helps if you talk out your problems."

"I don't know if I have a problem." The man brushed his hand slowly across his eyes. "Where do I start?"

"Let me do it for you," suggested Borgenese. "You ask questions when you feel like it. It may help you."

He paused, "You were found two weeks ago in the Shelters. You know what those are?"

The man nodded, and Borgenese went on: "Shelter and food for anyone who wants or needs it. Nothing fancy, of course, but no one has to ask or apply; he just walks in and there's a place to sleep and periodically food is provided. It's a favorite place to put people who've been retroed."

The man looked up. "Retroed?"

"Slang," said Borgenese. "The retrogression gun ionizes animal tissue, nerve cells particularly. Aim it at a man's legs and the nerves in that area are drained of energy and his muscles won't hold him up. He falls down.

"Aim it at his head and give him the smallest charge the gun is adjustable to, and his most recent knowledge is subtracted from his memory. Give him the full charge, and he is swept back to a childish or infantile age level. The exact age he reaches is dependent on his physical and mental condition at the time he's retroed.

"Theoretically it's possible to kill with the retrogression gun. The person can be taken back to a stage where there's not enough nervous organization to sustain the life process.

"However, life is tenacious. As the lower levels are reached, it takes increasing energy to subtract from anything that's left. Most people who want to get rid of someone are satisfied to leave the victim somewhere between the mental ages of one and four. For practical purposes, the man they knew is dead—or retroed, as they say."

"Then that's what they did to me," said the man. "They retroed me and left me in the Shelter. How long was I there?"

\*     \*     \*     \*     \*

Borgenese shrugged. "Who knows? That's what makes it difficult. A day, or two months. A child of two or three can feed himself, and no record is kept since the place is free. Also, it's cleaned automatically."

"I know that now that you mention it," said the man. "It's just that it's hard to remember."

"You see how it is," said the counselor. "We can't check our files against a date when someone disappeared, because we don't know that date except within very broad limits." He tapped his pen on the desk. "Do you object to a question?"

"Go ahead."

"How many people in the Solar System?"

The man thought with quiet desperation. "Fourteen to sixteen billion."

The counselor was pleased. "That's right. You're beginning to use some of the information we've put back into your mind. Earth, Mars and Venus are the main population centers. But there are also Mercury and the satellites of Jupiter and Saturn, as well as the asteroids. We can check to see where you might have come from, but there are so many places and people that you can imagine the results."

"There must be *some* way," the man said painfully. "Pictures, fingerprints, something."

"Something," Borgenese nodded. "But probably not for quite a while. There's another factor, you see. It's a shock, but you've got to face it. And the funny thing is that you'll never be better able to than now."

He rocked back. "Take the average person, full of unsuspected anxiety, even the happiest and most successful. Expose him to the retrogression gun. Tensions and frustrations are drained away.

"The structure of an adult is still there, but it's empty, waiting to be filled. Meanwhile the life of the organism goes on, but it's not the same. Lines on the face disappear, the expression alters drastically, new cell growth occurs here and there throughout the body. Do you see what that means?"

The man frowned. "I suppose no one can recognize me."

"That's right. And it's not only your face that changes. You may grow taller, but never shorter. If your hair was gray, it may darken, but not the reverse."

"Then I'm younger too?"

"In a sense, though it's actually not a rejuvenation process at all. The extra tension that everyone carries with him has been removed, and the body merely takes up the slack.

"Generally, the apparent age is made less. A person of middle age or under seems to be three to fifteen years younger than before. You appear to be about twenty-seven, but you may actually be nearer forty. You see, we don't even know what age group to check.

"And it's the same with fingerprints. They've been altered by the retrogression process. Not a great deal, but enough to make identification impossible."

*     *     *     *     *

The nameless man stared around the room—at Val Borgenese, perhaps fifty, calm and pleasant, more of a counselor than a policeman—out of the window at the skyline, and its cleanly defined levels of air traffic.

Where was his place in this?

"I guess it's no use," he said bleakly. "You'll never find out who I am."

The counselor smiled. "I think we will. Directly, there's not much we can do, but there are indirect methods. In the last two weeks we've exposed you to all the organized knowledge that can be put on tapes—physics, chemistry, biology, math, astrogation, the works.

"It's easy to remember what you once knew. It isn't learning; it's actually relearning. One fact put in your mind triggers another into existence. There's a limit, of course, but usually a person comes out of re-education with slightly more formal knowledge than he had in his prior existence." The counselor opened a folder on his desk. "We gave you a number of tests. You didn't know the purpose, but I can tell you the results."

He leafed slowly through the sheets. "You may have been an entrepreneur of some sort. You have an excellent sense of power ethics. Additionally, we've found that you're physically alert, and your reactions are well coordinated. This indicates you may have been an athlete or sportsman."

Val Borgenese laid down the tests. "In talking with you, I've learned more. The remark you made about fingerprints suggests you may have been a historian, specializing in the Twentieth Century. No one else is likely to know that there was a time in which fingerprints were a valid means of identification."

"I'm quite a guy, I suppose. Businessman, sportsman, historian." The man smiled bitterly. "All that ... but I still don't know who I am. And you can't help me."

"Is it important?" asked the counselor softly. "This happens to many people, you know, and some of them do find out who they were, with or without our help. But this is not simple amnesia. No one who's been retroed can resume his former identity. Of course, if we had tapes of the factors which made each person what he is...." He shrugged. "But those tapes don't exist. Who knows, really, what caused him to develop as he has? Most of it isn't at the conscious level. At best, if you should learn who you were, you'd have to pick up the thread of your former activities and acquaintances slowly and painfully.

"Maybe it would be better if you start from where you are. You know as much as you once did, and the information is up to date, correct and undistorted. You're younger, in a sense—in better physical condition, not so tense or nervous. Build up from that."

"But I don't have a name."

"Choose one temporarily. You can have it made permanent if it suits you."

\*     \*     \*     \*     \*

The man was silent, thinking. He looked up, not in despair, but not accepting all that the counselor said either. "What name? All I know is yours, and those of historical figures."

"That's deliberate. We don't put names on tapes, because the effects can be misleading. Everyone has thousands of associations, and can mistake the name of a prominent scientist for his own. Names unconsciously arrived at are usually no help at all."

"What do I do?" the man said. "If I don't know names, how can I choose one?"

"We have a list made up for this purpose. Go through it slowly and consciously. When you come to something you like, take it. If you chance on one that stirs memories, or rather where memories ought to be but aren't, let me know. It may be a lead I can have traced."

The man gazed at the counselor. His thought processes were fast, but erratic. He could race along a chain of reasoning and then stumble over a simple fact. The counselor ought to know what he was talking about—this was no isolated occurrence. The police had a lot of experience to justify the treatment they were giving him. Still, he felt they were mistaken in ways he couldn't formulate.

"I'll have to accept it, I suppose," he said. "There's nothing I can do to learn who I was."

The counselor shook his head. "Nothing that *we* can do. The clues are in the structure of your mind, and you have better access to it than we do. Read, think, look. Maybe you'll run across your name. We can take it from there." He paused. "That is, if you're determined to go ahead."

That was a strange thing for a police counselor to say.

"Of course I want to know who I am," he said in surprise. "Why shouldn't I?"

"I'd rather not mention this, but you ought to know." Borgenese shifted uncomfortably. "One third of the lost identity cases that we solve are self-inflicted. In other words, suicides."

\*     \*     \*     \*     \*

His head rumbled with names long after he had decided on one and put the list away. Attractive names and odd ones—but which were significant he couldn't say. There was more to living than the knowledge that could be put on tapes and played back. There was more than choosing a name. There was experience, and he lacked it. The world of personal reactions for him had started two weeks previously; it was not enough to help him know what he wanted to do.

He sat down. The room was small but comfortable. As long as he stayed in retro-therapy, he couldn't expect much freedom.

He tried to weigh the factors. He could take a job and adapt himself to some mode of living.

What kind of a job?

He had the ordinary skills of the society—but no outstanding technical ability had been discovered in him. He had the ability of an entrepreneur—but without capital, that outlet was denied him.

His mind and body were empty and waiting. In the next few months, no matter what he did, some of the urge to replace the missing sensations would be satisfied.

The more he thought about that, the more powerfully he felt that he had to know who he was. Otherwise, proceeding to form impressions and opinions might result in a sort of betrayal of himself.

Assume the worst, that he was a suicide. Maybe he had knowingly and willingly stepped out of his former life. A suicide would cover himself—would make certain that he could never trace himself back to his dangerous motive for the step. If he lived on Earth, he would go to Mars or Venus to strip himself of his unsatisfactory life. There were dozens of precautions anyone would take.

But if it weren't suicide, then who had retroed him and why? That was a question he couldn't answer now, and didn't need to. When he found out who he was, the motivation might be clear; if it wasn't, at least he would have a basis on which to investigate that.

If someone else had done it to him, deliberately or accidentally, that person would have taken precautions too. The difference was this: as a would-be suicide, he could travel freely to wherever he wished to start over again; while another person would have difficulty enticing him to a faroff place, or, assuming that the actual retrogression had taken place elsewhere, wouldn't find it easy to transport an inert and memory-less body any distance.

So, if he weren't a suicide, there was a good chance that there were clues in this city. He might as well start with that idea—it was all he had to go on.

He was free to stay in retro-therapy indefinitely, but with the restricted freedom he didn't want to. The first step was to get out. He made the decision and felt better. He switched on the screen.

Borgenese looked up. "Hello. Have you decided?"

"I think so."

"Good. Let's have it. It's bound to touch on your former life in some way, though perhaps so remotely we can't trace it. At least, it's something."

"Luis Obispo." He spelled it out.

\*      \*      \*      \*      \*

The police counselor looked dubious as he wrote the name down. "It's not common, nor uncommon either. The spelling of the first name is a little different, but there must be countless Obispos scattered over the System."

It was curious. Now he almost did think of himself as Luis Obispo. He wanted to be that person. "Another thing," he said. "Did I have any money when I was found?"

"You're thinking of leaving? A lot of them do." Val Borgenese flipped open the folder again. "You did have money, an average amount. It won't set you up in business, if that's what you're thinking."

"I wasn't. How do I get it?"

"I didn't think you were." The counselor made another notation. "I'll have the desk release it—you can get it any time. By the way, you get the full amount, no deductions for anything."

The news was welcome, considering what he had ahead of him.

Borgenese was still speaking. "Whatever you do, keep in touch with us. It'll take time to run down this name, and maybe we'll draw a blank. But something significant may show up. If you're serious, and I think you are, it's to your advantage to check back every day or so."

"I'm serious," said Luis. "I'll keep in touch."

There wasn't much to pack. The clothing he wore had been supplied by the police. Ordinary enough; it would pass on the street without comment. It would do until he could afford to get better.

He went down to the desk and picked up his money. It was more than he'd expected—the average man didn't carry this much in his pocket. He wondered about it briefly as he signed the receipt and walked out of retro-therapy. The counselor had said it was an average amount, but it wasn't.

He stood in the street in the dusk trying to orient himself.

Perhaps the money wasn't so puzzling. An average amount for those brought into therapy for treatment, perhaps. Borgenese had said a high proportion were suicides. Such a person would want to start over again minus fears and frustrations, but not completely penniless. If he had money he'd want to take it with him, though not so much that it could be traced, since that would defeat the original purpose.

The pattern was logical—suicides were those with a fair sum of money. This was the fact which inclined Borgenese to the view he obviously held.

Luis Obispo stood there uncertainly. Did he want to find out? His lips thinned—he did. In spite of Borgenese, there were other ways to account for the money he had. One of them was this: he was an important man, accustomed to handling large sums of money.

He started out. He was in a small city of a few hundred thousand on the extreme southern coast of California. In the last few days he'd studied maps of it; he knew where he was going.

*     *     *     *     *

When he got there, the Shelters were dark. He didn't know what he had expected, but it wasn't this. Reflection showed him that he hadn't thought about it clearly. The mere existence of Shelters indicated an economic level in which few people would either want or need to make use of that which was provided freely.

He skirted the area. He'd been found in one of the Shelters— which one he didn't know. Perhaps he should have checked the record before he came here.

No, this was better. Clues, he was convinced, were almost non-existent. He had to rely on his body and mind; but not in the ordinary way. He was particularly sensitive to impressions he had received before; the way he had learned things in therapy proved that; but if he tried to force them, he could be led astray. The wisest thing was to react naturally, almost without volition. He should be able to recognize the Shelter he'd been found in without trouble. From that, he could work back.

That was the theory—but it wasn't happening. He circled the area, and there was nothing to which he responded more than vaguely.

He would have to go closer.

He crossed the street. The plan of the Shelters was simple; an area two blocks long and one block wide, heavily planted with shrubs and small trees. In the center was an S-shaped continuous structure divided into a number of small dwelling units.

Luis walked along one wing of the building, turned at the corner and turned again. It was quite dark. He supposed that was why he wasn't reacting to anything. But his senses were sharper than he realized. There was a rustle behind him, and instinctively he flung himself forward, flat on the ground.

A pink spot appeared, low on the wall next to him. It had been aimed at his legs. The paint crackled faintly and the pink spot faded. He rolled away fast.

A dark body loomed past him and dropped where he'd been. There was an exclamation of surprise when the unknown found there was no one there. Luis grunted with satisfaction—this might be only a stickup, but he was getting action faster than he'd expected. He reached out and took hold of a leg and drew the assailant to him. A hard object clipped the side of his head, and he grasped that too.

The shape of the gun was familiar. He tore it loose. This wasn't any stickup! Once was enough to be retrogressed, and he'd had his share. Next time it was going to be the other guy. Physically, he was more than a match for his attacker. He twisted his body and pinned the struggling form to the ground.

That was what it was—a form. A woman, very much so; even in the darkness he was conscious of her body.

Now she was trying to get loose, and he leaned his weight more heavily on her. Her clothing was torn—he could feel her flesh against his face. He raised the gun butt, and then changed his mind and instead fumbled for a light. It wasn't easy to find it and still keep her pinned.

"Be quiet or I'll clip you," he growled.

She lay still.

* * * * *

He found the light and shone it on her face. It was good to look at, that face, but it wasn't at all familiar. He had trouble keeping his eyes from straying. Her dress was torn, and what she wore underneath was torn too.

"Seen enough?" she asked coldly.

"Put that way, I haven't." He couldn't force his voice to be matter-of-fact—it wouldn't behave.

She stared angrily at the light in her eyes. "I knew you'd be back," she said. "I thought I could get you before you got me, but you're too fast." Her mouth trembled. "This time make it permanent. I don't want to be tormented again like this."

He let her go and sat up. He was trembling, too, but not for the same reason. He turned the light away from her eyes.

"Ever consider that you could be mistaken?" he asked. "You're not the only one it happens to."

She lay there blinking at him, eyes adjusting to the changed light. She fumbled at the torn dress, which wouldn't stay where she put it. "You too?" she said with a vast lack of surprise. "When?"

"They found me here two weeks ago. This is the first time I've come back."

"Patterns," she said. "There are always patterns in what we do." Her attitude toward him had changed drastically, he could see it in her face. "I've been out three weeks longer." She sat up and leaned closer. She didn't seem to be thinking about the same things that had been on her mind only seconds before.

He stood up and helped her to her feet. She was near and showed no inclination to move away. This was something Borgenese hadn't mentioned, and there was nothing in his re-education to prepare him for this sensation, but he liked it. He couldn't see her very well, now that the light was turned off, but she was almost touching him.

"We're in the same situation, I guess." She sighed. "I'm lonely and a little afraid. Come into my place and we'll talk."

He followed her. She turned into a dwelling that from the outside seemed identical to the others. Inside, it wasn't quite the same. He couldn't say in what way it was different, but he didn't think it was the one he'd been found in.

That torn dress bothered him—not that he wanted her to pin it up. The tapes hadn't been very explicit about the beauties of the female body, but he thought he knew what they'd left out.

She was conscious of his gaze and smiled. It was not an invitation, it was a request, and he didn't mind obeying. She slid into his arms and kissed him. He was glad about the limitations of re-education. There were some things a man ought to learn for himself.

She looked up at him. "Maybe you should tell me your name," she said. "Not that it means much in our case."

"Luis Obispo," he said, holding her.

"I had more trouble, I couldn't choose until two days ago." She kissed him again, hard and deliberately. It gave her enough time to jerk the gun out of his pocket.

She slammed it against his ribs. "Stand back," she said, and meant it.

\*      \*      \*      \*      \*

Luis stared bewilderedly at her. She was desirable, more than he had imagined and for a variety of reasons. Her emotions had been real, he was sure of that, not feigned for the purpose of taking the gun away. But she had changed again in a fraction of a second. Her face was twisted with an effort at self-control.

"What's the matter?" he asked. He tried to make his voice gentle, but it wouldn't come out that way. The retrogression process had sharpened all his reactions—this one too.

"The name I finally arrived at was—Luise Obispo," she said.

He started. The same as his, except feminine! This was more than he'd dared hope for. A clue—and this girl, who he suddenly realized, without any cynicism about "love at first sight," because the tapes hadn't included it, meant something to him.

"Maybe you're my wife," he said tentatively.

"Don't count on it," she said wearily. "It would have been better if we were strangers—then it wouldn't matter what we did. Now there are too many factors, and I can't choose."

"It has to be," he argued. "Look—the same name, and so close together in time and place, and we were attracted instantly—"

"Go away," she said, and the gun didn't waver. It was not a threat that he could ignore. He left.

She was wrong in making him leave, completely wrong. He couldn't say how he knew, but he was certain. But he couldn't prove it, and she wasn't likely to accept his unsubstantiated word.

He leaned weakly against the door. It was like that. Retrogression had left him with an adult body and sharper receptiveness. And after that followed an urge to live fully. He had a lot of knowledge, but it didn't extend to this sphere of human behavior.

Inside he could hear her moving around faintly, an emotional anticlimax. It wasn't just frustrated sex desire, though that played a part. They had known each other previously—the instant attraction they'd had for each other was proof, leaving aside the names. Lord, he'd trade his unknown identity to have her. He should have taken another name—any other name would have been all right.

It wasn't because she was the first woman he'd seen, or the woman he had first re-seen. There had been nurses, some of them beautiful, and he'd paid no attention to them. But Luise Obispo was part of his former life—and he didn't know what part. The reactions were there, but until he could find out why, he was denied access to the satisfactions.

From a very narrow angle, and only from that angle, he could see that there was still a light inside. It was dim, and if a person didn't know, he might pass by and not notice it.

His former observation about the Shelters was incorrect. Every dwelling might be occupied and he couldn't tell unless he examined them individually.

He stirred. The woman was a clue to his problem, but the clue itself was a far more urgent problem. Though his identity was important, he could build another life without it and the new life might not be worse than the one from which he had been forcibly removed.

Perhaps he was over-reacting, but he didn't think so: *his new life had to include this woman.*

He wasn't equipped to handle the emotion. He stumbled away from the door and found an unoccupied dwelling and went in without turning on the lights and lay down on the bed.

In the morning, he knew he had been here before. In the darkness he had chosen unknowingly but also unerringly. This was the place in which he had been retrogressed.

It was here that the police had picked him up.

* * * * *

The counselor looked sleepily out of the screen. "I wish you people didn't have so much energy," he complained. Then he looked again and the sleepiness vanished. "I see you found it the first time."

Luis knew it himself, because there was a difference from the dwelling Luise lived in—not much, but perceptible to him. The counselor, however, must have a phenomenal memory to distinguish it from hundreds of others almost like it.

Borgenese noticed the expression and smiled. "I'm not an eidetic, if that's what you think. There's a number on the set you're calling from and it shows on my screen. You can't see it."

They would have something like that, Luis thought. "Why didn't you tell me this was it before I came?"

"We were pretty sure you'd find it by yourself. People who've just been retroed usually do. It's better to do it on your own. Our object is to have you recover your personality. If we knew who you were, we could set up a program to guide you to it faster. As it is, if we help you too much, you turn into a carbon copy of the man who's advising you."

Luis nodded. Give a man his adult body and mind and turn him loose on the problems which confronted him, and he would come up with adult solutions. It was better that way.

But he hadn't called to discuss that. "There's another person living in the Shelters," he said. "You found her three weeks before you found me."

"So you've met her already? Fine. We were hoping you would." Borgenese chuckled. "Let's see if I can describe her. Apparent age, about twenty-three; that means that she was originally between twenty-six or thirty-eight, with the probability at the lower figure. A good body, as you are probably well aware, and a striking face. Somewhat oversexed at the moment, but that's all right—so are you."

He saw the expression on Luis's face and added quickly: "You needn't worry. Draw a parallel with your own experience. There were pretty nurses all around you in retro-therapy, and I doubt that you noticed that they were female. That's normal for a person in your position, and it's the same with her.

"It works this way: you're both unsure of yourselves and can't react to those who have some control over their emotions. When you meet each other, you can sense that neither has made the necessary adjustments, and so you are free to release your true feelings."

He smiled broadly. "At the moment, you two are the only ones who have been retroed recently. You won't have any competition for six months or so, until you begin to feel comfortable in your new life. By then, you should know how well you really like each other.

"Of course tomorrow, or even today, we might find another person in the Shelter. If it's a man, you'll have to watch out; if a woman, you'll have too much companionship. As it is, I think you're very lucky."

Yeah, he was lucky—or would be if things were actually like that. Yesterday he would have denied it; but today, he'd be willing to settle for it, if he could get it.

"I don't think you understand," he said. "She took the same name that I did."

Borgenese's smile flipped over fast, and the other side was a frown. For a long time he sat there scowling out of the screen. "That's a hell of a thing to tell me before breakfast," he said. "Are you sure? She couldn't decide on a name before she left."

"I'm sure," said Luis, and related all the details of last night.

The counselor sat there and didn't say anything.

\*   \*   \*   \*   \*

Luis waited as long as he could. "You can trace *us* now," he said. "One person might be difficult. But two of us with nearly the same name, that should stick out big, even in a population of sixteen billion. Two people are missing from somewhere. You can find that."

The counselor's face didn't change. "You understand that if you were killed, we'd find the man who did it. I can't tell you how, but you can be sure he wouldn't escape. In the last hundred years there's been no unsolved murder."

He coughed and turned away from the screen. When he turned back, his face was calm. "I'm not supposed to tell you this much. I'm breaking the rule because your case and that of the girl is different from any I've ever handled." He was speaking carefully. "Listen. I'll tell you once and won't repeat it. If you ever accuse me, I'll deny I said it, and I have the entire police organization behind me to make it stick."

The counselor closed his eyes as if to see in his mind the principle he was formulating. "If we can catch a murderer, no matter how clever he may be, it ought to be easier to trace the identity of a person who is still alive. It is. *But we never try.* Though it's all right if the victim does.

"*If I should ask the cooperation of other police departments, they wouldn't help. If the solution lies within an area over which I have jurisdiction and I find out who is responsible, I will be dismissed before I can prosecute the man.*"

Luis stared at the counselor in helpless amazement. "Then you're not doing anything," he said shakily. "You lied to me. You don't intend to do anything."

"You're overwrought," said Borgenese politely. "If you could see how busy we are in your behalf—" He sighed. "My advice is that if you can't convince the girl, forget her. If the situation gets emotionally unbearable, let me know and I can arrange transportation to another city where there may be others who are—uh—more compatible."

"But she's my wife," he said stubbornly.

"Are you sure?"

Actually Luis wasn't—but he wanted *her* to be, or any variation thereof she would consent to. He explained.

"As she says, there are a lot of factors," commented the counselor. "I'd suggest an examination. It may remove some of her objections."

He hadn't thought of it, but he accepted it eagerly. "What will that do?"

"Not much, unfortunately. It will prove that you two can have healthy normal children, but it won't indicate that you're not a member of her genetic family. And, of course, it won't touch on the question of legal family, brother-in-law and the like. I don't suppose she'd accept that."

She wouldn't. He'd seen her for only a brief time and yet he knew that much. He was in an ambiguous position; he could make snap decisions he was certain were right, but he had to guess at facts. He and the girl were victims, and the police refused to help them in the only way that would do much good. And the police had, or thought they had, official reasons for their stand.

Luis told the counselor just exactly what he thought of that.

"It's too bad," agreed the counselor. "These things often have an extraordinary degree of permanency if they ever get started."

If they ever got started! Luis reached out and turned off the screen. It flickered unsteadily—the counselor was trying to call him back. He didn't want to talk to the man; it was painful, and Borgenese had nothing to add but platitudes, and fuel to his anger. He swung open the panel and jerked the wiring loose and the screen went blank.

There was an object concealed in the mechanism he had exposed. It was a neat, vicious, little retrogression gun.

\*    \*    \*    \*    \*

He got it out and balanced it gingerly in his hand. Now he had something else to work on! It was *the* weapon, of course. It had been used on him and then hidden behind the screen.

It was a good place to hide it. The screens never wore out or needed adjustment, and the cleaning robots that came out of the wall never cleaned there. The police should have found it, but they hadn't looked. He smiled bitterly. They weren't interested in solving crimes—merely in ameliorating the consequences.

Though the police had failed, he hadn't. It could be traced back to the man who owned it, and that person would have information. He turned the retro gun over slowly; it was just a gun; there were countless others like it.

He finished dressing and dropped the gun in his pocket. He went outside and looked across the court. He hesitated and then walked over and knocked.

"Occupied," said the door. "But the occupant is out. No definite time of return stated, but she will be back this evening. Is there any message?"

"No message," he said. "I'll call back when she's home."

He hoped she wouldn't refuse to speak to him. She'd been away from retro-therapy longer than he and possibly had developed her own leads—very likely she was investigating some of them now. Whatever she found would help him, and vice versa. The man who'd retroed her had done the same to him. They were approaching the problem from different angles. Between the two of them, they should come up with the correct solution.

He walked away from the Shelters and caught the belt to the center of town; the journey didn't take long. He stepped off, and wandered in the bright sunshine, not quite aimlessly. At length he found an Electronic Arms store, and went inside.

                              *    *    *    *    *

A robot came to wait on him. "I'd like to speak to the manager," he said and the robot went away.

Presently the manager appeared, middle aged, drowsy. "What can I do for you?"

Luis laid the retrogression gun on the counter. "I'd like to know who this was sold to."

The manager coughed. "Well, there are millions of them, hundreds of millions."

"I know, but I have to find out."

The manager picked it up. "It's a competitor's make," he said doubtfully. "Of course, as a courtesy to a customer...." He fingered it thoughtfully. "Do you really want to know? It's just a freezer. Not at all dangerous."

Luis looked at it with concern. Just a freezer—not a retro gun at all! Then it couldn't have been the weapon used on him.

Before he could take it back the manager broke it open. The drowsy expression vanished.

"Why didn't you say so?" exclaimed the manager, examining it. "This gun has been illegally altered." He bent over the exposed circuits and then glanced up happily at Luis. "Come here, I'll show you."

Luis followed him to the small workshop in the back of the store. The manager closed the door behind them and fumbled among the equipment. He mounted the gun securely in a frame and pressed a button which projected an image of the circuit onto a screen.

The manager was enjoying himself. "Everybody's entitled to self-protection," he said. "That's why we sell so many like these. They're harmless, won't hurt a baby. Fully charged, they'll put a man out for half an hour, overload his nervous system. At the weakest, they'll still keep him out of action for ten minutes. Below that, they won't work at all." He looked up. "Are you sure you understand this?"

It had been included in his re-education, but it didn't come readily to his mind. "Perhaps you'd better go over it for me."

The manager wagged his head. "As I said, the freezer is legal, won't harm anyone. It'll stop a man or an elephant in his tracks, freeze him, but beyond that will leave him intact. When he comes out of it, he's just the same as before, nothing changed." He seized a pointer and adjusted the controls so as to enlarge the image on the screen. "However, a freezer can be converted to a retrogression gun, and that's illegal." He traced the connections with the pointer. "If this wire, instead of connecting as it does, is moved to here and here, the polarity is reversed. In addition, if these four wires are interchanged, the freezer becomes a retrogressor. As I said, it's illegal to do that."

*   *   *   *   *

The manager scrutinized the circuits closely and grunted in disgust. "Whoever converted this did a sloppy job. Here." He bent over the gun and began manipulating micro-instruments. He worked rapidly and surely. A moment later, he snapped the weapon together and straightened up, handing it to Luis. "There," he said proudly. "It's a much more effective retrogressor than it was. Uses less power too."

Luis swallowed. Either he was mad or the man was, or perhaps it was the society he was trying to adjust to. "Aren't you taking a chance, doing this for me?"

The manager smiled. "You're joking. A tenth of the freezers we sell are immediately converted into retrogressors. Who cares?" He became serious. "Do you still want to know who bought it?"

Luis nodded—at the moment he didn't trust his voice.

"It will take several hours. No charge though, customer service. Tell me where I can reach you."

Luis jotted down the number of the screen at the Shelter and handed it to the manager. As he left, the manager whispered to him: "Remember, the next time you buy a freezer—ours can be converted easier than the one you have."

He went out into the sunlight. It didn't seem the same. What kind of society was he living in? The reality didn't fit with what he had re-learned. It had seemed an orderly and sane civilization, with little violence and vast respect for the law.

But the fact was that any school child—well, not quite *that* young, perhaps—but anyone older could and did buy a freezer. And it was ridiculously easy to convert a freezer into something far more vicious. Of course, it was illegal, but no one paid any attention to that.

This was wrong; it wasn't the way he remembered....

He corrected himself: he didn't actually remember anything. His knowledge came from tapes, and was obviously inadequate. Certain things he just didn't understand yet.

He wanted to talk to someone—but who? The counselor had given him all the information he intended to. The store manager had supplied some additional insight, but it only confused him. Luise—at the moment she was suspicious of him.

There was nothing to do except to be as observant as he could. He wandered through the town, just looking. He saw nothing that seemed familiar. Negative evidence, of course, but it indicated he hadn't lived here before.

Before what? Before he had been retrogressed. He had been brought here from elsewhere, the same as Luise.

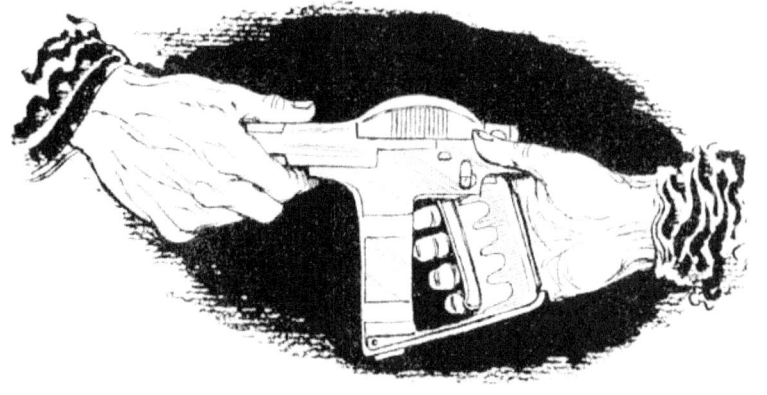

He visited the spaceport. Again the evidence was negative; there was not a ship the sight of which tripped his memory. It had been too much to hope for; if he had been brought in by spaceship, it wouldn't still be around for him to recognize.

Late in the afternoon, he headed toward the center of town. He was riding the belt when he saw Luise coming out of a tall office building.

*       *       *       *       *

He hopped off and let her pass, boarding it again and following her at a distance. As soon as they were out of the business district, he began to edge closer.

A few blocks from the Shelter she got off the belt and waited, turning around and smiling directly at him. In the interim her attitude toward him had changed, evidently—for the better, as far as he was concerned. He couldn't ignore her and didn't want to. He stepped off the belt.

"Hello," she said. "I think you were following me."

"I was. Do you mind?"

"I guess I don't." She walked along with him. "Others followed me, but I discouraged them."

She was worth following, but it was not that which was strange. Now she seemed composed and extraordinarily friendly, a complete reversal from last night. Had she learned something during the day which changed her opinion of him? He hoped she had.

She stopped at the edge of the Shelter area. "Do you live here?"

Learned something? She seemed to have forgotten.

He nodded.

"For the same reason?"

His throat tightened. He had told her all that last night. Couldn't she remember?

"Yes," he said.

"I thought so. That's why I didn't mind your following me."

Here was the attraction factor that Borgenese had spoken of; it was functioning again, for which he was grateful. But still, why? And why didn't she remember last night?

They walked on until she came to her dwelling. She paused at the door. "I have a feeling I should know who you are, but I just can't recall. Isn't that terrible?"

It was—frightening. Her identity was apparently incompletely established; it kept slipping backward to a time she hadn't met him. He couldn't build anything enduring on that; each meeting with her would begin as if nothing had happened before.

Would the same be true of him?

He looked at her. The torn dress hadn't been repaired, as he'd thought at first; it had been replaced by the robots that came out of the wall at night. They'd done a good job fitting her, but with her body that was easy.

It was frightening and it wasn't. At least this time he didn't have a handicap. He opened his mouth to tell her his name, and then closed it. He wasn't going to make that mistake again. "I haven't decided on a name," he said.

"It was that way with me too." She gazed at him and he could feel his insides sloshing around. "Well, man with no name, do you want to come in? We can have dinner together."

He entered. But dinner was late that night. He had known it would be.

*     *     *     *     *

In the morning light, he sat up and put his hand on her. She smiled in her sleep and squirmed closer. There were compensations for being nobody, he supposed, and this was one of them. He got up quietly and dressed without waking her. There were a number of things he wanted to discuss, but somehow there hadn't been time last night. He would have to talk to her later today.

He slipped out of the house and went across the court into his own. The screen he had ripped apart had been repaired and put back in place. A voice chimed out as he entered: "A call came while you were gone."

"Let's have it."

The voice descended the scale and became that of the store manager. "The gun you brought in was sold six months ago to Dorn Starret, resident of Ceres and proprietor of a small gallium mine there. That's all the information on record. I trust it will be satisfactory."

Luis sat down. It was. He could trace the man or have him traced, though the last might not be necessary.

The name meant something to him—just what he couldn't say. Dorn Starret, owner of a gallium mine on Ceres. The mine might or might not be of consequence; gallium was used in a number of industrial processes, but beyond that was not particularly valuable.

He closed his eyes to concentrate. The name slid into vacant nerve cells that were responsive; slowly a picture formed, nebulous and incomplete at first. There was a mouth and then there were eyes, each feature bringing others into focus, unfolding as a germ cell divides and grows, calling into existence an entire creature. The picture was nearly complete.

Still with eyes closed, he looked at the man he remembered. Dorn Starret, five-eleven, one hundred and ninety, flesh that had once been muscular and firm. Age, thirty-seven; black hair that was beginning to recede from his forehead. The face was harder to define—strong, though slightly hard, it was perhaps good looking. It was the eyes which were at fault, Luis decided— glinting often—and there were lines on the face that ought not to be there.

There was another thing that set the man apart. Not clothing; that was conventional, though better than average. Luis stared into his memory until he was able to see it. *Unquestionably the man was left-handed.* The picture was too clear to permit a mistake on that detail.

He knew the man, had seen him often. How and in what context? He waited, but nothing else came.

Luis opened his eyes. He would recognize the man if he ever saw him. This was the man who owned the gun, presumably had shot him with it, and then had hidden it here in this room.

He thought about it vainly. By itself, the name couldn't take him back through all past associations with the man, so he passed from the man to Ceres. Here he was better equipped; re-education tapes had replaced his former knowledge of the subject.

\*    \*    \*    \*    \*

The asteroid belt was not rigidly policed; if there was a place in the System in which legal niceties were not strictly observed, it was there. What could he deduce from that? Nothing perhaps; there were many people living in the belt who were engaged in legitimate work: miners, prospectors, scientific investigators. But with rising excitement, he realized that Dorn Starret was not one of these.

He was a criminal. The gallium mine was merely an attempt to cover himself with respectability. How did Luis know that? He wasn't sure; his thought processes were hidden and erratic; but he knew.

Dorn Starret was a criminal—but the information wasn't completely satisfactory. What had caused the man to retrogress Luis and Luise Obispo? That still had to be determined.

But it did suggest this: as a habitual criminal, the man was more than ordinarily dangerous.

Luis sat there a while longer, but he had recalled everything that would come out of the original stimulus. If he wanted more, he would have to dig up other facts or make further contacts. But at least it wasn't hopeless—even without the police, he had learned this much.

He went over the room thoroughly once more. If there was anything hidden, he couldn't find it.

He crossed the court to Luise's dwelling. She was gone, but there was a note on the table. He picked it up and read it:

*Dear man with no name:*

*I suppose you were here last night, though I'm so mixed up I can't be sure; there's so little of memory or reality to base anything on. I wanted to talk to you before I left but I guess, like me, you're out investigating.*

*There's always a danger that neither of us will like what we find. What if I'm married to another person and the same with you? Suppose ... but there are countless suppositions—these are the risks we take. It's intolerable not to know who I am, especially since the knowledge is so close. But of course you know that.*

*Anyway I'll be out most of the day. I discovered a psychologist who specializes in restoring memory; you can see the possibilities in that. I went there yesterday and have an appointment again today. It's nice of him, considering that I have no money, but he says I'm more or less an experimental subject. I can't tell you when I'll be back but it won't be late.*

*Luise.*

He crumpled the note in his hand. Memory expert. Her psychologist was that—in reverse. Yesterday he had taken a day out of her life, and that was why Luise hadn't recognized him and might not a second time.

\*　　\*　　\*　　\*　　\*

He leaned against the table. After a moment, he straightened out the note. A second reading didn't help. There it was, if he could make sense from it.

Luise and himself, probably in that order. There was no proof, but it seemed likely that she had been retrogressed first, since she had been discovered first.

There was also Dorn Starret, the criminal from Ceres who had hidden the gun in the Shelter that he, Luis, had been found in. And there was now a fourth person: the psychologist who specialized in depriving retrogression victims of what few memories they had left.

Luis grimaced. Here was information which, if the police would act on it properly ... but it was no use, they wouldn't. Any solution which came out of this would have to arise out of his own efforts.

He folded the note carefully. It would be handy to have if Luise came back and didn't know who he was.

Meanwhile, the psychologist. Luise hadn't said who he was, but it shouldn't be difficult to locate him. He went to the screen and dialed the directory. There were many psychologists in it, but no name that was familiar.

He pondered. The person who had retroed Luise and himself—what would he do? First he would take them as far from familiar scenes as he could. That tied in with the facts. Dorn Starret came from Ceres.

Then what? He would want to make certain that his victims did not trace their former lives. And he would be inconspicuous in so doing.

Again Luis turned to the screen, but this time he dialed the news service. He found what he was looking for in the advertisements of an issue a month old. It was very neat:

DO YOU REMEMBER EVERYTHING—or is your mind hazy? Perhaps my system can help you recall those little details you find it so annoying to forget.

MEMORY LAB.

That was all. No name. But there was an address. Hurriedly Luis scanned every succeeding issue. The advertisement was still there.

He was coming closer, very close. The ad was clever; it would attract the attention of Luise and himself and others like them, and almost no one else. There was no mention of fees, no claim that it was operated by a psychologist, nothing that the police would investigate.

Night after night Luise had sat alone; sooner or later, watching the screen, she had to see the ad. It was intriguing and she had answered it. Normally, so would he have: but now he was forewarned.

Part of the cleverness was this: that she went of her own volition. She would have suspected an outright offer of help—but this seemed harmless. She went to him as she would to anyone in business. A very clever setup.

But who was behind MEMORY LAB? Luis thought he knew. A trained psychologist with a legitimate purpose would attach his name to the advertisement.

Luis patted the retro gun in his pocket. Dorn Starret, criminal, and inventor of a fictitious memory system, was going to have a visitor. It wasn't necessary to go to Ceres to see him.

*    *    *    *    *

It was the only conclusion that made sense. Dorn Starret had retroed him—the gun proved that—and Luise as well. Until a few minutes ago, he had thought that she had been first and he later, but that was wrong. They had been retrogressed together and Dorn Starret had done it; now he had come back to make certain that they didn't trace him.

Neat—but it wasn't going to work. Luis grinned wryly to himself. He had a weapon in his pocket that was assurance it wouldn't work.

He got off the belt near the building he had seen Luise leaving yesterday. He went into the lobby and located MEMORY LAB, a suite on the top floor. It wasn't necessary, but he checked rental dates. The lab had been there exactly three weeks. This tied in with Luise's release from retro-therapy. Every connection he had anticipated was there.

He rode up to the top floor. There wasn't a chance that Starret would recognize him; physically he must have changed too much since the criminal had last seen him. And while Luise hadn't concealed that she was a retro and so had given herself away, he wasn't going to make that mistake.

The sign on the door stood out as he came near and disappeared as he went by. MEMORY LAB, that was all—no other name, even here. Naturally. A false name would be occasion for police action. The right one would evoke Luise's and his own memories.

He turned back and went into the waiting room. No robot receptionist. He expected that; the man didn't intend to be around very long.

"Who's there?" The voice came from a speaker in the wall; the screen beside it remained blank, though obviously the man was in the next room. For a commercial establishment, the LAB was not considerate of potential clients.

Luis smiled sourly and loosened the weapon in his pocket. "I saw your advertisement," he said. No name; let him guess.

"I'm very busy. Can you come back tomorrow?"

Luis frowned. This was not according to plan. First, he didn't recognize the voice, though the speaker could account for that if it were intentionally distorted. Second, Luise was inside and he had to protect her. He could break in, but he preferred that the man come out.

He thought swiftly. "I'm Chals Putsyn, gallium importer," he called. "Tomorrow I'll be away on business. Can you give me an appointment for another time?"

There was a long silence. "Wait. I'll be out."

He'd *thought* the mention of gallium would do it. True, the mine Starret owned was probably worthless, but he couldn't restrain his curiosity.

\*     \*     \*     \*     \*

The door swung open and a man stepped out, closing the door before Luis could see inside.

He had erred—the man was not Dorn Starret.

The other eyed him keenly. "Mr. Chals Putsyn? Please sit down."

Luis did so slowly, giving himself time to complete a mental inventory. The man *had* to be Dorn Starret—and yet he wasn't. No disguise could be that effective. At least three inches shorter; the shape of his head was different; his body was slighter. Moreover, he was right-handed, not left, as Starret was.

Luis had a story ready—names, dates, and circumstances. It sounded authentic even to himself.

The man listened impatiently. "I may not be able to help you," he said, interrupting. "Oddly enough, light cases are hardest. It's the serious memory blocks that I specialize in."

There was something strange about his eyes—his voice too. "However, if you can come back in two days, late in the afternoon, I'll see what I can do."

Luis took the appointment card and found himself firmly ushered to the door. It was disturbing; Luise was in the next room, but the man gave him no opportunity to see her.

He stood uncertainly in the hall. The whole interview had taken only a few minutes, and during that time all his previous ideas had been upset. If the man was not Dorn Starret, who was he and what was his connection? The criminal from Ceres was not so foolish as to attempt to solve his problems by assigning them to another person. This was a one-man job from beginning to end, or ought to be.

Luis took the elevator to the ground floor and walked out aimlessly on the street. There was something queer about the man on the top floor. It took time to discover what it was.

The man was not Starret—but he was disguised. His irises were stained another color and the voice was not his own—or rather it was, but filtered through an artificial larynx inserted painfully in his throat. And his face had been recently swabbed with a chemical irritant which caused the tissues beneath his skin to swell, making his face appear plumper.

Luis took a deep breath. Unconsciously he had noticed details too slight for the average person to discern. This suggested something about his own past—that he was trained to recognize disguises.

But more important was this: that the man was disguised at all. The reason was obvious—to avoid evoking memories.

The man's name—what was it? It hadn't even been registered in the building—he'd asked on his way out. And Luise couldn't tell him. She was no longer a reliable source of information. He had to find out, and there was only one way that suggested itself.

Luise was still in there, but not in physical danger. The police were lax about other things, but not about murder, and the man knew that. She might lose her memories of the past few weeks; regrettable if it happened, but not a catastrophe.

But who was the man and what was his connection?

He spent the rest of the day buying equipment—not much, but his money dwindled rapidly. He considered going back to the Shelter and then decided against it. By this time Luise would be back, and he would be tempted not to leave her.

After dark, when the lights in the offices went out, he rented an aircar and set it down on the top of the building.

\* \* \* \* \*

He walked across the roof, estimating the distances with practiced ease, as if he'd undergone extensive training and the apprenticeship period had been forgotten and only the skill remained. He knelt and fused two small rods to a portion of the roof, and then readjusted the torch and cut a small circular hole. He listened, and when there was no alarm, lifted out the section. There was nothing but darkness below.

He fastened a rope to the aircar. He dropped the rope through the hole and slid down. Unless he had miscalculated, he was where he wanted to be, having bypassed all alarm circuits. There were others inside, he was reasonably certain of that, but with ordinary precautions he could avoid them.

He flashed on a tiny light. He had guessed right; this was MEMORY LAB—the room he'd wanted to see this afternoon but hadn't been able to. In front of him was the door to the waiting room, and beyond that the hall. He swung the light in an arc, flashing it over a desk and a piece of equipment the nature of which he didn't know. Behind him was still another door.

The desk was locked, but he took out a small magnetic device and jiggled it expertly over the concealed mechanism and then it was unlocked. He went hurriedly through papers and documents, but there was nothing with a name on it. He rifled the desk thoroughly and then went to the machine.

He didn't expect to learn anything, but he might as well examine it. There was a place for a patient to sit, and a metal hood to fit over the patient's head. He snapped the hood open and peered into it. It seemed to have two functions. One circuit was far larger and more complicated, and he couldn't determine what it did. But he recognized the other circuit; essentially it was a retrogressor, but whereas the gun was crude and couldn't be regulated, this was capable of fine adjustment—enough, say, to slice a day out of the patient's life, and no more.

That fitted with what had happened to Luise. She had been experimented on in some way, and then the memory of that experiment had been erased. But the man had grown careless and had taken away one day too many.

He snapped the mechanism closed. This was the method, but he still didn't know who the man was nor why he found it necessary to do all this.

There was a door behind him and the answer might lie beyond it. He listened carefully, then swung the door open and went through.

The blow that hit him wasn't physical; nothing mechanical could take his nerves and jerk them all at once. A freezer. As he fell to the floor, he was grateful it was that and not a retro gun.

Lights flooded the place, and the man of the afternoon interview was grinning at him.

"I thought you'd be back," he said, pleased. "In fact, I knew you would."

\*    \*    \*    \*    \*

Somewhere he had blundered; but he didn't know how. Experimentally he wriggled his fingers. They moved a fraction of an inch, but no more. He was helpless and couldn't say anything. He wasn't quite sure at the moment that he wanted to.

"You were right, I didn't recognize you physically," continued the man. "Nevertheless, you gave yourself away. The name you used this afternoon, Chals Putsyn, is *my* name. Do you remember now?"

Of course. He'd chosen Chals Putsyn at random, because he'd had to say something, and everything would have been all right—except it actually hadn't been a random choice. The associations had triggered the wrong words into existence.

His mind flashed back to the time he'd discussed names with Borgenese. What had he said?

Putsy. But it wasn't Putsy—it was Putsyn.

"You're very much improved," said the real Chals Putsyn, staring curiously at him. "Let me recommend the retro treatment to you. In fact I'd take it myself, but there are a few inconveniences."

Yeah, there were inconveniences—like starting over again and not knowing who you were.

But Putsyn was right: he was physically improved. A freezer knocked a man down and kept him there for half an hour. But Luis had only been down a few minutes, and already he could move his feet, though he didn't. It was a phenomenally fast recovery, and perhaps Putsyn wasn't aware of it.

"The question is, what to do with you?" Putsyn seemed to be thinking aloud. "The police are intolerant of killing. Maybe if I disposed of every atom...." He shook his head and sighed. "But that's been tried, and it didn't make any difference. So you'll have to remain alive—though I don't think you'll approve of my treatment."

Luis didn't approve—it would be the same kind of treatment that Luise had been exposed to, but more drastic in his case, because he was aware of what was going on.

Putsyn came close to drag him away. It was time to use the energy he'd been saving up, and he did.

Startled, Putsyn fired the freezer, but he was aiming at a twisting target and the invisible energy only grazed Luis's leg. The leg went limp and had no feeling, but his two hands were still good and that was all he needed.

He tore the freezer away and put his other hand on Putsyn's throat. He could feel the artificial larynx inside. He squeezed.

He lay there until Putsyn went limp.

*     *     *     *     *

When there was no longer any movement, he sat up and pried open the man's jaws, thrusting his fingers into the mouth and jerking out the artificial larynx. The next time he would hear Putsyn's real voice, and maybe that would trigger his memory.

He crawled to the door and pulled himself up, leaning against the wall. By the time Putsyn moved, he had regained partial use of his leg.

"Now we'll see," he said. He didn't try to put anger in his voice; it was there. "I don't have to tell you that I can beat answers out of you."

"You don't know?" Putsyn laughed and there was relief in the sound. "You can kick me around, but you won't get your answers!"

The man had physical courage, or thought he did, and sometimes that amounted to the same thing. Luis shifted uneasily. It was the first time he'd heard Putsyn's actual voice; it was disturbing, but it didn't arouse concrete memories.

He stepped on the outstretched hand. "Think so?" he said. He could hear the fingers crackle.

Putsyn paled, but didn't cry out. "Don't think you can kill me and get away with it," he said.

He didn't sound too certain.

Slightly sick, Luis stepped off the hand. He couldn't kill the man—and not just because of the police. He just couldn't do it. He felt for the other gun in his pocket.

"This isn't a freezer," he said. "It's been changed over. I think I'll give you a sample."

Putsyn blinked. "And lose all chance of finding out? Go ahead."

Luis had thought of that; but he hadn't expected Putsyn to.

"You see, there's nothing you can do," said Putsyn. "A man has a right to protect his property, and I've got plenty of evidence that you broke in."

"I don't think you'll go to the police," Luis said.

"You think not? My memory system isn't a fraud. Admittedly, I didn't use it properly on Luise, but in a public demonstration I can prove that it does work."

Luis nodded wearily to himself. He'd half suspected that it did work. Here he was, with the solution so close—this man knew his identity and that of Luise, and where Dorn Starret came into the tangle—and he couldn't force Putsyn to tell.

He couldn't go to the police. They would ignore his charges, because they were based on unprovable suspicions ... ignore him or arrest him for breaking and entering.

"Everything's in your favor," he said, raising the gun. "But there's one way to make you leave us alone."

"Wait," cried Putsyn, covering his face with his uninjured hand, as if that would shield him. "Maybe we can work out an agreement."

Luis didn't lower the gun. "I mean it," he said.

"I know you mean it—I can't let you take away my life's work."

"Talk fast," Luis said, "and don't lie."

He stood close and listened while Putsyn told his story.

This is what had happened, he thought. This is what he'd tried so hard to learn.

"I had to do it that way," Putsyn finished. "But if you're willing to listen to reason, I can cut you in—more money than you've dreamed of—and the girl too, if you want her."

Luis was silent. He wanted her—but now the thought was foolish. Hopeless. This must be the way people felt who stood in the blast area of a rocket—but for them the sensation lasted only an instant, while for him the feeling would last the rest of his life.

"Get up," he said.

"Then it's all right?" asked Putsyn nervously. "We'll share it?"

"Get up."

Putsyn got to his feet, and Luis hit him. He could have used the freezer, but that wasn't personal enough.

He let the body fall to the floor.

He dragged the inert form into the waiting room and turned on the screen and talked to the police. Then he turned off the screen and kicked open the door to the hall. He shouldered Putsyn and carried him up to the roof and put him in the aircar.

*    *    *    *    *

Luise was there, puzzled and sleepy. For reasons of his own, Borgenese had sent a squad to bring her in. Might as well have her here and get it over with, Luis thought. She smiled at him, and he knew that Putsyn hadn't lied about that part. She remembered him and therefore Putsyn hadn't had time to do much damage.

Borgenese was at the desk as he walked in. Luis swung Putsyn off his shoulder and dropped him into a chair. The man was still unconscious, but wouldn't be for long.

"I see you brought a visitor," remarked Borgenese pleasantly.

"A customer," he said.

"Customers are welcome too," said the police counselor. "Of course, it's up to us to decide whether he *is* a customer."

Luise started to cross the room, but Borgenese motioned her back. "Let him alone. I think he's going to have a rough time."

"Yeah," said Luis.

It was nice to know that Luise liked him now—because she wouldn't after this was over.

He wiped the sweat off his forehead; all of it hadn't come from physical exertion.

"Putsyn here is a scientist," he said. "He worked out a machine that reverses the effects of the retro gun. He intended to go to everyone who'd been retrogressed, and in return for giving them back their memory, they'd sign over most of their property to him.

"Naturally, they'd agree. They all want to return to their former lives that bad, and, of course, they aren't aware of how much money they had. He had it all his way. He could use the machine to investigate them, and take only those who were really wealthy. He'd give them a partial recovery in the machine, and when he found out who they were, give them a quick shot of a built-in retro gun, taking them back to the time they'd just entered his office. They wouldn't suspect a thing.

"Those who measured up he'd sign an agreement with, and to the other poor devils he'd say that he was sorry but he couldn't help them."

Putsyn was conscious now. "It's not so," he said sullenly. "He can't prove it."

"I don't think he's trying to prove that," said Borgenese, still calm. "Let him talk."

Luis took a deep breath. "He might have gotten away with it, but he'd hired a laboratory assistant to help him perfect the machine. She didn't like his ideas; she thought a discovery like that should be given to the public. He didn't particularly care what she thought, but now the trouble was that she could build it too, and since he couldn't patent it and still keep it secret, she was a threat to his plans." He paused. "Her name was Luise Obispo."

\*     \*     \*     \*     \*

He didn't have to turn his head. From the corner of his eye, he could see startlement flash across her face. She'd got her name right; and it was he who had erred in choosing a name.

"Putsyn hired a criminal, Dorn Starret, to get rid of her for him," he said harshly. "That was the way Starret made his living. He was an expert at it.

"Starret slugged her one night on Mars. He didn't retro her at once. He loaded her on a spaceship and brought her to Earth. During the passage, he talked to her and got to like her a lot. She wasn't as developed as she is now, kind of mousy maybe, but you know how those things are—he liked her. He made love to her, but didn't get very far.

"He landed in another city on Earth and left his spaceship there; he drugged her and brought her to the Shelter here and retroed her. That's what he'd been paid to do.

"Then he decided to stick around. Maybe she'd change her mind after retrogression. He stayed in a Shelter just across from the one she was in. And he made a mistake. He hid the retro gun behind the screen.

"Putsyn came around to check up. He didn't like Starret staying there—a key word or a familiar face sometimes triggers the memory. He retroed Starret, who didn't have a gun he could get to in a hurry. Maybe Putsyn had planned to do it all along. He'd built up an airtight alibi when Luise disappeared, so that nobody would connect him with that—and who'd miss a criminal like Starret?

"Anyway, that was only part of it. He knew that people who've been retroed try to find out who they are, and that some of them succeed. He didn't want that to happen. So he put an advertisement in the paper that she'd see and answer. When she did, he began to use his machine on her, intending to take her from the present to the past and back again so often that her mind would refuse to accept anything, past or present.

"But he'd just started when Starret showed up, and he knew he had to get him too. So he pulled what looked like a deliberate slip and got Starret interested, intending to take care of both of them in the same way at the same time."

He leaned against the wall. It was over now and he knew what he could expect.

"That's all, but it didn't work out the way Putsyn wanted it. Starret was a guy who knew how to look after his own interests."

Except the biggest and most important one; there he'd failed.

Borgenese was tapping on the desk, but it wasn't really tapping—he was pushing buttons. A policeman came in and the counselor motioned to Putsyn: "Put him in the pre-trial cells."

"You can't prove it," said Putsyn. His face was sunken and frightened.

"I think we can," said the counselor indifferently. "You don't know the efficiency of our laboratories. You'll talk."

\*     \*     \*     \*     \*

When Putsyn had been removed, Borgenese turned. "Very good work, Luis. I'm pleased with you. I think in time you'd make an excellent policeman. Retro detail, of course."

Luis stared at him.

"Didn't you listen?" he said. "I'm Dorn Starret, a cheap crook."

In that mental picture of Starret he'd had, he should have seen it at once. Left-handed? Not at all—that was the way a man normally saw himself in a mirror. And in mirror images, the right hand becomes the left.

The counselor sat up straight, not gentle and easygoing any longer. "I'm afraid you can't prove that," he said. "Fingerprints? Will any of Starret's past associates identify you? There's Putsyn, but he won't be around to testify." He smiled. "As final evidence let me ask you this: when he offered you a share in his crooked scheme, did you accept? You did not. Instead, you brought him in, though you thought you were heading into certain retrogression."

Luis blinked dazedly. "But—"

"There are no exceptions, Luis. For certain crimes there is a prescribed penalty, retrogression. The law makes no distinction as to how the penalty is applied, and for a good reason. If there was such a person, Dorn Starret ceased to exist when Putsyn retroed him—and not only legally."

Counselor Borgenese stood up. "You see, retroing a person wipes him clean of almost everything he ever knew—*right and wrong*. It leaves him with an adult body, and we fill his mind with adult facts. Given half a chance, he acts like an adult."

Borgenese walked slowly to stand in front of his desk. "We protect life. Everybody's life. *Including those who are not yet victims.* We don't have the death penalty and don't want it. The most we can do to anyone is give him a new chance, via retrogression. We have the same penalty for those who deprive another of his memory as we do for those who kill—with this difference: the man who retrogresses another knows he has a good chance to get away with it. The murderer is certain that he won't.

"That's an administrative rule, not a law—that we don't try to trace retrogression victims. It channels anger and greed into non-destructive acts. There are a lot of unruly emotions floating around, and as long as there are, we have to have a safety valve for them. Retrogression is the perfect instrument for that."

Luise tried to speak, but he waved her into silence.

"Do you know how many were killed last year?" he asked.

Luis shook his head.

"Four," said the counselor. "Four murders in a population of sixteen billion. That's quite a record, as anyone knows who reads Twentieth Century mystery novels." He glanced humorously at Luis. "You did, didn't you?"

Luis nodded mutely.

Borgenese grinned. "I thought so. There are only three types of people who know about fingerprints today, historians and policemen being two. And I didn't think you were either."

Luise finally broke in. "Won't Putsyn's machine change things?"

"Will it?" The counselor pretended to frown. "Do you remember how to build it?"

"I've forgotten," she confessed.

"So you have," said Borgenese. "And I assure you Putsyn is going to forget too. As a convicted criminal, and he will be, we'll provide him with a false memory that will prevent his prying into the past.

"That's one machine we don't want until humans are fully and completely civilized. It's been invented a dozen times in the last century, and it always gets lost."

He closed his eyes momentarily, and when he opened them, Luise was looking at Luis, who was staring at the floor.

"You two can go now," he said. "When you get ready, there are jobs for both of you in my department. No hurry, though; we'll keep them open."

Luis left, went out through the long corridors and into the night.

*     *     *     *     *

She caught up with him when he was getting off the belt that had taken him back to the Shelters.

"There's not much you can say, I suppose," she murmured. "What can you tell a girl when she learns you've stopped just short of killing her?"

He didn't know the answer either.

They walked in silence.

She stopped at her dwelling, but didn't go in. "Still, it's an indication of how you felt—that you forgot your own name and took mine." She was smiling now. "I don't see how I can do less for you."

Hope stirred and he moved closer. But he didn't speak. She might not mean what he thought she did.

"Luis and Luise Obispo," she said softly. "Very little change for me—just add Mrs. to it." She was gazing at him with familiar intensity. "Do you want to come in?"

She opened the door.

Crime was sometimes the road to opportunity, and retrogression could be kind.

# The Deadly Ones

Originally Published In *Fantastic Universe*,
July 1954

*Rathsden. I'm sure the name means nothing to you. There are legends, of course—from old Germany and the greater Reich, colonial America even. But you can't prove anything very damaging or concrete with legends. And even when the story is otherwise correct, I've been careful to keep my name out of it. A clever person shuns publicity, though it may involve tampering with history. For all practical purposes the name Rathsden is unknown. I want it kept that way.*

# THE DEADLY ONES

I can't remember when the inspiration came. Probably it had lain for a long time dormant in the back of my mind, like a mole hibernating in midwinter. Warmed by the proper circumstances, it emerged at last in its full vigor to claim my attention.

I've always worked hard, but lately what I got out of my efforts you couldn't call a living. The Red Cross was largely responsible. You could never get me to say a good word for that agency—ever.

Still, I have made use of them, and in this case they made their contribution, though it was an unwitting one.

I gave the idea careful thought. From the beginning I knew I needed help. I'm not superhuman, not in the strict sense, thought I suppose I could give a good account of myself against Wells' Invisible Man, homo superior, or a new crop of mutants that will spring up some day soon.

I needed help, and I carried the problem to a council of my fellows. We discussed it thoroughly, and in the end, though they didn't give me their blessing, they consented to aid me.

The problem was the flying saucers, or rather how to force one to land. We debated the matter for a long time, but there didn't seem to be any way to do it. No jet could keep up with a saucer and present rockets were equally inadequate. Besides, we didn't have access to any of these machines.

Someone in the back of the council whose name I didn't catch suggested that if we couldn't force one to land, perhaps we could lure one down. It didn't matter how, as long as it remained on the ground for an hour or so, with its ports open. The rest would be up to me.

"Fine," I said. "What do you propose?"

"They're investigating, you know," he said, "in the western part of the country. Rocket bases, atom bomb sites, anything that indicates advanced technology. Let's give them another menace."

"Sounds good. What are they interested in?" He was a hard fellow to locate, and I didn't try to visualize his face. He came from Ireland, I believe.

"A spaceship," he said. "A very formidable creation, with an incredible drive."

There was nothing wrong with the basic concept. The ship wouldn't be real, of course. It would merely seem real from the air. We could accomplish that.

As for the drive, we could manage that too. In a little-investigated part of the spectrum we could create a low and steady output, suggesting that the drive was idling, ready for instant takeoff.

None of this was impossible for us.

We? Have I said that we're not human? We've existed for a long time on earth besides *Homo sapiens*, and he has only guessed that we are here. The ordinary limitations of man don't apply to us.

A few of us working together could create an illusionary spaceship, and an intriguing drive to go with it. This was something flying saucers couldn't resist. They'd come down when they found they couldn't investigate from their customary high-level flights.

I nodded at the fellow I couldn't see. "Excellent. However, when the saucer lands you'll have to maintain the illusion. Logistics are involved too."

"That's easy," he said. "But what if it isn't manned by robots as you've assumed? You can get inside all right, but a living creature will discover you."

I looked at the blank spot where I thought he might be. "Really, now. It *has* to be a robot. No living creature, except for us, can stand the accelerations we've observed."

"But what if we're wrong?" he persisted.

"In that case we'll have time for one quick look," I said. "If it *is* living and we're no match for it, we'll run like hell."

There was general laughter and the fellow raised no further objections. For all I know, he went home. The meeting broke up and everyone except a few volunteers left. We continued to discuss ways and means.

When the plans seemed foolproof, I got up. "Just a minute," another fellow I didn't recognize interposed. "Suppose everything works the way you say it will. The saucer lands, and we succeed in getting inside. What makes you think it will go back to the home planet?"

"Don't overlook our fake spaceship," I said. "If the robot investigator from the saucer found a real spaceship, that would be important information. It would be important enough to warrant a quick trip back to the local base, wherever that may be situated.

"But when the robot can't locate anything, in spite of the instruments, it will be dealing with top *priority* stuff. Logically it will report back to the prime evaluation center, on the home planet. I think I'm safe in anticipating a short journey."

"I hope so." He shook his head dubiously. "But what about us? We don't have to worry about humans, and probably those things out there haven't come close enough to learn about us. But they're pretty advanced. What if they should?"

"You think they can detect us when we're dematerialized?" I smiled. "Don't be naïve. Anyway, nothing risked, you know."

I shouldn't have said that. I talk too much. "Nothing gained." He completed the sentence for me. He didn't look altruistic. "Just what do we stand to gain?"

The others hadn't thought of it, and neither had I from, that angle. I ad-libbed. "It's not been good here lately. There's too many factors against us, agencies that I don't have to mention."

"Feast or famine, mostly the last. And what are we going to do after an atomic war, when the mutants come along? Are you sure we can compete with them? As bad as it is now, it can get worse." I paused to let the dire predictions sink in.

"Someone has to do it, and I intend to be the one to find new worlds for us," I said.

My confidence impressed the others, but not the heckler. "I can see that you'll find it for yourself. But how are you going to let us know?"

"Just now I can't communicate from here to Philadelphia," I said. "It's a harassing business, merely trying to stay alive. Here I haven't time to practice mental communication. But there the conditions will be ideal and I expect to develop myself so that I can reach out anywhere in the galaxy."

Objectively that was true. Subjectively I could have changed my mind about sharing my prize. They didn't think of that and I didn't mention it.

The last objection was silenced. They went about their preparations and I about mine.

\* \* \* \* \*

We set up the decoy in Illinois. No real reason, I suppose, except that most of us are allergic to the desert, the logical place to build a spaceport and ships. Deserts are hot, dry and bright, and there are few humans there. In our own way we're fond of men, though they may not think so.

Illinois it was, and if there was a note of incongruity in it, so much the better. A spaceship looked strange in the middle of the flat cornfields? Very well, it did. Let the robot investigator find out why it was there.

The creation was not difficult. There was a haze in the air and the fields were green, and the spaceship pointed a sleek nose towards the sky. It was impalpable from below. A farmer plowed right through the stern tubes without knowing they were there. An inconvenience only, we blacked him out as seen from above. The farmhouse we converted into a control tower and the barn became a disembarkation structure.

There were side manifestations, of course. Dogs growled uneasily and barked, then ran and hid in the woods. Roosters could not crow not hens lay eggs. Milk curdled, in cows and cans, and all the butter turned rancid. Unfortunately we don't often use our entire minds—and when we do there are peripheral effects. However, no human in the area noticed us, and life went on pretty much as usual.

Radio reception was poor all over North America, and television was disrupted for a thousand miles, The disruption was deliberately planned. We had to attract the attention of the saucers, and that was the easiest way to do it. The radiation was supposed to represent a power leak from out hypothecated interstellar drive.

They came the second night, and it was good that they did. The strain was telling on everyone in the project. It's not easy to keep up such a big illusion.

The flight of saucers wheeled across the sky, lights out and undoubtedly ready for action. They had located us all right, and the wanted to see just what it was we had. But they couldn't find out from the air no matter how many times they passed over.

It must have been quite a jolt. They had earth all pegged down to the last improvement in a self-locking nut. And suddenly here was something new which didn't belong.

Toward midnight, with five of them still skimming the clouds, the sixth came down. I was ready, and had everything I needed with me. The saucer landed in a field half a mile away. The vegetation burned invisibly where it settled. A section of the saucer opened, and a much littler saucer came out.

The little saucer was a robot. I was sure of that the instant I saw it, mostly because it had wheels. There is nothing to indicate that a life form can't have wheels, but it does pose a nice problem of what a living creature will use for bearings. It was a robot, then and it came out and headed for our ship, which was still holding together splendidly, needle nose pointing at the sky.

It was time for me to go to work. I started toward the big saucer.

"It's coming closer." This was the thought of the individual who had created the ship out of his own dematerialized atoms.

"Put out a force field and keep it away." He sounded shaky and I thought a wry jest would help, The containers I was carrying were heavy.

The ship snorted. "I wish I could. But seriously, how long do I have to stay here?"

"Keep it up," I said. "I've got lots of supplies."

The terror in his voice was real. "I don't like that thing. It's snooping around."

"Waken the farmer. Maybe he'll kick up a disturbance and the robot will investigate.

With a shotgun the farmer couldn't do much, but a lucky shot might put a wheel out of commission. The robot wouldn't like that.

"I can't make the farmer open his eyes. The saucer put him to sleep and I can't touch his mind."

The saucers had a good brand of hypnotism, if that's what it was. We knew they had space travel and now it was evident that they were equally advanced in other ways.

"Use your judgment," I told the ship. "Hold it as long as you can and then pretend to go out into space, or forward in time. Anything that will look good."

I needed time. I could have dematerialized where I stood, and rematerialized inside the saucer. But if I did, I would have to leave most of the supplies behind. A short journey, I had said. And that was true—short as far as interstellar distances are concerned. But it would be long by normal methods of reckoning, and I had to live through it. I couldn't abandon my supplies.

I succeeded in transporting all the food to a place just outside the large saucer before out ship disappeared. It didn't go out into space, nor into time as I expected. Instead it sank rapidly into the ground, and left no hole behind. This, I think, confused the robot. I heard it thrashing around in the cornfield, possibly in bewilderment.

I gathered some of the containers and carried them inside the saucer. It was lighted all right, and the lighting scheme was as weird as the interior. They used the spectrum below the red and above the violet. Why this should be so I don't know. I merely report what I found. Apparently they didn't react to what we consider visible light.

I adjusted my eyes.

I found an empty space which I assumed was for the storage of specimens. I put my food I there. Outside I went for more, and then back again. I repeated my trips until everything was loaded. Unpalatable food, of course, concentrated and not tasty, but it would last until I stepped out on the planet at the opposite end. After that there would be other problems.

I went outside for the last communication with my fellows. The ship I could examine later. I looked around. The control tower and disembarkation structure were still visible, though they were wavering in the dim light.

"Are you there?" I thought.

"I am." The control tower thought back. "I wish I wasn't."

"It's just a robot," I said reassuringly. "It's not interested in a building."

"Maybe not," conceded the control tower. "But it's inside examining sleeping people. I wish it would go away."

He was losing control of himself and that didn't suit my purpose. "It's just a machine. Hold on for a little longer."

He held on.

The robot left the illusionary control tower and headed toward the saucer. For a squat ungainly contrivance it covered the distance in an amazing fashion. I had barely time to get inside before it rumbled into the saucer. It was carrying something. We took off before I could see what it was.

We left earth smoothly, though any kind of takeoff would have suited me. Inertia had never been my problem. Neither was the possibility that the robot would discover me. I was certain tI didn't register on light-sensitive cells, and I had other tricks I could use if I had to.

The robot had tentacles I hadn't noticed before because they had been retracted. They weren't retracted now, and they held a farmer. He was unconscious.

The robot was monkeying around with the farmer, but it was hardly the time to interfere. Needles stabbed the farmer in several places. Withdrawing the blood and storing it, probably inside the robot.

The first needle were jerked out, and replaced by others. Again this was logical: pumping a fluid into the farmer's veins with the intent of suspending the life force until they reached the home planet.

The whole procedure made sense. When the robot couldn't find the spaceship it had taken someone in the vicinity for questioning. They'd be surprised what they'd learn from the farmer, though. Absolutely nothing! We had protected ourselves too well. The farmer's ordeal had no bearing on the success of my enterprise. Nevertheless I became slightly ill at the waste involved.

The robot dropped the farmer in a place similar to the one in which I had hidden my supplies. Then it crouched down and became motionless, waiting. There was nothing for it to do.

Nor for myself, either. We were out of the atmosphere and on our way.

                    *       *       *       *       *

The journey was six months of monotony. Avoiding the robot was easy because it didn't move. The ship was all mine but I couldn't make use of it. I puttered around, but there was nothing much to learn. The drive was in operation, and as long as it was, I couldn't get close. I had no idea of what it was or how it worked, but the force that surrounded it was, for me at least, and absolute barrier.

The rest of the saucer was equally confounding. There were several low-ceilinged compartments which held instruments at whose functions I could not guess. There were no star charts anywhere, but I had to assume the ship knew where it was going.

Whatever our destination, we were approaching it faster than light. Occasionally I looked out of the vision ports, and what I saw didn't resemble suns, though of course they were. It was the light shift which changed their appearance.

One day the saucer gave a lurch and we were simultaneously below the speed of light, and near our goal. Dead ahead was a multiple star system. Where it lay in relation to Earth I don't know. Within fifty to a thousand light-years I suppose.

For the first time in months the robot stirred, went to the farmer and began to work on him. I kept out of the way. It seemed the sensible thing to do. No matter how often I looked, I couldn't determine the location of the planet toward which we were bound. The ship knew, but I was in ignorance.

From behind, in the next compartment, came the labored sounds of the robot. Then there was another sound and it didn't come from the robot. I looked in. The farmer sat up, gazed around, understood some or little of what he saw. That understanding was enough for him. He collapsed. He was still breathing, though; in spasmodic gasps.

The revivification was a complete success. I decided to keep the man in mind. He was an important source of reserve strength.

My hopes leapt high when I saw the planet. It was something less than the size of Saturn, but much larger than Earth. It was large enough to support a tremendous population. I hadn't bargained for anything so good.

I had only a vague plan to go by. I had made the journey in complete safety, and that was important. My next move would depend on circumstances. I could dematerialize myself off the ship, and onto the planet. With an extreme expenditure of energy I could even take the remainder of my food supply with me.

But it didn't seem to be worth the effort. I had done all right so far by remaining quiet, and letting events occur as they would. I decided to see it through on the same basis. I stayed in the ship, and let it land.

That was not my first mistake, landing with the ship, If anything, the error began a thousand years earlier, in my infancy, the first night I saw the light of the moon. No one asked me to come. I did it voluntarily, for reasons my total personality found acceptable. In my own mind I added up the advantages in leaving Earth, and then schemed until I found a way to do it.

I had been dissatisfied with the way things were going among men. I objected to blood spilled uselessly. And so I had contrived to escape. Greener pastures? Not exactly. I don't like salads. Still the saying conveys something of the way I felt. Long before the ship landed it was too late, though I didn't know it.

*     *     *     *     *

The robot scurried about the saucer, chirruping mechanically and creaking. When it finished the duties it picked up the farmer, and carried him out. The man was still unconscious, but he began to scream.

Soon after it left, other robots came into the ship. Slightly different from the kind I had seen, they must have been repair robots. They went about tasks that were unfamiliar to me, and they talked.

This was new. I couldn't understand what they said until I found the speech center of one, and let my mind reach out, lightly.

"A master says there is a stowaway on one of the ships."

It was unforeseen. Nothing I had encountered could detect my existence without registering on my consciousness. These *masters* were going to be tougher than humans. I waited while the other replied.

"Do they know what ship he's on?"

My robot waved a tentacle. "There are ten thousand ships here, each waiting for a checkover before reassignment. Would you bother to search each ship?"

"Physically, you mean?" asked the other. "No. They will take him off as the ship leaves."

Getting me off was going to take some doing, though the *masters* didn't know it. They had gauged humans correctly, but they hadn't met me. Nevertheless I was uneasy.

"Why does he stay on the ship?" asked my robot.

The other chuckled. "Maybe he changed his mind, and wants to go home. He'll be surprised when he learns where he's bound for."

I'll admit I panicked then—because a robot chuckled. It's not the friendly sound you might think. And also because of what it said. I had no intention of going home, but I liked to think I could if I wanted to. Now I saw that, due to their system of rotating assignments, it was next to impossible to determine which ship was going back to Earth. I made up my mind quickly.

Several things happened simultaneously. I dematerialized myself where I was, and rematerialized tenuously inside the robot. At the same time I took control of its motor and brain centers.

I forced it away from the job, and commanded it to go to the storage space where the last of my food was hidden. The other robot didn't notice. I surmised they didn't take orders from each other but from someone above. For the moment *I* was above.

Out of the ship we went, and into the confusion of the repair shops. Nothing but ships and robots, and I'd had enough of these.

I needed a hiding place to rest, and plan my forays against the creatures of this planet. I rummaged hurriedly through the robot brain, and learned that we were near the edge of a large city. Without cataloguing all the information I received, I forced the robot through obscure alleys toward the open plain surrounding the city.

It was cramped and uncomfortable inside the robot even though I didn't exist as solid matter. And I had to operate blind. I couldn't adjust my sight to that of the robot, and had to function once removed from reality, through its incomplete senses.

The last alley we entered ended on the open plain. The robot rolled down it—and stopped. I couldn't see what was in front of us, but I could guess—one of the creatures of the planet, the things that made the flying saucers. Without hesitation I directed the robot to attack,

It didn't.

Its refusal was not unexpected. They would have been quite insane to build robots without installing some safeguards. It meant, however that the next step was up to me. I took it.

I dematerialized out of the robot and rematerialized facing my antagonist. On the average it takes me a few microseconds to evaluate a foe, and find his weakness. I looked longer than that. It was the first time I had seen anything that could destroy at a glance my confidence in my own survival capacity.

And there was no weakness.

*     *     *     *     *

What I did then was not cowardice, it was pure survival, the reaction of a nervous system shocked to the limits of endurance. I dematerialized myself from where I stood and rematerialized far out on the open plain. Twice I repeated the process until the city was out of sight over the horizon. The creature didn't follow, though it could have done so easily enough—if it had wanted to.

I know my strength. On Earth it's the source of legends—the shadowy half-believed stories of werewolves and vampires. Fact and fancy mixed together to chill the minds and hearts of men. For myself, and others like me, it's a distinct advantage to have our existence doubted. A victim paralyzed with fear, too shocked and demoralized to cry out, is easier to subdue.

But the strength I was so confident of is meaningless here. Crouched in the shadow of the boulder, the only shade on the arid plain, it suddenly dawned on me that the creatures who rule this planet knew about me from the beginning, when I thought I was hidden. It amused them I think.

I can't go back to the city and find the farmer. He's their meat. And I have limitations. I can't dematerialize myself off this planet. A few drops of fluid are left in the container with the Red Cross stamp on it, my last link with Earth.

I was born knowing the facts of *my* life. For a thousand years I've taken my food where and how I could get it. But these creatures are different, not only in body chemistry. They are tougher than Teflon skin and have hydrofluoric acid in their veins. I've always killed for food, but they—kill for pleasure. And their appearance exactly coincides with their character. I ought to know.

But there's one escape they forgot about, and I will take it. When they come hunting, they won't find me. Self-destruction is preferable to meeting those horrors face to face again.

# THE IMPOSSIBLE VOYAGE HOME

ILLUSTRATED BY DICK FRANCIS
ORIGINALLY PUBLISHED IN *GALAXY SCIENCE FICTION*,
AUGUST 1954

*The right question kept getting the wrong answer—
but old Ethan and Amantha got the right answer
by asking the wrong question!*

# THE IMPOSSIBLE VOYAGE HOME

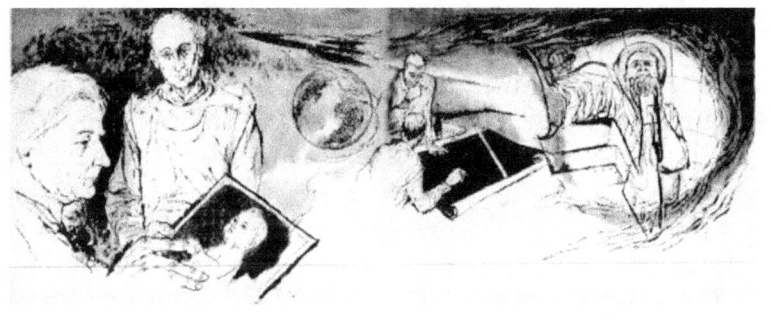

"Space life expectancy has been increased to twenty-five months and six days," said Marlowe, the training director. "That's a gain of a full month."

*Millions of miles from Earth, Ethan also looked discontentedly proud. "A mighty healthy-looking boy," he declared.*

Demarest bent a paperweight ship until it snapped. "It's something. You're gaining on the heredity block. What's the chief factor?"

"Anti-radiation clothing. We just can't make them effective enough."

*Across space, on distant Mars, Amantha reached for the picture. "How can you tell he ain't sickly? You can't see without glasses."*

*Ethan reared up. "Jimmy's boy, ain't he? Our kids were always healthy, 'specially the youngest. Stands to reason their kids will be better."*

*"Now you're thinking with your forgettery. They were all sick, one time or another. It was me who took care of them, though. You always could find ways of getting out of it." Amantha touched the chair switch.*

The planets whirled around the Sun. Earth crept ahead of Mars, Venus gained on Earth. The flow of ships slackened or spurted forth anew, according to what destination could be reached at the moment:

"A month helps," said Demarest. "But where does it end? You can't enclose a man completely, and even if you do, there still is the air he breathes and food he eats. Radiation in space contaminates everything the body needs. And part of the radioactivity finds its way to the reproductive system."

*     *     *     *     *

Marlowe didn't need to glance at the charts; the curve *was* beginning to flatten. Mathematically, it was determinable when it wouldn't rise at all. According to analysis, Man someday might be able to endure the radiation encountered in space as long as three years, if exposure times were spaced at intervals.

But that was in the future.

"There's a lot you could do," he told Demarest. "Shield the atomics."

"Working on it," commented Demarest. "But every ounce we add cuts down on the payload. The best way is to get the ship from one place to another faster. It's time in space that hurts. Less exposure time, more trips before the crew has to retire. It adds up to the same thing."

*On Mars, Amantha fondled the picture. "Pretty. But it ain't real." She laid it aside.*

*Ethan squinted at it. "I could make you think it was. Get it enlarged, solidified. Have them make it soft, big as a baby. You could hold it in your lap."*

*"Outgrew playthings years ago." Amantha adjusted the chair switch, but the rocking motion was no comfort.*

*Ethan turned the picture over, face down. "Nope. Hate to back you up, 'Mantha, but it ain't the same. There's nothing like a baby, wettin' and squallin' and smilin', stubborn when it oughtn't to be and sweet and gentle when you don't expect it. Robo-dolls don't fool anybody who's ever held the real thing."*

In the interval, Earth had drawn ahead. The gap between the two planets was widening.

"That's another fallacy," objected the training director. "The body can stand just so much acceleration. We're near the limit. What good are faster ships?"

"That's your problem," said Demarest. "Get me tougher crewmen. Young, afraid of nothing, able to take it."

It always ended here—younger, tougher, the finest the race produced—and still not good enough. And after years of training, they had twenty-five months to function as spacemen. It was a precious thing, flight time, and each trip was as short as science could make it. Conjunction was the magic moment for those who went between the planets.

It was the heredity block that kept Man squeezed, confined to Earth, Mars and Venus, preventing him from ranging farther. The heredity block was a racial quantity, the germ plasm, but not just that. Crew and passengers were protected as much as possible from radiation encountered in space and that which originated in the ship's drive. The protection wasn't good enough. Prolonged exposure had the usual effects, sterilization or the production of deformed mutations.

Man was the product of evolution on a planet. He didn't step out into space without payment.

\*    \*    \*    \*    \*

The radiation that damaged genes and chromosomes and tinier divisions also struck nerve cells. Any atom might be hit, blazing, into fission and decaying into other elements. The process was complicated. The results were not: the nerve was directly stimulated, producing aural and visual hallucinations.

Normally, the hallucination was blanked out. But as the level of body radioactivity increased, so did the strength of the vision. It dominated consciousness. The outside world ceased to have meaning.

The hallucination took only one form, a beautiful woman outside the ship, unclad and beckoning.

It was the image of vanished fertility that appeared once the person was incapable of reproducing *as a human.*

Why this was so hadn't been determined. Psychologists had investigated and learned only that it invariably occurred after too great exposure. There was another thing they learned. No, that had come first. This was the reason they had investigated.

In the Solar System, the greatest single source of radiation, including the hard rays, was the Sun. It was natural that the siren image should seem stronger in that direction, that it should fade or retreat toward its origin. No one had ever returned from compulsive pursuit of the illusionary woman, though in early days radio contact had been made with ships racing toward the Sun.

The heredity block was self-enforcing.

Deviously, the race protected itself, or something higher watched over it to assure *human* continuity. Marlowe wasn't sure which, but it was there.

"I think you're on the wrong track," he said. "Shield the ship completely and it won't matter how long the trip takes. The crew can work in safety."

Demarest grunted. "Some day we'll have an inertia-free drive and it won't matter how much mass we use. It does now. Our designs are a compromise. Both of us have to work with what's possible, not what we dream of. I'll build my ship; you find the right crew to man it."

Marlowe went back to his graphs. Machines could be changed, but the human body clung stubbornly to the old patterns. He couldn't select his crews any younger—but was there perhaps a racial type more resistant to radiation? Where? No place that he knew of. Maybe the biologists could produce one, he thought hopefully, and knew he was fooling himself. Human beings weren't fruit flies; by the time enough generations rolled around for the resistant strain to breed true— and leave a surplus to man the ships—he would be long dead and the problem solved.

The best of humanity would be dead, too, wiped out by sterilization.

Or the Solar System would be peopled by mutant monstrosities.

\*        \*        \*        \*        \*

Far away, and not concerned with the problem, Ethan shrugged resignedly. "Guess we'll have to get used to the idea— we just won't see him till he grows up—if we'll still be around."

"You've got years and years ahead of you, and not worth a thing the whole time!" Amantha snapped.

"Damnation," said Ethan wistfully, "I'd like to dandle him."

"Won't be the same when he grows up and comes here," Amantha conceded. "There I go agreein' with you! What's got into me?"

"Maybe we can get on the next slow ship. They run them once in a while for people with weak hearts." He considered. "Don't know whether Retired Citizens' Home will let us go, though."

"Retired Citizens!" She blew her nose scornfully. "They think we don't know it's just a home for the aged!" She threw away the tissue. "Think they'll let us?"

"It won't be them so much that'll stop us. Our hearts ain't too good and we haven't got much space time to use. We shouldn't have gone to Venus."

"We had to see Edith and Ed and their kids and we had to come back to Mars so we could be near John and Pearl and Ray. Let's not regret what we've done." She picked at the chair arm. "We've been here a long time, ain't we?"

Ethan nodded.

"Maybe they've forgotten we've only got a month left," she said eagerly.

"You sure it's a month?"

"Figure it out. It took longer when we went."

"Then it's no use. A slow ship is all we'd be allowed to take— and we wouldn't be allowed because it'd be more than a month."

"They won't remember every last minute we spent in space."

"They will, too," he stated. "They've got records."

"Maybe they lost them."

"Look, we've got kids and grandchildren here. They come around and see us. Do we have to go to Earth, 'specially when it'd be against the law?"

"That's just it," she argued. "We've seen all our other kids' kids. Ain't we going to see the youngest? How do we know his wife can take care of a baby? I can't sleep nights, thinking of it."

"Try catnaps during the day, like I do."

Amantha touched the button and the automatic chair stopped abruptly. "Are you going to try to get tickets or aren't you?"

"I'll think about it. Go ahead and rock."

"I won't," she said obstinately, "not even if it was the kind of chair you can rock yourself. I thought I married a man who'd make me happy."

"I've always done my best. Go ahead and rock."

"But will you try to get the tickets?"

Ethan nodded resignedly and felt better when the chair began to swing back and forth. There was no living with a woman when she didn't have peace of mind.

*     *     *     *     *

Amantha lay in bed, listening. Sometimes her hearing was very good, the way it used to be. Other times, it wasn't worth a thing. The way it came and went reminded her of when she was young and used to wonder why old folks couldn't hear. Now she could often lie next to Ethan and not even notice whether he was snoring. Tonight her hearing was good.

Footsteps came from the hall, creaky noises of someone trying not to make a sound. She'd lain awake many nights, hearing him come home. She knew who it was and for once she didn't mind. The Home for Retired Citizens had rules.

Careful, she thought. There's the bad spot where the floor's thin and bends when you step on it. Then when your foot comes off it, it goes ploinnnnng. They don't build right any more. Skimping and trying to save.

But there wasn't a sound. Ethan avoided it. When she thought of it, she realized he had a suspicious amount of skill— the skill of practice.

Ethan was fumbling at the door and she forgot her irritation. She slipped out of bed and swung the door open. He stumbled in against her. "'Mantha, they laughed—"

"Did you have anything to eat?" she broke in.

"Cup of that Mars coffee. But—"

"Don't talk till you get something hot inside. Empty belly, empty head."

"Can't eat stuff that comes out of the wall. I'll wait till breakfast."

She flicked the light on low and punched the selector. She took the glow-plate from under the bed and set it on the table.

As the food arrived, she heated it and began adding spices. "There—it ain't real food, but you can pretend."

Ethan pretended and, when the food was gone, wiped his lips and looked at her.

She nodded. "Now you can tell me—but keep your voice low. Don't wake anyone up."

Ethan stretched and creaked. "Went down to the Interplanet office and they wouldn't talk to me. Said there wasn't any ship leaving for the next ten months and they didn't sell tickets in advance. I kept pestering them and they got mad. They looked up our records and said we couldn't go anytime, except on a fast ship, and, considering our age, it was doubtful they'd let us. Didn't give up, though, and finally they said we might get a release from the man who'd take us. Maybe they wanted to get rid of me. Anyway, they sent me down to talk with one of the pilots."

*     *     *     *     *

Amantha approved. Go straight to the man responsible. Persistence could get you there.

"He talked real nice for a while," Ethan continued. "He explained he didn't own the ship and didn't have the say-so who he took. I knew you wanted to go real bad. I offered him the money we'd saved."

"*All* of it, Ethan?"

"Don't get mad. Figured it was worth it to you."

"Don't believe in paying extra," she mused, "but did you tell him we could borrow some if it wasn't enough?"

"Didn't get a chance. He started laughing, saying didn't I understand he got paid not just for each trip, but for all the years after that, when he was finished and had used up his time and couldn't work at the only thing he knew? Saying that he wouldn't risk that kind of security for any money and I was an idiot for believing he might." Ethan trembled.

"Never mind. He's an old fool."

"He's younger than Jimmy."

"Some people get wisdom when they're young."

Ethan sat morosely in the chair. "If Jimmy hadn't made that last trip, he'd be here and he'd have married a girl here and his kids would be here. We wouldn't have to worry about them."

"I guess so, but he was lucky anyway. They found out he wasn't as strong as he was supposed to be and wouldn't let him come back." She began clearing the dishes. "How'd they know he couldn't come back?"

"They got tests. They give them each trip."

She should have thought of it. They had tests. Because of tests, Jimmy was safe but distant. She sat down.

"Tired." Ethan yawned. "Let's go to bed."

"You go. I'm thinking."

Amantha went on thinking while he undressed and lay down. Sometimes it was difficult—things weren't as clear as they used to be. Tonight, though, she had no trouble managing her mind. A woman who had kids had to know her way around things. Presently, she said, "Tomorrow I'm going to bake."

Ethan stirred. "Won't do no good. Didn't say so, but there was a girl talking to the pilot when I got there. She was crying and begging him to take her to Earth next trip. Said she'd do anything if he would."

"Shame on her!" exclaimed Amantha. "But did it work?"

"She was young and pretty and still he wouldn't pay attention to her," said Ethan. "What chance would you have?"

"I'm going to bake tomorrow. In the morning, we're supposed to go for a walk. We'll take a big basket. Do you remember the old canal nobody goes near any more?"

There was no answer. Ethan was asleep. Now that she'd decided what to do, she lay down beside him.

\*     \*     \*     \*     \*

The sentry huddled in his post. It was insulated and supplied with oxygen, very much like a spacesuit. Though big for a spacesuit, it was a small place to spend hours in without relief. But there were compensations: never anything to do—except as now. He went to the mike.

"Get back," he shouted.

They paid no attention.

Swearing, he shouted again, turning up the volume. Even in the thin air, he had enough sound to blast them off their feet. But they kept on going. He poked the snout of his weapon through the porthole and then withdrew it. Who'd  given him those orders anyway? He didn't have to obey them. He clamped on his oxygen helmet and slipped into electric mitts and hurried outside.

"Where do you think you're going?" he demanded, standing in front of them.

"Hello," said Amantha. "Didn't see anyone around."

Damn senior citizens—they never used hearing aids. "You've got to turn around and go back," he said.

"Why?"

He was shivering and didn't see how they could stand it. Thin clothing and obsolete oxygen equipment. Oddly, they could take more than you'd think, though. Used to it, he supposed. "Come on in," he commanded gruffly. He wasn't going to freeze. They followed him into the post. "Didn't you see the signs to keep out?"

"But the ships aren't using the field. What harm are we doing?"

"Orders," he said. There were still a few pilots checking over their ships, making sure everything was in working condition before they were locked up. In a week, all flight personnel would be gone to the settlements, there to await the next round of voyages when Earth came near. They had it soft, while he, the guard, had to stay in cold discomfort.

"We're going to visit a friend of my son," said Amantha. "They were pilots together. Do you object?"

He didn't, but there were some who would. The order made sense with respect to little boys who would otherwise swarm over the field, falling off ships or getting stuck in rocket tubes.

"What have you got?" he asked, eying Amantha's parcel dubiously.

"I baked something." She opened a corner of the package and the smell drifted out. "Made it with Martian fruit. Not much of it around these days."

He sniffed and became hungry. That was queer—he'd eaten before coming on duty.

"Okay," he said. "You can go. Don't get caught or it's my neck." He stood closer to the old man and woman, and the package, too, and pointed out the window. "Act like you're leaving in case anyone's checking up. When you get near the line of ships, duck behind them and walk along until you find the right one. No one will see you except me."

Amantha pinched the package together. "I'd give you some, but I can't cut it before the pilot sees it."

"I guess you can't," said the sentry wistfully. "Maybe he won't eat all of it."

"May he won't. I'll bring you back what's left—if there *is* any left."

Long after they were gone, the sentry stood there, trying to analyze the indefinable odor. He was still standing there when the checkup squad marched in and arrested him for gross dereliction of duty.

*     *     *     *     *

"Go away," said the pilot, disappearing from the viewport. Ethan pounded on the hull with a rock. The pilot came back, twisting his face. "Stop it. I'll angle the rocket tubes around and squirt you with them."

Ethan raised the rock.

"Okay," said the pilot. "I'll talk to you, though I know what you want." Sullenly, he made the hatch swing open. He looked down at them. "All right, let's hear it."

"Got a present for you," said Ethan.

"Not allowed to take bribes unless it's money."

"Young man, where are your manners?" snapped Amantha.

"Haven't got any. It's the first thing they train out of you." The pilot started to jerk his head back, saw the rock and decided not to close the hatch. He glanced at the narrow ladder to the ground. "I'll take your present. Bring it up."

He stopped smirking as Amantha hitched up her skirts and, holding the package in one hand, swung up the ladder. Agile as goats and probably as sensible, he thought. He took hold of her as she neared the top.

"Grandma, you're too old to climb around. You'll break every brittle bone in your body if you fall."

"Ain't so brittle," said Amantha, making way for Ethan who had followed her. "My, it's cold!" She began shivering. "Invite us in to get warm."

"You can't go in. I'm busy. Hey, wait!" The pilot hurried after her into the control compartment.

Amantha was looking around when he arrived. "Cozy but kind of bare," she said. "Why don't you hang up pictures?"

"Most fabulous pictures you'll ever see are right there."

Amantha followed his glance. "Nothing but Mars. I can see that every day." She puzzled over it. "Oh, you're teasing an old woman. I didn't mean what you see out of the port, stars and planets and such. I'd want a picture of an Indian settin' on a horse."

"I'll bet!" muttered the pilot. "Get warm in a hurry. I've got work to do."

"You just go ahead," she said. "We'll set here and toast our toes. We don't aim to interfere."

"I'll stay," said the pilot hastily. "Let's have the present." He'd made a tactical error—he should have ignored the noise that went shimmering through the hull when the old man had pounded with a rock. No, it was nice to think he could have, but impossible. Patience was one of the things the aged did have and the young didn't.

Amantha set the package down. The pilot scrambled ahead of her and got the navigator's instruments off the desk and into the drawer.

She opened and displayed the contents.

"I baked it for you," she said. "It's a cake."

\*     \*     \*     \*     \*

He could see what it was. "Hate cake," he said. "Can't eat it."

"You'll eat this. Canalberry shortcake."

"Canalberry?" he asked, wrinkling his face. He smelled it and changed expressions in the middle of a wrinkle. Resolutely, he turned away from it and saw Ethan clearly, perhaps for the first time. It was the old man who had tried to bribe him a few days ago. They weren't as innocent as they seemed. What were they trying to do?

"Ain't you even going to taste it?" she urged.

He shuddered suspiciously. It smelled good, though he had told the truth about hating the stuff. Under other circumstances, he might have nibbled at a piece for politeness' sake.

"Can't. Doctor's orders."

"Diabetic? Didn't think they let them in space-service," said Amantha. "Funny, it's the same with Ethan. He can't eat sweets, either." She looked at her creation. "Seems a shame to bring it so far to somebody who can't touch it. Do you mind if I cut myself a slice?"

"Go ahead, Grandma."

"Amantha," she corrected him and brought out a knife and two small plates. He wondered if there was any significance. *Two* plates.

She laid a slice on the plate and poked at it with a fork that was also in the package. She put the fork down and picked up the cake.

"It don't taste right unless you eat it the way it was meant to be," she said.

He watched her in anguish. His nose quivered and his stomach rumbled. He shouldn't have let them in.

A crumb fell to the floor and Amantha reached for it. She straightened up, a berry in her hand.

"Canalberries," she said. "They're nearly all gone. Used to be you could hardly go anywhere without stepping in them."

She crushed the berry and the rich aroma swept devastatingly through the air.

"Sure you won't have some?" she asked, slicing the cake and placing it in front of him. When he finished that, he cut another, and another, until the cake was gone.

The pilot settled logily in a chair and dozed off. Amantha and Ethan watched him in silence.

The pilot got up and began to stretch lazily without seeming to notice them. The laziness disappeared and the stretch changed into a jerk that seemed to elongate his body. He sprang out of the compartment and went leaping down the corridor. When he came to the hatch, he didn't hesitate. The ladder was too slow. He jumped.

He landed on the sand, sinking in to his knees. He extricated himself and went bounding over the field.

"Never saw canalberries take so long," muttered Amantha. "Don't know what's wrong. Nothing's as good as it used to be."

She shook off her hat and closed the airlock.

"You don't need those nose plugs any more, Ethan. Come on, let's see if you remember."

*    *    *    *    *

Several hours later, she twirled unfamiliar knobs and, by persistence and beginner's luck, managed to get the person she wanted.

"You the commander?" Since he had a harassed look, she assumed he was. "Thought you might be worried about that poor boy."

"Madam, what do you want?" He scowled at the offscreen miscreant who had mistakenly summoned him. "I'm chasing criminals. I haven't got time to chat about old times."

"Don't sass me. I thought you might want to know how to stop that poor boy from running around."

The commander sat down. "What young man?" he asked calculatingly.

"Don't know his name," said Amantha. "He ran out of the ship before we could ask him."

"So *you're* the poisoner," said the commander coldly. "If he dies, neither your age nor your sex will make any difference."

"Just canalberries," Amantha assured him. "Reckon you wouldn't know about them."

"What are you talking about?"

"Canalberries. Used to be lots of them. Males, men and animals, just can't help eating them. Don't bother women or any other kind of females. Biologists used to tell us it was a seed-scattering device. Guess so. Won't hurt him none. Try bicarb and vinegar. It'll fix him up."

"For your sake, I hope it will!" said the commander. "He's in a bad way." He stabbed a pencil at her and his voice became stern. "If you follow directions, I'm sure I can get you off lightly."

"Think we will?" said Amantha.

The commander hurried on. "It's hard to find a ship in space. Stay where you are or, if you can, turn around and come back—*slowly*. We'll send a ship up and transfer a competent pilot to bring you down. Do you hear?"

"Real plain. You got good radios on these ships."

He smothered a growl. "Your lives are in danger. We're not going to chase out and rescue you unless you cooperate." It was an understatement. If they observed radio silence, search ships would never find them. They might not think of it, but he wouldn't bet. They were smart enough to steal the ship.

There was another thing. From what he'd learned from records, they were close to the exposure limit. Any moment now, they might go berserk, turning their course fatally toward the Sun. He had to be careful what he said.

"We'll get you out of this, but only if you help. I refuse to sacrifice men and waste their flight time, which is more precious than any ship, merely to save two senile incompetents. Is this clear?"

"I suppose," said Amantha. "We've got to go home."

The commander rubbed his hands. They weren't as stubborn as he feared. He'd rescue them.

"Good. I'll have men aloft in a few minutes."

"Guess it was you who didn't hear," she said. "Our home is on Earth."

## II

"There's no one here," said the robot blocking the door.

"We'll wait." Amantha tried to go inside. The robot wouldn't move.

It was dark and windy and, from the steps, they could see lights of houses glowing around them. Not many—it was near the edge of the little town. Farther away, over the hill, the ship nestled safely in a valley. No one had seen them land. They were sure of it.

Ethan removed his hat and his bent shoulders straightened. He seemed to grow taller.

"Rain," he said in awe. "Thirty years and yet I haven't forgotten what it's like."

"It's wet, that's what it's like," said Amantha. "Robot, let us in or I'll have Ethan take a wrench to you. He loves to tinker."

"I can't be threatened. My sole concern is the welfare of my charge. Also, I'm too large for any human to hurt me."

"Damnation, I'm soppin'!" complained Ethan. "It's better to remember the rain than to be in it."

"Wait till my son Jimmy gets back. He'll be ravin'. Makin' us stay out here and get soaked."

"Son? Is the Jimmy you refer to Pilot James Huntley?"

"Ex-pilot."

"Correct. But he's not at home. He took his wife to the hospital half an hour ago."

"So soon?" gasped Amantha. "Thought I taught him better than that. Women have got to rest between kids."

"It's not another child," said the robot with disinterest. "It has to do with one of the ills flesh is heir to and machines are not. Nothing serious."

Ethan fidgeted, turning up his collar. Water began flowing from the eaves. "Stop arguin' and let us in. Jimmy will turn off your juice when he finds you've kept his folks outside."

"Folks? He has none here. A mother and father living happily on Mars. They died quite recently, lost in space and plunging into the Sun."

"Make up your mind," Amantha said peevishly. "We ain't on Mars, we weren't happy and we didn't get lost and plunge into the Sun."

"I merely repeat—in sequence—the information I'm given or overhear. If it's inconsistent, so are humans. I'm used to it."

"'Mantha, they think we're dead," said Ethan. He wiped a raindrop away. "Poor Jimmy!"

A thin wail came from a crack in the door. The robot's eyes shone briefly, then dimmed.

"What's that?" asked Amantha. "Sounds like a baby. Thought you said no one was home."

"No responsible adult. Only a child. Because of that, I can admit no one except the parents—or a doctor if I decide one is needed." The robot whirred and drew itself up. "He's absolutely safe. I'm a Sitta."

"You sure are. Now get out of my way before I jab you. The kid's crying."

"He is, but it's no concern of yours. I'm better acquainted with infant behavior than any human can be. The pathetic sob merely means that the child wants attention. I was given no instructions to hold him."

*     *     *     *     *

Again the child cried. "Who needs to be told?" demanded Amantha. "Nobody gives grandmothers instructions."

"He's got a grandfather to cuddle him," added Ethan. "How far do you think we came to do it?"

"And he's not cryin' because he wants attention. Something's stickin' him and he's hungry. Don't you think a grandmother would know?"

"There's nothing that can stick him, but if, by accident, something sharp had gotten in his bed and if he were also hungry, he would sound like this." The Sitta hunched down and swiveled its head, giving an imitation. "You see? I do nothing but watch babies. It's built into me."

Inside the house, the child's tone changed, became querulous, listening. Interrogatively, it offered a single yowl.

"My analysis was correct. It wanted attention. The parents left so hurriedly, they forgot to give me permission. When I didn't come to investigate, the child stop—"

The wail burst forth with renewed vigor.

The robot rotated its head and the alert look flashed on and off. It stuttered, "I know w-what I'm doing. But I—I can tell only what has happened to my charge, n-never what *will*!" The Sitta rumbled bewilderedly. "Anticipation is beyond my capacity. The child *is* hurt and hungry. Please come in and help me."

Triumphantly, Amantha followed the robot into the house toward the nursery. She whispered to Ethan, "Sittas ain't smart. I reckon he never heard a bunch of babies together. If one cries, they all do."

The Sitta barred the path. "You seem sincere and are obviously an expert. But before you go in, understand this— attempt no harm to the being in there. I'm linked."

"You'll be unlinked if you don't stop acting balky," warned Amantha. She ducked under his arm and darted toward the crib.

"By linked, I mean that if anything happens that I require aid to handle, an alarm rings in Sittas Circle and help is on the way. Meanwhile, I can put out fires or carry him unharmed through concrete walls."

"Go ahead, run through a wall," invited Amantha abstractly, snatching up the child. "The darling's wet, too. Fetch me a diaper."

The robot fetched at her command. And when the child was quiet, even cooing, but with a sharp undertone of protest, Amantha settled back. "Now we've got to feed him."

"They didn't give me special instructions and I can't originate. If you hadn't come, I'd have had to contact a doctor."

Amantha handed the child to Ethan. "You hold him." She went into the kitchen.

Ethan tossed the child up. "Here we go," he bellowed. "Free fall. Got to start early to make a spaceman out of you." The Sitta stared at them, puzzled, as the infant shrieked with fear or joy. "Now if only Jimmy was here to see us," said Ethan, grinning proudly.

Jimmy didn't come back soon enough. The police arrived first.

*     *     *     *     *

Ethan wandered to the window. The ground was far below. He didn't want to think of what was outside the door.

"Don't mind jail myself—been in a few." He looked at Amantha. "Just for raising hell. Never thought I'd be responsible for putting *you* behind bars."

"It wasn't you," said Amantha, her back straightening. "Curious about it myself." Wisps of hair straggled over her face. "I mean why didn't we think of it on Mars? Didn't we know what they'd do?"

"I guess we didn't." Ethan cracked his knuckles contemplatively. "Did it occur to you?"

"No. I can't understand." She frowned, but it didn't help clarify what she was thinking about.

"We're criminals," said Ethan soberly. "Thieves."

"I don't mind for us. Jail's not much worse than the home for Retired Citizens. It's our grandson I'm thinking of."

"Don't worry. They won't do a thing to him." His eyes widened and he wiped off the sweat. "Oh. I see what you mean."

"Jailbirds," said Amantha. "We'll still be in here when he grows up. It's a fine way to help your kin. They'll never trust him with us in his family."

"Jailbirds," repeated Ethan mournfully. By some magic, his face cracked along the wrinkles and broke into a smile. "But once we flew," he whispered to himself.

The door opened and an official of some sort came in. Outside, Ethan caught a brief glimpse of guards.

Marlowe, chief training director of space pilots for Interplanet Transport, Inc., walked in silence across the room and eased tiredly into a chair behind the desk. He'd gotten the news late at night, having been the first one contacted. The ship that had been lost had showed up in the atmosphere. There couldn't be a mistake. No other flight was scheduled for months.

"Follow it," he had ordered and the trackers had kept it on the screen, flashing a message to the police as soon as they located where it landed. It was logical that it should go where it did, but he didn't think that anything about this flight was susceptible to a rational approach.

Marlowe's eyelids felt lined with sand, but that was as nothing compared to his mental irritation. The two oldsters were dead and the ship was vaporized in the Sun. But, of course, it wasn't true and he had to figure out why.

Others would be here to help him unravel the mystery, from Demarest on down. Meanwhile, he was first. There was a lesson to learn if he could figure out what it was. Damn these senile incompetents.

"Ethan and Amantha Huntley?" he asked. They didn't fit in with his preconceived picture.

"You the judge?" said Ethan. "I demand to see a lawyer. We've got our rights."

"Why don't you let our son in?" Amantha protested. "I know he's been dying to see us. You can't keep us locked up like this."

"Please! I've just come from a consultation with your son. You'll see him soon. As for being detained, you've been well treated. Most of the time, doctors have been examining you. Isn't that true?"

"What's that got to do with it?" challenged Ethan. "Never been sick a day in my life. Sure, my back hurts, and now and then my knees swell up. But it's nothing. We didn't ask for a doctor. Got our own on Mars. Young fellow, fifty or sixty."

\*     \*     \*     \*     \*

Facts contradicted each other. They were what Marlowe expected and yet they weren't. It was hard to determine. Records showed that if the old couple were not actually senile incompetents, they were close to it. Now that they'd returned the ship in good condition, legal action against them would be dangerous. Everyone had grandparents and knew that they were sometimes foolish. It was a spot to get out of as gracefully as the company could.

It was as training director for Interplanet Transport, however, that he was interested in them.

"You were in space for nearly four months," he said. "Few people take that much exposure to radiation at one time. We had to determine the state of your health. The evaluation isn't complete, but I think we can say you're in no immediate danger."

Did they understand? It was doubtful. No one else would have stolen the ship and attempted to bring it to Earth. But, damn it, they had done so, landing the ship on the outskirts of the little town, unobserved in the gathering storm.

The facts were painfully fresh in his mind.

"I'd like to know something of your background," said Marlowe. "What's your experience with spaceships?"

"Went to Venus in one," Ethan answered. "Also took a trip to Mars. Stayed there."

The old man had haunted the control compartment, watching how it was done. Some people did. But that was not a substitute for experience.

"That was long ago and you were a passenger. Anything more recent?"

"Nope. Except for this last trip."

That was what didn't make sense.

"Are you sure? Be honest. Check your memory."

The old man had once piloted jets. But it was not the same.

"No other experience," said Ethan. "Had training, though."

Marlowe knew it. Without training, no one could manage takeoff and landing. Somehow, the official search had failed to uncover this vital information. "Where did you take it?"

"Forget the name. Remember every word of it, though."

Marlowe nodded. It was often the case. Early memories were fresh and clear while later events blew over the enfeebled mind and left no trace. "But you didn't tell me where."

"Don't remember that part of it. It was a mighty good course. Wasn't accepted, even though I passed, after paying for my lessons in advance. They said I was too old."

Air lodged in his throat—Marlowe doubled over. If he'd heard rightly.... Good God, there were angels and correspondence courses that watched over the aged! No—give the credit to angels.

"I realized I wasn't as spry as I used to be," continued Ethan seriously. "Can't shoot off a planet or slam down on one the way your pilots do. We were at the far end of the field, quite a ways off. Everybody was busy with the pilot who was running around. They were trying to help him.

"Guess they didn't see us. They'd have laughed if they did. We went up slow, kind of wobbly. But we got off."

\*    \*    \*    \*    \*

The old man was beaming, proud of it. He didn't know it wasn't skill but the built-in safety factor, all the stabilizing mechanisms coming into play at once. Demarest, the chief of construction, had seen to it that the ships were well designed. Marlowe would have to commend him when he got here.

A thought occurred to the training director. If the stabilizing mechanisms were there, why not use them always? Of course, it wasn't that simple. Interplanetary ship stabilizers weren't effective at high speed.

Another thought crowded in. Why such high speed? That was something over which there was no choice. The protective atmosphere had to be left swiftly. The speed was added to at every opportunity. It was possible to slow down only at the last moment. Otherwise....

Otherwise what?

There was no escape from the conclusion—otherwise heredity was altered and mutations would result. Marlowe sat back. This was true without exception. It was the biggest factor that controlled the conditions of interplanetary flight. But—

*They'd had their children!*

Marlowe's pulse increased. As training director, he'd learned not to leap at things that merely looked good. He had to examine them carefully. But—well, it was a new approach, though he couldn't really expect anything from it. There was more to a crew than a pilot, more to space flight than one incredible lucky voyage, for angels took vacations, too.

"You weren't on duty at all times," Marlowe pointed out. "Then there's navigation."

"Don't sleep much," said Ethan. "Catnap once in a while." He thought it over. "When I did sleep, 'Mantha helped out." He looked at her. "I'm not the expert on navigation. You'd better ask her."

"*No!*" cried Marlowe.

"Why not? Just because I'm a woman?" Her eyes were bright.

"But who taught you navigation?"

Amantha sniffed. "Look here, young man, don't tell me what I can learn." She closed her eyes and imagination carried her back to the ship. "Lots of dials and gadgets—but I used to have near as many in my kitchen before they said I was too old to cook. Anyway, you don't have to figure it out on paper. If you look at things just right, you sort of know where you are."

*     *     *     *     *

Amantha folded her hands. "First, you take a big handful of the Sun's attraction and mix it with a bigger scoop of the gravitation of the planet you happen to be on. For us, that was Mars. Then you add a pinch of acceleration. That's what makes you rise. When you get out a ways, you decrease Mars and add more Earth and another pinch of Sun, stirring it around in your mind each day until it feels just right."

She smiled. "I never did hold with too much measuring."

The muscles in Marlowe's chest felt cramped from holding his breath in. While she spoke, he could almost believe she knew what she was doing, that she had a knack for it. Perhaps she did—brief flashes of clarity swept over her senile, beclouded mind. And the same with the old man. These instances of sanity—and luck—had pulled them through.

The ship was back, unharmed. He shouldn't ask for more. And yet—they had made it to Earth.

The chute in the desk clattered noisily and ejected a packet. Marlowe looked at it—it was for him. The full medical report; it had been slow in coming. But this was a small town. The doctor who had looked them over was good, though. Marlowe made certain of that.

He opened the report and read. When he finished, he knew that though luck and angels had been with them on takeoff and part of the passage—along with dimly remembered fragments of unrelated skills that had somehow coalesced into a working knowledge of how to run a ship—it wasn't the whole story. When they landed on Earth, it was no miracle. They had known what they were doing.

"What is it?" asked Ethan. "Habeas corpus?"

"No," said Marlowe. But in one sense it was, though of a kind that no mere judge could return a verdict on. He read the report again.

"No evidence of mental senility," it said in part. "Micro-samples of brain cells seem to be taken from someone about forty or fifty. Physical reactions are slow but firm and consistent. There are puzzling aspects. Certain obscure functions apparently are those of septuagenarians. Others are in keeping with the mental age. The weakest organs govern, of course; they should live another thirty years, as if they really were in their seventies. However, locomotion and judgment should not be impaired until the very end. Query: Are you sure these are the people I was supposed to examine? I couldn't find that deep, inoperable, though non-malignant tumor the man was supposed to have."

Marlowe folded and refolded the report. Radiation could kill. But it could also cure. It was a standard treatment. But never so drastic and not on the aged for this purpose. He had come at once on two monumental discoveries, both by accident. How many discoveries *were* accidental?

These two wouldn't live longer, but they would have a better life and in full possession of their senses.

"Sure, we borrowed—stole the ship," said Ethan abruptly, interrupting Marlowe's thoughts. "You got it back, but that don't change things. We've got money. We might have enough to pay for most of the fuel."

"It's not necessary. We'll charge it off as an experiment." Marlowe tried to frown. Perhaps he succeeded. "In return for not prosecuting, I want you to abandon your pension and go to work for Interplanet Transport."

Ethan's joints creaked as he sat up eagerly. "Work it off? Sounds fair." There were wrinkles on his face and there never would be any less, but they weren't as deep as they had been, not when they formed the network of a smile. "I can sweep out a ship. Maybe you'd even let me go on a trip once in a while. I could be a cabin boy."

They had been considered useless and incapable for so long that they still didn't realize what he was saying. They weren't childish, but they thought they were. Re-education would have to proceed slowly.

"I had a trip in mind for you," said Marlowe. "And Amantha will have to go to work, too."

"Young man, it's been a long time since I cooked anything but one canalberry shortcake, but you just watch what I can stir up."

"I've got just the place for you," Marlowe answered. "One more stipulation—don't talk about your experiences. If reporters come around, and I think they will, say merely that we traced the ship and, after conferring with you, decided to drop all charges. Understand?"

Amantha nodded. "Look bad for you, wouldn't it? Not guarding the ships any better than that, I mean."

He was thankful their minds had merely been resharpened, that they would never regain their original edge. She was right—it *would* look bad. Also, the company had competitors. And by the time *they* got wind of it, he wanted to have a head-start. Only a few of the aged would fit in with his plans, though the rest would benefit, and by more than a change of status.

Marlowe nodded. "That's it. Report tomorrow and we'll go over your assignments."

"Guess you don't know what we're like," said Ethan. "We've hardly seen our littlest grandson yet. What do you suppose we stole—experimented with the ship for?"

Marlowe watched them go and, as the door closed, began to write hurriedly. The others would be here soon. He wanted to have it summarized by the time they arrived.

Half an hour later, he looked at what he'd put down. It was on the back of the medical report.

"Memo: Change the design of our lastest ship. Instead of a heavy-hulled, superfast rocket, requiring the utmost in bodily coordination and stamina, reverse every specification. Permeability to radiation no objection."

He chuckled. Demarest would threaten to resign. It violated every precept he had ever learned. But the engineer would change his mind when he saw the rest of it.

\*    \*    \*    \*    \*

Marlowe read on: "Top speed need not be high. Emphasis should be placed on safety. Must be maneuverable by operators whose reactive time is not fast, but whose judgment and foresight are trustworthy. Stress simplicity.

"Memo No. 2: Inaugurate another class of service. In addition to fast speedy passages when planets are close, a freight system that can operate continuously is now possible. The planets will open up faster if a steady supply route can be maintained. Older passengers will be a mainstay, especially since therapeutic value is sure to be disclosed. Estimated time to prepare for first run— one year minimum.

"Memo No. 3: Recruiting. Do not overlook the most unlikely skill. It may indicate undisclosed ability of high order.

"Training: Blank. Improvise as you go along!"

Marlowe got up. He thought he heard planes overhead. If so, he had something for them. He'd have to argue, but he felt up to it. The sand had disappeared from his eyes. His step was lighter, too.

And that was because of another item he hadn't written down. He wouldn't forget.

He was in the mid-forties and would have to begin learning. It was the awkward age—too old—too young. He couldn't hope to pilot the murderously fast ships currently in use. And he couldn't take his place in the clumsy tubs that would soon be swinging between the planets, opening up space to commerce. He would have to wait, but what he learned now would be useful some day. It would be better integrated for having been long buried in his memory.

A vintage aspiration.

When he was immune to the mutating effects of radiation, old and nearly sleepless, he could retire from this career—into a better one.

# End as a World

Originally Published In *Galaxy Science Fiction*,
September 1955

# End as a World

Every paper said so in all the languages there were, I guess. I kept reading them, but didn't know what to believe. I know what I wanted to think, but that's different from actually knowing.

There was the usual news just after Labor Day. The dodgers were winning of losing, I forget which, and UCLA was strong and was going to beat everybody they met that fall. An H-bomb had been tested in the Pacific, blowing another island off the map, just as if we had islands to spare. Ordinarily this was important, but now it wasn't. They put stuff like this in the back pages and hardly anybody reads it. There was only one thing on the front pages and it was all people talked about. All I talked about, anyway.

It began long before. I don't know how long because they didn't print that. But it began and there it was, right upon us that day. It was Saturday. Big things always seem to happen on Saturdays. I ate breakfast and got out early. I had the usual things to do, mowing the lawn, for instance. I didn't do it, nor anything else, and nobody said anything. There wasn't any use in mowing the lawn on a day like that.

I went out, remembering not to slam the door. It wasn't much, but it showed thoughtfulness. I went past the church and looked at the sign that was set diagonally at the corner so that it could be read from both streets. There it was in big letters, quoting from the papers: THIS IS THE DAY THE WORLD ENDS! Some smart reporter had thought it up and it seemed so true that that was the only way it was ever said. Me? I didn't know.

It was a bright day. People were out walking or just standing and looking at the sky. It was too early to look up. I went on. Paul Eberhard was sitting on the lawn when I came along. He tossed me the football and I caught it and tried to spin it on my finger. It didn't spin. It fell and flopped out with crazy bounces into the street. The milk truck stopped, while I got it out of the way. I tossed the football back to Paul. He put his hand on it and sat there.

"What'll we do?" he said.

I made a motion with my hands. "We can throw the ball around," I said.

"Naw," he said. "Maybe you've got some comic books."

"You've seen them all," I said. "You got some?"

"I gave them to Howie." He said thoughtfully screwing the point of the ball into the center of a dandelion. "He said he was going to get some new ones, though. Let's go see." He got up and tossed the ball toward the porch. It hit the railing and bounced back into the bushes. That's where he usually kept it.

"Paul," called his mother as we started out.

"Yeah?"

"Don't go too far. I've got some things I want you to do."

"What?" he said patiently.

"Hauling trash out of the basement. Helping me move some of the potted plants around in front."

"Sure," he said. "I'll be back."

We went past another church on the way to Howie's. The sign was the same there. THIS IS THE DAY THE WORLD ENDS! They never said more than that. They wanted it to hang in our minds, something we couldn't quite touch but we knew was there.

Paul jerked his head at the sign. "What do you think of it?"

"I don't know." I broke off a twig as we passed a tree. "What about you?"

"We got it coming." He looked at the sky.

"Yeah, but will we get it?"

He didn't answer that. "I wonder if it will be bright?"

"It is now."

"It might cloud over."

"It won't matter. It'll split the sky." That was one thing sure. Clouds of anything weren't going to stand in the way.

We went on and found Howie. Howie is a Negro, smaller than we are and twice as fast. He can throw a football farther and straighter than anyone else on the team. We pal around quite a bit, especially in the football season.

He came out of the house like he was walking on whipped cream. I didn't let that fool me. More than once I've tried to tackle him during a practice game. Howie was carrying a model of a rocket ship, CO2 powered. It didn't work. We said Hi all around and then he suggested a game of keep-away. We'd left the football at Paul's and we couldn't so we walked over to the park.

We sat down and began talking about it. "I'm wondering if it will really come," said Paul. We all squinted up.

"Where'll the President watch it from?" I said. "He should have a good view from the White House."

"No better than us right here," said Howie.

"What about Australia? Will they see it there?" I said.

"They'll see it all over."

"Africa, too? What about the Eskimos?"

"It doesn't matter whether they actually see it or not. It will come to everyone at the same time."

I didn't see how it could, but I didn't feel like an argument. That's what they were saying on TV and you can't talk back to that.

"Everybody," said Howie. "Not just in this town, but all over. Where there are people. Even where they're not."

"You read that," said Paul.

"Sure," said Howie. "You lent me the comic books. It's even in them."

We didn't say much after that. I kept thinking of the man who made the H-bomb. I bet he felt silly and spiteful, blowing up an island. Somebody might have wanted to live on it if he'd just left it there. He must have felt mean and low when something really big like this came along.

We talked on for a while, but we'd talked it out long ago. There was really nothing new we could say. Every so often we'd look up at the sky, but it wasn't going to come until it got here.

Finally we drifted apart. There wasn't anything left to do. We walked home with Howie and then I went with Paul, leaving him to come back to my house. I looked at the lawn and without thinking about it got busy and mowed it. I surprised myself.

It was hot, or is seemed to me it was. I went in to eat. Ma came by and shut off the sound of the TV. I could still see the picture in the other room. The announcer was making faces, but, of course, I didn't hear what he said. He looked pretty funny, I thought. I thought we were all probably pretty funny, I thought, moving our mouths and blinking our eyes and waving our hands. Only nothing real was coming out. Not yet, anyway.

"Sit still," said Ma. "It will happen without your help. It's going to be all right."

"Think so?" I said. She would have told me anything to keep me quiet. She gets nervous when I fidget.

"I think so," she said, giving me my allowance. It was early for that. Usually I didn't get it until after supper. "Why don't you go uptown and watch it from there?"

"Maybe I will," I said, dabbling my hands in the water at the sink. "Are you going to go?"

"Of course I'm not. Why should I get into that mob? I can watch it just as well from here."

Sure she could. But it was not the same. Everybody I knew was going to be there. I changed shirts before I left. I took a rag and wiped the dust from my shoes. I wasn't trying to be fussy ot dressed up or anything. I just thought I should do it.

There was shade and sun on the streets and a few big clouds in the sky.

A car slowed up and stopped besides me. The window rolled down and Jack Goodwin leaned toward me. "Going up town?"

"Yeah."

"Want a lift?"

"Sure." Actually I didn't. I'd rather have walked, looking around as I went.

Jack Goodwin grinned as I got in. He's got gray hair, where he has hair. The rest is bald. He looked me over. "I don't see any comets on your shoulders," he said gravely.

"I never had any," I said. Some people seem to think everyone under seventeen is a kid.

"You'll be needing them," he said.

"Maybe," I said. I ought to have walked.

I never knew how slow a day could pass. I suppose I should have slept late and kept busy doing something. This was worse than putting on a uniform and waiting until game-time.

At least there was a coach on the field to tell you what to do as you ran through the drill.

Jack Goodwin stopped at a light. I had a notion to get out. But I didn't. Goodwin grinned again as the light changed and we started up. "I don't blame you for being edgy," he said. "It's the suspense. If we only had some way of knowing for sure, radio maybe."

"There's no radio," I said. "The calculations have been checked."

"Sure, but maybe there's something we forgot. Or don't know. All sorts of things can go wrong."

He must have talked on and on, but I didn't listen. Howie and me and Paul had gone over everything he was saying.

"Thanks," I said as he stopped and I got out.

"Don't mention it," he said. He nearly scraped the rear fender of the car as he drove off. It was a new car, too. He wasn't so bad. Maybe he was just worried.

I wandered to the newsstand and looked at magazines and pocketbooks. Old lady Simpson didn't ask me if I was going to buy and didn't chase me away. She was busy arguing with some customers. Even so it was the first time she didn't pay attention to me when I came in. I had a good chance to look at things I never buy. There was nothing in them I wanted to see. I was thirsty. I had a Coke and was still thirsty. I asked for a glass of water, drank half of it and went out.

Down the street there was a TV set in a store window. I watched it. They were showing a street in India, people looking up. They flashed all around, to Italy, China, Brazil. Except for their clothes, it wasn't much different from here. They were all looking up.

I did the same. For the first time I noticed there was a slight overcast. Big billowing clouds had passed, but this was worse. I hoped it would clear away in time. Not that it really mattered.

It was more crowded than usual for Saturday, but at the same time it was quiet. People were shopping, but they weren't really buying much or else they bought it faster. Nobody wanted to miss it. They all seemed to have one eye on their lists and another on the clock.

Howie and Paul came up the street and we nodded and said something. A few other boys from the school passed by and we stopped. We gathered together. It was getting closer—and the space between the minutes was growing longer and longer.

I looked at Paul's watch. He said it was on the minute. I decided there was time to go in and get a candy bar. All of a sudden I was hungry. I didn't know where it came from. I'd had to stuff down lunch not long ago. And now I was hungry.

I went to a store and had to fight my way in. People were coming out. Not just customers, but the clerks and owner, too. There was a big television screen inside, but nobody wanted to see it on that. They wanted to be outside where it would happen to them. Not just see it, have it happen. The store was empty. Not closed—empty.

I turned and rushed out to join the others. I couldn't miss it. There were still minutes to go, but suppose there had been a miscalculation. I knew what that would mean, but even so I had to be there. I would almost die, too.

Now we were all looking up-all over the world people were, I suppose. It was quiet. You could hear them breathing.

And then it came, a flash across the sky, a silver streak, the biggest vapor trail there ever was. It went from this side to that side in no time. It split the sky and was gone before the shock blast hit us. Nobody said anything. We stood there and shivered and straightened up after the rumbling sound passed.

But there was the vapor trail that stretched farther than anyone could see. It would go around the world at least once before it came to an end somewhere in the desert. I saw my science teacher—he was trying to smile, but couldn't. And then there was the pharmacist who had wanted to be a research chemist, but wasn't good enough.

In front of me, old Fred Butler, who drives the bus to Orange Point and King City, cracked his knuckles. "He did it," he whispered. "All the way to Mars and back. Safe and right on schedule." He jumped in the air and kept jumping up. He hadn't been that high off the ground in several years. He never would be again unless he took an elevator. And I knew he hated elevators.

Factory whistles started blowing. They sounded louder than Gabriel. I wondered if he heard them. I grabbed hold of the nearest person and started hugging.  I didn't know it was the snooty girl from the next block until she hugged back and began kissing me.  We yelled louder than the factory whistles.  We had a right.

It was just like the papers said:  This was the day the world ended—

And the Universe began.

# BOLDEN'S PETS

ILLUSTRATED BY DIEHL
ORIGINALLY PUBLISHED IN *GALAXY SCIENCE FICTION*,
OCTOBER, 1955

*The price of life was a life for a life—
which was all the reward the victim looked for!*

# BOLDEN'S PETS

His hands were shaking as he exhibited the gifts. If he were on Earth, he would be certain it was the flu; in the Centaurus system, kranken. But this was Van Daamas, so Lee Bolden couldn't say what he had. Man hadn't been here long enough to investigate the diseases with any degree of thoroughness. There were always different hazards to overcome as new planets were settled.

But whatever infection he had, Bolden was not greatly concerned as he counted out the gifts. He had felt the onset of illness perhaps an hour before. When he got back to the settlement he'd be taken care of. That was half a day's flight from here. The base was equipped with the best medical facilities that had been devised.

He stacked up the gifts to make an impressive show: five pairs of radar goggles, seven high-velocity carbines, seven boxes of ammunition. This was the natives' own rule and was never to be disregarded—it had to be an odd number of gifts.

The Van Daamas native gazed impassively at the heap. He carried a rather strange bow and a quiver was strapped to his thigh. With one exception, the arrows were brightly colored, mostly red and yellow. Bolden supposed this was for easy recovery in case the shot missed. But there was always one arrow that was stained dark blue. Bolden had observed this before—no native was ever without that one somber-looking arrow.

The man of Van Daamas stood there and the thin robe that was no protection against the elements rippled slightly in the chill current of air that flowed down the mountainside. "I will go talk with the others," he said in English.

"Go talk," said Bolden, trying not to shiver. He replied in native speech, but a few words exhausted his knowledge and he had to revert to his own language. "Take the gifts with you. They are yours, no matter what you decide."

The native nodded and reached for a pair of goggles. He tried them on, looking out over fog and mist-shrouded slopes. These people of Van Daamas needed radar less than any race Bolden knew of. Living by preference in mountains, they had developed a keenness of vision that enabled them to see through the perpetual fog and mist far better than any Earthman. Paradoxically it was the goggles they appreciated most. Extending their sight seemed more precious to them than powerful carbines.

The native shoved the goggles up on his forehead, smiling with pleasure. Noticing that Bolden was shivering, he took his hands and examined them. "Hands sick?" he queried.

"A little," said Bolden. "I'll be all right in the morning."

The native gathered up the gifts. "Go talk," he repeated as he went away.

*   *   *   *   *

Lee Bolden sat in the copter and waited. He didn't know how much influence this native had with his people. He had come to negotiate, but this might have been because he understood English somewhat better than the others.

A council of the natives would make the decision about working for the Earthmen's settlement. If they approved of the gifts, they probably would. There was nothing to do now but wait—and shiver. His hands were getting numb and his feet weren't much better.

Presently the native came out of the fog carrying a rectangular wicker basket. Bolden was depressed when he saw it. One gift in return for goggles, carbines, ammunition. The rate of exchange was not favorable. Neither would the reply be.

The man set the basket down and waited for Bolden to speak. "The people have talked?" asked Bolden.

"We have talked to come," said the native, holding out his fingers. "In five or seven days, we come."

It was a surprise, a pleasant one. Did one wicker basket equal so many fine products of superlative technology? Apparently it did. The natives had different values. To them, one pair of goggles was worth more than three carbines, a package of needles easily the equivalent of a box of ammunition.

"It's good you will come. I will leave at once to tell them at the settlement," said Bolden. There was something moving in the basket, but the weave was close and he couldn't see through it.

"Stay," the man advised. "A storm blows through the mountains."

"I will fly around the storm," said Bolden.

If he hadn't been sick he might have accepted the offer. But he had to get back to the settlement for treatment. On a strange planet you never could tell what might develop from a seemingly minor ailment. Besides he'd already been gone two days searching for this tribe in the interminable fog that hung over the mountains. Those waiting at the base would want him back as soon as he could get there.

"Fly far around," said the man. "It is a big storm." He took up the basket and held it level with the cabin, opening the top. An animal squirmed out and disappeared inside.

Bolden looked askance at the eyes that glowed in the dim interior. He hadn't seen clearly what the creature was and he didn't like the idea of having it loose in the cabin, particularly if he had to fly through a storm. The man should have left it in the basket. But the basket plus the animal would have been two gifts—and the natives never considered anything in even numbers.

"It will not hurt," said the man. "A gentle pet."

*     *     *     *     *

As far as he knew, there were no pets and very few domesticated animals. Bolden snapped on the cabin light. It was one of those mysterious creatures every tribe kept in cages near the outskirts of their camps. What they did with them no one knew and the natives either found it impossible to explain or did not care to do so.

It seemed unlikely that the creatures were used for food and certainly they were not work animals. And in spite of what this man said, they were not pets either. No Earthman had ever seen a native touch them nor had the creatures ever been seen wandering at large in the camp. And until now, none had been permitted to pass into Earth's possession. The scientists at the settlement would regard this acquisition with delight.

"Touch it," said the native.

Bolden held out his trembling hand and the animal came to him with alert and friendly yellow eyes. It was about the size of a rather small dog, but it didn't look much like one. It resembled more closely a tiny slender bear with a glossy and shaggy cinnamon coat. Bolden ran his hands through the clean-smelling fur and the touch warmed his fingers. The animal squirmed and licked his fingers.

"It has got your taste," said the native. "Be all right now. It is yours." He turned and walked into the mist.

Bolden got in and started the motors while the animal climbed into the seat beside him. It was a friendly thing and he couldn't understand why the natives always kept it caged.

He headed straight up, looking for a way over the mountains to avoid the impending storm. Fog made it difficult to tell where the peaks were and he had to drop lower, following meandering valleys. He flew as swiftly as limited visibility would allow, but he hadn't gone far when the storm broke. He tried to go over the top of it, but this storm seemed to have no top. The region was incompletely mapped and even radar wasn't much help in the tremendous electrical display that raged around the ship.

His arms ached as he clung to the controls. His hands weren't actually cold, they were numb. His legs were leaden. The creature crept closer to him and he had to nudge it away. Momentarily the distraction cleared his head. He couldn't put it off any longer. He had to land and wait out the storm—if he could find a place to land.

Flexing his hands until he worked some feeling into them, he inched the ship lower. A canyon wall loomed at one side and he had to veer away and keep on looking.

Eventually he found his refuge—a narrow valley where the force of the winds was not extreme—and he set the land anchor. Unless something drastic happened, it would hold.

*    *    *    *    *

He made the seat into a bed, decided he was too tired to eat, and went directly to sleep. When he awakened, the storm was still raging and the little animal was snoozing by his side.

He felt well enough to eat. The native hadn't explained what the animal should be fed, but it accepted everything Bolden offered. Apparently it was as omnivorous as Man. Before lying down again, he made the other seat into a bed, although it didn't seem to matter. The creature preferred being as close to him as it could get and he didn't object. The warmth was comforting.

Alternately dozing and waking he waited out the storm. It lasted a day and a half. Finally the sun was shining. This was two days since he had first fallen ill, four days after leaving the settlement.

Bolden felt much improved. His hands were nearly normal and his vision wasn't blurred. He looked at the little animal curled in his lap, gazing up at him with solemn yellow eyes. If he gave it encouragement it would probably be crawling all over him. However, he couldn't have it frisking around while he was flying. "Come, Pet," he said—there wasn't anything else to call it—"you're going places."

Picking it up, half-carrying and half-dragging it, he took it to the rear of the compartment, improvising a narrow cage back there. He was satisfied it would hold. He should have done this in the beginning. Of course he hadn't felt like it then and he hadn't had the time—and anyway the native would have resented such treatment of a gift. Probably it was best he had waited.

His pet didn't like confinement. It whined softly for a while. The noise stopped when the motors roared. Bolden headed straight up, until he was high enough to establish communication over the peaks. He made a brief report about the natives' agreement and his own illness, then he started home.

He flew at top speed for ten hours. He satisfied his hunger by nibbling concentrated rations from time to time. The animal whined occasionally, but Bolden had learned to identify the sounds it made. It was neither hungry nor thirsty. It merely wanted to be near him. And all he wanted was to reach the base.

The raw sprawling settlement looked good as he sat the copter down. Mechanics came running from the hangars. They opened the door and he stepped out.

And fell on his face. There was no feeling in his hands and none in his legs. He hadn't recovered.

*     *     *     *     *

Doctor Kessler peered at him through the microscreen. It gave his face a narrow insubstantial appearance. The microscreen was a hemispherical force field enclosing his head. It originated in a tubular circlet that snapped around his throat at the top of the decontagion suit. The field killed all microlife that passed through it or came in contact with it. The decontagion suit was non-porous and impermeable, covering completely the rest of his body. The material was thinner over his hands and thicker at the soles.

Bolden took in the details at a glance. "Is it serious?" he asked, his voice cracking with the effort.

"Merely a precaution," said the doctor hollowly. The microscreen distorted sound as well as sight. "Merely a precaution. We know what it is, but we're not sure of the best way to treat it."

Bolden grunted to himself. The microscreen and decontagion suit were strong precautions.

The doctor wheeled a small machine from the wall and placed Bolden's hand in a narrow trough that held it steady. The eyepiece slid into the microscreen and, starting at the finger tips, Kessler examined the arm, traveling slowly upward. At last he stopped. "Is this where feeling ends?"

"I think so. Touch it. Yeah. It's dead below there."

"Good. Then we've got it pegged. It's the Bubble Death."

Bolden showed concern and the doctor laughed. "Don't worry. It's called that because of the way it looks through the X-ray microscope. It's true that it killed the scouting expedition that discovered the planet, but it won't get you."

"They had antibiotics. Neobiotics, too."

"Sure. But they had only a few standard kinds. Their knowledge was more limited and they lacked the equipment we now have."

The doctor made it sound comforting. But Bolden wasn't comforted. Not just yet.

"Sit up and take a look," said Kessler, bending the eyepiece around so Bolden could use it. "The dark filamented lines are nerves. See what surrounds them?"

Bolden watched as the doctor adjusted the focus for him. Each filament was covered with countless tiny spheres that isolated and insulated the nerve from contact. That's why he couldn't feel anything. The spherical microbes did look like bubbles. As yet they didn't seem to have attacked the nerves directly.

While he watched, the doctor swiveled out another eyepiece for his own use and turned a knob on the side of the machine. From the lens next to his arm an almost invisible needle slid out and entered his flesh. Bolden could see it come into the field of view. It didn't hurt. Slowly it approached the dark branching filament, never quite touching it.

The needle was hollow and as Kessler squeezed the knob it sucked in the spheres. The needle extended a snout which crept along the nerve, vacuuming in microbes as it moved. When a section had been cleansed, the snout was retracted. Bolden could feel the needle then.

*     *     *     *     *

When the doctor finished, he laid Bolden's hand back at his side and wheeled the machine to the wall, extracting a small capsule which he dropped into a slot that led to the outside. He came back and sat down.

"Is that what you're going to do?" asked Bolden. "Scrape them off?"

"Hardly. There are too many nerves. If we had ten machines and enough people to operate them, we might check the advance in one arm. That's all." The doctor leaned back in the chair. "No. I was collecting a few more samples. We're trying to find out what the microbes react to."

"*More* samples? Then you must have taken others."

"Certainly. We put you out for a while to let you rest." The chair came down on four legs. "You've got a mild case. Either that or you have a strong natural immunity. It's now been three days since you reported the first symptoms and it isn't very advanced. It killed the entire scouting expedition in less time than that."

Bolden looked at the ceiling. Eventually they'd find a cure. But would he be alive that long?

"I suspect what you're thinking," said the doctor. "Don't overlook our special equipment. We already have specimens in the sonic accelerator. We've been able to speed up the life processes of the microbes about ten times. Before the day is over we'll know which of our anti and neobiotics they like the least. Tough little things so far—unbelievably tough—but you can be sure we'll smack them."

His mind was active, but outwardly Bolden was quiescent as the doctor continued his explanation.

The disease attacked the superficial nervous system, beginning with the extremities. The bodies of the crew of the scouting expedition had been in an advanced state of decomposition when the medical rescue team reached them and the microbes were no longer active. Nevertheless it was a reasonable supposition that death had come shortly after the invading bacteria had reached the brain. Until then, though nerves were the route along which the microbes traveled, no irreparable damage had been done.

\* \* \* \* \*

This much was good news. Either he would recover completely or he would die. He would not be crippled permanently. Another factor in his favor was the sonic accelerator. By finding the natural resonance of the one-celled creature and gradually increasing the tempo of the sound field, the doctor could grow and test ten generations in the laboratory while one generation was breeding in the body. Bolden was the first patient actually being observed with the disease, but the time element wasn't as bad as he had thought.

"That's where you are," concluded Kessler. "Now, among other things, we've got to find where you've been."

"The ship has an automatic log," said Bolden. "It indicates every place I landed."

"True, but our grid coordinates are not exact. It will be a few years before we're able to look at a log and locate within ten feet of where a ship has been." The doctor spread out a large photomap. There were several marks on it. He fastened a stereoscope viewer over Bolden's eyes and handed him a pencil. "Can you use this?"

"I think so." His fingers were stiff and he couldn't feel, but he could mark with the pencil. Kessler moved the map nearer and the terrain sprang up in detail. In some cases, he could see it more clearly than when he had been there, because on the map there was no fog. Bolden made a few corrections and the doctor took the map away and removed the viewer.

"We'll have to stay away from these places until we get a cure. Did you notice anything peculiar in any of the places you went?"

"It was all mountainous country."

"Which probably means that we're safe on the plain. Were there any animals?"

"Nothing that came close. Birds maybe."

"More likely it was an insect. Well, we'll worry about the host and how it is transmitted. Try not to be upset. You're as safe as you would be on Earth."

"Yeah," said Bolden. "Where's the pet?"

The doctor laughed. "You did very well on that one. The biologists have been curious about the animal since the day they saw one in a native camp."

"They can *look* at it as much as they want," said Bolden. "Nothing more on this one, though. It's a personal gift."

"You're sure it's personal?"

"The native said it was."

The doctor sighed. "I'll tell them. They won't like it, but we can't argue with the natives if we want their cooperation."

Bolden smiled. The animal was safe for at least six months. He could understand the biologists' curiosity, but there was enough to keep them curious for a long time on a new planet. And it was his. In a remarkably short time, he had become attached to it. It was one of those rare things that Man happened across occasionally—about once in every five planets. Useless, completely useless, the creature had one virtue. It liked Man and Man liked it. It was a pet. "Okay," he said. "But you didn't tell me where it is."

The doctor shrugged, but the gesture was lost in the shapeless decontagion suit. "Do you think we're letting it run in the streets? It's in the next room, under observation."

The doctor was more concerned than he was letting on. The hospital was small and animals were never kept in it. "It's not the carrier. I was sick before it was given to me."

"You had something, we know that much, but was it this? Even granting that you're right, it was in contact with you and may now be infected."

"I think life on this planet isn't bothered by the disease. The natives have been every place I went and none of them seemed to have it."

"Didn't they?" said the doctor, going to the door. "Maybe. It's too early to say." He reeled a cord out of the wall and plugged it into the decontagion suit. He spread his legs and held his arms away from his sides. In an instant, the suit glowed white hot. Only for an instant, and it was insulated inside. Even so it must be uncomfortable—and the process would be repeated outside.

The doctor wasn't taking any chances. "Try to sleep," he said. "Ring if there's a change in your condition—even if you think it's insignificant."

"I'll ring," said Bolden. In a short time he fell asleep. It was easy to sleep.

* * * * *

The nurse entered as quietly as she could in the decontagion outfit. It awakened Bolden. It was evening. He had slept most of the day. "Which one are you?" he asked. "The pretty one?"

"All nurses are pretty if you get well. Here. Swallow this."

It was Peggy. He looked doubtfully at what she held out. "All of it?"

"Certainly. You get it down and I'll see that it comes back up. The string won't hurt you."

She passed a small instrument over his body, reading the dial she held in the other hand. The information, he knew, was being recorded elsewhere on a master chart. Apparently the instrument measured neural currents and hence indirectly the progress of the disease. Already they had evolved new diagnostic techniques. He wished they'd made the same advance in treatment.

After expertly reeling out the instrument he had swallowed, the nurse read it and deposited it in a receptacle in the wall. She brought a tray and told him to eat. He wanted to question her, but she was insistent about it so he ate. Allowance had been made for his partial paralysis. The food was liquid. It was probably nutritious, but he didn't care for the taste.

She took the tray away and came back and sat beside him. "Now we can talk," she said.

"What's going on?" he said bluntly. "When do I start getting shots? Nothing's been done for me so far."

"I don't know what the doctor's working out for you. I'm just the nurse."

"Don't try to tell me that," he said. "You're a doctor yourself. In a pinch you could take Kessler's place."

"And I get my share of pinches," she said brightly. "Okay, so I'm a doctor, but only on Earth. Until I complete my off-planet internship here, I'm not allowed to practice."

"You know as much about Van Daamas as anyone does."

"That may be," she said. "Now don't be alarmed, but the truth ought to be obvious. None of our anti or neobiotics or combinations of them have a positive effect. We're looking for something new."

It should have been obvious; he had been hoping against that, though. He looked at the shapeless figure sitting beside him and remembered Peggy as she usually looked. He wondered if they were any longer concerned with him as an individual. They must be working mainly to keep the disease from spreading. "What are my chances?"

"Better than you think. We're looking for an additive that will make the biotics effective."

*       *       *       *       *

He hadn't thought of that, though it was often used, particularly on newly settled planets. He had heard of a virus infection common to Centaurus that could be completely controlled by a shot of neobiotics plus aspirin, though separately neither was of any value. But the discovery of what substance should be added to what antibiotic was largely one of trial and error. That took time and there wasn't much time. "What else?" he said.

"That's about it. We're not trying to make you believe this isn't serious. But don't forget we're working ten times as fast as the disease can multiply. We expect a break any moment." She got up. "Want a sedative for the night?"

"I've got a sedative inside me. Looks like it will be permanent."

"That's what I like about you, you're so cheerful," she said, leaning over and clipping something around his throat. "In case you're wondering, we're going to be busy tonight checking the microbe. We can put someone in with you, but we thought you'd rather have all of us working on it."

"Sure," he said.

"This is a body monitor. If you want anything just call and we'll be here within minutes."

"Thanks," he said. "I won't panic tonight."

She plugged in the decontagion uniform, flashed it on and then left the room. After she was gone, the body monitor no longer seemed reassuring. It was going to take something positive to pull him through.

They were going to work through the night, but did they actually hope for success. What had Peggy said? None of the anti or neobiotics had a positive reaction. Unknowingly she had let it slip. The reaction was negative; the bubble microbes actually grew faster in the medium that was supposed to stop them. It happened occasionally on strange planets. It was his bad luck that it was happening to him.

He pushed the thoughts out of his mind and tried to sleep. He did for a time. When he awakened he thought, at first, it was his arms that had aroused him. They seemed to be on fire, deep inside. To a limited extent, he still had control. He could move them though there was no surface sensation. Interior nerves had not been greatly affected until now. But outside the infection had crept up. It was no longer just above the wrists. It had reached his elbows and passed beyond. A few inches below his shoulder he could feel nothing. The illness was accelerating. If they had ever thought of amputation, it was too late, now.

$$* \quad * \quad * \quad * \quad *$$

He resisted an impulse to cry out. A nurse would come and sit beside him, but he would be taking her from work that might save his life. The infection would reach his shoulders and move across his chest and back. It would travel up his throat and he wouldn't be able to move his lips. It would paralyze his eyelids so that he couldn't blink. Maybe it would blind him, too. And then it would find ingress to his brain.

The result would be a metabolic explosion. Swiftly each bodily function would stop altogether or race wildly as the central nervous system was invaded, one regulatory center after the other blanking out. His body would be aflame or it would smolder and flicker out. Death might be spectacular or it could come very quietly.

That was one reason he didn't call the nurse.

The other was the noise.

It was a low sound, half purr, half a coaxing growl. It was the animal the native had given him, confined in the next room. Bolden was not sure why he did what he did next. Instinct or reason may have governed his actions. But instinct and reason are divisive concepts that cannot apply to the human mind, which is actually indivisible.

He got out of bed. Unable to stand, he rolled to the floor. He couldn't crawl very well because his hands wouldn't support his weight so he crept along on his knees and elbows. It didn't hurt. Nothing hurt except the fire in his bones. He reached the door and straightened up on his knees. He raised his hand to the handle, but couldn't grasp it. After several trials, he abandoned the attempt and hooked his chin on the handle, pulling it down. The door opened and he was in the next room. The animal was whining louder now that he was near. Yellow eyes glowed at him from the corner. He crept to the cage.

It was latched. The animal shivered eagerly, pressing against the side, striving to reach him. His hands were numb and he couldn't work the latch. The animal licked his fingers.

It was easier after that. He couldn't feel what he was doing, but somehow he managed to unlatch it. The door swung open and the animal bounded out, knocking him to the floor.

He didn't mind at all because now he was sure he was right. The natives had given him the animal for a purpose. Their own existence was meager, near the edge of extinction. They could not afford to keep something that wasn't useful. And this creature was useful. Tiny blue sparks crackled from the fur as it rubbed against him in the darkness. It was not whining. It rumbled and purred as it licked his hands and arms and rolled against his legs.

After a while he was strong enough to crawl back to bed, leaning against the animal for support. He lifted himself up and fell across the bed in exhaustion. Blood didn't circulate well in his crippled body. The animal bounded up and tried to melt itself into his body. He couldn't push it away if he wanted. He didn't want to. He stirred and got himself into a more comfortable position. He wasn't going to die.

\*       \*       \*       \*       \*

In the morning, Bolden was awake long before the doctor came in. Kessler's face was haggard and the smile was something he assumed solely for the patient's benefit. If he could have seen what the expression looked like after filtering through the microscreen, he would have abandoned it. "I see you're holding your own," he said with hollow cheerfulness. "We're doing quite well ourselves."

"I'll bet," said Bolden. "Maybe you've got to the point where one of the antibiotics doesn't actually stimulate the growth of the microbes?"

"I was afraid you'd find it out," sighed the doctor. "We can't keep everything from you."

"You could have given me a shot of plasma and said it was a powerful new drug."

"That idea went out of medical treatment a couple of hundred years ago," said the doctor. "You'd feel worse when you failed to show improvement. Settling a planet isn't easy and the dangers aren't imaginary. You've got to be able to face facts as they come."

He peered uncertainly at Bolden. The microscreen distorted his vision, too. "We're making progress though it may not seem so to you. When a mixture of a calcium salt plus two antihistamines is added to a certain neobiotic, the result is that the microbe grows no faster than it should. Switching the ingredients here and there—maybe it ought to be a potassium salt—and the first thing you know we'll have it stopped cold."

"I doubt the effectiveness of those results," said Bolden. "In fact, I think you're on the wrong track. Try investigating the effects of neural induction."

"What are you talking about?" said the doctor, coming closer and glancing suspiciously at the lump beside Bolden. "Do you feel dizzy? Is there anything else unusual that you notice?"

"Don't shout at the patient." Bolden waggled his finger reprovingly. He was proud of the finger. He couldn't feel what he was doing, but he had control over it. "You, Kessler, should face the fact that a doctor can learn from a patient what the patient learned from the natives."

But Kessler didn't hear what he said. He was looking at the upraised hand. "You're moving almost normally," he said. "Your own immunity factor is controlling the disease."

"Sure. I've got an immunity factor," said Bolden. "The same one the natives have. Only it's not inside my body." He rested his hand on the animal beneath the covers. It never wanted to leave him. It wouldn't have to.

"I can set your mind at rest on one thing, Doctor. Natives are susceptible to the disease, too. That's why they were able to recognize I had it. They gave me the cure and told me what it was, but I was unable to see it until it was nearly too late. Here it is." He turned back the covers and the exposed animal sleeping peacefully on his legs which raised its head and licked his fingers. He felt that.

*    *    *    *    *

After an explanation the doctor tempered his disapproval. It was an unsanitary practice, but he had to admit that the patient was much improved. Kessler verified the state of Bolden's health by extensive use of the X-ray microscope. Reluctantly he wheeled the machine to the wall and covered it up.

"The infection is definitely receding," he said. "There are previously infected areas in which I find it difficult to locate a single microbe. What I can't understand is how it's done. According to you, the animal doesn't break the skin with its tongue and therefore nothing is released into the bloodstream. All that seems necessary is that the animal be near you." He shook his head behind the microscreen. "I don't think much of the electrical analogy you used."

"I said the first thing I thought of. I don't know if that's the way it works, but it seems to me like a pretty fair guess."

"The microbes *do* cluster around nerves," said the doctor. "We know that neural activity is partly electrical. If the level of that activity can be increased, the bacteria might be killed by ionic dissociation." He glanced speculatively at Bolden and the animal. "Perhaps you do borrow nervous energy from the animal. We might also find it possible to control the disease with an electrical current."

"Don't try to find out on me," said Bolden. "I've been an experimental specimen long enough. Take somebody who's healthy. I'll stick with the natives' method."

"I wasn't thinking of experiments in your condition. You're still not out of danger." Nevertheless he showed his real opinion when he left the room. He failed to plug in and flash the decontagion suit.

Bolden smiled at the doctor's omission and ran his hand through the fur. He was going to get well.

\*     \*     \*     \*     \*

But his progress was somewhat slower than he'd anticipated though it seemed to satisfy the doctor who went on with his experiments. The offending bacteria could be killed electrically. But the current was dangerously large and there was no practical way to apply the treatment to humans. The animal was the only effective method.

Kessler discovered the microbe required an intermediate host. A tick or a mosquito seemed indicated. It would take a protracted search of the mountains to determine just what insect was the carrier. In any event the elaborate sanitary precautions were unnecessary. Microscreens came down and decontagion suits were no longer worn. Bolden could not pass the disease on to anyone else.

Neither could the animal. It seemed wholly without parasites. It was clean and affectionate, warm to the touch. Bolden was fortunate that there was such a simple cure for the most dreaded disease on Van Daamas.

It was several days before he was ready to leave the small hospital at the edge of the settlement. At first he sat up in bed and then he was allowed to walk across the room. As his activity increased, the animal became more and more content to lie on the bed and follow him with its eyes. It no longer frisked about as it had in the beginning. As Bolden told the nurse, it was becoming housebroken.

The time came when the doctor failed to find a single microbe. Bolden's newly returned strength and the sensitivity of his skin where before there had been numbness confirmed the diagnosis. He was well. Peggy came to walk him home. It was pleasant to have her near.

"I see you're ready," she said, laughing at his eagerness.

"Except for one thing," he said. "Come, Pet." The animal raised its head from the bed where it slept.

"Pet?" she said quizzically. "You ought to give it a name. You've had it long enough to decide on something."

"Pet's a name," he said. "What can I call it? Doc? Hero?"

She made a face. "I can't say I care for either choice, although it did save your life."

"Yes, but that's an attribute it can't help. The important thing is that if you listed what you expect of a pet you'd find it in this creature. Docile, gentle, lively at times; all it wants is to be near you, to have you touch it. And it's very clean."

"All right, call it Pet if you want," said Peggy. "Come on, Pet."

It paid no attention to her. It came when Bolden called, getting slowly off the bed. It stayed as close as it could get to Bolden. He was still weak so they didn't walk fast and, at first, the animal was able to keep up.

*     *     *     *     *

It was almost noon when they went out. The sun was brilliant and Van Daamas seemed a wonderful place to be alive in. Yes, with death behind him, it was a very wonderful place. Bolden chatted gaily with Peggy. She was fine company.

And then Bolden saw the native who had given him the animal. Five to seven days, and he had arrived on time. The rest of the tribe must be elsewhere in the settlement. Bolden smiled in recognition while the man was still at some distance. For an answer the native shifted the bow in his hand and glanced behind the couple, in the direction of the hospital.

The movement with the bow might have been menacing, but Bolden ignored that gesture. It was the sense that something was missing that caused him to look down. The animal was not at his side. He turned around.

The creature was struggling in the dust. It got to its feet and wobbled toward him, staggering crazily as it tried to reach him. It spun around, saw him, and came on again. The tongue lolled out and it whined once. Then the native shot it through the heart, pinning it to the ground. The short tail thumped and then it died.

Bolden couldn't move. Peggy clutched his arm. The native walked over to the animal and looked down. He was silent for a moment. "Die anyway soon," he said to Bolden. "Burned out inside."

He bent over. The bright yellow eyes had faded to nothingness in the sunlight. "Gave you its health," said the man of Van Daamas respectfully as he broke off the protruding arrow.

It was a dark blue arrow.

\*     \*     \*     \*     \*

Now every settlement on the planet has Bolden's pets. They have been given a more scientific name, but nobody remembers what it is. The animals are kept in pens, exactly as is done by the natives, on one side of town, not too near any habitation.

For a while, there was talk that it was unscientific to use the animal. It was thought that an electrical treatment could be developed to replace it. Perhaps this was true. But settling a planet is a big task. As long as one method works there isn't time for research. And it works—the percentage of recovery is as high as in other common ailments.

But in any case the animal can never become a pet, though it may be in the small but bright spark of consciousness that is all the little yellow-eyed creature wants. The quality that makes it so valuable is the final disqualification. Strength can be a weakness. Its nervous system is too powerful for a man in good health, upsetting the delicate balance of the human body in a variety of unusual ways. How the energy-transfer takes place has never been determined exactly, but it does occur.

It is only when he is stricken with the Bubble Death and needs additional energy to drive the invading microbes from the tissue around his nerves that the patient is allowed to have one of Bolden's pets.

In the end, it is the animal that dies. As the natives knew, it is kindness to kill it quickly.

It is highly regarded and respectfully spoken of. Children play as close as they can get, but are kept well away from the pens by a high, sturdy fence. Adults walk by and nod kindly to it.

Bolden never goes there nor will he speak of it. His friends say he's unhappy about being the first Earthman to discover the usefulness of the little animal. They are right. It is a distinction he doesn't care for. He still has the blue arrow. There are local craftsmen who can mend it, but he has refused their services. He wants to keep it as it is.

# Mezzerow Loves Company

ILLUSTRATED BY EMSH
ORIGINALLY PUBLISHED IN *GALAXY SCIENCE FICTION*,
JUNE 1956

*There were pride and indignation in Mezzerow's mission to
Earth and yet a practical reason ...
but maybe he should have let bad enough alone!*

# MEZZEROW LOVES COMPANY

The official took their passports, scanning the immense variety of stamps he had to choose from. He selected one with multicolored ink that suited his fancy and smeared it against the small square of plastic.

"Marcus Mezzerow?" he asked, glancing at the older man and back at the passport. His lips quivered with amusement at what was printed there. "There seems to be a mistake in the name of the planet," he said. "It's hard to believe they'd call it Messy Row."

"There is a mistake," said Marcus heavily. "However, there's nothing you can do about it. It's listed as Messy Row on the charts."

The official's face twitched and he bent over the other passport. He was slow in stamping it. "Wilbur Mezzerow?" he asked the young man.

"That's me," said Wilbur. "Isn't it a terrible thing to do? You'd almost think people on Earth can't spell—or maybe they don't listen. That's why Pa and me are here."

"Wilbur, this man is not responsible for our misfortune," said Marcus. "Neither can he correct it. Don't bore him with our problems."

"Well, sure."

"Come on."

"Welcome to Earth," said the official as they walked away. He caught sight of a woman coming toward him and cringed inwardly before he recognized that she, too, had just arrived from one of the outer worlds. He could tell because of the absence of the identifying gleam in her eyes. On principle he'd stamp her passport with dull and dingy ink.

     \*     \*     \*     \*     \*

Wilbur scuffled along beside his father. He hadn't attained his full growth, but he was as tall though not as heavy as Marcus. "Where are we going now?" he asked. "Get the name changed?"

"Don't gawk," said Marcus, restraining his own tendency to gaze around in bewilderment. Things had changed since his father had been here. "No, we're not. It's simple, but it may take longer than we think. We have to act as if Earth is an unfriendly planet."

"Hardly seems like a planet."

"It is. If you scratch deep enough under those buildings, you'll find soil and rock." Even Marcus didn't know how deep that scratch would have to be.

"Seems hard to believe it was once like—uh—Mezzerow." Wilbur was looking at the buildings and pedestrians streaming past and the little flutter cars that filled the air. "Bet you can't find any place to be alone in."

"More people are alone within ten miles of us than you have ever seen," said Marcus. He stopped in front of a building and consulted a small notebook. The address agreed, but he looked in vain for a name. There wasn't a name on any of the buildings.

Nevertheless, this ought to be it. They'd been walking for miles and he had checked all the streets. He spoke to Wilbur and they went inside.

It was a hotel. The Universe over, there is no mistaking a hotel for anything else. Continuous arrivals and departures stamp it with peculiar impermanency. A person might stay twenty years and yet seem as transient as the man still signing the registry.

A clerk sauntered over to the Mezzerows. He was plump, but the shoulders of his jacket were obviously much broader than he was. "Looking for someone?" he inquired.

"I'm looking for the Outer Hotel," said Marcus.

"This is a hotel," the clerk said, raising his shoulders and letting them fall. One shoulder didn't come down, so he grasped the bottom of the sleeve and pulled it down.

"What's the name?"

The clerk yawned. "Doesn't have a name—just a number. No hotel has had a name for the last hundred years. Too many of them."

"My father stayed at the Outer Hotel fifty years ago, before he left to discover a new planet. It was at this address."

The clerk, wary of his shoulder pads, shrugged sideways. It gave him a bent look when one shoulder stayed back. "Maybe it wasn't a hundred years ago," he said to his fingernails. "Anyway, they don't have names now."

"This must be the old Outer Hotel," Marcus decided. "We'll stay here."

The clerk's aplomb was not as foolproof as he imagined. It slipped a trifle. "You want to stay here? I mean *really?*"

"Why not?" growled Marcus. "You have room, don't you? It seems like a decent place. I don't have any other recommendations."

"Certainly it's decent and we have room. I thought you might be more comfortable elsewhere. I can recommend an exclusive men's hotel to you."

"We are plain people and don't want anything exclusive," said Marcus. "Register us, please."

"I don't do menial tasks," said the clerk with an offended laugh. "I'm here for the sole purpose of imparting class to the hotel. Take your registry problems to the desk robot."

Wilbur looked curiously at the pudgy clerk as he walked away, smiling coyly at the passersby. "Pa, how can a man like him make this place seem classy?"

"Son, I don't know," said Marcus heavily. "Earth has changed since your grandfather described it to me. I don't propose to find out what's the matter with it. We'll just take care of our business and go home."

*    *    *    *    *

They signed at the desk, giving their baggage claim checks to the robot, who assured them that everything would be zipped straight to their room from the spaceport.

In spite of Wilbur's protests that he wasn't tired, that he was just getting used to walking again after being cramped in the ship, they went to their rooms to freshen up. Thus they missed the noontime exodus of workers from the buildings around them.

Marcus had food sent up, but didn't eat much, though initially he had been hungry. The lot 219 steaks were excellent in appearance, nicely seared and thick. Inside, they were gray and watery, with an offensive taste, obviously tank-grown. After a few bites, Marcus abandoned the meat and ate vegetables. These, though ill-flavored and artificially colored, he could eat without suspicion.

Wilbur consumed everything before him, ending by looking hungrily at the steak on his father's plate. Marcus hastily shoved the trays in the disposer slot. If he had time before he left Earth, he meant to find out what a "lot 219" steak was. He hoped it wasn't what he thought.

When they were ready, they dropped to the ground floor. The clerk who gave class to the hotel was nowhere in sight. They went out into the street and headed for the tall spire of Information Center. It was a landmark they couldn't miss. Every human who thought of visiting Earth was familiar with it. If a question couldn't be answered there, it was beyond the scope of human knowledge.

There were many more women than men on the streets. Marcus noted it, but didn't think it unusual. He had heard that women had more free time in the middle of the day on planets that had been settled for a long time. He walked on with a long stride, oblivious to the feminine glances he and his son attracted.

At Information Center, he consulted the index at the entrance, jostled by people from thousands of planets who were doing the same. The red line on the floor led to the planet section, which was what he wanted. Keeping check on Wilbur, who showed a tendency to wander, he followed it to the end.

The end was an immense room with innumerable small booths. Instinctively, Marcus distrusted booths; more than anything else, they resembled vertical coffins. Growling to Wilbur to stay close by, he went inside and closed the door. He inserted a coin and made the selection.

A harried face appeared on the viewplate. "Does your question require a human answer?"

"It certainly does," said Marcus. "I didn't come nine hundred and forty-seven light-years to be befuddled by a robot."

The harried face barked something unintelligible in another direction and then turned back to Marcus. "Very well. Question?"

"I want to request a change. My planet—"

"Planet? Change?" repeated the face. It disappeared and a finger took its place. The finger rifled rapidly down a vertical index. It stopped and stabbed and the index popped open. "Go to building P-CAF." The finger snatched a slip out of the open space and dropped the slip in a slot. "Go to the platform at the rear of this building. Take any tube with P-CAF on it. Apply at that building for the change."

Marcus wasn't surprised, but he felt annoyed. "Can't you make the change here? I don't like being shoved around."

"We are not authorized to make changes. We are merely what our name implies; we have the information to direct you to the proper sources. The slip I gave you is a map of the general vicinity of the place you want. You can't get lost."

"You gave me no map," snapped Marcus. The voice didn't answer him, though the finger still waved on the viewplate. He couldn't argue very well with a finger. The plate burped and a slip dropped out of the slot below it. Only then did he release the lever, allowing the finger to vanish.

*     *     *     *     *

Marcus studied the map. P-CAF (Planets; changes, apply for) was between M-AVO (Marriages; alternate variations of) and M-AAD (Marriages; annulment and divorce).

Hastily, he stuffed the map in his pocket as Wilbur pressed the door, trying to look at what he had in his hand. It was nothing for a growing boy to see.

It wasn't a good map, since it didn't show where the building was in relation to the rest of the city. The transportation tube would take him there, but he'd have to find his own way back.

The tube that whisked them to P-CAF was occupied mainly by Outers, a circumstance that made the crowded uncomfortable trip more bearable. Marcus didn't talk to the others—their interests were worlds apart—but he felt closer to them than to the strange, frantic people of Earth.

P-CAF was neo-drive-in classical, a style once in vogue throughout the Universe. With Wilbur following, Marcus plunged in. It seemed strange that he had come nine hundred odd light-years for a matter that, once stated, would only take a few matters of some minor official's time. And yet it was necessary. For years, he had been writing requests without results.

It was not as crowded as Information Center. The booths were wider and Marcus decided they both could squeeze in. It was a historic moment: Wilbur should be present. After several trials, they did get in together.

The official who came to the plate was as relaxed as the other had been harried. "Planets; changes, apply for," he said. He had perfected the art of raising one eyebrow.

"That's why we're here," said Marcus, fumbling in his jacket. He was jammed against Wilbur and couldn't get his hand in his pocket.

"Land masses reshaped, oceans installed, or climate recycled?" asked the official.

"We don't want the climate changed," said Wilbur. "We've got lots of it—rain, hail, snow, hot weather. All in the same day—though not in the same place. It's a big planet, nearly as big as Earth."

"Wilbur, I'll do the talking," declared Marcus, still struggling to reach his pocket.

"Yes, Pa. But we don't want the continents reshaped. We like them as they are. And we've got enough oceans."

"Wilbur," Marcus said sharply, pulling his hand free. He held up a tattered chart.

"Are you sure you know what you do want?" asked the relaxed man with a yawn.

"I'm coming to it," said Marcus. "Fifty years ago, my father, Mathew Mezzerow, discovered a planet. Things being the way they were then, planet stealing and such, Captain Mezzerow didn't come back and report it. He settled on it right there, securing for his heirs and descendants a proper share of the new world."

"What do you expect for that, a medal?"

"He could have had a medal. Being practical, he preferred a part of the planet. Since then, we have become a thriving community. But we're not growing as fast as we should. That's why I'm here."

"You've come to the wrong place," said the man. "P-EHF is what you want."

"Planets; economic help for? No, we don't want that kind of aid. However, there is one insignificant mistake that has been hindering us. People don't settle the way they should. You see, though Captain Mathew Mezzerow didn't return to report his discovery in person, he did send in a routine claim. That's where the mistake was made. Naturally he named the planet after himself. Mezzerow. Mezz—uh—row. The second *e* is almost silent, hardly pronounced at all. But what do you think somebody—a robot, probably—called it?"

"I can't guess."

"Messy Row," said Marcus. "It maligns a good man's name. We're stuck with it because somebody bobbled."

\*     \*     \*     \*     \*

"I admit it isn't pretty," said the official with a cautious smile. "But I can't see that it affects anything. One name is as good as another."

"That's what you think," Marcus retorted. "I can see how the robot made the mistake and I'm not blaming it. My father sent in a verbal tape report. Mezzerow could sound a little like Messy

Row. Anyway, it's had a bad effect on the settlers. Men come there because it sounds easy and relaxed, which it is, of course, to a point. But women avoid it. They don't like the sound of the name."

"Then it's really women you're concerned with," said the official. A cold glazed stare had replaced his indifference. "In any event, you've come to the wrong place. We reconstruct planets. Names are out of our jurisdiction."

"It makes things bad when there aren't enough women," continued Marcus. "Some men leave when they can't find anyone to marry." He crumpled the old chart in his hands. "It's not merely that, of course. Simple justice demands that a great man's name be properly honored."

"You've come to the wrong place for justice," said the official. "P-CAF doesn't make this kind of an adjustment. Let's see if I can't refer you to someone else." He rested his head on his hand. Then he straightened up, snapping his fingers. "Of course. If you want the name of a planet changed, you go to Astrogation; charts, errors, locations of."

"You do?" Marcus asked dubiously. Life on Mezzerow had not prepared him for the complexities of governmental organization.

"Certainly," said the official, happy that he had solved the problem. "Don't thank me. It's what I'm here for. Go to A-CELO."

"Where is it?"

The official frowned importantly and turned to the great vertical file that Marcus was learning to associate with all departments of the government. He stabbed his finger at a space, but nothing opened. "Seem to be all out of reference slips," he said with a casual lack of surprise. "Come back tomorrow and I may have some. It's quitting time now."

"Do I have to come back? A-CELO may be on the other side of the city from here."

"It may be," said the official, reaching for his jacket. "If you don't want to waste time, buy a map from an infolegger. It'll be a day old, but chances are it should be accurate on most things." The plate snapped off, leaving Marcus and his son staring at nothing.

Marcus got up and left the booth. "What's an infolegger?" asked Wilbur as he followed him.

"They move things fast on Earth," said Marcus tiredly. He hadn't realized how wearing it could be to chase down the thread of responsibility in a government that had many things to look after. "An infolegger doesn't know any more about it than you do, but he'll sell you information that you can ordinarily get free from the government."

"But who buys from him?"

"Fools like me who get tired of running around. We'd better get back to the hotel."

"I wish we were on Messy—Mezzerow," said Wilbur wistfully. "Ma would have dinner ready now."

"I keep forgetting your appetite. All right, we'll eat as soon as we find a restaurant."

\*     \*     \*     \*     \*

They found one a block away. It was easy enough to walk there. It was stopping that was hard. Marcus made his way to the side of the street and hauled Wilbur in out of the stream of pedestrians. Inside there was one vacant table which they promptly took, oblivious to the glares of those who were not so fast afoot.

Marcus studied the menu at length. To his disappointment, there was no lot 219 steak listed. Instead there were two other choices, a lot 313 and a miscellany steak. Marcus looked up to see that his son had already dialed his order. Questioning revealed that Wilbur had missed his afternoon snack and thought that a full portion of one steak and half of the other would compensate for his fast. "Vegetables, too," said Marcus.

"Pa, you know I don't like that stuff."

"Vegetables," said Marcus, watching to make sure his son selected a balanced diet. After deliberation, he decided on a high protein vegetable plate for himself, though ordinarily he liked meat. He couldn't get that idea out of his mind.

The low rectangular serving robot scurried up and began dispensing food with a flurry of extensibles. Marcus noted that the steaks were identical with those served in the hotel. "Waiter, what is the origin of those steaks?"

"The same as all meat. Hygienically grown in a bath of nutrients that supply all the necessary food elements. Trimmed daily and delivered fresh and tender, ready for instant preparation."

"I'm familiar with the process," snapped Marcus, wincing as his son chewed the gray, watery substance. "What I asked was the origin, the ultimate origin. From what animals were the first cells taken?"

"I don't know. No other protein source is so free from contamination."

"Will the manager know?"

"Perhaps."

"Tell him I would like to see him."

"I'll pass the request along. But it won't do any good. The manager can't come. It's a robot attached to the building."

"Then I'll go to it," said Marcus, rising. "Keep the food warm. How do I get there?"

"The manager shouldn't be disturbed," said the robot as it placed thermoshields over the food. "It's the small room to the rear, at the right of the kitchen."

Marcus found the place without difficulty. The manager lighted up as he came in. The opposite wall blinked and a chair swung out for him. "Complaint?" said the manager hollowly. The manager was hollow.

"Not exactly," said Marcus, repeating his request.

The manager meditated briefly.

"Are you an Outer?"

"I am."

"I thought so. Only Outers ask that question. I'll have to find out some day."

"Make it today," said Marcus.

"An excellent thought," said the manager. "I'll do it. But this is a chain restaurant and so you'll have to wait. If you don't mind the delay, I'll plug in one of our remote information banks."

Marcus did mind delay, but it was worse not knowing. He waited.

*    *    *    *    *

"I have it," said the robot after an interval. "There is great difficulty feeding a city this large. In fact, there is with all of Earth—it's greatly overpopulated."

"So I understand," mumbled Marcus.

"The trouble began forty-five or fifty years ago with the water supply," said the robot. "It was sanitary, but there was too great or not great enough concentration of minerals in it. Information isn't specific on this point. The robots in control of the tanks found that beef, pork, lamb and chicken in all their variety would not grow fast enough. Many tanks wouldn't grow at all.

"The robots communicated this fact to higher authorities and were told to find out how to correct the situation. They investigated and determined that either the entire water-system would have to be overhauled, or a new and hardier protein would have to be developed. Naturally, it would require incalculable labor to install a new water-system. They didn't recommend it."

"Naturally," said Marcus.

"The situation was critical. The city had to be fed. The tank robots were told to find the new protein. Resources were thrown open to them that weren't hither-to available. In a short time, they solved the problem. About half of the tanks that were not growing properly were cleaned out and the new protein placed in them. The old animal name system was outmoded so the new lot number system was devised and applied to every tank regardless of its ultimate origin."

"Then nobody has any idea what they're eating," said Marcus. "But what was that new protein? That's what I want to know."

"It was hardy. It came from the most adaptable creature on Earth," said the robot. "And there was another factor in favor of it. The flesh of all mammals is nearly the same. But there are differences. The ideal protein for a meat-eating animal is one which exactly matches the creature's own body, eliminating food that can't be fully utilized."

Marcus closed his eyes and grasped the arm of the chair.

"Do you feel ill?" inquired the managing robot. "Shall I call the doctor? No? Well, as I was saying, there was already a supply of animal tissue on hand. It was this that the robots used. It's funny that you're asking this. Not many people are so curious."

"They didn't care," snarled Marcus. "As long as they were fed, they didn't ask what it was."

"Why should they?" asked the robot. "The tissue was already well adapted to growth tanks. Scrupulously asceptic, in no way did it harm the original donors who were long since dead. And there was little difference in the use of it, anyway. No one would hesitate if he were injured and needed skin or part of a liver or a new eye. This was replacement from the inside, by a digestive process rather than a medical one."

"The robots took tissue from the surgery replacement tanks," said Marcus. "Do you deny it?"

"That's what I've been telling you," said the robot. "A very clever solution considering how little time they had. However only about half of the tanks had to be replaced."

"Cannibals," said Marcus, nearly destroying the chair as he hurled it away from him.

"What's a cannibal?" asked the robot.

But Marcus wasn't there to answer. He went back to the restaurant, under control by the time he reached the table. He couldn't tell Wilbur because Wilbur had finished eating except for the vegetables which were mostly untouched. Marcus sat down and took the shields off the food, looking at it gloomily.

"Pa, aren't you going to eat?" asked Wilbur.

"As soon as I get my breath back," he said. It wasn't bad when he ate, but the mere thought of food was distasteful. He glanced sternly at his son. "Wilbur, hereafter you may not order meat. As long as we are on Earth, you will ask for eggs."

"Just eggs?" said Wilbur incredulously. "Gee, they're real expensive here. Anyway, I don't like them without a rasher of—"

"Eggs," said Marcus. Another thought occurred to him. "Sunny-side up. No cook can disguise that."

\*       \*       \*       \*       \*

The sky was dark when they left the restaurant. After work, traffic had abated and the entertainment rush hadn't come on the streets, which were now curiously silent and deserted. Marcus caught sight of the tall spire of Information Center glistening against the evening sky.

"Where are we going?" asked Wilbur.

"To the hotel. We have a hard day's work tomorrow."

"Can we walk? I mean, we can't see anything in the tubes."

"It's a long walk."

"It's right over there. I've walked farther before breakfast."

Marcus noted with approval that Wilbur had used the Information Center as a landmark to deduce the correct location of the hotel. His training showed. Even in the confusion of the city, he wouldn't get lost. "It's farther than you think, but we'll walk if you want. It may be our last evening on Earth. At least, I sincerely hope so."

They went on. In time they saw what there was to see. It was a city, vast and sprawling, but still just another city Man had created. The buildings were huge, but constructed as all buildings had to be, out of stone and steel, concrete and plastic. Women were beautiful, tastefully gowned and coiffured, but it was easy to see that they were merely women. Shops were elaborate and fanciful, but there was a limit to what they displayed, an end to the free play of fancy.

By the time they realized they were tired, they were close to the hotel. There wasn't any use in seeking transportation, since they'd get where they were going almost as fast either way. They had kept to the main thoroughfares since there was more to see. But Marcus had quickly accustomed himself to the pattern of streets and as they neared their destination he saw a short cut which they took.

It was getting late and the street was dark. He began to wonder whether they should have come this way. He decided they shouldn't have. A faint red flash from the doorway indicated that his tardy decision was sound but useless. His knees tingled where the red flash struck him and in the middle of a stride he felt he didn't have any feet. He fell forward, trying to shield Wilbur. Wilbur was falling, too, and they collided on the downward arc.

Hands seized him, lifting him up. He was in no condition to struggle. Besides it wasn't safe. A tingler wasn't a lethal weapon, but it could have unpleasant effects if used carelessly or hastily. He didn't think they were in any real danger and it was best not to provoke their captors.

*       *       *       *       *

By the time he had recovered sufficiently to be aware of what was going on, he found he had been carried to a space between two buildings, hidden from the street by a masonry projection. Wilbur was sitting beside him and a dim light played on them.

"Don't move," said a voice that made an effort to be rough and hard, but failed by an octave. Now that Marcus thought of it the hands that had lifted him were small and soft. Their captors were women. The disconnected impressions of the city seemed to fall into a pattern. He was not greatly surprised at what was happening.

The light moved closer and Marcus could make out the figure of the woman who held it. Behind her were others—all women. But even delicate hands were capable of leveling a tingler. "Don't say anything," he said to his son in a low voice. Wilbur nodded dazedly.

"No whispering," barked the soprano, shining the light directly in his eyes. "Now, are either of you married?"

Marcus sighed; so that was it. Poor Earth was in a bad way when a pudgy unattractive clerk could get a high-salaried job solely because he was male.

"Answer me," demanded the high unsteady voice. "Are either of you married? On Earth, I mean."

Marcus could see her clearly, now that his eyes had become accustomed to the light. She was young, barely out of her teens.

"What kind of question is that? When you're married, you're married. It doesn't matter where you are." On Earth, apparently, it did.

"Outers," she exclaimed happily. "I've always hoped I'd find one. They're real men. Now let's see, which one shall I take?" She flashed the light on Wilbur, who squirmed and blinked.

"He's younger and will probably last longer," she said critically. "On the other hand, he'll be clumsy and inexperienced."

She turned to Marcus. "You need a shave," she said crisply. "Your beard is turning gray. I think I'll take you. Older men are nice."

"You can't have me," said Marcus. She was near and he could have taken both the weapon and the light from her. But he couldn't stand, much less walk, and there were other women in the background, all armed probably, watching the girl who seemed to be their leader. "You see, I am married. Wilma wouldn't like it, if I took another wife."

"Not even just for the time you're on Earth? It isn't much to ask." She turned the light on herself. "Am I unattractive?"

She was not outstandingly beautiful, but since she was dressed as scantily as law allowed and fashion decreed Marcus could see her desirability. "How old are you?" he asked.

"Old enough," she said. "In eleven months, I'll be twenty-one."

"You're pretty," said Marcus. "If I were fifteen or twenty years younger—and not married—I'd come courting."

"But you did," she said in amazement. "Why did you come down a dark street, if you weren't looking for romance?"

\*      \*      \*      \*      \*

This, it seemed, is what passed for romance on Earth. Men must be outnumbered at least three to one. It tied in with what he had so far observed. "I'm sorry for your trouble," he said.

"But you must remember that we're Outers. We're not familiar with your customs. We were merely taking a short cut to our hotel."

She gestured in sullen defeat. "I suppose it was a mistake. But why can't I have him, then? He's not married."

"He isn't, nor will he be for some time. He has barely turned seventeen. I won't give my permission."

"He's your son? Then you are experienced. Are you sure you won't reconsider me—just while you're on Earth? I told you I don't like young men. Maybe that's because my father was an older man."

"I'm sure he was," said Marcus. "However that's no reason to find me irresistible." He tried to stand, but his legs were rubbery and he sat down quickly.

She looked at him with concern. "Does it hurt? I guess we gave you the strongest charge." She handed him the light and went to the women who were standing some distance behind her. He heard her whispering. Presently she came back.

She knelt beside him and began rubbing his legs. "I sent them away," she said. "They're going to look for someone else. It was my turn to propose to whomever we captured, but now you spoiled it."

He smiled at her earnestness. "I'm sure you deserve better than you're apt to find with these strange methods of courtship. However I think you should help my son. You gave him a charge, too."

"I bet I did," she said scornfully. "Don't worry about him. Kids recover easily."

"Should I clout her, Pa?" asked Wilbur as he stood up, bending his knees gingerly. "She had no business shooting us."

"She didn't, but you have no business talking like that. Touch her and I'll wallop you."

The girl ignored Wilbur, putting her arms around Marcus and helping him to his feet. From the girl's reaction to him you'd never think so, but he was getting old. The first step was proof of it. He could walk unaided, but it felt as if someone were pulling pins out of his legs at the rate of two or three a second.

"I'll go with you to the hotel," said the girl. "There are probably other marriage gangs out. If they see me with you, they'll think I've already made my catch."

Marcus frowned in the darkness. Wilbur was getting entirely the wrong idea about women. He'd find it difficult to adjust to the different conditions at home. Marcus told the girl their names and asked hers.

"Mary Ellen."

"That's all, Mary Ellen?"

"Of course, I have a last name, but I'm hoping to change it."

He sighed in resignation. "Mary Ellen, we won't discuss marriage again. Is this clear? However I have plans for you. I'll get in touch with you before we leave Earth." They were nearing a brightly lit thoroughfare and he felt safer.

"I was hoping you'd say that," she said wistfully. She dug into a tiny purse and handed him a card. "You'll notice there's another name on it, too. That's Chloe, my half-sister. She's smart and I like her, but I hope you don't like her—not better than me, anyway."

"I'm sure I won't. But why half-sister? I'd think it would be rather difficult for your mother to marry again."

"Of course she couldn't," she said scornfully. "No woman's allowed more than half a—"

"Mary Ellen!"

"All right, I won't say it," she said crossly. "But you asked."

\*     \*     \*     \*     \*

He could fill in the missing information. With women drastically outnumbering men, husbands had to be shared. Men were allowed more than one mate, but women never were. Perhaps the development of polygamy had been inevitable.

Earth was the center of a vast and spreading civilization. Men went out to settle the newly discovered planets while, for the most part, women tended to remain behind. More than that, there were some women who came to Earth from planets that had been settled longer, attracted by the glamor of an older civilization and high-paying jobs, never realizing until they got there the other conditions that went with it.

Earth's dilemma was therefore a partial solution to one of the problems of his own planet. But the important problem, getting the name changed to Mezzerow, was harder than he had anticipated. He wasn't looking forward to tomorrow.

He noticed Mary Ellen glancing curiously around. "Is there anything wrong?" he asked.

"Nooo. It's just sort of funny that you'd stay here—in the heart of the unmarried girls' residential district." She grinned at him. "Maybe I'd better go in with you."

"I think you'd better," he said. That's what the pudgy clerk had meant. He should have listened to him and gone to the men's hotel.

The lobby was crowded with women, many of whom, he suspected, had been waiting for their return. On a man-starved planet, word got around. Perhaps he was imagining it, but he thought he heard an audible sigh of disappointment when they came in with Mary Ellen. She had more than repaid them for the few anxious moments she had caused. Much more, though she didn't know it yet.

They went directly to their rooms and Marcus sent Wilbur inside, lingering at the door to talk with the girl. "Should I come in?" she asked hopefully. "I'm really sorry about your legs."

"You will not come in, Mary Ellen. I don't trust myself alone with you."

"You mean it?"

"I was never more sincere." He almost believed it himself.

"We don't *have* to get married if you're not going to be here long enough to make it worthwhile," she said happily. "I was thinking—"

He glanced warningly inside the room.

"He's a big nuisance," she whispered. "Look. I've got to work tomorrow, but in the evening I'll be free. Put the kid on a merry-go-round and come and see me, huh?" She threw her arms around Marcus and kissed him passionately. Then she turned and ran down the hall.

Marcus shook his head and went into his room.

\*     \*     \*     \*     \*

In the morning, Marcus had little difficulty contacting an infolegger. For a rather large sum, a map purporting to show the location of A-CELO exchanged hands. For another sum, a map of the principal transportation tubes was added to it. Both were assuredly out of date in many respects, but were probably correct in the one detail Marcus was concerned with.

They started rather late to avoid the morning rush. There were some transportation complications. At the first trial they arrived at the wrong section of the city. After consultation with various passengers and robot way stations, they got it straightened out. Penciling corrections on the map, they retraced their route, making only one mistake along the way. This mistake was not their fault. A transfer junction had been relocated since they had passed through it on the way out.

They got to their destination in good time, perhaps faster than if they had used the services of Information Center. A-CELO was also an example of neo-drive-in classical. But instead of resembling something appropriate, say a five or six pointed star, it appeared to be a mere jumble of children's curv-blocks. A closer look convinced Marcus that his first appraisal had been wrong. Originally it must have been built to house another A-function. Perhaps A-WR (Anatomy; woman, reclining).

Whatever it was on the outside, A-CELO was confusion within. Marcus found it impossible to get near the question booths. Robots scurried about in seemingly useless tasks and workmen shouted orders that no one paid attention to. In the midst of the dust and turmoil, one man stood on a platform and watched the frantic effort with bored serenity.

"Moving," he said automatically as Marcus approached.

"Where to?"

"I don't know. It depends on whom we can bump."

\*     \*     \*     \*     \*

Marcus paled visibly. They were moving and didn't know where. Another day and his map was useless. And if this man was right, even Information Center wouldn't know where A-CELO was tomorrow. "Isn't there a planning commission?" he said. "Don't they tell you where to move?"

The man shrugged. "There's a planning commission. But they had too many responsibilities and had to move to a larger building, the same as we're doing. Until they get settled, everyone's on his own." The man spoke quietly into the mike and the tempo of the removal robots accelerated. He turned back to Marcus and added an explanation: "Three exploration ships returned yesterday, loaded to the brim with micro-data. That's why we have to move."

Marcus rubbed his face. He could see it posed a problem. It was not merely the storage of new data, the data also had to be made available to the public. This required new offices, human supervisors, robot clerks.

That was the way they did things on Earth, but he wished they'd waited a few days. "You can't be moving this stuff out on the streets. Somebody must have an idea where you're going. Tell me who he is. I've got to find out where you'll be tomorrow."

"Oh, no. If you found where we're moving, you'd learn who we're going to bump," said the man with cheerful cunning. "They'd take steps to repel us. Can't have that." The man scratched his head. "Tell you, if you're really honest—if you're not a department spy—I can show you how to take care of your business today."

"I'm an Outer," said Marcus. "I don't care about your squabbles. I want to get something settled and get out of here."

"You look like an Outer," said the man. "Here's what you do. Part of the department is still functioning. Go to the side entrance. Question booths there are open." He turned back to the mike and barked orders that had no visible effect on anything.

*     *     *     *     *

The man was partly wrong. The side entrance was open, but corridors and booths were jammed with displaced information seekers. Marcus was not easily discouraged. By now he was accustomed to the vast machinations required for the simplest things. He went to the back entrance. It, too, was jammed, but after a short desperate struggle he squeezed into a booth, leaving Wilbur to hang on the outside.

The official who answered him was sleepy and harassed, a difficult expression. He yawned and took his feet off the desk to acknowledge the call and then a robot removed the desk. He had no place to put his feet so he kept them firmly on the floor as if he expected that, too, to vanish.

Marcus stated the request clearly, spreading the chart for the man to see. "Here is the original from which the photo-tape was made and sent to Earth with his comments. I don't know what happened here. Perhaps the tape was fuzzy or it may have been fogged in transit by radiation. Or it may have been faulty interpretation on the part of a robot."

The official peered out of the view plate. "Messy Row. Mezzerow. Ha, ha." He laughed perfunctorily and got up to pace. A robot came near the chair and he sat down hastily.

"Here, you can see that in his own hand he spelled it Mezzerow," said Marcus. "He named it after himself as every explorer is entitled to do once in his career. I ask that in simple justice the mistake be corrected. I have a petition signed by everyone on the planet."

The official waved the documents back. "It doesn't matter who signed," he said. "We don't allow these things to influence our decision." He put his head in his hand though he had no desk for his elbow. His lips moved soundlessly as he framed the reply.

"I want to give you an insight to our problems," he said. "First, consider pilots. There are all sorts of beautiful names for planets. Plum Branch, Coarsegold, Waves End, but there's only one Messy Row. It's a bright spot on their voyage. They look at the charts and see it—Messy Row. They laugh. Laughter is a therapeutic force against the loneliness of space. The name of your planet is distinctive."

"We don't care for the distinction," said Marcus. "It's got so bad, we call it Messy Row ourselves, when we're not thinking. Who's going to settle on a planet they laugh at?" The official didn't seem to hear. Marcus adjusted the volume control, but there didn't seem to be anything wrong with the sound or the volume.

"This is only a small part of it," continued the man. "Do you have any idea how many charts we print? You would have us make them obsolete. Think of the ships roaming through space, many never touching Earth. How can we reach them with corrected charts?"

"I'm glad you said corrected charts," said Marcus. "But corrected charts shouldn't be any harder to deliver than new ones—which, you'll admit, you're always making."

"I can't compromise our famous accuracy for the whims of a few selfish individuals," said the official. He stood up and this time the robot whisked the chair away. He smiled and reached out his hand for the familiar vertical file. The file wasn't there, but a robot was. It took his hand and tried to lead him away. He shook himself loose. "You can see we're busy. Come back when we're not in the midst of an upheaval. I might consider a request that at present I must turn down." He walked briskly away, leaving Marcus with a fine view of an empty room—until a robot came and took the viewplate to the other end.

Marcus eased out of the booth. Wilbur was waiting with an anxious face. "I know it's past noon," he said gloomily to his son. "We'll get something to eat. Eggs." Wilbur knew better than to protest.

*    *    *    *    *

They left A-CELO before the removal robots arrived at the rear section. In the quiet of a nearby restaurant Marcus considered the problem anew. The mission hadn't been entirely a failure. He could accomplish one important task without the aid of any government agency. In fact, it was better if he didn't ask their help.

But he owed something to the memory of Captain Mathew Mezzerow. Mezzerow his father had called the planet—and Mezzerow it was going to be.

There was also Wilma. She had arrived when both she and the settlement were quite young. Courted and feted and proposed to endlessly, she had found the excitement of being the center of attention irresistible. She hadn't minded the name then, not since she was the prettiest, most attractive girl there. There weren't many others.

But she had changed as Messy Row had grown. They had four sons now, Wilbur the oldest. Four sons. She was not concerned whether they would marry. Her sons were smart and handsome and belonged to the best family—they would experience no trouble in finding wives. But if they did she could always take them visiting—to a planet on which there was no woman shortage.

Once she had been slightly giddy, even after they were married. Marcus had often wondered how her lashes could possibly remain intact when other men came near. She had outgrown that phase and when the chrysalis burst it revealed a different woman.

Out of the flirtatious girl came the homemaker. Everything near her was immaculate. Fences around the house were whitewashed and the lawns were always mowed. Inside, everything was as tidy as a pin. Mud was never tracked in. Wilma no longer approved of Messy Row as the name of any planet on which she lived.

Marcus had to have help. Someone who lived on Earth would know the proper approach better than he. He fished out the card Mary Ellen had given him and the longer he looked the more certain he was that he had found the person. It was not Mary Ellen. It was her sister.

Mary Ellen and Chloe—no last names given. Apparently this was custom, the way unmarried girls informed the world that they were looking for mates. In addition to their names was the address at which they both lived.

There was also the occupation of each. Mary Ellen was a junior attendant, whatever that was. But Chloe was far more important. She was an astrographer, a senior supervisor astrographer.

Marcus ate rapidly, a definite plan materializing with each bite. Chloe was the key. With her aid, he should be able to change Messy Row. He smiled reflectively. With what he had to offer she would certainly consent to help him—even if it was illegal.

\*      \*      \*      \*      \*

Mary Ellen was not at home, but Chloe was and she welcomed them. Marcus truthfully explained how they'd met her sister. Chloe commented unfavorably on the marriage gangs and, though Marcus agreed, he received the remarks in silence. It was not for him to change the mores of Earth. Society had to work with what there was.

Chloe was small and dark in contrast to the larger blonde Mary Ellen. She was older, too. Once she must have been quite pretty, but instead of easing graciously into the poise of maturity she had been forced into the early thirties without a husband. The struggle showed.

She was cordial when they came in and even more cordial when he finished outlining his plan. "Yes, something can be done," she said quietly. "I will set up the organization and ship them out in groups of ten. I have a vacation in a few months and Mary Ellen and I will come then." She glanced at him anxiously. "That is, if you think I'm needed."

"You are," he assured her. "We need wives, mothers, skilled technicians. I can't think of anyone who will fit the description better."

"Then you'll see me again," she said. "And not merely for the reasons you think. You see, I have a high-salaried job and could have been married before this. But it didn't seem right. I want to feel I'm of some use to a civilization that seems to have forgotten people like me exist."

"Mezzerow needs you," he said. "I was thinking of a man I know. Joe Ainsworth, a quiet thoughtful fellow of about thirty-five or thirty-seven. His trouble has been that he likes pretty women who are also intelligent. I'll have him keep an eye out for you."

She smiled and the transformation took place. She *was* pretty. Marcus wondered whether there was such a person as Joe Ainsworth. There must be, in kind if not in name.

"So much for that," said Chloe briskly. "The rest of your plan for Messy Row is a fine example of muddy thinking. In the first place I work for a private company, not the government."

"But you make government charts."

"True. But let me show you what I mean. What's the code number of the chart Messy Row is on?"

Marcus quoted it from memory. The code of a map on which a given system could be found was almost as important as the name.

Chloe closed her eyes. "No," she said when she opened them. "That's done in another department. I couldn't possibly change it to Mezzerow."

"But if you changed it, the name would stay," said Marcus. "I'll give you money to see that it gets done. Once it's on the map nobody will say anything. Even if they do notice, all they'll know is that there's a conflict between early and late editions. They'll have to go directly to the source to straighten it out. And we're the source."

Chloe smiled fleetingly. "It's never done that way. Do you think they'd send nine hundred and forty-seven light-years to find whether the name is Messy Row or Mezzerow?" She crossed her legs and they were nice legs. There had to be a Joe Ainsworth.

"It won't work," said Chloe. "I can't make the change myself or even bribe someone to do it." She noticed his dejection and touched his hand. "Don't be discouraged. There's another way. An Outer wouldn't think of it because he doesn't know what goes on behind the scenes."

"I've seen enough to give me a good idea," said Marcus.

"I wonder. Have you noticed that when you ask for information you are always answered by a human? And just as obviously he doesn't know. He has to contact a robot and relay the information along."

\*    \*    \*    \*    \*

He hadn't thought of it. The omnipresent vertical file was, in reality, a robot memory bank. Why not give the robot a voice and dispense with innumerable men and women? The question was on his face when he looked at Chloe.

"Robots are logical—nothing more," she said. "Most questions can't be given black and white answers. There must be an intermediary who understands the limitations of the mechanical mind to interpret it to the public."

"I don't see how this is going to help me," he said.

"You've been trying to get an official to say that you're right and he'll see that the change is made. Abandon that approach. He'll never take the time. Write your request."

"For forty years we've been writing. That's why I'm here."

Chloe smiled again. "The number of letters received by the government in one year reaches a remarkable total. Or perhaps the total isn't huge when you consider how many humans in the Universe there are. Anyway, off-planet letters are never opened, because there's no way to tell from the outside which are important. So they're all pulped and used as nutrients in food tanks."

Marcus nodded dubiously. "I see. Anyone who thinks he has something important will come here ... as I did. And if he isn't satisfied he tries to go over the head of whoever refused the request. This volume is still great, but it's small enough to be processed without falling hopelessly behind."

"Exactly. And if you phrase your request properly there's a good chance it will be granted, even if it is foolish."

"This isn't foolish," said Marcus, rubbing his hands. "I've got all the facts. I can write them in my sleep."

"Who said anything about facts?" said Chloe. "The worst thing you can do is to give them facts. Don't you see what I'm trying to tell you?"

Marcus took a deep breath. "No," he said.

"Let's go over it again. Mathew Mezzerow discovered a planet and named it after himself. Does this mean anything? Not really. Does it mean anything that Messy Row will be settled more slowly because of the name? Again no. Thousands of other planets will gain the settlers that Messy Row loses. The robot will refuse a request based on facts and from the government's viewpoint will be justified."

"But you just said robots don't handle requests."

"Face to face they don't. You would resent it as an arrogant bureaucracy being told you couldn't have something by a robot. But you don't see who processes written requests. And in these matters the government uses robots because they're more efficient."

It was too complex for Marcus. Robots processed written requests, but not those made in person. Robots were logical and only logical and therefore ordinarily should not be appealed to on the basis of reason.

He swallowed hard and looked at Chloe. "What should I do?" he asked.

"Emotion," she said. "Robots don't understand emotion. But they can and have been built to recognize emotion. On a minor matter such as this, you need to overload the emotion recognition factor.

"Merely identify the planet. Then stress not the justice of your claim but the anguish you've suffered. Make it extreme—paint a picture of the misery the error has already caused and will continue to cause. If you make it strong enough, the robot will set aside rational processes and grant the request."

*     *     *     *     *

It began to be clear. As the government grew in size and complexity and contact with the governed parts became more tenuous, greater reliance had to be placed in logic, machine-made logic. But machines could not hope to encompass all the irrationality of Man. And irrational demands were apt to cause trouble. Pride was irrational, and so was the greater part of human misery.

Therefore, in minor matters, the government had provided a safety valve for irrational requests. Only in minor matters, men still decided important issues. But in the innumerable small decisions that had to be made daily, robots would set aside their logical process if a strong emotion were present.

"Pa," said Wilbur from the corner in which he had been squirming sleepily.

"Not now, Wilbur," growled Marcus. "I suppose you're hungry." In his mind he was composing the request. It was unlike anything he'd written.

"I think there's something in the kitchen," said Chloe, but Marcus hastily refused. Even on her salary she couldn't afford to serve eggs.

Mary Ellen came in just then. She slouched in dispiritedly, cloak drooping about her. "Hi, sis," she said as she opened the door.

Then she saw Marcus and revived abruptly. She flung herself across the room and into his lap, wrapping her arms around him. "Mark, dear," she said, smiling cattily over his head at her sister.

Marcus sighed regretfully. Heaven knew what the boy in his innocence would tell his mother. He worked himself loose from the girl's embrace and explained why he was here.

"Then we're going to Messy Row?"

"In a few months," said Chloe. "Marcus is setting up a perpetual fund to help those who can't pay their fare."

"Oh, I'll go," said Mary Ellen, looking steadily at Marcus. "But you needn't expect me to get married."

Marcus smiled to himself. She was dramatizing. When she found her choice wasn't limited she would scarcely remember him. There was, if Marcus now recalled correctly, a Joe Ainsworth, twenty-four or five. What made him seem older, when Marcus had first thought of him, was his prematurely gray hair. The two should be a perfect match. Chloe could not have Joe Ainsworth after all, but there'd be another for her.

"Please change, Mary Ellen," said Marcus. "We're going to dinner."

"All of us?"

"Certainly all of us," said Marcus dryly, noting her disapproval.

* * * * *

As she left he began discussing with Chloe what he should say in the request. Apparently there were nuances he didn't understand because he still didn't have it settled to his satisfaction when Mary Ellen returned.

"I'm ready," she said, pirouetting for his approval.

She was ready, but not for a quiet little dinner. "I suggest a wrap for your shoulders," he said. She made a face, but went to get one.

"How long will it take to get this through?" he asked Chloe.

"Four to six *years*. There's a backlog."

"Four to six *years*?" he repeated incredulously? He began to see that the loophole the government had provided was very small indeed. Who would bother, even if he felt strongly about it, when he knew it would take so long?

"That's going through regular channels." Chloe frowned and smoothed her hair. "You may be very lucky though. Today, just today, we might find a much faster way. You said they are moving A-CELO?"

"They are," he said, hoping he knew what she meant. This was a golden opportunity that might never come again.

"Then they'll be busy through the night. A workman should have access to the master robot."

Marcus smiled. "I'm an excellent workman."

"You'll need me, too. You won't recognize what you're after."

"Granted. Is it dangerous?"

"Not physically. But there's a severe penalty for tampering with government property. There's an even heavier one for trying to get your case considered ahead of schedule."

He could see why this was so. He could also see that Chloe was the kind of person Messy Row needed. She knew what she was getting into, but didn't hesitate. "Then you should come with me. But stay in the background. Promise me you'll try to get away if I'm caught."

She shrugged. "If you're caught you'll need help on the outside."

Mary Ellen came back, a transparent shimmering wrap over her shoulders. She was blonde and dazzling. "Where are we going? I'm so happy."

Marcus loosened his collar and sat down. "Dinner's off, except for you two. Chloe and I have work to do. Mary Ellen, take Wilbur back to the hotel for me. Watch after him."

"You want me to?" she asked despondently.

"I asked you to."

"Then I will." She arched her back, and it was a splendid arch. She swirled around, pausing at the door. "Come on, brat," she snarled.

"Pa, I can get along—" said Wilbur. Marcus looked at him and he left with Mary Ellen.

"We haven't much time," said Marcus when they were alone. "First we have to write the request. I'll need your help."

Chloe took the cover off a small machine in the corner. She sat down and turned toward him. "We have to emphasize anguish and suffering."

"Misery," suggested Marcus.

"Misery is a good strong word," she agreed. "It isn't used much lately. You should have this acted on in hours instead of years."

"It will be nice," said Marcus. "I can't think of any name as bad as Messy Row." Slowly he began to speak of the misery resulting from the error. Making corrections as they went, Chloe typed it on the tape.

*      *      *      *      *

Marcus Mezzerow felt the weight of forty-three years roll away. He was tired, but it was relaxed tiredness that comes with achievement. It had been easy to walk into A-CELO and become part of the bustle and confusion. It had even been easy to locate the master robot that processed decisions on chart names. But the rest hadn't been easy even with Chloe to guide and counsel him.

The master robot was one of the last things to be moved. It was located deep in the sub-sub-basement, ordinarily inaccessible. It was a ponderous contrivance, awkward to move and quite delicate. Truck robots backed up to it and under it, lifting it up. Technicians and extra workmen swiftly began disconnecting it from the building. Marcus was one of those extra workmen and he did his job as well as the others. But he didn't get an opportunity to insert his request in the machine.

Chloe sauntered past in shapeless work clothes, winking as she went by. She attracted no attention because there were many women around. Marcus got ready, moving to the front of the machine, feeling the spool in his pocket. A technician stared suspiciously at him, but there wasn't anything definite to object to.

Chloe leaned against the wall, moving the switch next to her with her elbow. Immediately standby circuits cut in, but the flicker of lights caused a commotion. The technician next to Marcus whirled, shouting at Chloe who looked startled and tired. The tiredness was real.

In the few free seconds he had, Marcus put the spool in the machine close to the top. It jammed the remaining spools closer together, but the machine was built to compensate for overloads. There should be no trouble from this.

The spool itself was another thing Chloe had helped him with. Normally requests were received on paper and had to be transcribed. She had enabled him to bypass one stage altogether.

They worked on after the shouting episode. At the first rest break they walked up to the street level, pausing in a dimly lighted hall to strip off their outer work clothing which they disposed of. They were no longer workmen. They were pedestrians who had passed by and wandered in to see what was happening. They didn't belong in the building and were told to leave, which they did.

And so it was late when Marcus entered the hotel. There was no one around, for which he was thankful. He didn't feel like fending off women at this hour of the morning. He went up and let himself in quietly. Wilbur was asleep in the adjoining room and the door between them was open. He closed it before turning on the light, which he adjusted to the lowest level. Perhaps by this time the master chart robot was in a new location, grinding out decisions. Messy Row was or soon would be a thing of the past.

"Pa," Wilbur called as Marcus removed a shoe.

"Yes. I'm back. Go to sleep."

"Did you get it done?"

"It's finished. We're taking the next ship out."

"Tomorrow?"

"If there's one scheduled tomorrow."

"Before we say good-by?"

Marcus could hear the bed rustle as Wilbur sat up. "We'll send them a note. Anyway they'll be on Mezzerow in a few months."

*       *       *       *       *

The door opened and Wilbur stood there, his face white and his eyes round and serious. "But I gotta say good-by to Mary Ellen."

Marcus took off the other shoe. He should have known not to leave them alone. His only excuse was that he had been thinking of other things. "I thought you didn't like her," he said.

"Pa, that was because I thought she didn't like me," said Wilbur. "But she does. I mean—" He leaned heavily against the doorway and his face was long and sad.

Marcus smiled in the near darkness. The boy had been around girls so seldom he didn't know how they behaved. He had mistaken a normal reaction to the opposite sex for something more. Nevertheless it had worked out nicely. Wilbur would not remember who it was that Mary Ellen had really pursued. With the feverish egotism of youth he would retain only the memory of the interest she'd shown in him. A kiss would haunt him for years. "Am I to understand you made love to her?" he asked sternly, amused at his own inaccuracy.

"Oh, Pa," said Wilbur. "I kissed her."

"These affairs pass away."

"I still gotta say good-by," said Wilbur.

"We'll see," said Marcus. Not if he could help it, would they. It would be a terrible thing if, on parting, Mary Ellen would throw her arms around him, ignoring Wilbur. She was too young to understand what it might mean to someone even younger than herself. Marcus went to sleep with the satisfaction of a man who is in full control of destiny.

In the morning there was no need for subterfuge. A ship was going near Mezzerow. Not directly to it, the planet wasn't that important. But it was merely a short local hop from one of the planets on the schedule. Mezzerow. After all these years he could call it by the rightful name without feeling provincial.

The excitement of the return trip shook Wilbur out of his preoccupation with Mary Ellen. Marcus packed and had the luggage zipped to the space port. He called Chloe and completed the financial arrangements and left a message for her sister who was at work.

And then they were at the port, entering the ship. There was a short wait before takeoff. They settled in the cabin and Wilbur promptly went to sleep. Food, sleep, girls; it was all a young man had time for.

But Marcus couldn't rest though he was tired. He wanted to hear the schedule announced. By this time the correction should have been made. The rockets started, throbbing softly as the tubes warmed up. Wilbur awakened with a start, sitting on the edge of the acceleration diaphragm. "Do you think they'll announce it?" he asked.

"I think so," said Marcus. The Universe would know that it was Mezzerow.

The rockets throbbed higher; the cabin shook. Weren't they going to call the schedule? The intercom in the cabin rasped.

They were. "Bessemer, Coarsegold," said the speaker.

"Get on the acceleration couch," said Marcus as he did so himself.

"Noreen, Cassalmont," the speaker droned. But now there was too much interference from the rockets. The thrust pressed Marcus deep into the flexible diaphragm. The announcer shouted, but the blood was roaring in his ears.

Marcus felt himself sliding into the gray world of takeoff.

\*    \*    \*    \*    \*

Then they were out among the stars and the sensation of great weight rolled away. Marcus sat up.

"We didn't hear it," said Wilbur, swinging his legs.

"We didn't. But they announced it."

"I wish I'd heard," said Wilbur.

It was bothering Marcus, too. "The thing to do is to find out," he said. They went into the corridor. The rockets were silent; the star drive had taken over. The solar system was behind them, indistinguishable from the other stars.

The pilot was busy and nodded his head, asking them to wait while he set the controls. He flipped levers and after an interval turned around. "Can I help you?" he asked.

"We didn't hear the schedule," said Marcus. "The rockets were too loud."

The pilot smiled apologetically. "You know how it is—last minute corrections on the charts. We had to wait until new ones were delivered, just before takeoff."

The oppression that had been hovering near lifted a little. "I understand," said Marcus. "Would you tell me if Mezzerow was one of the corrections?"

The pilot turned to the list and ran his finger down the line. He looked and looked again. "No Mezzerow here," he said.

The oppression had never been far away. It came back. "No Mezzerow?" said Marcus bleakly.

"No, but I'll check." The pilot bent over the list. "Wait. Maybe this is why I didn't see it. Take a look."

Marcus looked where the pilot was pointing. Above the fingernail, in bold black letters, was the name.

MISERY ROW (Formerly Mezzerow—changed to avoid confusion with    a family name.)

"Thanks," said Marcus faintly. "That's what I wanted to know."

They went to the cabin in silence. Marcus closed his eyes but that didn't shut out the new name. Nothing could.

"That's not as nice as it was," said Wilbur. "What do you suppose was wrong?"

"I don't know," said Marcus. But he did know. Fourteen times, or was it eleven, he had used one word. He had tried to overload the master robot with emotion and he had succeeded.

He had given it one outstanding impression: Misery.

"What'll we do?" said Wilbur. "Go back and change it?"

"No," said Marcus. "We'll leave it as it is. When you grow up and take my place, you can try your hand at it if you want."

Women would get there regardless of what it was called. Chloe would realize what had happened and anyway he'd write. She'd see that they got to the right place. And with women for the men who wanted to settle, they'd get along.

Besides, there was the element of uncertainty. He had thought nothing could be quite as bad as the old name ... until this. He shuddered to think what the next change might be like.

"Will it be all right?" asked Wilbur anxiously.

"It has to be all right," said Marcus, his voice strong with resignation. "We're going home to Misery Row."

# Second Landing

Originally Published In *Amazing Science Fiction Stories*, January 1960

*A gentle fancy for the Christmas Season—an*
*oft-told tale with a wistful twistful of Something*
*that left the Earth with a wing and a prayer*

# SECOND LANDING

Earth was so far away that it wasn't visible. Even the sun was only a twinkle. But this vast distance did not mean that isolation could endure forever. Instruments within the ship intercepted radio broadcasts and, within the hour, early TV signals. Machines compiled dictionaries and grammars and began translating the major languages. The history of the planet was tabulated as facts became available.

The course of the ship changed slightly; it was not much out of the way to swing nearer Earth. For days the two within the ship listened and watched with little comment. They had to decide soon.

"We've got to make or break," said the first alien.

"You know what I'm in favor of," said the second.

"I can guess," said Ethaniel, who had spoken first. "The place is a complete mess. They've never done anything except fight each other—and invent better weapons."

"It's not what they've done," said Bal, the second alien. "It's what they're going to do, with that big bomb."

"The more reason for stopping," said Ethaniel. "The big bomb can destroy them. Without our help they may do just that."

"I may remind you that in two months twenty-nine days we're due in Willafours," said Bal. "Without looking at the charts I can tell you we still have more than a hundred light-years to go."

"A week," said Ethaniel. "We can spare a week and still get there on time."

"A week?" said Bal. "To settle their problems? They've had two world wars in one generation and that the third and final one is coming up you can't help feeling in everything they do."

"It won't take much," said Ethaniel. "The wrong diplomatic move, or a trigger-happy soldier could set it off. And it wouldn't have to be deliberate. A meteor shower could pass over and their clumsy instruments could interpret it as an all-out enemy attack."

"Too bad," said Bal. "We'll just have to forget there ever was such a planet as Earth."

"Could you? Forget so many people?"

"I'm doing it," said Bal. "Just give them a little time and they won't be here to remind me that I have a conscience."

"My memory isn't convenient," said Ethaniel. "I ask you to look at them."

*     *     *     *     *

Bal rustled, flicking the screen intently. "Very much like ourselves," he said at last. "A bit shorter perhaps, and most certainly incomplete. Except for the one thing they lack, and that's quite odd, they seem exactly like us. Is that what you wanted me to say?"

"It is. The fact that they are an incomplete version of ourselves touches me. They actually seem defenseless, though I suppose they're not."

"Tough," said Bal. "Nothing we can do about it."

"There is. We can give them a week."

"In a week we can't negate their entire history. We can't begin to undo the effect of the big bomb."

"You can't tell," said Ethaniel. "We can look things over."

"And then what? How much authority do we have?"

"Very little," conceded Ethaniel. "Two minor officials on the way to Willafours—and we run directly into a problem no one knew existed."

"And when we get to Willafours we'll be busy. It will be a long time before anyone comes this way again."

"A very long time. There's nothing in this region of space our people want," said Ethaniel. "And how long can Earth last? Ten years? Even ten months? The tension is building by the hour."

"What can I say?" said Bal. "I suppose we can stop and look them over. We're not committing ourselves by looking."

They went much closer to Earth, not intending to commit themselves. For a day they circled the planet, avoiding radar detection, which for them was not difficult, testing, and sampling. Finally Ethaniel looked up from the monitor screen. "Any conclusions?"

"What's there to think? It's worse than I imagined."

"In what way?"

"Well, we knew they had the big bomb. Atmospheric analysis showed that as far away as we were."

"I know."

"We also knew they could deliver the big bomb, presumably by some sort of aircraft."

"That was almost a certainty. They'd have no use for the big bomb without aircraft."

"What's worse is that I now find they also have missiles, range one thousand miles and upward. They either have or are near a primitive form of space travel."

"Bad," said Ethaniel. "Sitting there, wondering when it's going to hit them. Nervousness could set it off."

"It could, and the missiles make it worse," said Bal. "What did you find out at your end?"

"Nothing worthwhile. I was looking at the people while you were investigating their weapons."

"You must think something."

"I wish I knew what to think. There's so little time," Ethaniel said. "Language isn't the difficulty. Our machines translate their languages easily and I've taken a cram course in two or three of them. But that's not enough, looking at a few plays, listening to advertisements, music, and news bulletins. I should go down and live among them, read books, talk to scholars, work with them, play."

"You could do that and you'd really get to know them. But that takes time—and we don't have it."

"I realize that."

"A flat yes or no," said Bal.

"No. We can't help them," said Ethaniel. "There is nothing we can do for them—but we have to try."

"Sure, I knew it before we started," said Bal. "It's happened before. We take the trouble to find out what a people are like and when we can't help them we feel bad. It's going to be that way again." He rose and stretched. "Well, give me an hour to think of some way of going at it."

*     *     *     *     *

It was longer than that before they met again. In the meantime the ship moved much closer to Earth. They no longer needed instruments to see it. The planet revolved outside the visionports. The southern plains were green, coursed with rivers; the oceans were blue; and much of the northern hemisphere was glistening white. Ragged clouds covered the pole, and a dirty pall spread over the mid-regions of the north.

"I haven't thought of anything brilliant," said Ethaniel.

"Nor I," said Bal. "We're going to have to go down there cold. And it will be cold."

"Yes. It's their winter."

"I did have an idea," said Bal. "What about going down as supernatural beings?"

"Hardly," said Ethaniel. "A hundred years ago it might have worked. Today they have satellites. They are not primitives."

"I suppose you're right," said Bal. "I did think we ought to take advantage of our physical differences."

"If we could I'd be all for it. But these people are rough and desperate. They wouldn't be fooled by anything that crude."

"Well, you're calling it," said Bal.

"All right," said Ethaniel. "You take one side and I the other. We'll tell them bluntly what they'll have to do if they're going to survive, how they can keep their planet in one piece so they can live on it."

"That'll go over big. Advice is always popular."

"Can't help it. That's all we have time for."

"Special instructions?"

"None. We leave the ship here and go down in separate landing craft. You can talk with me any time you want to through our communications, but don't unless you have to."

"They can't intercept the beams we use."

"They can't, and even if they did they wouldn't know what to do with our language. I want them to think that we don't *need* to talk things over."

"I get it. Makes us seem better than we are. They think we know exactly what we're doing even though we don't."

"If we're lucky they'll think that."

\*      \*      \*      \*      \*

Bal looked out of the port at the planet below. "It's going to be cold where I'm going. You too. Sure we don't want to change our plans and land in the southern hemisphere? It's summer there."

"I'm afraid not. The great powers are in the north. They are the ones we have to reach to do the job."

"Yeah, but I was thinking of that holiday you mentioned. We'll be running straight into it. That won't help us any."

"I know, they don't like their holidays interrupted. It can't be helped. We can't wait until it's over."

"I'm aware of that," said Bal. "Fill me in on that holiday, anything I ought to know. Probably religious in origin. That so?"

"It was religious a long time ago," said Ethaniel. "I didn't learn anything exact from radio and TV. Now it seems to be chiefly a time for eating, office parties, and selling merchandise."

"I see. It has become a business holiday."

"That's a good description. I didn't get as much of it as I ought to have. I was busy studying the people, and they're hard to pin down."

"I see. I was thinking there might be some way we could tie ourselves in with this holiday. Make it work for us."

"If there is I haven't thought of it."

"You ought to know. You're running this one." Bal looked down at the planet. Clouds were beginning to form at the twilight edge. "I hate to go down and leave the ship up here with no one in it."

"They can't touch it. No matter how they develop in the next hundred years they still won't be able to get in or damage it in any way."

"It's myself I'm thinking about. Down there, alone."

"I'll be with you. On the other side of the Earth."

"That's not very close. I'd like it better if there were someone in the ship to bring it down in a hurry if things get rough. They don't think much of each other. I don't imagine they'll like aliens any better."

"They may be unfriendly," Ethaniel acknowledged. Now he switched a monitor screen until he looked at the slope of a mountain. It was snowing and men were cutting small green trees in the snow. "I've thought of a trick."

"If it saves my neck I'm for it."

"I don't guarantee anything," said Ethaniel. "This is what I was thinking of: instead of hiding the ship against the sun where there's little chance it will be seen, we'll make sure that they do see it. Let's take it around to the night side of the planet and light it up."

"Say, pretty good," said Bal.

"They can't imagine that we'd light up an unmanned ship," said Ethaniel. "Even if the thought should occur to them they'll have no way of checking it. Also, they won't be eager to harm us with our ship shining down on them."

"That's thinking," said Bal, moving to the controls. "I'll move the ship over where they can see it best and then I'll light it up. I'll really light it up."

"Don't spare power."

"Don't worry about that. They'll see it. Everybody on Earth will see it." Later, with the ship in position, glowing against the darkness of space, pulsating with light, Bal said: "You know, I feel better about this. We may pull it off. Lighting the ship may be just the help we need."

"It's not we who need help, but the people of Earth," said Ethaniel. "See you in five days." With that he entered a small landing craft, which left a faintly luminescent trail as it plunged toward Earth. As soon as it was safe to do so, Bal left in another craft, heading for the other side of the planet.

*       *       *       *       *

And the spaceship circled Earth, unmanned, blazing and pulsing with light. No star in the winter skies of the planet below could equal it in brilliancy. Once a man-made satellite came near but it was dim and was lost sight of by the people below. During the day the ship was visible as a bright spot of light. At evening it seemed to burn through the sunset colors.

And the ship circled on, bright, shining, seeming to be a little piece clipped from the center of a star and brought near Earth to illuminate it. Never, or seldom, had Earth seen anything like it.

In five days the two small landing craft that had left it arched up from Earth and joined the orbit of the large ship. The two small craft slid inside the large one and doors closed behind them. In a short time the aliens met again.

"We did it," said Bal exultantly as he came in. "I don't know how we did it and I thought we were going to fail but at the last minute they came through."

Ethaniel smiled. "I'm tired," he said, rustling.

"Me too, but mostly I'm cold," said Bal, shivering. "Snow. Nothing but snow wherever I went. Miserable climate. And yet you had me go out walking after that first day."

"From my own experience it seemed to be a good idea," said Ethaniel. "If I went out walking one day I noticed that the next day the officials were much more cooperative. If it worked for me I thought it might help you."

"It did. I don't know why, but it did," said Bal. "Anyway, this agreement they made isn't the best but I think it will keep them from destroying themselves."

"It's as much as we can expect," said Ethaniel. "They may have small wars after this, but never the big one. In fifty or a hundred years we can come back and see how much they've learned."

"I'm not sure I want to," said Bal. "Say, what's an angel?"

"Why?"

"When I went out walking people stopped to look. Some knelt in the snow and called me an angel."

"Something like that happened to me," said Ethaniel.

"I didn't get it but I didn't let it upset me," said Bal. "I smiled at them and went about my business." He shivered again. "It was always cold. I walked out, but sometimes I flew back. I hope that was all right."

In the cabin Bal spread his great wings. Renaissance painters had never seen his like but knew exactly how he looked. In their paintings they had pictured him innumerable times.

"I don't think it hurt us that you flew," said Ethaniel. "I did so myself occasionally."

"But you don't know what an angel is?"

"No. I didn't have time to find out. Some creature of their folklore I suppose. You know, except for our wings they're very much like ourselves. Their legends are bound to resemble ours."

"Sure," said Bal. "Anyway, peace on Earth."

SPECIAL PREVIEW!

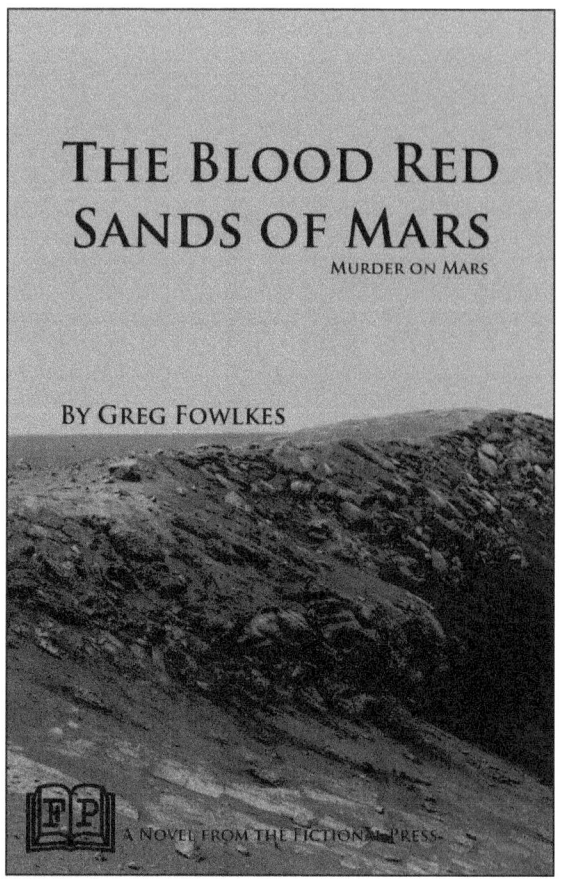

# THE BLOOD RED SANDS OF MARS
## MURDER ON MARS

## A NOVEL BY GREG FOWLKES

# THE BLOOD RED SANDS OF MARS

The wind was blowing again against the west wall of the hut. He could hear the grains of sand abrading the thin aluminum skin that protected him from the outside. Through the window, half frosted from the continuous onslaught of sand and dust, he could see clouds of dust obscuring the sky. The sky was a pastel pink, a color no sky had any right to be. The wind, despite its 120 kph. velocity, made only a thin howl as it blew over the half buried cylinder of the hut.

McKernan lay on his cot trying not to admit that he was awake. It was a losing battle. After a few minutes he surrendered and glanced over at the clock sitting on the crate next to his bed. The dim red digits of the LED display read 7:58. It was too early to get up, too late to go back to sleep. He rolled over, shivering at the cold. The temperature couldn't have been more than ten degrees Celsius inside the hut. For the twentieth time he thought to himself that he would have to fix the heater before winter—if he could get the parts. Either that, or put in more insulation—if he could find that. The cold finally forced the decision to get up.

Standing, he felt the cold plastic floor beneath his bare feet. With his foot he fished the worn and patched pants from beneath the cot and pulled them on. He dug underneath his pillow and came up with a switchblade knife that he stuck in his pocket before drawing on the turtleneck sweater that had lain next to his pants. The cold feel of the cloth did nothing to dispel the cold from his body. From the crate he picked up a shoulder holster with a small automatic pistol and put it on. McKernan drew the weapon, worked the slide once, and after examining it perfunctorily, placed it back in the holster. Satisfied, he pulled on a worn pair of leather boots and placed another knife in a sheathe between his skin and the boot top.

Dressed, he went over to the shelf that served as counter and table. He put a pan of beans onto the heating unit and got a soysteak from the small refrigerator that held up one end of the shelf. The steak went into the frying pan on the other heating element. An egg would have been nice, but at the current price of three dollars apiece it was an extravagance that he would have to put off for a while.

As the food cooked he drew a liter of water from the spigot in the corner of the hut and watered the plants in the garden under the window. The carrots and tomatoes were doing nicely. He smiled briefly because it would be good to have fresh vegetables for a change. The big, leafy oxygen plants were doing well, too. He would be able to cut down on his oxygen ration this month and save some money.

He took the beans off the heating element and replaced them with the coffee pot. The beans were still half cold, but he wasn't in the mood to hassle with them. He only had the two heating elements, and he didn't want to have to wait for his coffee. He forced down the beans and then wolfed down the steak. It almost tasted like real beef, but then maybe his memories were fading. As usual, the coffee tasted terrible and tepid, too. The air pressure in the hut was too low for water to boil properly.

He finished his meal and scraped the remnants of food into the pressure vessel that served as a compost heap. The gauge on its neighbor showed that he had almost half a tank of methane. He'd be able to sell that soon and use the money for something useful, like a still. Completing his rounds, the gauges on the life support systems showed that everything was still working at keeping him alive. He went back to the pots and scrubbed them clean with sand. That, at least, was plentiful and cheap.

He checked his watch against the clock. It was time to get going. Pulling on his jacket he went to the airlock at the corridor end of the hut. After checking the gauge to make sure that there was pressure on the other side, he undogged the latches and stepped through. Closing the door behind him, he repeated the process with the outer hatch, latching both doors behind him. The outer door he locked with a heavy padlock.

He had entered a low tubular corridor made of the same aluminum foil and plastic foam construction as the hut. The walls, however, were even thinner, and no pretense was made of heating it. He could see his breath condensing in front of him as he began to walk down its length. It was a hell of a way to live, he reflected, not for the first time. But then, it had been hell living in L.A. where he'd been born, with brown air, rats, a chronic shortage of water, and overcrowded tenements. He had made his choice, but sometimes it seemed as though life was a continual shiver.

The corridor was pierced at regular intervals by hatches identical to his own. The huts behind the hatches were identical, too, except for the modifications the owners had made to make them more livable. This part of the city was old, dating back a couple of decades to the first days of the settlement when it had been part of a scientific base. The scientists had departed, at least from that corridor, and been replaced by those who had the money to buy or rent the huts from the Trust Authority. Maintenance was pretty much left up to the residents.

Along the sides and overhead ran the pipes and conduits that pumped in the gases, liquids, and power necessary for sustaining life. The whole system looked as jury rigged and fragile as it actually was, though surprisingly few people died whenever the system failed. Martians were a cautious lot. One didn't talk much about injuries. Accidents on Mars didn't leave many.

A hundred meters down the tube he came to an airlock. Going through the same ritual that he had used on his front door, he went through to another length of corridor indistinguishable from the one he had just left. Continuing on, he passed through two more airlocks until he entered a corridor that sloped downward. The hatches were farther apart, and larger. Signs overhead indicated the businesses or functions that were carried out behind them. The air was warmer because the corridor was buried beneath the sand which provided insulation. At the end of the tunnel was a larger airlock set into a wall of fused silica bricks, the first substantial piece of construction he had met that morning.

Passing through the portal was like entering another world, which in a way he had. This was the public Mars, the planet seen by the corporation men and the officials of the Trust Authority. It was also the planet seen by tourists, the brave new colony, man's first outpost on another planet. The tourists didn't really care to see the hut town. They were part of the same world as the corporation men and the government types. It still took a great deal of money or power to reach Mars.

The difference was more than one of degree. For one thing, the temperature was a comfortable twenty. For another, the walls were flat and met the floors and ceilings at right angles, unlike the inflated skins of the huts and corridors. With a little imagination it could almost be an enclosed shopping mall on earth, though the presence of fused silica blocks was more prevalent than any architect would allow.

The most important difference, however, was the sight of people scurrying along. He hadn't met anyone in the outer corridors. People rarely lingered there because of the cold. Now, McKernan could see at least twenty people and it was still fairly early. No airlocks interrupted this corridor. Extending for two hundred meters in either direction, it was twenty meters wide and ten high, the largest enclosed volume on the planet. Arrayed along its length were the offices and store fronts of the corporations that owned Mars, as well as the more prosperous saloons and bordellos.

One day the Trust Authority promised that the whole city would be like that, with apartments and condominiums for the ordinary workers, but neither the Authority or the corporations had yet come up with the money. For the moment all that existed was the one street of a few blocks.

McKernan headed towards the Authority's offices which dominated one end of the mall, but turned aside at the last moment when he noticed that a small, dark doorway was open. He knew that he should resist the temptation, but he was not in a very disciplined mood. He went through the doorway into the darkness beyond.

———————————

Finnegan's was the only real, honest bar on Mars. There were any number of saloons and even a cocktail lounge in the Mars Sheraton, but only one quiet, dark place where a man could drink in peace. McKernan felt the need for some of that peace at the moment.

He sat down on one of the stools before the only mahogany bar on Mars. Finnegan, himself, was behind the bar, though in fact he almost always was, no matter what the hour. The bartender looked up and greeted the newcomer, "Good morning, constable. Beer or whiskey?"

"It's too early for beer. It's too early for whiskey, but give me a shot, anyway."

Finnegan poured out a shot glass of amber liquid and placed it before McKernan and then stood back polishing a glass while he studied the man opposite him.

McKernan knocked back half the glass before he spoke. When he did, there was a bitter edge to his voice. "Sometimes I wonder if it's worth it, Finnegan. I could be back on a planet fit for human life."

"Could you, now, constable?" Finnegan said, putting down the glass and picking up another in equally gleaming condition. "If mother earth was such a bed of roses, why are you here?"

He breathed on the glass and examined it against the light for a moment, then looked at McKernan with the same intentness. "You're here because you're not the sort to live off the dole or to spend your life with another man being your boss. Instead you'll spend your life trying to make this planet a fit place to live and retire in twenty years with a nice pension. Now drink up and get to work, laddy."

"Yeah, sure. Sorry to burden you with my problems. Early morning depression, I guess. See you." He finished off the shot and left five dollars in Authority script on the bar.

---

The bite of the whiskey so early in the morning didn't really help his disposition, but it did give him enough courage to make it to the office. The morning ritual at Finnegan's was becoming too much of a habit. His three years on Mars were beginning to show.

The jail wasn't in the brick part of the Authority building, but in the complex of pneumatic architecture that sprawled behind it. The huts were old—older than his own—but dated back to the days when governments had not begrudged a few billions for exploration, back before space had to show a profit. For that reason, they were sound and well insulated, though a bit tacky looking.

The jail consisted of two huts joined together, one for offices, the other for the two makeshift cells and storage. Ferris was the only one there when he walked in, a young kid, younger than he had been himself when he had come to Mars. He was still impressed enough with his responsibilities and had not yet been worn down by the grim realities to take his job in any way but seriously.

Ferris greeted him with a solemn, "Good morning, sir," with a stress on the sir. As a three year veteran of Mars, Ferris looked on his boss with more than a touch of awe.

"Anything exciting happen overnight?" McKernan didn't really expect much. A few fights in the saloon district, a knifing maybe if things got out of hand. Petty thievery, or perhaps not so petty. He looked at Ferris and saw a flash of excitement in his eyes that the younger man was trying hard to suppress in order to match the hard bitten image he had of his superior.

"Yes, sir. We've got a murder on our hands."

"Another knifing down at Thelma's?" he asked, naming an infamous saloon and bordello that figured in a quarter of all the police reports.

"No. A prospector was found out on his claim yesterday, over on the far side of Olympus Mons. He was shot, Inspector."

That was bad, McKernan thought. People on Mars weren't supposed to have guns. With the thin skins of most buildings and a hostile atmosphere outside that would support life exactly as long as you could hold your breath, they were dangerous, and not just to the targets. The Authority had made them illegal and the corporations had been more than willing to agree. They weren't easy to get—not something that could be picked up casually or made, like a knife. Even without the details it sounded like the work of a real criminal and not just a squabble over a claim or a woman.

"Okay. Let me have the report. I'll take a look at it."

He took the folder from Ferris who looked a bit crestfallen. He probably expects me to go rush off to the outside and track down the murderer like an Indian scout, McKernan thought. He'd learn in time. Mars was a big planet and a dangerous one, but because of its nature there were also very few places that a man could run to and none where he could hide indefinitely.

He was leafing through the report when he came to his door. For the thousandth time he read, "Inspector Erik McKernan, Chief Constable." Mother would have been proud, he thought sardonically. She had hated the L.A. cops like all the other residents of the barrio. He went through the door into the little cubicle that was his real home. There, sitting at his desk, he began to read the report, sketchy though it was, to look for some explanations.

**Available now! Visit www.TheFictionalPress.com for more information, or buy it in both print and electronic format at your favorite online bookstore!**

## Other Science Fiction Novels by Greg Fowlkes

The Fictional Detective

The Blood Red Sands of Mars: Murder on Mars

The Laws of Magic: A Wizard at Law Novel.

The Ghost in the Machine: A wizard at Law novella

Ice Vikings

Cargo from Paradise

Tequila Visions

# Also From Resurrected Press
## SCIENCE FICTION AUTHORS RESURRECTED

### FYFE RESURRECTED - THE STORIES OF H. B. FYFE
Stories from the Golden Age of Science Fiction by the author of D-99. dealing with the interaction of humans and aliens on far off worlds in ways that were as creative as they were imaginative.

### SCHMITZ RESURRECTED - SELECTED STORIES OF JAMES H. SCHMITZ
Includes "An Incident on Route 12", "Watch the Sky", "The Other Likeness", "The Star Hyacinths", "Oneness", "The Winds of Time", "Ham Sandwich" and "Gone Fishing".

### SHECKLY RESURRECTED - THE EARLY STORIES OF ROBERT SHECKLEY
Resurrected Press has collected some of the best of these from the 50's including "Warrior Race", "The Leech", "Watchbird", "Warm", "Diplomatic Immunity", "The Hour of Battle", "Besides Still Waters", "Keep Your Shape", "One Man's Poison", 'Ask a Foolish Question", "Cost of Living", "Death Wish Forever".

### DICK RESURRECTED - THE EARLY STORIES OF PHILIP K. DICK
Early stories from the author of the novels that inspired "Blade Runner," "Total Recall," and "A Scanner Darkly".

### HAMILTON RESURRECTED - CLASSIC STORIES OF EDMOND HAMILTON
Edmond Hamilton was one of the most popular writers during the 30's and 40's, the period that saw the first flowering of modern science fiction.

### SMITH RESURRECTED - SELECTED STORIES OF EVELYN E. SMITH TON
During an era when women rarely appeared in science fiction magazines, Evelyn E. Smith appeared regularly in the pages of Galaxy and Fantastic Universe. Resurrected Press is proud to return these stories to print.

# The Fictional Detective
by Greg Fowlkes

## Who killed Ezekial O. Handler?

A beautiful dame, a hard-boiled private eye − and a dead body.

It started like any other case. When a famous writer dies in a mysterious car crash, private detective Frank Slade is called in to find answers, but all he finds is more questions. Who killed Ezekial Handler? Who is Janet Nielsen and why is she so interested in finding out? Who is leaving the neatly typed clues? And as Slade tries to find answers to these questions he starts to wonder if the ultimate answer will threaten his very existence.

## Read about it in
## The Fictional Detective

Visit www.thefictionaldetective.com

## About Resurrected Press

This classic book was handcrafted by Resurrected Press. Resurrected Press is dedicated to bringing high quality classic books back to the readers who enjoy them. These are not scanned versions of the originals, but, rather, quality checked and edited books meant to be enjoyed!

## Introducing The Fictional Press

The Fictional Press is a small, independent press specializing in the publication of fictional works by emerging authors. If you are interested in bringing your fictional works to life in print as well as electronically, contact us! We can help!

www.ingramcontent.com/pod-product-compliance
Lightning Source LLC
Chambersburg PA
CBHW070400260626
47161CB00001B/214